W9-BHW-079

The Bride Sale

CANDICE HERN

The BRIDE SALE

AVON BOOKS
An Imprint of HarperCollins*Publishers*

AVON BOOKS
An Imprint of HarperCollins*Publishers*
10 East 53rd Street
New York, New York 10022-5299

ISBN: 0-7394-2277-4

Printed in the U.S.A.

To Casey Mickle,
whose help throughout this endeavor
was invaluable, from its earliest inception
at a Greenwich Village tapas bar
to final editing.

I could not have done it without her.

Chapter 1

Cornwall
October 1818

"C'mon, me laddies. What'm I bid fer this fine bit o' flesh?"

" 'Alf a crown!"

Raucous laughter almost drowned out the auctioneer's rude response to the opening bid. James Gordon Harkness, fifth Baron Harkness, leaned against the rough granite wall of the village apothecary shop just off Gunnisloe market square. The lane and its shops were deserted; most of the villagers and market-day travelers had gathered in the square to watch the livestock auction. James nibbled on the last bit of savory meat pie as his servant loaded the carriage boot with the day's purchases: several bolts of local wool, a few hammered copper cook pots, two large bags of seed, a brace of pheasant, a basket of smoked fish, and three cases of wine.

"Two pounds!"

James licked the pastry crumbs from his long fingers as he listened to the auction taking place around the corner. The voices of auctioneer and bidders rang clearly in the crisp air of early autumn.

"Two pounds ten."

"Aw, c'mon," a female voice shouted above the din. "The poor cow be worth more'n that, you bleedin' idiot."

"Not to my man, she ain't," another female replied, eliciting howls of laughter from the crowd.

"Two pounds fifteen!"

This was followed by more laughter and the ear-splitting din of what had to be the banging of dozens of tin kettles. Village women often took up the old tradition of kettle banging to encourage more intense bidding. It must be some prime bit of flesh indeed, James mused as the rhythmic clanging grew louder.

A stiff breeze chased a flutter of red birch leaves down the lane, and James brushed back a lock of thick black hair blown forward by the wind. He watched the leaves skitter away, but kept his ear to the auction in the square.

"Three pounds!"

As he listened, James savored the fragrant scent of freshly baked cinnamon buns and meat pies, of roasting pig and rabbit shank, of fresh cider and ale. The delicious smells and the sounds of gaiety and fierce bartering inevitably drew his thoughts to earlier times, when he might have enjoyed such a day, when he would have been a welcome participant. Now he would not willingly walk into a crowd that size, a crowd of people who knew him, knew who and what he was.

He seldom ventured into Gunnisloe at all, though it was the closest market town. He preferred the larger, more distant markets of Truro or Falmouth, where he was not as well-known. But he had business in Gunnisloe today. Taking advantage of market day, he had sent his footman into the stalls to purchase a few household goods. While the markets bustled and thrived in the village square, James had kept his distance. He was in no mood to endure the strained silence, the wary glances, the hushed whisperings that would inevitably follow his entry into the public square.

The footman closed the boot and locked it, then opened the carriage door and stood aside. James pushed away from the granite wall and walked toward the open door. He replaced his curly brimmed beaver on his head and tugged it low against the wind.

"Four pounds!"

"Don't 'ee dare bid on her, Danny Gower, lest 'ee want yer heart ripped clean outa yer chest."

Peels of laughter and more banging of tin kettles followed this interesting pronouncement. James halted his ascent into the carriage. What on earth was going on? He had never before heard a crowd behave in such a strangely boisterous manner at an auction. What the devil was so special about this particular cow?

His curiosity got the better of him, and he stepped away from the carriage. Just one look was all he wanted. Just to see for himself what all the fuss was about. Just one quick look and he would be on his way.

"Five pounds!"

James walked the few steps to the end of the lane and peered around the corner, hoping no one would notice him. He quickly removed his beaver, realizing the tall, elegant hat would act as a beacon, drawing the attention of the simply dressed villagers and miners. But he needn't have worried. When he moved to the edge of the crowd of perhaps two hundred people or more, no one paid him the least mind.

For a moment he savored the once-familiar hustle and bustle of Gunnisloe on market day. Makeshift pens lined one side of the square where cattle and sheep were exhibited for auction. Many were already being rounded up and led away by their new owners. In one corner, several dozen individuals and families sat at long trestle tables and benches that were lined up in a herringbone pattern and sheltered from the wind by a temporary awning of striped canvas stretched over wooden poles. The substantial figure of Mag Puddifoot threaded her way among the tables, ladling out portions of her famous furmity pudding, just as she had done since James was a boy. Colorful carts and stalls selling all manner of goods and produce dotted the rest of the square's perimeter. Sweet and pungent aromas from the food vendors—stronger and more seductive here than in the adjacent lane—caused James to forget for an instant why he had made so bold as to enter the square in the first place.

"Six pounds!"

James's gaze darted warily through the crowd as he moved closer. No one had yet noticed him. All eyes were on the stone plinth next to the market cross where the auctioneer, old Jud Moody, stood with one arm raised and stirring the air, punctuating the banging of the kettles and urging the crowd on to higher bids. In Jud's other hand was a leather harness attached to the neck of a woman.

A woman.

What in blazes was going on here?

The men in the crowd were actually offering up bids of purchase for a *woman*. Not a prized bit of livestock after all, but a flesh-and-blood human being.

A wife sale.

He had read of wife sales among the lower classes who could not afford a legal divorce. He knew, too, that the courts turned a blind eye to such illegitimate proceedings, and even the subsequent remarriage of either party. Yet there appeared to be no prearranged buyer here, as was normally the case. This poor woman was being offered up for bid like a broodmare or a common packhorse.

His own disgrace almost paled when compared to such an infamous transaction. Almost. But here were the good people of Gunnisloe, steeped in their salt-of-the-earth Methodist prudery, now sunk so low.

And they dared to judge *him*? The self-righteous, hypocritical prigs. These same people who dashed into doorways at the very sight of him, clutching their terrified children to their breasts, unwilling to forgive his sins, obviously had no scruples about subjecting one of their own to such a sinful public display.

But as he looked more closely at the woman on the plinth, she did not appear to belong to one of the local mining or farming families. She wore a heavy blue cloak that appeared, even from a distance, to be a high-quality, well-tailored garment, along with a bonnet lined in a matching blue fabric. Both garments seemed to identify her as something other than a common laborer, or even a tenant farmer's wife. Could the clothing have somehow been procured to bring a better price at auction? To make her appear more attractive?

"Seven pounds!" a man shouted. He was a stranger to James. He looked to be a tinker or peddler of some kind, standing next to a large draft horse laden with packs overflowing with tin utensils. James supposed that the sanctimonious locals would blame this whole iniquitous business on foreigners and itinerants, or even the recent influx of new workers for the copper mines. Surely their high-principled and upstanding neighbors and acquaintances would never become involved in such a shocking affair. Not the fine moor folk, who owed him their wages from the mines and the tenant cottage roofs over their heads, but who would not so much as doff their hats in his direction. Not these stolid Cornishmen, so full of Christian charity and human compassion.

"Seven pounds ten!" This bid came from Sam Kempthorne, one of his own tenant farmers, who leered at the woman with a distinctly lascivious glint in his eye. So much for Christian charity.

"Eight pounds!" the tinker retaliated.

"Eight pounds ten."

The woman stood stiff and unmoving on the old

stone platform. Her head was bent, the deep poke brim of the bonnet shadowing her features. Despite her outward immobility, James did not miss the slight contraction of her shoulders at each shouted bid. He was reminded of a soldier he had once watched being flogged for some minor infraction, stoically submitting to each stroke of the lash.

He looked behind her and saw a well-dressed young man standing to the side of Jud Moody. The man's eyes were wide with what might have been fear. They scanned the crowd and then pinned Moody with a frantic look of desperation.

"C'mon, lads," old Moody shouted to the crowd after nodding at the young man. "Her may be a stranger an' all, even a foreigner from up-country. But tedn't no common hedge whore, she. Her be quality, I'm tellin' 'ee. Can't sham breedin' like that. Goes down to the very bone. Wife of a gen'l'mun, too. Worth more'n a piddlin' few quid, by God. Gimme a real bid, a reas'n'ble bid."

"Give us a better look at 'er, then!" a man's voice shouted.

Old Moody tugged on the halter attached to the woman's neck, causing her head to jerk up for a brief moment. "C'mon, dearie," he said. "Show 'em wot yer offerin'."

She looked younger than James had expected, perhaps in her mid-twenties. Darkish hair was just barely visible beneath her bonnet. Her eyes appeared to be dark as well, though James was not close enough to be certain. She again lowered her gaze, and appeared to be terrified. No, not quite terrified, he decided as he studied her further. Fear drained her face of all color, but there was also the merest hint of defiance in the tight jaw and in the square set of her shoulders when Moody pulled on the halter. And in the way she jerked her neck and pulled right back, causing Moody to bobble, unbalanced, for a moment. Good for her, James thought. Good for her.

"See wot a fair one her be," Moody continued. "Fine-lookin'. Still got all her teeth," he added as he chucked her chin. "Young, too. An' built just right to warm one o' yer beds. See here." The auctioneer pulled away her cloak and ran his hand suggestively over the front of her dress, stretching the fabric of the bodice taut across her bosom.

James took a step forward just as Mag Puddifoot, distracted from her furmity, scowled and shook a long wooden spoon toward the auctioneer. "Here, now!" she shouted in an outraged tone. But the well-dressed young man had already slapped away Moody's hand.

"Don't you touch her," the man said. The wind had whipped the open cloak over the woman's shoulder. The husband reached over and gently pulled the cloak around her again. She shrugged away his touch.

How odd, James thought, that a man who would so callously offer up his wife as mere chattel should exhibit even that small act of consideration.

"Ah," Moody said. "See wot a *lady* her is. Worth a good deal more'n a scrubby handful o' coins, an' this here gen'l'mun knows it. Ain't likely to let her go fer a measly few yellow boys, is 'ee, sur?"

The husband stared at Moody for a moment, then dropped his gaze and shook his head.

"C'mon, then, lads," Moody continued. "Who be willin' to pay fer a real lady to wive? Who'll tip me twen'y pounds?"

"Twen'y quid? That be a price fit fer a fine dollymop, not a wife!"

The crowd burst into laughter.

"Then buy her fer yer dollymop, Nat," old Moody replied.

Nat Spruggins, one of James's own tributers from Wheal Devoran, stood grinning like a fool as other men pounded him on the back with encouragement.

"Naw," Nat replied above the laughter. "Me wife wouldn't like it!"

"Nor an' I wouldn't!" replied Mrs. Spruggins, who stood nearby. "Gor, Nattie, y'ain't got 'nuff wind at night to plow yer own field, much less 'nother man's."

More laughter followed.

"Best 'ee should find a bach'ler, Jud Moody," another female voice cried out. "Ain't no wife gonna like it no more'n Hildy Spruggins."

"C'mon, then, all 'ee bach'lers," Moody continued. "Who among 'ee needs a fair, young wife, then? Already broke in by this here fine gen'l'mun. Knows her way about a man's bed, I reckon. Don't she, sur?"

The young man glowered angrily at Moody, but then looked away and said nothing. The bastard.

"I'll give ten quid!"

"Cheelie Craddick, don't be insultin'. A real lady to warm the bed o' the likes of 'ee? An' fer a piddlin' ten quid? Don't make me laugh! God's teeth, man, her be worth at least as much as yer best horse! A'right, then. Who else'll bid? C'mon, boys. Tip me a *real* bid. Who'll go twen'y quid?"

"So why he be sellin' her, anyway?" another man's voice rose above the hubbub. "Does her be some kinda shrew or sumthin'? Wot fer be this here feller so hell-bent on gettin' rid of her?"

"Now, Jacob," Moody replied. " 'Ee knows how the quality be. Gets tired o' the same woman ever' night. Wants variety and all. An' so, this here fine gen'l'mun is willin' to give her up fer a fair price, and let one o' you lucky lads have a go at her. So, who'll it be, then?"

James frowned at the coarse words, even as the notion crossed his mind that he might enjoy having a go at her himself. But he was, of course, an even bigger bastard than this diddling husband, so it was no surprise that such a foul notion would enter his head.

He looked more closely at the tethered female. Was she truly a woman of quality? A woman of his own class? James had never heard of a wife sale among the gentry. The husband's appearance was that of an affluent, well-tailored young man about Town. His manner was slightly skittish, even a little embarrassed.

What kind of man would do this to his own wife? How could he discard her so easily, humiliate her so publicly? What about his vows? What about his honor?

Brought up short by the absurdity of such a harsh appraisal, James chuckled mirthlessly to himself. Who was *he* to question a man's honor? What right did *he* have to pass judgment on another man's treatment of his wife? So what if the young man was prepared so casually to abandon her? So what if he decided to humiliate her in so public a fashion? So what if he was imbecile enough not to realize how lucky he was to have her, and how empty a man's life could be without a wife by his side? So what? It was nothing to James. It was no concern of his.

"Wot 'bout Big Will?" a female voice shouted. "He could use a wife, an' fer certain ain't no one else'd have him!"

The crowd erupted in laughter once again. James followed a sudden movement toward the opposite edge of the square, where the hulking figure of Will Sykes, Gunnisloe's smithy, stood staring at the harnessed woman on the plinth. His beefy arms—bare to the shoulder and covered with thick black hair, soot, grease, and God only knew what else—were crossed over his broad chest.

"How 'bout it, Big Will?" Moody said as several men pushed the huge man forward. "Wot else yer gonna spend yer blunt on? Here be a nice, soft female jus' waitin' fer yer tender touch."

The blacksmith glared slack-jawed at the young woman, who kept her eyes averted. Big Will Sykes had lived in Gunnisloe his entire life and had always been a competent blacksmith. But his size, his general lack of intellect, and his peculiar notions of personal hygiene had made him the butt of local jokes for years. The women teased him from afar, but none would go near him.

"Wot says 'ee, Will?" old Moody cajoled. "A woman of yer own at last. A real lady, too."

Big Will licked his lips and James felt a momentary tightening of his stomach. Did he pity the woman? Did he care? No. He did not. It was none of his concern what happened to her. It was none of his concern if the young husband happened to be a cad of the first degree, who allowed his wife to be ogled by that great slobbering animal, and who was ready to toss away his responsibilities to the highest bidder. Was James so confident of his own sense of honor? Did he honestly believe that he was himself incapable of such perfidy?

What a foolish notion, when he was in fact guilty of much more.

Urged on by the other men, Big Will edged closer to the plinth.

"She be yers fer twen'y pounds," Moody said. "A bargain she be, too. God knows 'ee won't never do no better."

"That be a lotta money," Big Will said, shaking his large head slowly side to side.

"Ah, but not fer the likes of 'ee, Will," Moody replied. "Got plen'y of the ready stashed away, 'ee does. Make decent money at forge. And all the district knows 'ee ain't spent a ha'penny in years. Besides, look at her, man. *Look* at her!"

Big Will continued to stare while the women in the crowd snickered and began beating their tin kettles once again. "Will! Will! Will!" the men shouted in time to the banging kettles. Will turned to the crowd and grinned, obviously pleased at being the center of attention.

"Will! Will! Will!"

The square throbbed with the hellish din until James could feel it through the soles of his boots.

"Will! Will! Will!"

With each shout and clang of kettles, the crowd surged forward slightly, closing in on the plinth.

More revelers entered the square and James was jostled from behind. He had to scramble to keep his balance as the mob continued to push, push, push ahead in rhythm with the pounding of kettles and the pulse of a hundred chanting voices.

"Will! Will! Will!"

The big man nodded at last and turned to the auctioneer. Old Moody held up his hand for silence, and the kettle banging gradually ceased.

"Aw right," Will said in his thick, toneless voice. He continued to leer at the woman who stood as still as Lot's wife. She had not raised her head once during all the commotion. "Twen'y quid, then."

Cheers and laughter rose from the crowd, and were soon drowned out by more kettle banging. James looked around him, astonished that these people, many of whom he'd known his entire life, were so eager to see this unknown, unsuspecting young woman thrust into the filthy, beefy arms of Will Sykes. They were going to let it happen; in fact, they were encouraging it to happen with no little enthusiasm.

James's glance darted between the woman and her husband. She stood ramrod straight against the rising wind, her head still bent down. Her hands were clasped tightly in front of her, their trembling the only outward sign of her anguish. Rarely had James witnessed such courage, even on the battlefields of Spain. And the wretched husband was going to let this thing happen. The young fool made no move to stop it.

It took Jud Moody some minutes to coax the raucous crowd to quiet. "Twen'y pounds from Big Will

Sykes," he said at last. "Does I have any more bids, then?"

The silence following the auctioneer's question sliced through James's gut like a French bayonet. Good Lord, what was wrong with him? He did not know this woman. He did not care what happened to her. It was none of his affair. If a young woman was about to be sold—*sold,* for God's sake!—to the most repulsive man in all of Cornwall, then so be it. It was nothing to James.

Still, she had not raised her head. She had no idea what fate awaited her. No idea at all. James wrenched his gaze from her and looked at the husband. The man had paled and looked as though he was about to be ill as he stared wide-eyed at Big Will. But he said nothing.

It was time to leave. James had no wish to remain for the last act of this hideous little drama.

But he could not seem to turn away.

"No more bids, then?" Moody repeated.

A knot began to form in James's stomach. His gaze raked the grinning, laughing crowd, whipped up by the wind and the excitement of the bidding like participants in some frenzied pagan ritual.

He looked once more at the tethered woman, rigid and trembling before the impassioned mob.

Damnation.

"If I has no more bids, then, the lady be sold—"

"I'll give one hundred pounds!"

A collective gasp rose from the crowd, followed by an ominous hush. Verity Osborne Russell looked up for the first time since mounting the plinth.

The gathering in the market square appeared incongruously small compared to the monstrous horde she had imagined. She had seen them, of course, when Gilbert had first led her into the square. But once the halter had been placed around her neck, everything had changed. The crowd had swelled and swelled into a hostile, taunting mob. To acknowledge them would have been to acknowledge what was happening, which Verity could not bring herself to do. And so she had resolutely refused to look up.

But she had felt thousands of sneering eyes raking her from head to toe, groping her with their prurient regard as surely as the auctioneer had with his wretched hands. And the rhythmic chanting had risen to such a pitch that Verity had felt herself shrinking beneath the enormous weight of that one hideous, united voice.

And the ear-shattering din of a hundred metal drums. For one irrational moment, she had believed they might take those sticks and spoons and whatever else they used to pound their kettles and turn them on her. She had actually feared for her life.

But Verity no longer interested them. All eyes had turned toward the tall, dark-haired man who stood at the back of the crowd. The man who had, apparently, just offered one hundred pounds for her.

He placed a high-crowned black hat upon his head, and it served as some sort of signal to the crowd. They parted before him like the Red Sea before the staff of Moses. He did not move forward, but seemed to glare straight at Verity. An uncontrollable shiver of apprehension danced down her spine. Her moment of terror was not yet over.

"Well, then," the auctioneer said into the silence. No longer that of the eager, bantering pitchman, his voice had become hesitant, almost strained. "One hun'red pounds from Lord Harkness."

Lord Harkness? He was a titled gentleman? A nobleman? A small bubble of hope rose up in Verity's chest. Perhaps he had come to put a stop to this unspeakable exhibition. Perhaps he was a true gentleman who was not about to allow this nightmare to continue. Perhaps he meant to bring Gilbert to his senses.

But no. His unwavering gaze was fixed on her. Not on the rowdy crowd that had tormented her. Not on the loathsome auctioneer. Not on Gilbert. His interest was all on Verity. This nobleman was not her savior. He had bid on her. He meant to purchase her.

"Don't suppose any o' the rest of 'ee can outbid His Lordship, eh?" the auctioneer said. After only the briefest of pauses, he continued. "The lady be sold, then, to Lord Harkness fer the gen'rous sum o' one hun'red pounds."

Sold.

A renewed and heart-pounding panic engulfed her. She had been sold. Sold.

The word reverberated in her head, louder than the crash of ten thousand metal drums, overpowering everything that had gone before. *Sold.*

It was impossible. This was the nineteenth century, for God's sake. Such things simply did not happen in these modern times, in this modern, enlightened Britain. Did they?

And yet she had just been sold. Like a horse at Tattersall's. Like a bonnet in a milliner's window or a sweetmeat from a confectioner. Like a slave.

Verity heard Gilbert's sigh of relief behind her. She had been sold and her husband was relieved. Was it because he was rid of her at last? Because he could now turn her over to a nobleman instead of the local blacksmith? Because he would receive one hundred pounds for her rather than a mere twenty?

It did not matter. Nothing about Gilbert mattered anymore.

Verity concentrated on the dark stranger now advancing through the crowd. The hat shadowed his face, so she was unable to get a good look at him. But something in the way he moved was arresting—an almost threatening kind of animal grace, an imperious arrogance. The unnerving silence of the crowd gave way to hushed whisperings as he walked toward the plinth. Those he passed watched him with eyes wide and mouths agape, stepping back as though afraid to get too close. Neighbor nudged neighbor and whispered in each other's ears. Children clung to their parents. Some pointed and giggled nervously.

The man ignored their reactions and strode ahead with a haughty arrogance that implied they had every right to be afraid.

Verity watched his maddeningly slow approach and every muscle in her already tense body tightened until she began to quiver like a bow string. She made a tiny, instinctive movement toward Gilbert—but her husband was no longer available to her. He never had been, really. Whatever tenuous ties bound them had been loosened the moment he put the halter around her neck, then severed completely with the single word "sold."

Verity clenched her hands tighter, locked her elbows and knees in an attempt to control her body. But the tighter she held herself, the more she trembled. She could not stop shaking.

The man continued his slow progress through the square. She overheard several muffled exclamations of "Lord Heartless!" But surely the auctioneer had called him Harkness. It was only her own anxiety that twisted the name into something more sinister.

But, dear Lord, how the people seemed to fear him. Who was he? And was she truly to be turned over to him like some prime bit of horseflesh, to this strange man who seemed to strike terror in the hearts of those who knew him?

Sold.

She could not stop the trembling. It overtook her completely: down into her belly until she felt queasy, and up into her throat so that she could not seem to swallow. She tried to stop it, to hold herself still, but it only seemed to get worse. Every muscle was held so taut she began to feel the sticky dampness of perspiration from the effort. Her petticoat clung to her legs and a trickle of moisture inched down the back of her neck. The wind against her damp skin chilled her. And still she trembled. Her whole body shook uncontrollably. She could not seem to stop it.

She must get hold of herself. She must not show her fear to this man, for perhaps he was one of those men who thrived on it. With slow, jerky movements, she reached up and grabbed the edges of her cloak and pulled it close about her, twisting her hands into the fabric to disguise their shaking.

When he reached the plinth, Verity saw the man's face clearly for the first time. It was harsh and angular and frowning. Heavy black brows beetled over intense blue eyes that skewered her to the spot, rapier sharp. When at last he jerked his glance away toward Gilbert, Verity let out a ragged breath. Her heart thundered in her ears. Surely he would hear it and know her fear.

"Are you the husband?" he asked in a deep, cultured voice.

She heard a shuffling movement behind her. "Yes."

"You wish to be rid of your wife?"

"Yes."

A wave of white-hot anger swept through Verity at that moment, almost smothering her fear. If she could have managed it, Verity would like to have swung around and slapped her husband full across the face. How dare he wish to be rid of her? It was not as though she had ever wanted him. Their marriage had been arranged by their fathers before they had even laid eyes on each other. If truth be told, during these last two interminable years she had often wished to be rid of Gilbert. But *she* had not been allowed to do so, simply because she wished it.

"You will sell her to me for one hundred pounds?" the dark man asked.

Gilbert moved forward so that he was standing beside Verity. Without moving, she slanted her eyes toward him. He removed his hat and ran his fingers through his fair hair.

"Well, as to that . . ." He paused, smoothed his hair, and replaced the hat upon his head, adjusting it to a cocky angle. He darted a glance toward Verity. "A hundred pounds will get you the woman," he said. "Another hundred will get you her things."

Verity heard a sharp intake of breath from the dark man. "Another hundred pounds?" he said in a voice edged with steel.

"It . . . it's a bargain, you see," Gilbert said. "I have her trunk of clothes and personal things in my coach. For a hundred pounds she can take them with her. 'Tis a fair price. It would cost you more than that to outfit her, would it not?"

The dark stranger fixed Gilbert with a look of such fury she thought he must be scorched by its intensity. She shuddered and tightened her grip on the cloak.

After what seemed minutes, the man reached into his coat and brought out a velvet sovereign purse. He fingered it briefly, then flung it roughly at Gilbert. "Take the whole bloody thing," he said. "There's over two hundred pounds in it. Take it and be off. Leave her trunk behind."

Gilbert pocketed the purse and stepped closer to Verity, who had not yet been able to move a muscle. "All right," he said. "I'll go. Verity, I—"

"Hold on, there, gen'l'mun," the auctioneer interrupted. "Can't just take the money an' be off like that. There be papers 'ee both got to sign first."

"Ah. Yes. Right," Gilbert said, still looking at Verity. "I had almost forgot."

"Follow me, then," the auctioneer said.

He and Gilbert turned toward the rear of the plinth. Verity was obviously meant to go with them, but she could not move. The trembling had subsided somewhat, but she could not move. She stood stiff as a statue, her feet screwed to the spot. If she could take but one step, then she might be able to take another, and then another, until she was running away. Away from this nightmare.

But she could not move.

"Wait!" The dark stranger strode up the two steps and stood directly in front of Verity. He reached out for her, and Verity's heart lurched in her chest. But then his hands circled the leather halter around her neck and began to unfasten it. "There is no need for this," he said. He slid the halter from her neck and tossed it into the crowd below.

Verity closed her eyes and let out a long, shuddery breath, then flexed her neck. After one more deep breath she eased the tight hold on the muscles in her shoulders, her back, her arms, her legs. Inch by inch, the tension in her body was gradually released until she stood composed and still. The trembling had stopped. She slowly untangled her fingers from the folds of the cloak and stretched them wide, then reached up to touch her throat where the halter had been. Panic no longer paralyzed her. She could move now. She could walk. She could walk away.

But she did not. The dark man looked at her with an unreadable expression. Inexplicably, she wanted to smile at him, but he stepped behind her to join Gilbert and the auctioneer. Verity pressed her fingers to her lips and wondered what had got into her. She turned and walked toward the men as they leaned over a small table at the rear of the plinth. She stepped closer and saw that they examined a parchment sheet. A deed of sale, no doubt. The disposition of her future.

Gilbert wrote a few lines on the parchment and handed the quill to the dark man. He dipped it in the tiny inkwell and scrawled something quickly. Verity leaned in closer for a better look—a glimpse into her fate.

> *I, Gilbert Russell, doth agree to part with my wife, Verity Russell, née Osborne, to James Gordon, Lord Harkness, for the sum of two hundred pounds, in consideration of relinquishing to him all rights, obligations, property claims, services, and demands whatsoever.*

And so she was to be transferred from one man to the next like a plot of land.

Verity did not for one minute believe that such a document legitimized the transaction. It could not possibly be legal. Could it? She watched as the auctioneer prepared a second copy of the document. Gilbert and Lord Harkness signed this one as well. The auctioneer sprinkled both documents with sand and handed one to each gentleman. Gilbert folded his copy and tucked it into his jacket. Lord Harkness stared at his copy, frowning, as if the words were incomprehensible to him.

He looked up and caught Verity's eye. For the briefest instant, their gazes locked. An unexpected hint of emotion—was it pity?—flickered across his eyes, but was gone in a blink. She might have imagined it, for he was scowling again before he turned away to speak with Gilbert.

After a few terse words Lord Harkness looked toward Verity again, but did not meet her eyes. "Let us be on our way," he said. "I believe we are quite through here."

Indeed, she was quite through. The life she had known, all that was familiar and routine, was over.

Lord Harkness stepped down from the plinth. He did not touch her, did not take her arm, but made it clear that he expected her to follow. Verity took a deep breath and moved to do so.

"Verity, wait."

She stopped at the sound of Gilbert's voice but did not turn around. She would not look at him. She never wanted to look at him again.

"I . . . I'm sorry, Verity," he said behind her in an uncertain voice. "It was the only way."

She did not understand how it could be so, but did not care. She was as anxious to be rid of him as he apparently was to be rid of her. She wanted to be gone. She wanted this to be over.

"Well," he continued, "at least now you are free of me."

Verity said nothing, and walked away from her husband for the last time.

She took two hesitant steps toward the edge of the plinth, and stopped. Lord Harkness waited below. After a moment, he reached up a hand to her, silently offering to help her down the steps.

Verity looked at that gloved hand and knew that if she took it, she would be tacitly accepting his protection. She had no idea what role he had in mind for her—mistress, servant, prisoner, slave? He may have a deed of sale, but she would never belong to him. He may own her body, but he would never have her soul. Never.

She clasped her hands at her waist and thrust out her chin. Slowly and cautiously, for her muscles had begun to seize up again with tension, she descended the steps on her own, ignoring his proffered hand. Lord Harkness quirked a brow, and his mouth twisted into what looked like a smirk. But he had turned around and walked on before she could be sure.

He did not turn back to see that she followed. He apparently had no doubt that she would do so. He had removed her halter and turned his back on her, making certain that she knew she was free to stay behind, and knowing that she would not. How could he be so sure of her? How could he know that she would not run away?

Verity's eyes darted about the crowded square, and she knew there was nowhere else to go. Not among these people, who had mocked her, tormented her, insulted her. At least Lord Harkness had done none of those things.

She would go with him. For now.

The whispering began as the crowd parted for them, as they had done for him earlier.

". . . Lord Heartless . . ."

"Ea! Poor thing."

"Wot'll become of her?"

"How long will she . . ."

"Lord Heartless . . ."

". . . her, too?"

"Do you suppose he will . . ."

"The poor creature, her . . ."

". . . another victim?"

"God help her."

Shaken by the half-heard whispers and concerned frowns, Verity clasped her hands together so tightly her fingernails dug painfully into her palms. Dear Lord, what was she headed for? What did these people believe he was going to do with her? Determined not to let the crowd see her fear, she kept her head high and followed the tall figure striding ahead. Yet for all her outward composure, she might as well have been riding through the square in a tumbril headed for the scaffold. She did not care to consider how close to the truth such an end might be.

Horrible, disjointed images invaded her mind, whispered childhood memories as incomprehensible now as then, but frightening in their implications. Hushed secrets from the last century about the Hellfire Club, about the Marquis de Sade, about white slavery.

Was this to be her fate? To be sacrificed to the whims of this dark stranger, to suffer unspeakable acts at his hand? To be tortured or even killed?

For some unaccountable reason—pride? stubbornness?—she did not want to die. Though she had nothing in particular to live for, she wanted to live.

With a determined tilt of her chin, she followed Lord Harkness to a plain, unmarked black carriage waiting in a nearby lane, blessedly removed from the market crowd. A coachman in white leather breeches, striped waistcoat, and dark jacket held the horses' heads while a footman opened the carriage door.

Once again, Lord Harkness offered his hand to assist her into the carriage, but she ignored him and he stepped aside to speak with the coachman. When the footman, a strapping ginger-haired fellow with an open, friendly face, offered to hand her up, she did not hesitate to accept.

Inside, the coach was elegant but not opulent. The seats and walls were upholstered in tufted blue velvet, the trimmings plain brass and mahogany. Its comfort was a blessing after the poor equipage Gilbert had hired for the journey to Cornwall.

But she must not allow a friendly footman and comfortable coach to confuse the situation.

The carriage began to bounce slightly. They must be loading the boot. Verity prayed that her trunk was intact, for it held practically everything she owned. She understood now why Gilbert had told her to pack so thoroughly: He had known she would not be coming back.

The carriage door opened and the young footman stuck his head in. "Pardon me, ma'am," he said. "But we had to unload these here cases o' wine to make room for yer trunk. Nuthin' fer it but to stack 'em here." He proceeded to pile three wooden crates on the seat opposite.

Dear God, was Lord Harkness a drunkard, too? Her father had seldom taken more than a glass at mealtime. Three cases of wine would have lasted him a year. How quickly would Lord Harkness drink his way through it? And was she to play some role in his drunken debaucheries?

The subject of her thoughts launched himself into the coach, seated himself next to her, and pulled the door behind him. His thigh brushed against hers, and Verity flinched as though singed. She scooted across the bench as far as she could and pressed up against the side panel. She fixed her gaze out the window, studying the plain granite wall that faced her.

"Are you . . . quite comfortable?" Lord Harkness asked.

Verity nodded without turning to look at him.

"Pendurgan is less than five miles away," he continued in an awkward-sounding tone. "We should be there in three-quarters of an hour or so."

Pendurgan. Even the name was frightening. She was going to a place called Pendurgan with a man called Heartless. Heaven help her.

The carriage lurched and pulled away. Verity grabbed the strap and hung on for her life.

Chapter 2

James drummed his fingers on the window ledge of the carriage. He had never felt so stupid in all his life. He had just bought and paid for a young woman. Now, what the devil was he supposed to do with her?

What had possessed him to do such a rash, impulsive thing? He should have known better. He ought to have stayed out of it, walked away from the market square without a second thought. God knows, he had no business bringing a young woman into his home. Not after all that had happened. And yet he had signed a paper accepting full responsibility for her. How could he have done such a damned fool thing?

And how was he to explain her to his household? He couldn't exactly trot her out like a new race horse, or deposit her in Mrs. Tregelly's care as though she were a new kitchen maid. Blast it all, he wished she were in fact some scruffy bit of baggage that could be dumped in the scullery and forgot about. But it had been obvious that she was of his own class, gentry at the very least. She had to be dealt with. Somehow.

And there was Agnes to consider. How was he to explain her to Agnes?

By morning everyone from Liskeard to Truro would have heard the tale, each making his own conclusions about James's plans for the woman. It did not take a superior mind to anticipate what those conclusions would be.

Bloody hell. He was to be the center of a scandal once again.

He looked over at her, but she was turned, pressed close against the door panel. No doubt she wished to avoid even the slightest contact with her new—what? Owner? But she was not his slave. Employer? She was not his servant, either. Husband? Certainly not.

What the devil was she, then? And what the hell was he supposed to do with her?

She would not even look at him, for God's sake. He might have known what to do if she had been a weepy, fragile young thing who looked to him for security, who clung to him as her savior after such a public humiliation. He would not have minded that, to have her cling to him. He recalled the full bosom revealed by Moody's hands. But she did not cling. She did not sob or swoon. Neither did she rant or shout about the injustice of her circumstances.

She did none of those things, damn her eyes, and so he did not know what to do.

She kept one hand at her waist, gripping the edge of her cloak, while the other held on to the strap so tightly James thought she might rip it out of the panel. And she kept her gaze fixed firmly out the window, the poke of her bonnet shielding her face.

He had, though, got a pretty good look at her—Verity, the husband had called her—when he stood before her at the base of the old market cross. She had been all huge brown eyes, wide with apprehension, set in a face of unnatural pallor. Though she tried to stand tall, she was slightly below average in height, the top of her head coming to just below his chin. And she had been shivering as violently as though just lifted from an icy sea. He recognized the great effort of will it had cost her to bring the trembling under control. She made the effort still, with her tight hold on the strap.

If only she would look at him. If only she would say something.

It occurred to James that he had yet to hear the sound of her voice. She had not uttered a single word during the entire ugly proceedings. Not to her husband. Not to Jud Moody. Certainly not to him.

As the carriage clattered and bounced over the broad granite cobbles of Gunnisloe's main road, he wondered what sort of voice she might have. He supposed it depended on where she was from. Moody had called her a foreigner, but that merely meant she was not Cornish. James gazed out the window at the squat, close-built granite cottages lining the narrow road and thought how bleak and colorless this part of Cornwall must appear to a stranger.

In some irrational way, her continued silence irritated him. He felt certain she would not speak or in any way acknowledge him, or their situation, until it was absolutely necessary. She was all wrapped up in a fierce sort of pride that had allowed her to survive the spectacle at Gunnisloe. She would not break just yet.

At any other time he might have admired such strength of character, but he was not disposed to such nonsense just now. Her quiet self-control, her infernal dignity, began to grate on his nerves. She was an enormous inconvenience, an unwanted and awkward responsibility he cursed himself for taking on.

And so, as the carriage lumbered along, the awkward silence continued, punctuated by the rattle of the windows and the clanging of the swingle bar as they left Gunnisloe behind and passed onto the deeply rutted, muddy road.

James wondered irritably if he should break the silence. But why should he make the effort when *she* was the one complicating his life? Besides, she—Verity, he remembered—was clearly frightened. Her savage grip on the leather strap signaled the level of her anxiety.

Of course she feared him. The bloody fools in Gunnisloe had seen to that. She had heard their malicious whispering and hollow concern—these same people who had been ready to toss her over to Will Sykes. But the big smith was merely gross and filthy, essentially harmless. They considered James the worst sort of monster, as though they feared he meant some kind of harm to her.

And the truly frightening thing was, they might be right.

His gaze wandered and took in the passing landscape. Damnation. He ought to have told his coachman to take the longer, southern route to Pendurgan, along the lush banks of the river. This road ran straight through one of the harsher stretches of Bodmin Moor. She probably thought he was escorting her to some kind of devil's lair.

As he watched her, James realized the view out her window was even more ominous than his own view of the faraway tors. For in the distance stood the ruined buildings of Wheal Zelah, a mine that had played out in his grandfather's time. The derelict windlass and crumbling engine house were a common enough sight in Cornwall, but what would this woman make of them, and of the slender chimney starkly silhouetted against the purple sky of dusk? And the slack heaps arranged like pyramids at the base? For one unacquainted with mines it must surely appear strange and godforsaken.

The coachman slowed the horses and edged toward the side of the road as though to allow another carriage to pass. Few carriages besides his own ever took this road, so James leaned toward his companion to get a better look out her window, where the other vehicle would pass. She flinched as his shoulder touched hers. He muttered a Cornish oath and pulled away at once, silently damning the woman for making him feel so awkward. "I beg your pardon," he said under his breath.

The carriage came to a complete stop to allow an approaching mule train to pass. James gave a soft but thoroughly wicked chuckle over what she would make of *this* peculiar sight. The big gray mules marched in pairs with panniers of copper ore slung over their backs. The panniers were stuffed full, a sight that brought a brief smile to James's face, for it was his ore, from his mines.

The wind carried the distant sounds of Wheal Devoran upon it: the low rattle and clang of the draught bob pumping water up from the lowest reaches of the earth, slightly muffled by the mizzling rain that had begun to fall. It was the sound of a working mine and gladdened the heart of any true Cornishman.

" 'Tis a good lode this year," he murmured.

The woman started at his words but did not turn around. Damn her skittish hide. He would keep his mouth shut until they had reached Pendurgan.

In the meantime, he must devise a plan. His servants dared not question him. But Agnes . . . He would have to tell her something. He must contrive some reasonable explanation of how he had left for Gunnisloe alone and returned with a young woman in tow.

And then he must determine how he was to keep away from her.

Damn, damn, damn.

The last of the mules trudged past the carriage, led by two unsmiling men whose faces and clothes were caked in mud, giving them a dark, almost featureless appearance. They wore broad, stiff-looking hats with odd little stubs of candles stuck on the brims.

A shiver fluttered down Verity's spine. What sort of place was this? She had grown up in the lush wolds of Lincolnshire, where the landscape was as different from this desolate spot as it could possibly be. Even Gilbert's home in Berkshire, though ramshackle and remote, had been nestled in the wooded downs. Nothing in her life had prepared her for such a place as this, with hardly a tree in sight, and those solitary few naked and black, as cheerless as the land. It was grim and alien, with its curious ruins and rocky moors, everything a harmonious gray.

And as though Lord Harkness had arranged it especially for her, it began to rain in earnest. A hard wind buffeted the coach so that it swayed and rocked along the rutted road. Verity sat huddled in her corner as they were pitched from side to side, and the sound of the wind mingled with the creaking of the carriage to create a shrill and mournful howl.

She kept a firm grip on the leather strap. She ought to have wrenched her gaze from the distressing, inhospitable landscape, but then she might have been tempted to shift her concentration to the silent stranger at her side. She could not ignore his closeness, or the jolt of apprehension that shook her like a sort of electrical shock each time the rocking of the coach caused her thigh to brush up against his.

The carriage slowed as the rain beat down more violently. Its wheels flung up mud from the road to splatter the window. Within minutes the view of the forbidding moorland had become entirely obscured.

Verity turned away from the window at last, closed her eyes, and imagined that when she opened them, she would find the sunny skies and gentle green wolds of Lincolnshire.

A slight movement at her side caused her to open her eyes. Curious, she slanted her gaze toward Lord Harkness, keeping her head forward so he would not notice. She shifted a fraction of an inch, just so she could peek at him beyond the brim of her poke bonnet. He, too, stared straight ahead. He had tossed his tall beaver onto one of the crates on the opposite bench. His hair looked black as a crow's wing in the gray light of the carriage. It grew long over his ears and hung slightly over the high collar of his shirt. It appeared to be dusted with silver at the temples, but that may have been a trick of the light. His profile showed a firm jaw and a strong nose with a slight bump along the ridge. She could not see his eyes, and indeed had no wish to do so, recollecting that brief but intense moment when their eyes had met in the town square.

Suddenly the coach lurched sharply, pressing Verity against the back of the bench as it began to climb a steep slope. The rain pounded hard against the windows, washing away most of the mud and revealing a view that caused her to gasp in surprise. The stark moorland gave way, at the top of the hill, to a thick, dark woodland. Though black and looming, as sinister as all she had seen during the journey from the town, the woodland nevertheless appeared incongruous after so much emptiness. The copse of trees seemed to spring magically straight out of the granite moor.

Verity knew in her heart that hidden among that grim-looking forest was her destination: Pendurgan.

"Ah, we are almost there," Lord Harkness said, startling Verity while she peered curiously out the window. "That is Pendurgan just ahead. My home."

As the carriage reached the crest of the hill, they entered a lush knoll encompassed by trees—chestnut trees, if she was not mistaken. Imagine that. Chestnut trees thriving in all that granite. Someone had gone to a great deal of trouble to protect—or hide?—the house.

And then she saw it. It did not look so much like a house as like a small, ancient castle. Squat and gray, its thick, embattled walls were pierced in only two places by high, narrow, slit windows. The rest, seemed to be unbroken, unadorned, unimpeachable granite. The structure appeared to rise up from the very stone beneath its feet.

Dear Lord. It was the sort of place one entered and never left, sinister and malevolent. The thick walls would close upon one like a prison.

The carriage drove through an arched gateway in the thick outer wall into a large inner courtyard. Though less imposing than the outside—at least there were windows, lots of windows—it still appeared a harsh, unwelcoming, rough-looking building.

The carriage came to a halt, and the ginger-haired footman swung open the door on her side and pulled down the step. Verity warily took his hand and climbed down. The rain fell hard upon the gravel drive, and she clutched her cloak close about her as she stood beside the carriage, uncertain what to do.

"Bring her trunk round to the great hall, Tomas," Lord Harkness said to the footman in a loud, sharp voice. "Jago, take the coach round back to the kitchen and unload the rest. Then get these horses out of the rain."

He turned quickly to Verity, grabbed her upper arm, and tugged her in the direction of a set of huge wooden doors. It was the first time he'd touched her, and she flinched slightly at the roughness of it. Not from fear, for she knew it had more to do with getting them both out of the rain than with any sort of brutality. There was something else, though, that caused her to flinch, caused her skin beneath his fingers to prickle and flush. She could not name what it was, but it frightened her as much as anything else that had happened this day.

Lord Harkness gave a sort of growl and stopped in his tracks. Tightening the hold on her arm, he turned her to face him. "Dammit," he snapped, "let us get one thing straight. While you are at Pendurgan, Mrs. . . . what was it? Russell? Mrs. Russell?"

"No!"

The word was uttered before she could check it. But after all that had happened this day, the name was anathema to her.

Lord Harkness glared at Verity through the curtain of rain that poured off the brim of his hat. A deep scowl beetled his brow as though he wanted to snap her head off for speaking at all.

"No," she repeated. She could hardly breathe from the effort of speaking even that single word. She wanted to say more, to explain about the name, but the very thought of speaking to this dark stranger who'd brought her to this forbidding place was liable to set her whole body to trembling once again.

"Verity Osborne," was all she could manage.

"You can call yourself anything you bloody well like," he said in an angry tone. "Anything, so long as we can get the hell out of this rain."

"Verity Osborne," she repeated, relieved at the more controlled tone she'd managed. The tiny victory gave her the will to stand taller and actually look him in the eye.

"Fine," he replied sharply. "Splendid. But you will be *Mrs.* Osborne while at Pendurgan. There'll be the devil of time explaining your arrival in any case," he continued in the same angry tone, brushing away the rain from his face. "But I refuse to have it put about that I have brought an unchaperoned young *miss* into my home. God almighty, that's the last thing I need."

With that, he tugged again on her arm and led her to the big doors that now stood open. A plump, silver-haired woman in a dark blue dress and white apron held the door. "My lord!" she exclaimed, her hands fluttering in agitation. "Come in quickly before you catch yer death."

Lord Harkness pushed Verity ahead until they were safely inside an enormous hall. The woman looked at her quizzically. "My lord?" she asked.

"Is the yellow bedchamber made ready for a guest, Mrs. Tregelly?" he asked in a curt, sharp tone as he removed his hat and shook the rain from his coattails.

"Yes, my lord," the woman replied. " 'Twas only last week we aired the mattresses and laid down fresh linen."

"Good. This is Mrs. Osborne. She will be staying with us for a while. Tomas, bring along her trunk and show Mrs. Osborne the way to the yellow bedchamber. Mrs. Tregelly, a word, if you please."

Without so much as a backward glance at Verity, he left the room. Mrs. Tregelly regarded Verity with a puzzled look, and then followed Lord Harkness. Verity stood in the entry hall, dripping rain all over the floor, and prayed the woman would come back. She had seemed so . . . normal. Grunting, the ginger-haired footman heaved the trunk onto his back. "This way, ma'am," he said.

Tomas, moving slowly with his heavy burden, led Verity across the broad hall. A fire in an enormous fireplace at one end provided the only light. It was difficult to make out details, but the room appeared to have a high beamed ceiling and dark paneling halfway up the whitewashed walls. Above the paneling, on every wall, hung row upon row upon row of swords, pikes, battle-axes, spears, rifles, and pistols of every kind. Scattered among the weapons were bits of armor—breastplates, helmets, and shields. Everything was polished to a sheen and glistened in the light of the fire.

"There be a candle on table just over there, ma'am," Tomas said, nodding toward a long trestle table placed against one of the walls. "Gets fair dark in these hallways. Best if 'ee takes a candle."

Verity picked up the candle and lit it by the fire, then followed Tomas as he led her into a dark corridor. They came at last to a stairway, the poor footman grunting and gasping with his burden. After a moment to catch his breath at the top of the stairs, he led her down another hallway and finally to an open doorway. "Here 'tis," he said, and stood aside waiting for Verity to enter. She hesitated, loath to go willingly into what might be her prison cell. At Tomas's plaintive look, she straightened her shoulders and walked into the room. The footman followed quickly behind and, with a groan, deposited her trunk near the foot of the bed. He then quickly set about making a fire in the fireplace.

"Is there anything else 'ee needs, ma'am?" he asked after he had initiated a roaring blaze.

Verity glanced about her. It was not at all what she had expected. "No," she said at last, still unprepared to trust her voice with more than a word or two.

"Very good, then," Tomas replied. "They dines at six, ma'am. It just be getting on five, so 'ee has a chance to rest up a bit. I'll make sure someone comes to get 'ee just afore six."

He bowed and left the room, closing the door behind him.

Verity sank down onto the edge of the bed with a sigh. It was a comfortable, if old-fashioned, bedchamber. The furnishings looked to be of a style at least a century old, heavy and dark. The bed and the windows were curtained with exquisite crewelwork on faded yellow cloth. The coffered ceiling was low, and the walls were hung with tapestries. The overall effect was dark, but somehow almost cozy.

But the chaos of her emotions robbed her of any sense of comfort. Seemingly normal servants, the offer of dinner, this lovely old room—none of it was in keeping with the forbidding granite exterior, the sinister-looking hall of weapons, or the mysterious master of Pendurgan himself. Which was the true face of Pendurgan? And which was the true nature of her own fate?

Verity sat unmoving on the bed for several minutes, too unsettled to stir. She considered unpacking her trunk, just to have something to do, to help keep her mind off the events of the last few hours. But to unpack would be tantamount to admitting defeat, to accepting this strange and dreadful situation. She lost track of time as she sat there on the bed, her mind a blank, as though waiting for someone to tell her what to do.

Finally she rose mechanically, untied her bonnet, and placed it on the bed. Then she removed her damp cloak and draped it over a chair near the fire. She had held her hands out to the flames to warm them when she heard the door behind her open. Startled, she straightened and turned around to find a dark figure silhouetted in the door frame. It was a woman, tall and thin, with her arms folded across her chest. She stepped into the room.

The light from the fire showed her to be an older woman with a pinched face and silver hair swept up in a style of some thirty years ago. She wore a simple black bombazine gown with no more ornament that a stark white fichu at the neck. She made an altogether strange and startling appearance, and Verity stared at her as though she were an apparition.

"So," the woman said at last, her voice dripping with disdain, "you are the one he brought here." Her eyes raked Verity from head to foot in a most insolent manner.

Who was this woman? Her manner of speech, if not her words, was refined, without the thick Cornish accent of Tomas or the softer Cornish of Mrs. Tregelly. She was certainly not a servant—a servant would never use such an impertinent tone. Unless, of course, it was directed to another servant. That must be it. Despite the comfortable bedchamber and apparent hospitality, she was to be a servant after all. But what sort of servant?

Unnerved by the woman's brazen scrutiny, Verity could only stare.

"Hmph. And you're not even pretty," the woman said, her sharp gaze taking in Verity's soaked hem and flattened hair. Unconsciously, Verity smoothed back stray wisps of hair at her temples and tucked them behind her ears. Why did this peculiar old woman care so much about her looks? Unless . . . unless she was being inspected for her suitability in a role where a woman's looks, and body, were of primary importance?

"Nothing like Rowena. Nothing at all. *She* was a beauty." The woman continued to glare at her in such a disquieting manner that Verity finally dropped her gaze to the floor. "Well, you will discover the truth about him soon enough." She turned quickly and walked away, the black skirts rustling with her brisk movement. When she reached the door, she paused and looked over her shoulder. "And then, by heaven," she said, "you will rue the day you ever came to Pendurgan."

Verity sank down on the bed and decided she'd had enough. She must get out of this place. Somehow, she had to escape. There was no one to help her; so she must be calm and she must think, without giving in to the wave of utter helplessness that threatened to overcome her. She was not used to taking matters into her own hands, and had generally allowed others to direct her life—her governess, her father, her husband.

But now she must take charge of her own fate. She was twenty-three years old, healthy, and reasonably sensible. She had never in all her life suffered an attack of nerves or indulged in a fit of the vapors. Now was not the time to give in to weakness.

Verity took a deep breath, pushed herself off the bed, and strode across the room to the door. Had the woman in black locked it behind her? Was she a prisoner? But of course she was—she was here against her will, was she not? It was merely the degree of confinement that was in question.

Verity grasped the doorknob and turned it. The door opened. She uttered a small sigh of relief and stepped into the hallway. It was lighted at intervals by brass wall sconces—and was perfectly empty. She was neither locked in nor guarded.

After one last look down the empty hallway, she quietly closed the door and walked across the room to the windows along the far wall. She swept back the heavy drapery and gazed out. Dusk had settled into darkness, and rain hammered against the mullioned panes, making it difficult to see anything outside. But there were no bars. Just simple, old-fashioned casement windows with ordinary sliding locks that had no more sinister purpose than to hold fast against the wind and rain. There even appeared to be a large tree adjacent to the window, several of its limbs within easy reach.

It was almost too easy.

Was she perhaps overreacting, finding evil where none existed? Could it be that there was nothing truly out of the ordinary about this household, that she was in fact perfectly safe? After all, would Lord

Harkness have made escape so apparently effortless if he truly meant harm to her, to confine her?

No, no, no, she thought, giving herself a mental shake. She could not allow herself to become complacent through the lack of bars on the windows and the absence of guards at her door, nor by the genial footman and sweet-faced housekeeper. She would not be lured into believing in her own safety. It could be a ruse. A trap. A trap that would be sprung once she had become comfortable, resigned, vulnerable.

No. She would persevere. She was going to leave—this very evening, if possible.

She peered out the window, squinting against the rain. No doubt the view was every bit as forbidding as it had been from the carriage. But Verity was willing to brave almost anything, just to be free of this place and this untenable situation.

She started at a loud rapping on the bedchamber door. Before she could respond, it was opened by a young girl with unruly wisps of red hair peeking out from beneath a mobcap.

"Evenin', ma'am," the girl said with a wary smile. "I brung hot water an' such for 'ee." She entered the room and placed the steaming brass canister on the washstand, along with a stack of white towels and a bar of soap.

Verity stared at the girl. What was this? Another seemingly friendly face and false amenities to lull her into comfort?

But hot water and soap sounded like heaven on earth. Verity felt not only grimy, but violated by the events of the day. Nothing would feel so good as to wash it all away.

The girl raised questioning brows at Verity's silence. "Thank you," Verity murmured. Though tension still gripped the back of her throat, only the slightest tremble colored her voice. Perhaps the girl would not notice.

"I'm to help 'ee unpack, too, ma'am, an' to see that ever'thin' be comfort'ble for 'ee."

So Verity was not to be a servant. But if not a servant, then what? The only answers that came to mind fueled her determination to flee.

"Thank you," Verity said, her voice still more tentative than she would have liked. She drew the curtain back down over the window, realizing she could see nothing to help her in her plan. She needed information. Perhaps the girl could be useful, if Verity could get her to talk. "Thank you," she repeated, more controlled this time.

"Mrs. Tregelly, she do say I'm to maid 'ee whilst yer at Pendurgan, ma'am," the girl said and bobbed an awkward curtsey. "My name's Gonetta." She stood facing Verity, hands behind her back, head lowered.

"A pretty name," Verity said. "Most unusual."

The girl shrugged. " 'Tis but an old Cornish name, ma'am. Common 'nuff round these parts."

"Not common to me, I'm afraid," Verity said, reaching for any topic that might get the girl talking. "I've never been to Cornwall, and so the language and names are quite new to me." She attempted a friendly smile.

The girl smiled readily in return. "I do hear tell," she said while fussing with the towels, "that folks from up country do find it hard to get their tongues round our words ofttimes. But don't 'ee be worrin' none. If 'ee do be stayin' awhile, 'ee be gettin' used to it soon 'nuff."

Staying awhile.

"Meanwhile, 'ee just tells us to slow down when our talk's not so clear. Now, me brother Tomas—he do be the footman what brung yer trunk up—he don't be sayin' much anyhow, so 'ee ought not have no trouble wid him. But me . . . Ma tells me I do rattle on fast as can be most times, but I'll try to be extra careful with 'ee, ma'am, 'ee bein' a foreigner an all."

Al tray tuh bay exter cawrfil wid ee, mum, ee bain ah furriner an awl. The accent was thick and unusual to Verity's ear, as hard to decipher as that of a Yorkshireman.

It was difficult not to smile at this seemingly ingenuous young girl, regardless of her role in this drama. But Verity had her own role to consider, and not necessarily the one assigned her. She would never have thought herself capable of dissimulation of any kind, but at the moment she thought she might be capable of any number of things, just to get out of here.

She forced a wider smile. "Thank you, Gonetta. I am very pleased to make your acquaintance. And I am—"

"Miz Osborne. I do know all about 'ee, ma'am."

Verity winced as though slapped. Of course, she would already be the subject of servants' gossip. What must they all think of her, a woman purchased at auction?

"Ma do say as how 'ee be his lordship's cousin and all," Gonetta went on. "And as how 'ee lost yer husband real sudden, like. I do be right sorry to hear that, ma'am. And as how 'ee had no place else ter go.

'Tis a real shame, 'tis, all that grief and hardship fallin' down on 'ee all at once, like."

So, she was to be Lord Harkness's cousin? She had wondered how he would explain her sudden appearance, or even if explanations were necessary. For all she knew, it might have been common enough for him to bring home unknown young women. She had assumed she would be acknowledged as his lordship's doxy, and that she would, in fact, be precisely that. Perhaps it was still the plan, but he was masking his intentions with this cousin story.

She shivered at the thought of all that implied, but it did not matter. Verity did not intend to stay around long enough to find out.

"Ea, but listen at me!" Gonetta exclaimed, blushing to the roots of her carroty hair. "I do got no right to be sayin' such things to 'ee. Beg pardon, ma'am, but me tongue it do run on sometimes." She caught her lower lip in her teeth, apparently flustered at the perceived breach of familiarity.

Gonetta's nervous babbling was precisely what Verity needed at the moment. Fortunately, no prompting was necessary.

" 'Tis a fine old place, Pendurgan be," Gonetta went on, looking up once again. "Old as the tors, almost. I do hope 'ee will be likin' it here," she added shyly. "I'll be startin' the unpackin' now."

"Thank you, Gonetta." At the girl's request, Verity retrieved the trunk key from her reticule and reluctantly passed it to her. Verity turned away, not wanting to be distracted by her possessions and all that they meant to her now that she was alone and cast adrift, without resources, without friends.

Somehow, after Gonetta's careful unpacking, Verity must gather up only what she could comfortably carry. She would have to resign herself to leaving the rest behind.

"I wonder, Gonetta," Verity said, forcing a cheerful tone to her voice, "if you could tell me a bit about Pendurgan and this area of Cornwall. I've never been to the West Country, you see, and it is quite unfamiliar to me. As we drove to Pendurgan it was dark and rainy and I could not see much. But I confess the land looked quite barren and rocky."

"Oh, 'ee must o' come from the north, then," Gonetta said as she gently shook out a favorite muslin frock and hung it in the wardrobe. It was probably too frivolous a garment and would have to be left behind. "Through the moor," Gonetta continued. " 'Tis a shame 'ee came in that way. 'Tis craggy and harsh in that direction, to be sure. But look here." She stepped to the window and drew back the curtain. "Oh, it do be too dark to see much, but honest, 'tis quite lovely from the south. There do be gardens and lawns out this way, and the river runs just at the edge of the estate, over there," she said, pointing to the east.

"Oh." Verity quelled her excitement. A river! If she could make her way outside, it would be simple enough to follow a river. "I did not know there was a river nearby," she said with feigned nonchalance. "We came from . . . oh, goodness. I cannot recall the name of the town."

"Gunnisloe, ma'am. Not much of a town, 'cept on market day when folks do come from all over."

Yes, Verity knew all about market day in Gunnisloe. She would not attempt escape in that direction. "Are there other towns or villages nearby, along the river?"

"Oh, yes, ma'am," Gonetta replied. "The next big town up river do be Bodmin, o' course. But St. Perran's be only a step away to the south. That do be our village, St. Perran's. Not much more'n a few cottages, the church, an' a kiddly or two. Mostly miners do live in the village proper. The tenant farmers do be more spread out."

"Farmers? There is farming at Pendurgan?"

"Oh, yes, ma'am. Did his lordship not tell 'ee?" Gonetta clucked her tongue as she folded a muslin and lace cap. "Jus' like a man to be more interested in the mines an' all that fancy machinery. But, yes, there do be good farmin' here. We do grow wheat and barley, and do keep a small herd of sheep."

Verity was encouraged by this information. The land she had seen on the carriage ride to Pendurgan could not have supported a bean, much less healthy crops of wheat. And if they kept sheep then there must be grazing land. It would be much less dreadful, she thought, to escape over familiar-looking farmland than across the rocky moors.

"I must say," she said, "it certainly sounds different from the land we rode through today."

"Like night an' day it do be, ma'am," Gonetta replied. "Night an' day. Just wait till 'ee do see it in the morning and 'ee'll know what I do mean."

Verity hoped to be well on her way before morning. "I long to see it," she said. "Tell me, Gonetta. We entered through a courtyard into a sort of great hall—"

"The Killin' Hall."

A chill crept down Verity's spine. "Killing Hall?"

"Aye," Gonetta said, placing Verity's ivory brush and comb on the washstand. "Did 'ee ever see so many awful old weapons an' such? I do call it the Killin' Hall cuz I figure them things done their fair share o' killin' over the years."

"Indeed," Verity said, "but not lately, one hopes."

"Oh no, ma'am," Gonetta said emphatically. "Mrs. Tregelly, she do keep us polishin' 'em to such a shine. Like as not she do be the first to murder anyone what do touch 'em."

"That is certainly reassuring," Verity murmured. "But how does one get out to the south side," she continued, "where the gardens are? I tend to rise early and may want to take a walk around the place, explore a bit."

"Oh, 'ee do just go downstairs like when 'ee do first come," Gonetta said, "only don't be goin' toward the Killin' Hall. Go left from the stairs past the lib'ary and out the south entrance."

"And can I get to the river from the gardens?"

"Oh, aye. The grounds skirt the river. 'Ee can't miss it. 'Tis a pretty sight in the early hours, 'tis."

"Will I be any trouble if I wander very early?" Verity asked. "Will the entrances be locked?"

Gonetta stopped folding a chemise and looked up. "Locked? Lord bless me, nuthin' do be ever locked at Pendurgan. Who be gonna break inta this sturdy old place, perched way up here all by itself? Ha! Don't 'ee worry 'bout nuthin', ma'am. We be safe as milk up here. Just 'ee wander about all 'ee wants."

Verity savored the tiny burst of newborn confidence. Though Gonetta made it sound not at all difficult, it would surely be the hardest move Verity had ever made—striking out on her own, friendless, with little more than pin money and a few trumpery pieces of jewelry to sustain her.

But she would be away from this place. Away from him.

She could do it.

"What would 'ee be wearin' for dinner, ma'am? Shall I be havin' somethin' pressed for 'ee?"

Dinner? Good Lord. The momentary rush of elation collapsed like a house of cards. She had been tricked by the early darkness into forgetting that she had an entire evening ahead of her before she could effect an escape. An entire evening she was no doubt meant to spend in the company of Lord Harkness and perhaps the woman in black.

No. Not now, just when she had screwed up what little courage she had to do this. She might lose her nerve if she had to face that man again.

"Oh, Gonetta," she said, not even having to feign a tone of distress, "would you see if I might have a tray in my room? I really am quite fagged to death and do not believe I am up to dressing for dinner."

"Yes, ma'am. I'll be bringin' a tray up m'self, an' a nice pot o' tea to soothe yer bones. Then we be tuckin' 'ee up all right and tight so's 'ee do be getting' a nice long rest. If 'ee do need anythin' whilst I do be gone, 'ee just do pull that there cord by the bed and I do be up in two shakes."

As soon as the door closed behind the girl, Verity slumped against the bedpost with relief. She would not have to see him again. She would not have to face those menacing brows and piercing blue eyes. The man called Heartless would not be able to frighten her out of doing what had to be done.

She began to rummage through her clothes, deciding what she would carry with her on her escape.

Chapter 3

James sat with his back to the smoldering fire and read the same paragraph for the third time. It was no use. He could not concentrate on the essay. He let the book fall open on his lap and closed his eyes. But he would not sleep yet. He fought it, as ever, unwilling to surrender without a struggle to the inevitable nightmares. He was not sleepy in any case. His mind was in turmoil.

He reached into the pocket of his waistcoat and fingered the bill of sale from the auction. The crisp parchment rustled loudly, inviting him to read it one more time. But there was no need. He had memorized the words some hours ago, and those words plagued him, kept him awake.

All rights. Obligations. Property claims. Services and demands. Obligations. Obligations.

The wretched document would probably not hold up in a court of law. Even so, his signature was there for all to see, and declared that he freely accepted this . . . this obligation, regardless of the legalities involved. He was a gentleman, after all, and—

His own cynical chuckle interrupted that absurd train of thought. Lord Heartless, a gentleman? There were many who would dispute that fine point.

James tucked away the loathsome parchment in his waistcoat pocket. It had been many long years since he had considered himself either noble or honorable. So, why not just give the woman an apron and a mop, put her to work in the scullery, and be done with foolish anxiety?

Obligations.

What was he to do about Verity Osborne?

He had told Mrs. Tregelly she was a distant cousin down on her luck. The sweet old woman had never once questioned how he had just happened to stumble upon his cousin unexpectedly in Gunnisloe. It was a ludicrous fiction. She had no doubt already heard the tale of the auction from Tomas, but could be trusted to uphold James's story with the staff and neighbors. It would be widely known as a charade, but Mrs. Tregelly would maintain that charade with her dying breath. She was one of the few people who had not turned their backs on him almost seven years ago, and her fierce loyalty was an enigma to James. He had done nothing to deserve it, yet he had come to count on it.

He sighed and slid down further in the chair. Stretching his arms out, he flexed his tired muscles and linked his hands behind his neck.

He must have a serious conversation with Verity Osborne tomorrow and settle on their story, not to mention their living arrangements. The cousin tale would have to do, with some embellishment of details for veracity. Though, God knew, by tomorrow the whole county would surely be aware of how she came to be at Pendurgan.

It had disappointed him when she had asked for a tray in her room. He had somehow conceived a notion that beneath her prim and docile exterior lurked a scrappy little thing with more backbone. Well, he supposed she had been through enough for one day. He could hardly begrudge her an evening alone. Besides, Agnes had been in one of her moods. The added tension of Verity Osborne's presence would have been more than he could bear in one evening.

But what of tomorrow?

Or rather, today, he mused as the old lantern clock behind him chimed three times.

An odd shuffling sound in the hallway brought his thoughts up short. Someone was coming. Lobb usually left him alone until dawn. What would make him wander down at this hour?

But whoever approached was more light-footed than James's valet, a large man whose heavy tread was unmistakable. Who, then?

James sat up and cocked an ear toward the library door, which stood slightly ajar. By the time the small shadowy figure passed the opening, he knew who it was.

"And where do you think you're going, Verity Osborne?"

The footsteps came to an abrupt halt and he heard a sharp intake of breath. She did not move.

"I think you had better come in," he said, "and tell me what is going on. If you are leaving, I have a right to know."

After a long, silent moment, the library door swung open. A heavily draped figure stepped tentatively into the darkened room. A weighty bag of some sort caused her to list slightly to the left. With slow, deliberate movements, she set it on the floor and clasped her hands at her bulky waist. She kept her gaze lowered.

James waited for her to speak.

"What right?" she asked, her voice low and tremulous. But of course, she was afraid of him. They had all made her afraid of him.

"I beg your pardon?"

He watched her swallow. She straightened her back and raised her chin, almost visibly gathering her courage. "What right do you have to know where I'm going?" When she lifted her gaze to look directly at him, her dark eyes caught the light of the dying fire, and for an instant he could have sworn he saw a glint of defiance there. It must have been a trick of the light, for as she continued to look at him, she was clearly frightened, and as twitchy as a bunny under the nose of a fox.

"I truly wish to know," she continued. "What rights do you suppose that sham transaction in the village square gives you?" Her voice quavered a bit, but she did not look away. "Do you mean to convince me there was anything remotely legal about what took place?"

James stared up at her, astonished. Earlier, she'd seemed hardly capable of speech at all. Yet here she was, still shaken and scared, but able to speak not only in a reasonably rational and articulate manner, but with a hint of challenge as well.

So, she was a scrappy bit of baggage after all. Now that he was faced with it, though, he was not at all sure he liked the idea of a female with spirit. A quiet, docile, shrinking sort of creature would have been so much easier to pack off to the scullery and ignore.

Her large brown eyes gazed steadfastly into his own, attempting a look to match the note of challenge in her voice. But they betrayed her with the merest flicker of apprehension, quickly masked. She certainly was a proud little article.

But not so little, James considered as his eyes roamed up and down her strangely large figure. She had seemed perfectly normal-sized in Gunnisloe, if a bit on the short side. He recalled once again the moment Jud Moody had pulled her dress tight across her bosom to reveal her figure to that randy mob. She had appeared very nicely formed, not unusually plump. But now—

By God, the foolish woman seemed to be wearing every article of clothing that would not fit in her bag! Garment upon garment had been layered on so that she looked as broad and square as an engine house.

"It does not matter whether it is legal," he said at last. "I put my name to a document that"—*traps,* he almost said—"obliges me to take responsibility for you. It also, by the way, makes me responsible for your debts. Before you go tearing off, I should like to know what precise obligations I have taken on."

She cocked her head to one side and drew her brows together in a deep vee of puzzlement. "I have no debts," she replied.

"I am happy to hear it. You put my mind greatly at ease."

"Then may I go now?"

James heaved a theatrical sigh. "Madam, if I allow you to go haring off in the middle of the night, in an area I suspect to be completely foreign to you, how can I be assured of your safety? There is no moon, I believe it is still raining, and you have no idea where you are. Anything could happen to you. You might slip on one of the cliffs and drown in the river, for instance." He swept his gaze up and down her lumpy figure. "Hell, if you were to fall down with all those clothes on, you'd never be able to get up. You'd just roll around like a turtle on its back."

Coals in the grate shifted and a burst of firelight illumined her face momentarily. He could swear that a smile twitched at the corners of her mouth.

"Or you could fall into an empty mine shaft," he continued, "and break your neck." The incipient smile died as her mouth set into a grim line. "You could be set upon by drunken miners who would have no regard for your virtue, or your life."

She seemed to pale at his words. "And if anything like that happened, it would be my fault and my fate. No one would be to blame."

"I would," James said.

"Why?"

He fished out the bill of sale and waved it before her. "Have I not signed a paper, madam," he said, almost shouting, "making me responsible for you? It would go hard with me if some mischief should occur to you while under my protection."

She glared at him through narrowed eyes, but James could read the indecision and confusion there as plain as a barn fire on a dark night. She didn't know what to do.

And neither did he. Why not just let her go? It would certainly solve a huge dilemma. What made him play this role of noble protector? He almost laughed at the absurdity of it.

"Of course, if you have someplace to go," he said in a mocking tone, "I would not dream of stopping you. Indeed, I seem to be making gross assumptions without any foundation. I must apologize for being so precipitous. Perhaps you have friends or family in the area? If so, I would be happy to take you to them in the morning. There is no need for you to tramp out alone on such a night."

She dropped her gaze and looked at her feet. Ha! He had her.

"*Do* you have someone to go to?" he prompted.

She continued to watch her toes for a moment. Finally, she looked up and met his eyes. "No, my lord," she replied in a soft voice. "I have no friends in the West Country."

Something in her manner—her pride? her courage?—goaded him into mocking her, daring her to go, pushing her to admit defeat. "Well then," he said in a tone sure to convey his scorn, "perhaps you have friends somewhat more distant to whom you wish to go? And you meant to hire a chaise in town for the journey?"

"No, my lord."

"No friends or family anywhere to take you in?"

"No, my lord."

"Well." James tapped his chin with steepled fingers and beetled his brow. "Well. That is most unfortunate. Ah, but perhaps you meant to hire a companion and find a cottage of your own so that you could live independently. Is that what you had planned, *Mrs.* Osborne?"

"No, my lord."

"Do you in fact have the means to live independently?"

"No, my lord."

"I thought not. I suspect if you had, your husband would have taken it for himself, would he not?"

"Yes, my lord."

"Well then, madam, what *had* you planned to do? Where the devil were you going in the dead of night in the middle of Cornwall?"

"I was going to follow the river into the next town," she said, attempting a dignified posture beneath the heavy layers of clothing.

"Bodmin?"

"I suppose so."

"And what did you plan to do in Bodmin?" he asked.

"Look for employment, some sort of position. Then, as I earned a bit of money I could begin to pay you back the two hundred pounds."

What the devil? "I beg your pardon?"

"The two hundred pounds you . . . you paid for me."

"Good God, woman, you are not an indentured

servant! Do not concern yourself with the two hundred pounds."

"I should not wish to be beholden to you, my lord," she said. "I will pay you back. If it takes me the rest of my life, I will pay you back. But I must find employment first."

James clucked his tongue and shook his head. The foolish, prideful woman. What was she thinking? "Mrs. Osborne, have you no wits? In the first place, the money was not given to you but to your husband. You are in no way beholden to me. You may come or go as you please."

Her eyes widened. What had she expected? That he would keep her under lock and key? But of course that must be precisely what she had thought, otherwise she would not be trying to escape like a criminal in the middle of the night, decked out like the rag-and-bone man.

"And in the second place," he continued, his voice rising along with his aggravation, "the only way you would find the river in the pitch of dark is by falling straight into it. There is not a gentle riverside for at least a half mile downriver. Here at Pendurgan, it's a straight drop off steep cliffs."

Verity chewed on her lower lip, and James knew she was wavering again.

"See here," he said with weary resignation, "if you truly wish to go to Bodmin in the morning, I shall take you. I don't recommend it, but it shall be as you wish. Do not forget, though, that I do have this document," he said, patting his waistcoat pocket, "and I am bound to take it seriously. I am responsible for you. I would prefer that you stay here at Pendurgan so that I can be certain of your safety."

"Stay as what?" she asked.

"I beg your pardon?"

"Stay as what? Your servant? Your . . . your . . ."

"My cousin," he snapped. He was growing impatient with this game. "I have told the staff you are a distant relation down on her luck. A recent widow. You are to use that identity while you remain at Pendurgan."

She stared at him with those big doe eyes of hers, clearly suspicious of every word he spoke. "That's all?" she asked. The tiniest note of challenge had crept into her voice. "A poor relation making herself useful?"

"If you like."

"And that is all you will expect of me? Nothing more?"

He allowed his gaze to travel up and down her boxy, padded figure. "Well," he said, "we shall just have to wait and see, won't we?"

Verity sat huddled in an oversized wing chair by the fire, wrapped in a thick blanket. Soft gray light crept through the edges of the heavy window curtains. Morning, finally. Almost time to go.

She had trudged back upstairs after her encounter with Lord Harkness, disoriented and confused, but ready to grab at the opportunity he offered. Rain continued to pelt the windows, and an occasional clap of thunder rumbled through the old stone walls and rattled the casement. After a while, she had stretched out on the bed, just to rest for a few hours. But exhaustion must have overcome her, for she had fallen asleep.

Dreams of banging kettles and crowds of leering people pushing toward her—closer, closer, closer—disturbed her sleep, and her own screams brought her awake. After two such nightmares, she had given up and moved to the chair, where she sat and spun fantasies about the new life ahead of her. But her thoughts kept returning to the master of Pendurgan.

Lord Harkness was both intriguing and a little frightening, but perhaps one was the same as the other. Last night she had sat in this same chair by the fire and waited for him to come. Still unclear why he had purchased her—but certain he must have some kind of sinister motive, she expected that he might come to her in the night.

Instead, he had left her alone.

He had been toying with her. Surely he suspected she would try to leave. Why else would he have been skulking in the library at that ungodly hour? He sat there the whole time as calm as you please, as though he had expected her. And he had called her name from behind the library door before he could possibly have seen her. How had he known it was she?

He had looked almost ghostly when she entered the room, a dark silhouette against the fire behind him. With the light coming from behind, she could make out little more than the arrogant line of his jaw and the languid tilt of his head. But she had needed no firelight to know his lip was curled in a disdainful smirk. The very air had crackled with his mockery.

Verity rose from the chair, stretched her stiff muscles, and walked to the window. She drew back the heavy curtains to find morning had indeed broken, tinting the gray sky a pale pink in the east. The view she met brought her up short and a tiny gasp escaped her lips.

This could not possibly be the same desolate place she had been brought to the previous evening. The vista that stretched before her was lush, green, and wooded. Terraced lawns edged with flowers dropped away from the house and gave way to a plantation of trees, some still awash in their autumn colors.

If not for the girl's words the night before, Verity could easily have believed she had dreamed the whole trip to Cornwall and now was back in Berkshire.

If the rest of Cornwall looked more like this than like the colorless granite town where she had been auctioned, she might find some pleasure in starting a new life here.

Her trunk still stood near the foot of the bed. The clothes she had bundled and worn for her attempted escape were still flung in a corner. She untied the bundle and had begun to toss the clothes in the trunk when a soft rapping on the bedchamber door startled her out of her work. Recalling the strange woman in black the night before, she froze.

The little maid, Gonetta, walked in, and Verity let out her breath with a whoosh.

The girl bobbed a curtsy, her eyes downcast. "I come to see if 'ee did be awake yet," she said. "I brung some hot water." She walked to the washstand and set down the brass canister. She tested the water and let out a soft sort of wail. "Ea, it do be cool already! I must've took too long."

She looked up with an expression of such distress it appeared she might burst into tears. "I had to go . . . I went somewheres else first and I hadn't ought to have done that. I be right sorry, ma'am. I'll go get more and do bring it right up."

"Don't trouble yourself. This water will be just fine."

"It won't be no trouble," the girl said, her voice high-pitched and unnatural.

"Thank you, but this water will do very nicely," Verity said. "It was kind of you to bring it."

Gonetta looked up and watched as Verity flung more clothes into the trunk. "Here, now," the girl said in a shocked tone. "Wot yer doing? Y'ain't leavin', is 'ee?"

"Yes, Gonetta, I am. Lord Harkness has agreed to drive me to Bodmin today. I have decided I would be more comfortable making my own way rather than living off my . . . my cousin's charity." She did not know why she felt obliged to explain anything to this young servant, but it just seemed to burst out.

"Oh," Gonetta said, her tone now almost desolate. "I be right sorry to hear that, ma'am. Right sorry. Here, let me help 'ee with them clothes."

The girl moved to stand in front of the trunk and pulled out one of the wrinkled dresses. She shook it out, turned to the wardrobe, and hung it up. When she had repeated the process with two other dresses, Verity put a hand on her arm to stop her.

"Gonetta," she said, "I am going, not staying. The dresses must go into the trunk, not the wardrobe."

The little maid looked up at Verity and her face crumpled. "Ea, Miz Osborne," she wailed, "I do be so sorry. It be just . . . j-just—" She dropped her face into her hands and began to sob.

Good heavens, what was all this?

In any other situation, Verity would not have thought twice before putting her arms around the girl and comforting her. But there was nothing normal about this situation or this place. She was not prepared to trust anyone at Pendurgan. This might be some charade to put her off-guard.

Yet the girl seemed genuinely distressed. Sobs wracked her small frame in a manner Verity was almost certain could not have been pretense.

After an uncomfortable moment, Verity touched Gonetta's arm and guided her to the edge of the bed. With a nod of her head, she indicated that the distraught girl should sit down. "There now," Verity said, somewhat awkwardly, "what's the trouble? I hope I have done nothing to—"

"It be n-not about 'ee, ma'am."

"Oh."

Gonetta looked up. "Oh, I m-meant no d-disrespect, ma'am. I be right sorry 'ee be leavin' so soon. I liked 'ee right off, I did. Happy to maid 'ee. B-but that be not it. Y'see . . . y'see . . ."

Her voice became choked with tears and she could not go on. Verity stood back, feeling unbearably oafish, and let her cry, convinced this was sincere anguish and not some calculated deception. She wondered what could have upset the girl so.

When Gonetta's sobs quieted to gentle tears, Verity said, "Tell me, please. Tell me what has upset you so."

Gonetta looked up, wiped her nose on her sleeve, and hiccoughed. "I can't help it, Miz Osborne," she said in a trembly voice. "It be me littlest brother, Davey. He do be real sick and Ma says he be d-dyin'. He be only just gone on five, y'see, and always do be such a hellion, beggin' yer pardon, ma'am. I can't bear to see him sick and dyin'. Not little Davey."

The girl's sobs tore at Verity's heart. "What is wrong with him, Gonetta?" she asked in a soft voice.

"He got the putrid sore throat and it just do get worse and worse. We can't get nothin' down him. And now it be gone to a real bad fever."

"What does the doctor say?" Verity asked. "Has he given Davey any physicks or other preparations to reduce the fever?"

Gonetta gave a plaintive wail. "We ain't got no doctor just now, ma'am. Dr. Trefusis, he had to go to Penzance on some fam'ly business. So we ain't had nobody to doctor poor Davey."

"You've had no one to help you with Davey? No one at all?" Verity asked, appalled that no local doctor was available. "Is there no village apothecary?" Gonetta shook her head. "What about local healers, green women, herbalists?" Gonetta furrowed her brow in puzzlement, as though she did not understand, then shook her head again. Verity sighed.

What should she do? Could she stand by and allow the child to die through sheer ignorance? Verity had some skill with herbs and knew a few remedies that could possibly help the boy.

Yet to remain and help would delay her departure from Pendurgan. Nothing was more important than to get away from this place.

Except that a little boy was perhaps dying.

"What have you been doing to care for him?" she asked.

"Just bathin' him to keep his skin cool, givin' him tea and honey, when he can swallow it."

Those things could only make him comfortable. Nothing they were doing would help to break the fever or heal the infected throat.

She began to pace the length of the room. Any sort of delay almost scared her to death. What if she was never able to leave?

Dear God, what should she do?

"I believe I may have something to help him," she said at last. She could not let the boy die. Gonetta stared at her, wide-eyed. "Do you recall seeing some muslin pouches," Verity asked, "when you unpacked my trunk yesterday?"

"Them little sachets, ma'am? I put some in each of the bureau drawers to keep yer things fresh."

Verity cocked a brow and almost smiled. Sachets, indeed. Some of them positively reeked. She pulled open each drawer and rummaged around until she had located all her herbal pouches.

"Does Cook keep fresh honey in the larder, Gonetta?"

"Aye, she do," the girl replied with a puzzled look, her eyes red-rimmed and puffy. "Why?"

"With this," Verity said, holding up one of the pouches, "and this one, too, along with a bit of honey, I can make up a syrup that might help your brother."

"Truly?" Gonetta asked, her eyes large with wonder. " 'Ee can make him better? He don't got to die?"

Verity must be careful not to give false hope. She was no magician. "I cannot promise anything, you understand," she said. "It depends on how far along the sickness is. But I have always had good luck with my hyssop infusions and horehound syrups."

Now that she had committed herself, she was anxious to get on with it. Perhaps her departure from Pendurgan would be only briefly postponed. Gonetta helped her to dress quickly, and within a quarter hour, she was bending over the young freckle-faced Davey.

He was tucked up in his mother's bed in the servants' quarters. With his hair as red as his sister's, Verity had no trouble imagining him as a tiny hellion. But not at the moment. A lump formed in her throat as she examined him. Gonetta held a candle close to his mouth while Verity held open his jaw and peered down his throat. It was scarlet as a poppy, but she could see no white patches. Even so, the child was burning up with fever, his breathing raspy. She hoped it was not too late.

The old woman in Lincolnshsire who'd taught Verity about herbs had often recommended other treatments as well for this type of disease. Verity instructed Mrs. Chenhalls, who was not only Davey's mother but also Pendurgan's cook, to bathe her son's feet and legs with warm water, and then to wrap his throat in wool. This would keep the distraught woman occupied while Verity prepared the herbals.

With Cook now unavailable, Verity enlisted the aid of Mrs. Tregelly. The housekeeper led the way into the ancient-looking, high-beamed kitchen. A huge open hearth dominated one wall, fitted with a swinging chimney crane and rows of adjustable pot hangers above the low, crackling fire.

The two women rummaged through the larders and located jars of honey. Mrs. Tregelly grabbed several pots from the wall rack, sending the rest of the cook pots swinging and banging loudly against one another.

Verity froze.

Cold wind whipped across her face and her neck was jerked roughly by the auctioneer's tug on the leather harness. The shouting from below was almost deafening. The crowd pressed in on her, pushing forward with each clang, clang, clang. Closer and closer until she could hardly breathe.

"Mrs. Osborne?"

The housekeeper's words broke the spell. Verity's hand clutched at her throat, where the harness had cut into her neck. Disoriented, she gazed about the perfectly ordinary kitchen and into the concerned gray eyes of Mrs. Tregelly.

"Are you all right, ma'am?"

Verity took a deep, shuddery breath and shook off her lingering uneasiness. "Yes. Yes, I'm fine, Mrs. Tregelly."

Pots of water were set to boil on the modern close-fire range, oddly out of place in this centuries-old kitchen. Verity opened one of her muslin pouches and sniffed to confirm it was indeed hyssop. She added a small amount to one of the pots of boiling water to begin an infusion. In another pot, she added the horehound in preparation for a honey syrup. For good measure, she added a pinch of horehound to the infusion as well.

She could have done all this almost mechanically, years of expertise driving her actions. Instead, Verity focused her attention on every simple detail of the well-known process: the crisp leaves crushed fine between her fingers, the precise balance of dried leaves to flower tops, the aroma as the herbs infused the water, indicating the proper proportions of horehound. The simple and blessedly familiar routine pushed the anxiety of delay from the forefront of her thoughts. Here, in this role, she was in control.

"I do hope this helps the child," Mrs. Tregelly said. "He be such a wee scamp, and always up to some kind of mischief, but he has a sweet nature, too. It would go hard with all of us to lose him." She wrinkled her nose at the strong camphorlike odor that now permeated the kitchen.

"I'll do my best to help," Verity said, watching the other pot as the liquid boiled down.

" 'Tis our good fortune that you happen to be here just now," Mrs. Tregelly said, "with the doctor away and all. And that you brought along all these herbs."

"Yes," Verity replied absently as she checked the steeping hyssop. "I tossed them in my trunk because I did not know—" She had been about to say that she had not known how long she and her husband would be away from home. "You never know when they will come in handy," she muttered.

"How is it you know so much about healing, Mrs. Osborne?" the housekeeper asked.

"Oh, I'm not exactly a healer, Mrs. Tregelly. But I

do know my herbs, and some of them happen to have great healing properties."

"I'm afraid I know very little about herbs," the older woman said. "Cook grows some for the kitchen, and I use lavender and sage and such throughout the house to sweeten the air and the linens. But that is the extent of my knowledge, I fear."

"Perhaps Cook has some of the best healing herbs right there in her kitchen garden."

"Perhaps she does," Mrs. Tregelly replied. "But likely she don't know it, else she would have made these concoctions herself to help her little boy."

" 'Ee could teach us."

Verity looked up from her reduction into the anxious eyes of young Gonetta, who had just entered the kitchen. Verity shook her head. "Here," she said ladling the hyssop infusion into a teacup. "Take this to your brother. Be sure he drinks as much as he can. He will not like the taste, but see that he drinks a good portion."

Gonetta dashed away to her brother's sickroom, her hand covering the teacup to keep it from sloshing.

While Verity began to mix the reduced horehound liquid with honey, Mrs. Tregelly watched in interest. "It is almost as strong-smelling as the infusion, is it not?" Verity said. "But the honey makes it go down easier. After drinking the hyssop, Davey will no doubt be glad to swallow something sweeter."

"Netta was right."

"About what?"

"You could teach us some of your skills. We'd be that grateful. There be no telling when Dr. Trefusis will return."

Verity shook her head and continued to stir the honey. "I'm sorry," she said quietly. "I will not be staying long."

Mrs. Tregelly clucked her disappointment but did not press the matter. A few minutes later, Gonetta bounded back into the kitchen. "He do be takin' it!" she exclaimed. "He don't like it, but Ma be gettin' it down him."

"That's good," Verity said. "Now find me a jar or a crock to hold this syrup. We'll see what else we can get down him."

When they returned to the sickroom, Mrs. Chenhalls smiled up at Verity, her eyes moist with emotion. "Thank 'ee, ma'am, fer helpin' my boy," she said. "See here? His breathin' do be better already. No more wheezin'. He goin' to be all right now, in't he?"

Verity leaned over the bed and touched the boy's cheek. He'd been bathed and wrapped up warmly. It was much too soon to know if the fever would break. Simply inhaling the steam of the infusion, with its heavy camphor aroma, would momentarily ease the child's breathing. But it was a temporary relief at best.

"I cannot promise anything, Mrs. Chenhalls. These remedies should make him more comfortable, allow him to breathe easier for a time. But please do not get your hopes up too soon. I cannot guarantee a cure. He is a very sick little boy. We will just have to wait. Now, see if you can get him to swallow a spoonful of this syrup. Then give him more infusion every hour. Be sure it is warm. And give him a teaspoon of the syrup every three hours. If he gets any worse, there are other treatments we can try."

"Thank 'ee, ma'am," Mrs. Chenhalls said. "Thank 'ee. I do be grateful 'ee come to stay with us. *Gras e dhe Dhew. Drusona!*"

Verity darted a questioning look at the woman's daughter, but the girl kept her eyes averted. "She do thank God that 'ee came," Gonetta whispered.

"Come along," Verity said, eager to escape the emotions that tugged at her. "Let me teach you and Mrs. Tregelly how to make more of these remedies, so you can tend to Davey after I leave."

Gonetta followed in silence. While Verity gave instructions for making both the infusion and the syrup, Gonetta did no more than nod now and then. Mrs. Tregelly made precise notes.

"Now, the only problem," Verity said, "is the supply of hyssop. I have enough horehound to leave with you. It takes very little to make the syrup. But I do not have much hyssop left. Do you suppose your mother has hyssop in her kitchen garden, Gonetta?"

"Don't know, ma'am. Wouldn't know it if I seen it."

"But I would," Verity replied. "Let's take a look."

Gonetta led her to a tidy, prosperous kitchen garden just beyond the scullery door to the outside. There were rosemary, sage, parsley, dill, fennel, thyme, tarragon, lovage, tansy, and lemon verbena. Verity scanned the plantings for the familiar tall stalks of hyssop. Sure enough, there they stood, next to their minty relatives.

"See here," Verity said, breaking off a leaf and rubbing it between her fingers. "You have everything you need. This is hyssop, which is used in the warm infusion. But I used dried leaves. You must double the amount if you use fresh leaves. Can you remember that?"

"Prob'bly not," Gonetta replied in a petulant tone. "I do think 'ee ought to stay. Then 'ee can take more time to teach us and make sure we don't do somethin' bad wrong. We do be simple folk, not educated like 'ee. We do need 'ee to help us, 'specially with no doctor an' all."

The girl's plaintive tone was almost more than Verity could bear. She wanted to help, she really did, for against her better judgment she found herself growing quite fond of Gonetta. And she could not forget the grateful, trusting look in Mrs. Chenhalls's eyes.

Even so, she could not do as they wished. It was impossible.

"I cannot stay, Gonetta," she said without looking at the girl. "I am leaving Pendurgan, as I've told you. Today, if I can finish my packing and locate his lordship."

" 'Ee don't *have* to go. Not yet. 'Ee could stay just till Davey be better, like."

"Oh, Gonetta." Verity steeled herself against the doleful look in the girl's eyes. She had to leave Pendurgan. She had to get away from Lord Harkness, who, whatever his motives, still made her decidedly uneasy.

"*Please,* ma'am. Davey woulda died if 'ee didn't been here. We do *need* 'ee, Miz Osborne. Please don't go."

"Gonetta—"

"Please, ma'am. Stay. His lordship won't mind. Will 'ee, my lord?"

Verity stiffened.

"Not in the least," said a deep voice behind her.

James watched her tight shoulders relax somewhat as she brought her discomposure under control. Even from behind he could see her chin tilt up at that defiant angle he'd seen last night. He could not suppress a mocking smile as she turned around.

But the smile slid from his face, leaving his mouth slightly agape. It was the first time he had seen her in full light without a bonnet shielding her face, and without a heavy cloak or that ridiculous mountain of clothing of last evening. He had not realized how attractive she was. He might almost call her beautiful, though she did not have sort of the fair-haired porcelain beauty he generally preferred.

Her hair, the color of rich, black coffee, swept off her face in deep waves. A few wayward wisps escaped at the nape of her long, slender neck. So lovely a neck, he thought, should never be hidden by bonnets—or be encased in a leather harness. She had a full mouth, a straight nose, and clear, fine-textured skin that made him think of Devonshire cream. Her large brown eyes—now glaring at him while he stood gaping like a schoolboy—were fringed with long lashes and set off by perfectly arched brows. They reminded him of the beautiful Spanish girls who had attached themselves to his regiment years ago.

He swallowed hard and tried not to think about how long he had been without a woman.

"Am I to understand that your brother is better?" he asked Gonetta, attempting to ignore Verity and the way his blood heated up at the very sight of her.

"It do look that way, my lord," Gonetta replied. "Miz Osborne here, she fixed him right up."

"Did she, indeed?"

"She did make med'cine fer him, outa plants and all. She know just what he did need and, sure 'nuff, it worked."

"It is too early to tell—" Verity began.

"Davey, he gonna be jus' fine now," Gonetta interrupted. "I do know it, my lord. Miz Osborne here, she cured him."

"Well, then," James said, "that is good news. I had sent to Bodmin for a physician for Davey. Perhaps when he arrives later today the boy won't be in such a bad way. We are most grateful to you, cousin."

Verity's gaze narrowed at the word "cousin," but she said nothing. She was going to be difficult about the ruse. But, by God, if she stayed under his roof, it would be as his relation. He would not have the servants gossiping about her as if she were his lightskirt, though that was, no doubt, precisely what they assumed her to be.

"In any case," he went on, "I would feel better if a physician examined him. I am sure Davey will need to be bled if he is to fully recover. I doubt Mrs. Osborne is prepared to—"

"You will *not* have him bled!"

Startled by this outburst, James cocked a brow at Verity. So, despite the obvious anxiety she still felt in his presence, certain issues seemed almost involuntarily to fire her spirit. Interesting.

"He is much too weak," she continued in a more diffident tone. She fingered the plant in her hand with jittery movements and did not meet his eyes.

"Bleeding him will only make him weaker, less able to fight off the fever."

He glared at her in disbelief. What nonsense was this? "I beg your pardon, cousin, but surely the boy must be bled."

She looked up at him. "I—I disagree," she replied, her voice unsteady. "He will recover more quickly with good strong herbals and *no* bleeding."

"What the devil are you talking about?" James said. "That is without doubt the most preposterous bit of rubbish I ever heard. Pure quackery." Her attitude took him by surprise. In spite of these little bursts of spirit, he would have guessed her to be more commonsensical than crackbrained. But then, she *had* tried to escape Pendurgan in the pouring rain, weighted down with layer upon layer of heavy clothing. Perhaps she was something of a loose screw after all. Damn. That was all he needed.

"Everyone knows that bleeding is necessary to excise bad humors from the body," he went on in a tone that, even to his own ears, sounded overly pedantic. "Physicians have been bleeding patients for centuries."

"And most of their patients die," Verity said.

"Not from being bled."

She looked up at him again. "How do you know?" she asked. Tension showed in her face, in the angle of her spine, and in her hand, tightly gripping the plant stalk as if it were a weapon.

"How can anyone know," she said, "if a patient dies from illness or from increased weakness to fight the illness, brought about by bleeding? My mother—" She stopped for a moment, then took a deep, shuddery breath and continued. "My mother was bled to death by well-meaning physicians. She had an inflammation of the lungs and was never allowed to recover her strength, but was bled and bled until there was nothing left of her. Oh, she might have died eventually, but nothing will convince me that her death was not hastened by constant bleeding."

A loud sob from Gonetta interrupted this remarkable speech. "Is Davey goin' to die, then?" she wailed. "If doctor come and bleed him, is he goin' to die after all?"

Verity looked over Gonetta's shoulder straight into James's eyes. She raised her brows and sent him a look that dumped responsibility for the answer squarely in his lap. Damn. If he allowed the doctor to bleed Davey now, and the boy subsequently died, James would be the villain once again. Responsible for yet another child's death.

By God, he would not face that again. Let this opinionated little harridan take the blame for whatever happened.

"Cousin," he crooned as he swept her a bow, "I defer to your superior judgment in this matter."

Verity looked momentarily abashed, then returned her attention to Gonetta. "I do not think it is a good idea to have Davey bled," she said. "It is best that we allow the healing properties of the herbals to take hold first. If he does not show any improvement, then we may discuss with the physician what is to be done next."

"Then 'ee will stay, ma'am," Gonetta asked, "to make sure nothin' do go wrong?"

Ha! Gonetta had her there. James guessed that she

was desperate to leave; now it would seem churlish of her to go. He watched Verity struggle with the decision. Her very mobile face registered helplessness, frustration, anger, and finally resignation. She would stay.

He should be pleased. He could oversee her welfare more easily if she stayed on at Pendurgan. Then why was he cursing himself for not getting a doctor sooner so that she could be on her way without a qualm?

"Very well," she said at last, her body visibly sagging with the weight of her decision. The depth of her frustration shone clearly in her dark eyes, now bright with unshed tears. "Very well. I will stay for the time being. But only until Davey is up and about again."

"Oh, thank 'ee, ma'am! Thank 'ee. Ma will be so happy. But 'ee do got to stay long enough to teach us 'bout them plants. There do be others hereabouts wot could use yer help, I reckon. Do 'ee know how to help with stiff joints and such?"

"Well, yes. There's—"

"Then 'ee could surely help Old Grannie Pascow, who do get too stiff to walk sometimes. What 'bout a bad stomach? Can 'ee help that, too?"

"There are herbs that will ease a bilious stomach. But—"

"Then Hildy Spruggins'll need yer help, too, 'cuz her stomach do be always botherin' her somethin' terrible. And what 'bout burns and cuts and bruises and sprained muscles and boils and dropsy and colic?"

Verity sighed. "Herbal remedies may be of some help in all of those cases, but—"

"Well, there do always be somebody wot's got one of them things wrong wid 'em," Gonetta said. "There do be a powerful lot 'ee has to teach us, ain't there? Could take a long time."

James wondered where this young girl had learned the art of manipulation so thoroughly. She had Verity pinned to the wall.

He would have been amused if a sudden anxiety hadn't gripped him as thoroughly as Davey's fever. Verity was being coerced into staying at Pendurgan indefinitely.

She appeared to be as torn as he was. She chewed absently on the nail of one finger. Two deep furrows marked her brow.

"Well?" Gonetta prompted. " 'Ee be stayin', then?"

Verity threw up her hands in a gesture of resignation. Her eyes had the look of those of a soldier packing up his kit in forced retreat. "All right," she said. "I will agree to stay. But only until Davey has recovered and I've taught you and your mother a few basic herbals. If," she added emphatically, looking directly at James, "his lordship has no objections?"

"You *know* you are welcome to stay, cousin," James said, his voice surprisingly even, considering the state of his nerves. "As I have told you."

Verity sniffed disdainfully, then turned toward one of the plants. "Let us take some hyssop with us," she said to Gonetta. "Your brother will need more of it very soon."

James produced a pocket knife that Verity used to cut several stalks of the hyssop plant. With a now purposeful stride she led them all back to the kitchen. James leaned against the wall next to the hearth, his arms crossed over his chest, as he watched Verity instruct Gonetta in caring for the herbs.

James had no reason to stay and watch. He had much to do about the estate and ought to check on the new pump at Wheal Devoran. In fact, he knew he should get away from Verity Osborne as quickly as possible, and stay away. But something about her piqued his interest. Something more than her physical appeal, though, God knew, there was that. His lip curled into a sneer as he considered how predictably base it was for the biggest scoundrel in Cornwall to lust after the first new woman to cross his path in over six years.

He ought not be interested in her at all. It could only lead to trouble. And yet she intrigued him.

He had always been drawn to the soft, fragile, feminine sort of female for whom he could feel protective. Rowena had been such a woman: fair and delicate as a May blossom. But there was nothing particularly delicate about Verity. Though their strange association gave him every right to feel protective of her, she did not encourage it. Beneath the uncertainty and fear she showed remarkable self-possession in the way she stood up to him, in the way she faced the inevitable decision to stay. Or perhaps it was not true courage, but merely pride.

He wondered what it would take to make her crack.

Just then, Agnes swept into the kitchen like a storm cloud, gathering her black skirts about her as though afraid to touch anything. James groaned. He had never before known her to venture into the kitchen. Why now, of all times?

"What is going on?" she said, her brows drawn together like thunderbolts into a deep scowl. "I demand to know where Cook is. I have been waiting this past hour to review the day's menu. And now I am forced to come"—she looked around the room, her mouth puckered in distaste—"down here. James, what are you doing here? I demand to know what is going on."

"I am sorry no one thought to alert you, Agnes," James said. "But Cook's youngest son, Davey, has taken very ill."

"Well," she said, dismissing such a trifle with a pettish shrug, "does that mean the entire household must come to a halt? Where is Mrs. Tregelly?"

"She is with Cook and Davey," James said, holding on to his temper with difficulty. "Shall I send her up to you to discuss the menus?"

"Yes, do that." Agnes turned toward Verity, who was looking at her as though she beheld an apparition. "What is *she* doing here?" Agnes asked, her voice rigid with icy disdain.

There was no easy way out of this. Agnes had to meet Verity sooner or later.

He moved toward Agnes, took her firmly by the arm, and steered her toward the shelves where Verity and Gonetta had been hanging bunches of hyssop. She resisted, but he tugged her along nevertheless.

"Agnes," he said, "allow me to make known to you Mrs. Verity Osborne. She is a cousin of mine who has come to stay with us at Pendurgan."

Agnes looked down the length of her nose at Verity, as though she held a quizzing glass trained on an insect.

"Cousin," he continued, "may I present to you my mother-in-law, Mrs. Agnes Bodinar." When Verity flashed him a startled look, he added, "Mrs. Bodinar is the mother of my late wife. She lives here at Pendurgan."

Verity collected herself quickly. She laid aside the herbs and brushed her hands on her blue wool skirts. She then very calmly offered her hand to Agnes. "I am pleased to be introduced to you, Mrs. Bodinar. At last."

James wondered what she meant by that. "Have you met already, then?"

"Mrs. Bodinar stopped by my room last night to welcome me to Pendurgan," Verity said, her eyes never leaving Agnes's.

Good Lord. What had Agnes done?

"But she left before I learned her name," Verity continued, cool as could be in the face of James's formidable mother-in-law. He would have expected her to be frightened of Agnes, who, Lord knew, frightened most everyone else with little more than a glance. Yet after that initial moment of well-concealed shock, Verity did not tremble at the sight of the old woman; her voice did not quaver.

"I am so happy to know who you are, Mrs. Bodinar. I wanted to thank you for being the first to welcome me." Verity continued to hold out her hand, though Agnes looked as if she'd rather touch a toad.

"Hmph! Cousin, indeed."

She would, of course, know the true story of how Verity came to be here. All of Cornwall would know it by now. But James was determined that in his own household, at least, the charade of the poor relation would be maintained.

"Yes, my dear," he said. "A distant cousin, but a relation, nonetheless. I trust you will afford her the same respect you would show any guest at Pendurgan."

Agnes turned away from Verity without a word. "Send Mrs. Tregelly to me at once," she said to James as she gathered her skirts about her and headed out of the kitchen. The rustle of fabric rang out in the silence of the cavernous room. At the doorway she stopped, turned around, and fixed Verity with a piercing gaze.

"Doxy!" she hissed, and left the room.

Chapter 4

The place was growing on her. The gardens of Pendurgan, even as winter approached, were full of wonders, especially for one with an eye for herbs and other useful plants.

With little more asked of her than to tend to Davey and provide herbal instructions to Gonetta and her mother, Verity had had plenty of time to explore the grounds in the five days since her arrival. She wandered freely through the terraces on the south side of the house—the only formal gardens at Pendurgan—to the winding paths that snaked through the heavily wooded lower grounds, ending in an ancient-looking granite wall that overlooked the river below. To the east were apple orchards and plots of winter vegetables.

Even with the fading autumn colors and the drab

gray of its granite and slate buildings, Pendurgan had a certain beauty.

The place was growing on her.

Verity tucked her cloak snugly about her against the chill air as she meandered along a narrow path in the lower grounds, her favorite of all the gardens. Heavily wooded with golden ash, oak, white thorn, larch, and copper beech, its paths twisted and turned, leading to unexpected broad vistas or intimate rustic alcoves, to fishponds and tiny thatched pavilions. She paused near an old slatestone dovecote to watch two white doves flutter out from the corbel in the domed roof. Following their flight, her eyes were drawn to a patch of Scotch broom farther down along the path. She hitched her basket upon her hip and considered the various uses she could make of even the dry wintry branches.

Clipping the stalks with the hand shears borrowed from Mrs. Chenhalls, Verity considered the Pendurgan cook and her family. Davey's fever had broken and he continued to recover, slowly but steadily. Verity's meager talents with herbs had been lauded as a near miracle. The fact that she had stood firm against the physician from Bodmin, who had indeed wanted to have the boy bled, only made Verity's star shine brighter among the Chenhalls family.

This small victory had given Verity a great deal of satisfaction, and not only for the boy's sake. She had begun to discover an unexpected bit of backbone she never realized was there.

It took little effort to settle into complacency among the friendly red-haired family who, along with the sweet-faced Mrs. Tregelly, kept Pendurgan running smoothly. Though it was by no means a large estate, Verity had been surprised at the small number of servants. Was the staff so limited because no others wished to work for a man everyone called Lord Heartless?

It was easy to ignore such suspicions with the Chenhalls family, especially Gonetta, who was cheerful and bright and eager to keep Verity at Pendurgan indefinitely. Verity had long ago abandoned the notion that the girl was part of some grand conspiracy—to make her feel welcome, to make her feel safe, to make her want to stay. To make her so complacent she would not notice the evil web being spun around her until she was trapped and the spider pounced. Never in all her life had Verity been prone to such bizarre fantasies.

But it was not all fantasy.

The fearsome Mrs. Bodinar was no figment of Verity's imagination, and stood in sharp contrast to the amiable staff. She glared, she sneered, she huffed, and she generally made herself disagreeable. When she spoke at all, when they took meals together in the evenings, it was to offer some criticism or to make some remark about having to share a roof with her son-in-law's trollop.

Verity had chosen not to respond to such attacks. She wasn't sure what to say in any case. Agnes Bodinar surely was not the only one at Pendurgan who assumed Verity was Lord Harkness's mistress.

So far, however, she was not.

The fact was, she rarely saw him. He spent much time away from the house, apparently at the mines, and kept very much to himself when he was at home.

But when she did see him, his presence still had the ability to unnerve her.

He watched her. She constantly felt him watching her with those cool blue eyes in a way that made her decidedly uneasy, in a way that made her think he would surely come at night to claim his rights, by purchase, of her body.

He had not done so, however, and Verity did not know what to make of it.

She watched him, as well. She often caught herself studying his long elegant fingers with their dusting of dark hair, or his angular profile with the strong, almost Roman nose, or the blue-black sheen of his longish hair in the candlelight, or the oddly attractive sprinkling of silver at his temples. He was not handsome in any sort of conventional way. Even so, there was something compelling about a face with cynical, vivid blue eyes set amid hard planes that might have been carved out of the local granite.

She ought not to notice such things. She ought to keep far away from him, for an air of danger hung thickly about him.

Perhaps that was what drew her, what fascinated her. He was dangerous, like no one she had known before, and she did not know when he might make his move. So there could be no complacency at Pendurgan until Verity understood this dark stranger and the role he intended her to play.

She arranged the broom stalks in the basket along with the other plants she'd collected and began the walk back to the house. She would go by way of the rear entrance to drop off the plants in the makeshift stillroom she'd arranged in one corner of the old kitchen. Tomorrow she would use the broom and comfrey roots to instruct Mrs. Chenhalls and Gonetta in the preparation of various oils and decoctions for stiff or swollen joints.

The wind whipped her skirts as she walked up the narrow, winding path through an archway in the old stone wall. Broader paths, lower walls, and open gateways led finally to the rear of the house and the kitchen garden. The wind picked up and blew strongly against her, almost taking off her bonnet. Verity dipped her head and held down the brim of the hat, using it to shield her face. Fighting her flapping skirts and the cloak billowing behind her like a sail, she hurried along with bowed head, following the familiar gravel path through the herb garden.

"Here now, what's this?"

Verity bumped against something solid and found that her blind steps had led her straight into the barrel chest of a man. He grasped her elbows to steady her, and she looked up into the eyes of Rufus Bargwanath, the steward at Pendurgan. She had been introduced to him briefly a few days earlier by Mrs. Tregelly but had not seen him since. He was a burly Cornishman of middle age with thick brown hair peppered with gray, a slightly bulbous nose, and a florid complexion. She had disliked him on sight.

He had a small office in the kitchen wing and must have stepped outside without Verity seeing him. He kept one hand on her elbow while he removed his hat with the other. "Ah. Mrs. Osborne, is it not?"

A sneer curled his lip as he emphasized the word "Mrs.," and a twinge of alarm crawled up Verity's spine. His indolent gaze roamed over her body and came to rest on the basket clutched tightly against her breast. Verity became uncomfortably aware of the strong wind molding the thin woolen dress against her body like a second skin. She squirmed, but his grip held firm.

"I had not realized Harkness had put you to work in the kitchen," Bargwanath said. He did not speak in the friendly broad Cornish of the Chenhalls family but in a rough, gravelly, thoroughly unpleasant voice with only a hint of the local accent in the long vowels. He gave her elbow a suggestive squeeze. "I thought he had *other* plans for you," he said.

A lecherous grin revealed a small mouth over-crowded with yellowed teeth. His breath stank of tobacco and onions. Verity wrenched her arm from his grasp. "Excuse me, Mr. Bargwanath," she said, then stepped around him and hurried toward the back entrance. His jeering laughter rang out behind her.

She raced through the larders and sculleries and into the welcoming warmth of the ancient kitchen. Mrs. Chenhalls stood in front of the enormous open hearth and looked up at Verity's entrance.

"Afternoon, Miz Osborne. Ogh! Been out gatherin' more herbs, have 'ee?"

When Verity reached the corner where she had stored plants and other materials for her herbal preparations, she set the basket down and pressed a hand to her chest. Panting as though she'd been running, she took a moment to compose herself. She braced both hands against the wooden counter and inhaled the fragrant aromas of roasting meat and freshly baked bread.

"I've been to the lower grounds," she said at last,

then untied her bonnet and hung it on a wall hook. She did not look up as she spoke, knowing her face must still be flushed from the steward's coarse words. "I found several good plantings down there that will be useful. I will tell you and Gonetta all about them tomorrow, and show you where to find them. If the weather's clear."

Mrs. Chenhalls turned back to the hearth and began adjusting a roasting spit between two stout iron fire dogs angled against the back wall. She chattered on about the capricious Cornish weather while Verity emptied her basket and began to tie the plants and roots into bunches. She only half listened to the woman's thickly accented words, her thoughts distracted by the disturbing encounter with the steward.

This was the only time she'd been truly frightened since that nightmarish first night. Since then, Agnes had been merely unpleasant, and Lord Harkness had kept his distance. Though Verity remained wary of both of them, neither had done anything to physically threaten or frighten her.

Oh, how she wished she was an ordinary guest in an ordinary household filled with ordinary people. Then there would be nothing to stop her from complaining to her host about the steward's impertinent behavior.

But there was nothing remotely ordinary about her situation.

How could she complain about the steward's insolent manner to a man whose very presence made her more uncomfortable still?

She fought back the disagreeable feeling of vulnerability. She would not give in to helplessness again.

She had come astonishingly far in overcoming her normally submissive nature. She would not give in now.

Verity finished organizing the plants, a routine that acted as a soothing balm to her taut nerves, then stood chatting with Mrs. Chenhalls about Davey's progress. The boy was still weak and a hacking cough lingered, but he was much better now that the fever had passed. Verity reminded the cook to keep the boy warm, promised to stop by to visit with him after supper.

"He'll be that pleased, he will," the cook said. "Think 'ee do be his very own ministerin' angel, *re Dhew*. He do be awful keen to get out o' bed, bless him."

"Oh, but it is too soon," Verity said.

"Aye, but he do be too young to know he in't quite well yet. If 'ee tells him to stay put, though, he'll listen. The boy'll listen to 'ee, if not his own Ma."

Verity smiled. "I'll do my best."

She left the kitchen thinking how fond she'd grown of the little red-haired boy who always grinned up at her impishly despite his illness. The small accomplishment of Davey's recovery banished all thoughts of the wretched steward, and a glimmering of pride brought a smile to her lips as she passed through the Great Hall on her way to the main stairway.

The smile faded and her breath caught when she saw Lord Harkness enter the hall from the outside. Verity did not know why he still unnerved her so, when he had not given her any real cause to fear him. She did not, in fact, fear him. What frightened her was her own foolish reaction to him each time she saw him.

He took off his hat and gloves and placed them on the small table near the door before he turned and saw her. For a long moment, their gazes locked and neither spoke.

"Cousin," he said at last, and she let out the breath she'd unconsciously held. He seemed uncertain what else to say; she could have sworn he was as uncomfortable as she was. It puzzled her to think why.

"How is your patient?" he asked.

"Improving. The fever has passed and now he must simply regain his strength, poor thing. But he is a fighter, I think."

"Yes, the lad's a true Cornishman. We're a tough race." Some unreadable emotion flickered in his eyes for an instant, then disappeared. "Most of us," he said. "Thank you again for being such a help to him."

"It was my pleasure," she said.

"Was it?" His eyes narrowed and regarded her intently. "I wonder."

Verity tried, she really tried, to hold his gaze, to demonstrate some of the new backbone that had lately made her so proud. She did not want him to know how much he rattled her. But she was no match for those cold blue eyes and had to look away.

"If you will excuse me," he said, "I have work to do." He walked past her toward his library. She heard the door close behind him.

She wished she knew what he was thinking, what he wanted of her. Anything was better than this uncertainty. At least she had held his gaze, she thought as she approached the landing on her way upstairs to her bedchamber. But was it due to strength of will or simple fascination for a man who was still little more than a dark stranger?

Silly girl. This old place was growing on her all right. It was making her foolish.

"And what could you possibly have to smile about?"

Agnes Bodinar stood on the landing looking down at Verity. She wore her usual black dress and familiar black expression. Her mouth puckered with disdain, and the contemptuous look in her gray eyes caused Verity to halt in mid-stride.

"Well?"

"It was nothing," Verity replied. She gripped her bonnet tightly in both hands and stood her ground, just as surely as she had with Lord Harkness. "Nothing at all."

"Hmph!" Agnes snorted. "I should hope not." She stepped off the landing onto the stair where Verity stood and brought her face to within inches of Verity's. Verity sucked in her breath and inhaled the fragrance of face powder and starch. The older woman's eyes narrowed, her brows knit together so tightly they formed deep furrows down the center of her forehead.

"You've no cause to smile. You're not safe here," she hissed, wagging a bony finger next to her nose. "He's evil, I tell you. Evil!"

She leaned away from Verity and eyed her from head to foot. "I don't care what lover's lies he may have whispered in your ears, or how much he's paying you. I'm only telling you to be on your guard if you know what's good for you. The man's a devil! He means you nothing but harm, mark my words."

I thought he had other plans for you, the steward had said.

"You should leave this place," Agnes continued. "Leave while you can."

Verity turned away from Agnes and bounded up the stairs. When she reached her bedchamber, she slammed the door closed and sank heavily back against it.

Yes, she ought to leave. These shifts between normalcy and nightmare and back again were too much for her. She thought again of sinister plots, of attempts to so confuse her that she didn't care what happened.

She would leave this place after Davey was fully recovered. She could not bear this bizarre game of wits any longer. She wasn't yet certain what the stakes were, but she knew they were high. And she was bound to lose.

The problem was, she did not know what sort of loss she faced. Would she ultimately lose her life? Would she merely lose her virtue? Or would she finally, inexorably lose her mind?

Thick smoke filled his nostrils and burned the back of his throat. The night air throbbed with the ceaseless din of gunfire. Shot and shell whistled through the ranks, but James held his men back while the first column stormed the breach. Through the veil of smoke and screaming men, he watched as the brigade was cut to shreds by the French guns.

A handful of intrepid souls scrambled across the trenches dug on either side of the breach where two twenty-four-pounders hurled grape at the attackers. After two more shattering rounds, the big guns fell silent. With only their bayonets, the stubborn men of the 88th must have dispatched the gunners. It was time to move. At Picton's signal, James waved his men forward onto the ramparts.

"Go!" he shouted as they ran past.

And then the earth exploded beneath him.

Balls of fire fell at his feet, and a heavy, sizzling mass knocked him to the ground. Pain in his left leg shot all the way up his shoulder and down again. Flames erupted all around him, catching everything combustible and sending off smaller explosions every few seconds. Two burning figures ran toward him, completely engulfed. Was one of them Hughes, his sergeant?

He had to help them.

The smell of burning flesh assaulted his nose and he thought he was going to be sick. But there was no time for such weakness. He had to get to his men. He had to help them.

But he couldn't move. Dammit, he couldn't move. Something pinned him to the ground. He flexed his back to shake it off, and a charred, smoldering arm fell across his face. Shuddering, he flung it away and swallowed hard against the bile that rose in his throat.

Still, the burning figures approached. Still, James could not move and the pain in his pinned leg had become an agony. One of the figures screamed his name and collapsed in a flaming heap a few feet away. A horrific wail pierced the air, subsided to a whimper, then fell silent.

James stretched out an arm toward him. "Hughes!" he cried out. "Hughes!"

The blackened form of his young sergeant stirred, limbs still licked with flames. The head moved.

But when the face lifted, it was not that of the young soldier looking back at him. It was Rowena. His beautiful Rowena, her face twisted in pain and despair. James watched in immobilized horror as she sat up. He saw the limp form of their son, Trystan, cradled in her arms. Her mouth formed the word, "Please!"

He struggled again to free himself, to go to them, but the burden on top of him seemed to push down, push down, until he could barely breathe. He had to get to them. He had to save them. They would die without his help. And Hughes and all the rest. They needed him. They all needed him.

But he could not move.

Rowena let out a long, mournful cry, and burst into flames.

"No!" James shouted, his eyes flying open as he struggled against the weight pushing down on him.

But it was only the blanket and counterpane, now hopelessly tangled with his thrashing. He fell back against the pillows and let his breath out in a whoosh. His body was covered in sweat and he felt as though he'd sprinted all the way up the hill to Pendurgan.

Damnation. Would he never be free of the dreams?

As usual he'd stayed awake last night as long as possible, having learned that the deep sleep of exhaustion, or occasionally of drunkenness, was often dreamless. But sometimes the nightmares came anyway, usually in the morning just before waking.

The bed chamber door opened quietly and Samuel Lobb entered. "Morning, m'lord."

James grunted a reply and burrowed deeper into the pillows, trying to shake off the dream images. But it was useless. They were always there, skirting around every conscious thought during waking hours and interrupting what passed for sleep. They were constant reminders of his weakness, his cowardice, his shame.

He heard the manservant walk to the fireplace and begin stoking the coals.

"Another bad 'un, m'lord?"

Poor old Lobb had suffered through many a bad night with James. More than anyone, Lobb understood about the dreams. He'd been at Ciudad Rodrigo, though as his batman and not therefore in the thick of fighting. Shortly after the explosion, when the 3rd Division stormed the retrenchments and took the town, Lobb had searched through the bloody, scorched mass of bodies and found James. He had pulled off the charred corpses whose weight had pinned James to the ground and carried his semiconscious employer to safety.

Lobb understood about the dreams.

"You'll be needin' this, m'lord." He set a steaming mug on the table next to the bed. Strong black coffee laced with brandy and a few other ingredients that Lobb kept to himself: his remedy for a particularly bad night.

James shrugged off the bedcovers and reached for the mug. "Thank you."

He took a long swallow and let the brandy soothe his nerves while the coffee prepared him to take on the day. He did not know what he would do without Lobb.

He was suddenly struck by an errant thought. "Lobb," he said, "I've heard it whispered about that Mrs. Osborne suffers nightmares, too. Do you know if it's true?"

The manservant pulled a fresh shirt from the clothespress and shook it out. He looked over at James, his brow furrowed as though he was hesitant to speak. James arched a questioning brow. "I believe it was true at first, m'lord," Lobb said at last. "Several of us heard her cries at night."

James winced, wondering what role he played in the woman's nightmares.

"But I could not say if it is still true," Lobb went on. "I have not personally heard her cry out these last few nights."

"If you do, perhaps you ought to send her some of this," James said, holding up the steaming mug. "It might help."

"Yes, m'lord."

James crawled out of bed and settled into the business of washing and shaving. His thoughts drifted to Verity Osborne. Despite her cries in the night, she seemed to have settled in quite comfortably. The staff doted on her, possibly because of the recovery of the Chenhalls boy. As far as he could tell, she had been true to her word about instructing them in the preparation of her herbal remedies. He had often seen her gathering plants, though he made a point of keeping his distance. Those deep brown eyes and the long white column of her neck bedeviled him.

But he studied her closely during the evenings when she took supper with him and Agnes. She never flinched during Agnes's frequent taunts, never spoke out to correct the impression that she was his mistress. She sat silent and dignified, the prideful angle of her jaw a clear refusal to be intimidated. Perhaps it was merely false bravado, though, with no real strength beneath it. After all, she did have nightmares.

When James had dressed and breakfasted, he made his way to the steward's office to check on the progress of the winter threshing. Rufus Bargwanath was a rough character at best, but a decent steward. Old Tresco, steward since James was a boy, had left after the tragedy in 1812. It had been difficult to get anyone to work at Pendurgan after that. Bargwanath knew it, and took advantage of the situation by requiring a salary far beyond his worth. James paid it just the same. He had no choice.

He found Bargwanath at his desk, his office in its usual disarray. James spent a half hour going over the stocking of fresh straw for the winter, and the progress of ditching and hedging.

Satisfied that Bargwanath had it all well in hand, James took his leave. When he reached the office door, the steward called out to him.

"I chanced upon that new warming pan o' yers yesterday," Bargwanath said. "You keepin' her all to yerself, or what?"

James spun around. "Watch your mouth, Bargwanath. Mrs. Osborne is a relation of mine and you will treat her with respect."

The steward gave a crack of laughter and leaned back in his chair, hands clasped behind his neck. "You don't expect nobody round here to fall fer that cousin story, do you? Hell, we all know how she come to be here. *And* what you paid for her. I just figured since you had her workin' in the kitchen that she was fair game."

"How dare you!" James took a step toward the desk, reining in the fury that had him ready to throttle the man.

"Looks to have a bit of spirit, she does. I like that in a woman, don't you?"

James placed both palms down on the desk and leaned forward. He fixed the man with a glare he'd honed to perfection in the army, a glare that had sent soldiers scurrying to do his bidding. "Keep your hands off her, Bargwanath," he said, his voice edged with steel, "if you know what's good for you. She has not been put 'to work,' as you call it. She is a guest at Pendurgan and I expect you to treat her accordingly. Do I make myself clear?"

Bargwanath shrugged indolently. "Sure, sure. I was only askin'."

James held the man's gaze for several long moments before Bargwanath lowered his eyes. He stormed out of the office, furious with the steward and his bloody impertinence. If he ever heard that Bargwanath had laid so much as a finger on Verity Osborne, he would kill the man with his bare hands. The very thought of him touching her twisted his gut into knots.

Too keyed up to check on the work at Wheal Devoran, James decided to ride off his anger. Jago Chenhalls saddled Castor for him, and James took off for the moors.

He'd ridden as far as one of the high tors before he slowed down. Caressing the gelding's damp neck, James let him walk, guiding him carefully along the ridge of broken and balancing granite rocks, of deep horizontal joints and sharp protrusions. Ageless and inviolable, the place never failed to inspire him, to exert its inexplicable power over him. There was a spiritual quality to it, elemental and secret. It was a place of ancient tombs and stone circles, of ghosts and piskeys, of legend and lore.

He led Castor slowly down the gentle slope of the rugged, boulder-strewn hill, allowing himself to absorb the spirit of the moor. Despite all the bad he'd seen and felt and wrought in his life, there was still this. There was still Cornwall.

James continued down through dun-colored wastes dotted with the deep green of furze, and onto the sweep of upland where the transition from moorland to cultivated countryside was abrupt and dramatic. He was on Pendurgan land now.

He saw a rider coming his way. When the familiar figure of Alan Poldrennan drew closer, James brought Castor to a halt and awaited the approach of the only man in the world he could rightly call his friend.

"Harkness! Well met," Poldrennan said as he reined in the bay mare. His genial smile was a welcome distraction. "Are you on your way home?"

James looked up at the darkening sky and realized he had been out on the moors for hours. "Damn," he said. "I hadn't realized it was so late. I must have lost track of time." A look of concern flickered in Poldrennan's eyes. James sighed. "It's all right, Alan. I was just wandering the moor, deep in thought."

Poldrennan smiled. "And so are you expected at home, or would you care to follow me to Bosreath and share a bottle with me? A bottle and a bird, perhaps?"

"By God, I think I will," James replied.

"Splendid!"

The two men turned their horses to the west toward Poldrennan's neighboring estate. "I haven't seen you in over a sennight." Poldrennan slanted a look at James. "I believe there have been changes at Pendurgan. Was it those changes that kept you so deep in thought you lost track of time?"

"I suppose you've heard the whole sorry tale?"

"News travels swiftly around here," Poldrennan replied. "I suspect there are few who have not heard some version of the tale. I'd be interested to hear what really happened."

As they rode toward Bosreath, James told his friend about the auction.

"What made you do it?" Poldrennan asked. "Were you thinking perhaps that she might . . . that you would . . . Well, dammit, I suspect it's been a while since you were with a woman. Was that why you bought her?"

James bristled. "No! No, of course not. That's not it at all. At least . . . at least I don't think it is." He slapped his thigh angrily. Castor misunderstood and set off at a gallop. James reined him in, crooned an apology in his ear, and waited for Poldrennan to catch up. "Damnation," he continued as though there'd been no interruption to their conversation. "Don't you think I've been asking myself the same question for the last week? Why? Why did I do it?"

"And?"

"And I still don't know." He flung up a hand in a vague gesture of frustration. "All I can tell you is that something inside me could not bear to see that poor woman handed over to Big Will Sykes. It made my stomach turn to think of it. And before I knew what I was doing, I'd bought her myself."

"Sykes, eh?" Poldrennan shuddered and began to chuckle. "I suppose I might have done the same," he said. "The man's disgusting." They rode on in silence for a few moments before Poldrennan spoke again. "And so it was not merely an impulse, but your honorable instincts that drove you to do it. To rescue her from a worse fate."

"Ha! I do not believe honor had anything to do with it. I suspect it was something much more base at work." He cast his friend a sheepish glance. "She's a frightfully good-looking woman."

"And yet I gather you have not acted on these baser instincts?"

"No."

"You see? You are honorable after all."

"No."

"But she's frightfully good-looking."

"Yes."

"And so what do you intend to do?"

"Stay away from her."

"Sounds honorable to me."

"Not honorable. Cowardly." James gave a disdainful snort. Poldrennan knew the depths of James's cowardice. He'd been in Spain. He'd been in Cornwall six years ago. He knew the truth. "I can't trust myself around her," James went on. "What if . . . what if during . . . Well, what if I harmed her? How could I live with that again?"

Poldrennan reined in to a halt. When James had done the same, Poldrennan reached over and placed a hand on his arm. "You must stop punishing yourself, Harkness. That was over six years ago. And it has not happened again."

"How do you know?"

"I know. So do you. It will not happen again. She is safe with you."

James flicked the reins and urged Castor into a gallop along the path to Bosreath. "I wish I could believe that."

"All right, Gonetta. I am ready."

The girl flashed Verity a brilliant smile, adjusted her bonnet, and reached for one of the large baskets they'd prepared. She walked toward the scullery door with a bounce in her step. When she realized Verity was not following, had not in fact moved, Gonetta turned, smiled again, and raised her eyebrows in a sign of encouragement.

Verity needed all the encouragement she could muster.

"C'mon, then," Gonetta said and headed out the door.

Verity took one last deep breath and followed. Was she making a horrible mistake? Should she stay behind?

Gonetta had told her that the villagers would be

grateful for her knowledge of homemade remedies for common ailments, but Verity doubted the girl's confidence in the villagers' reception. These were small, close-knit communities who did not take well to strangers. Not only was she a "foreigner," but one who'd come to Cornwall under peculiar circumstances. What sort of welcome could she truly expect from these cautious, insulated people who likely believed her to be Lord Harkness's mistress? What if some of them had been at the auction and seen her? What if some of them had been among the kettle-banging, surging crowd that still haunted her dreams?

But this was old ground. Verity had been over it and over it in her mind before finally agreeing to Gonetta's enthusiastic invitation. Besides, she had become restless. Even with Pendurgan's extensive grounds and gardens, she felt confined. A small part of her welcomed this excursion, regardless of its outcome.

And so here she was on her way to call on some of the good people of Pendurgan's village of St. Peran's.

Leaving the formal grounds of Pendurgan, Verity was comforted to find the lane flanked on both sides by green fields crisscrossed with hedgerows. It seemed so very normal. So very English. What had happened to all that bleak granite moorland they'd passed through on their way to Pendurgan? She looked right and left, but saw only lush countryside.

She caught Gonetta's puzzled glance. "Wot 'ee lookin' fer, then?"

Verity smiled and shrugged. "I was just remembering all that granite wasteland we drove through on our way to Pendurgan. Did I imagine it?"

Gonetta stopped, took Verity by the shoulders, and swung her around toward the house. "See there?" she said and pointed to a hill beyond Pendurgan. Higher even than Pendurgan's own hill, it was crowned with great rock outcroppings weathered into all manner of fantastic shapes and littered with masses of fallen rock.

"That do be the High Tor," Gonetta said. "It do be a kind o' trick o' the landscape, Pa says, the way 'ee can't see it at all from Pendurgan. But from here it do loom up big in the distance. That do be what 'ee seen comin' from Gunnisloe."

"It's amazing," Verity said. "I was beginning to think I'd dreamed it."

"The moor do be a queer place," Gonetta said. "It do play tricks on 'ee. Or the piskeys do. Lots o' folks get piskey-led on the moor, clean lost in land they been walkin' fer their whole lives. They'll run 'ee in circles, the piskeys will. But this lane to St. Perran's, it do be straight and clear. No odd turns for piskeys to hide in."

Verity smiled at the girl's perfectly serious notion of faeries. At least she assumed that was what a piskey must be. "And what's that?" Verity asked, pointing to two tall, slender structures rising from the stone rubble at the base of the western slope.

"Them stacks? Why, that do be Wheal Devoran."

"The mine?"

"Aye, one o' his lordship's copper mines."

Gonetta stood patiently while Verity studied the odd structures, starkly elegant amid the rough landscape. A thin stream of smoke, or perhaps it was steam, rose from one of the chimneys and drifted toward the desolate tor.

"Wheal Devoran do be where most of the menfolk round here work," Gonetta said. "Them as don't farm. Most o' the girls, too. I do be one o' the lucky ones, workin' up at big house. Better'n a bal-maiden at mine."

So the mysterious lord of the manor not only provided farms for his tenants to work but also employment for the rest of the population. "If Lord Harkness employs most of the local people," Verity wondered aloud, "why is he so disliked? I know he is called Lord Heartless. Why?"

Gonetta's face went blank as an egg. She shrugged, then continued walking down the lane.

The girl's guarded attitude toward Lord Harkness caused all Verity's earlier doubts and fears to swirl momentarily like a sinister fog in her brain. What was the mystery of the lord of Pendurgan, the mystery that only Agnes Bodinar dared speak of?

"C'mon, then," Gonetta said, and Verity turned to follow her, more curious than ever about the black-haired man with the penetrating blue eyes.

In this direction, toward the village, they were once again surrounded by fields of green. What a study in contrasts was this strange land. And its people.

She could see the village in the near distance. As they grew closer, Verity began to feel very much a foreigner. Here was no familiar warmth and charm of the wold villages of her youth, or even those of Berkshire where she'd spent the last two years. There were no whitewashed cottages and no thatched roofs. No timber framing or vine covered walls.

Instead, it was a miniature version of the frightful Gunnisloe. Graceless, squat cottages of rough granite with slate roofs were scattered haphazardly along random dirt paths branching off the main lane. Boxy, utilitarian structures with no character and little individuality, they stood colorless, drab, and uninviting.

On a slight rise at the far end of the cluster of cottages stood the church. Built of the same slate and granite as the cottages, it was only slightly more refined. The square tower was topped with four finials that looked like rabbits' ears from a distance. The few trees in the village seemed to be clustered near the church.

"Here do be the Dunstan cottage," Gonetta said. "We'll stop here first." She lowered her voice and leaned close to Verity. "Jacob Dunstan do work one o' the pump engines at Wheal Devoran. It do make his wife think they be better'n some since he don't have to work a pitch like most of t'others. She do put on airs, sometimes. Afternoon, Miz Dunstan," she added in a louder voice.

A stocky dark-haired woman in a plain blue dress and white apron stood in the doorway of the stone cottage. She did not reply to Gonetta's greeting and eyed Verity suspiciously.

"I brung Miz Osborne to meet 'ee, from up to Pendurgan. She do be a cousin of his lordship's come to stay awhile."

The woman gave a muffled snort that told Verity how much she believed the cousin relationship. Verity braced herself for an uncomfortable afternoon.

Gonetta ignored the woman's rudeness and turned toward Verity. "This here do be Ewa Dunstan, ma'am. Her husband, Jacob, he do work up at Wheal Devoran."

"Above ground," Ewa Dunstan was quick to add, "in the engine house."

Verity reached out a hand. "How do you do, Mrs. Dunstan? I am pleased to meet you."

The woman looked momentarily abashed, but finally took Verity's hand. "How do 'ee do?" she said.

"Ma baked an extra batch of fuggan and asked me to bring some," Gonetta said. She reached into her basket, pulled out one of the wrapped cakes, and offered it to Ewa Dunstan. "I been tellin' Miz Osborne how Ma's fuggan cakes be the best in district. Can 'ee credit it? Miz Osborne never had no fuggan before she do come here. Guess they don't have it where she do come from."

"Indeed?" Ewa said. "And where do 'ee come from, ma'am?"

"I grew up in Lincolnshire," Verity said in as pleasant a tone as she could manage, determined to rise above the scorn of a miner's wife. "But I have grown very fond of Mrs. Chenhalls's fuggan. They are delicious."

"Brought some more stuff, too," Gonetta said. She pulled out one of the muslin packets they had prepared, and regaled Ewa Dunstan with tales of Verity's knowledge of herbs. Verity interrupted a lengthy discourse on Davey's miraculous recovery.

"I understand the local physician is still away," she said, "and so I thought perhaps to distribute these packets of herbs to the village families. They can be used to make an infusion for common head colds that are bound to strike as winter approaches."

Verity proceeded to give Ewa Dunstan directions in how to make and dispense the infusion, and the dour woman began to unbend slightly.

"I been bothered with the toothache," she said. "Don't s'pose 'ee got somethin' to help fer that?"

Verity told her that she could indeed recommend a gargle and would prepare the ingredients and deliver them tomorrow. She took out a small notebook and pencil and scribbled a note to herself.

Grateful, Ewa went so far as to invite Verity in for a dish of tea. Gonetta replied before Verity could say a word.

"That be right kind o' 'ee, Miz Dunstan," she said, "but we do got to deliver these here cakes and pouches to rest o' village. Miz Osborne, she made up a special tea, though, that I do be hopin' we can convince Old Grannie to brew up. Come on down to her cottage in a while and try some."

Gonetta had spoken of Old Grannie Pascow as a sort of matriarch of the village, and Verity was anxious to make a good impression on the elderly woman. As they left Ewa Dunstan, Verity asked Gonetta if it was quite proper to invite someone to Mrs. Pascow's without the old woman's consent. Gonetta laughed.

" 'Ee'll see how it do be soon 'nuff," she said. "All the women do end up at Old Grannie's anyhow. Don't need no invitation."

The visit to Ewa Dunstan marked the pattern of the rest of the visits through the village and the outlying tenant farms. Initial wariness gave way to politeness and sometimes downright friendliness. And everyone had an ailment or complaint of some kind. Hildy Spruggins had stomach pains, Dorcas Muddle's baby suffered colic and gas, Lizzy Trethowan's husband had strained a back muscle while repairing a hedgerow, Annie Kempthorne endured severe menstrual cramps, and Borra Nanpean's daughter had a chronic cough.

Verity filled her notebook with lists of preparations for the villagers. She ultimately felt welcome in each cottage by farmer's wife and miner's wife alike. By the time they had made their way to Old Grannie Pascow's cottage, Verity was almost giddy with relief.

The old woman's cottage was no different from the rest: a simple stone square with plain gabled roof and small, wood-frame windows. Despite the austere exteriors, however, each cottage had been warm and cozy inside.

Grannie Pascow stood in the doorway as though expecting their arrival. A short, plump, silver-haired woman of indeterminate age, she had a formidable nose and small, dark eyes that missed nothing. She stood regal as a queen during Gonetta's brief introductions, then, with a sweep of an arm, invited them inside.

It was clear why they'd been expected. Several of the village woman Verity and Gonetta had visited earlier were already seated inside, clustered around a large hearth. The low-beamed ceiling made the room appear smaller than it was. A corner staircase indicated that a second floor had been accommodated beneath the steep gable of the roof. Gonetta had told

Verity that Grannie's grandson and family shared the cottage with her.

Grannie Pascow moved slowly to the chair nearest the fire. It was a high-backed wooden armchair, the only armchair in the room. The old woman eased herself stiffly into the seat of honor.

Gonetta touched Verity lightly on the arm. "I best leave 'ee alone here," she whispered, "and return to Pendurgan. It do be gettin' on afternoon and Mrs. Tregelly'll have my hide if I don't get them grates cleaned. I don't want 'ee feelin' bound to hurry on my account. Take yer time here. The way back do be easy enough, I do think."

A pang of anxiety struck Verity at the thought of being left alone with these women, but it passed when she caught Borra Nanpean's friendly smile and realized she'd be fine. Gonetta transferred a few remaining items from her basket to Verity's, made her polite farewells, and quietly left the cottage.

"Come sit here by me, Verity Osborne," Grannie Pascow said, patting the worn rush seat of the chair next to her.

Verity stepped across Ewa Dunstan and Lizzy Trethowan and took her seat by the old woman. After more introductions, she offered the last of the fuggan cakes to Grannie, along with a pouch of elderberry and rosehip tea she'd brought with her from Berkshire. Grannie thanked Verity and handed both to Kate Pascow, her granddaughter-in-law, and asked her to brew the tea and slice the cake.

"I do heard 'ee knows 'bout herbs," Grannie said. *Ah d'heerd ee naws boot harbs*. Verity's ear was becoming accustomed to the peculiar Cornish notion of grammar, and the local accent with its long R's and rolling vowels, with its quizzical lift at the end of each sentence, the almost musical way a final syllable was drawn out and up. Even so, she had to strain to understand every word. "Ever'body claimin' 'ee do be goin' to fix 'em up with some remedy or t'other," Grannie Pascow continued. "Where'd 'ee learn so much? From yer ma?"

"There was an elderly woman in the village where I grew up," Verity said, pleased to begin with such a comfortable and welcome topic, even knowing it was Grannie's way of uncovering pertinent details of family and station and connections. "Her name was Edith Littleton and she was the local green woman. My mother was prone to illness, and so I took an interest in Edith's work, hoping to help my mother. Edith took me under her wing as a child and taught me everything I know."

"We do be most grateful fer that knowledge just now," Grannie Pascow said, "with no doctor in the district and only that fool surgeon Mr. Trevenna at the mine." She shifted her hip awkwardly in the chair and stretched out one leg toward the fire.

"I beg your pardon, Mrs. Pascow—"

Verity was interrupted by laughter from all around, including Grannie Pascow. It was the first time the old woman had cracked a smile, and a sheaf of deep creases spread across each cheek like a fan. It transformed her totally, and reminded Verity so much of her beloved Edith that she almost cried.

" 'Ee go callin' me Miz Pascow and I be lookin'

'round to see who 'ee be talkin' to. Just call me Grannie. Ever'body else do. Or Old Grannie. They does call me that behind my back and think I be too ancient to know. But I don't care none. I *be* old."

Verity smiled. She was going to like Grannie Pascow. "What I was going to say, Grannie, is that I couldn't help but notice the stiffness in your hip. Gonetta told me that you suffered from rheumatism. I hope you won't think it too impertinent of me, but I took the liberty of making up this oil for you."

She reached in her basket and pulled out a small corked bottle of brownish-yellow liquid and handed it to Grannie. The old woman held it up to the firelight, turning it first one way, then another, as if it were something rare and precious.

"I've had great success with this mixture," Verity continued. "The oil is heated with branches of broom, chamomile flowers, and comfrey roots. Massage it into your joints, then lie quietly for a half hour or so and you will feel much better, I promise you."

Grannie's dark eyes had grown wide with wonder as she continued to stare at the small bottle. The room grew silent. Finally, the old woman cocked her head toward Verity and smiled. "I will use this, child," she said. "Yes, I will. It be most kind of 'ee, Verity Osborne. I be that grateful to 'ee, child."

The women began to pepper her with medical questions and Verity had to remind them she was no physician. She deftly steered the conversation to their own families, their farms, their children. Grannie Pascow sat silent during most of the conversation, directing the distribution of tea and cake by her granddaughter-in-law. Though she seldom spoke, she listened intently, her eyes on Verity more often than not. Finally, while Hildy Spruggins chattered on about how her son Benjie was now working at Wheal Devoran, Grannie held up her hand for silence. Hildy's mouth shut like a trap.

"I won't be mincin' words, Verity Osborne," Grannie said. "Tedn't no point. Here it be, then: we all do know how 'ee come to be at Pendurgan."

Verity's heart sank to her toes. She held her breath and waited for the other shoe to drop.

"None of us got the right to ask 'bout that bit o' business in Gunnisloe. Some been there, anyway. Hildy been there with her Nat." Hildy Spruggins hung her head and blushed scarlet. "Annie, too," Grannie continued. "I already done spoke harsh to ever'body here'bouts fer their part. 'Twas shameful. Pure shameful." Her eyes narrowed as they moved from woman to woman, castigating each with no more than a glance. She let the awkward silence fill the room before returning her attention to Verity.

"But I do tell 'ee to yer head that I think 'ee do be a fine woman, Verity Osborne," she said. "Coulda been that 'ee stayed up to the big house and never concerned yerself wid us village folk. A woman like 'ee, a gentleman's daughter, wid education and fine manners, 'ee might've ignored us, never set foot on our plain dirt floors. Like some. 'Ee didn't have to come down here wid yer remedies and advice, but 'ee did and we do all be thankful fer it."

Murmurs of agreement came from all around the room.

"Thing is," Grannie went on, "wot's done be done an' there be no changin' it now. I just want to make myself easy about yer being up there an' all. I wouldn't want to hear of no harm coming to 'ee. So you tell Grannie straight right now, and I'll not be askin' 'ee again. Do everythin' be all right with 'ee in that house? Do that boy be treatin' 'ee right?"

Chapter 5

His head throbbed. He pushed the heels of his palms against his eyes and tried to make the pain go away. The pounding only intensified, continuous Howitzer rounds fired from inside his head and slamming into the backs of his eyeballs.

James groaned. *Oh, God, not again.* A sick dread churned in his gut. He took in deep gulps of cool air to combat the nausea that always came with the headache. When he was fairly certain he was not going to be sick, he finally opened his eyes.

He was on the moor. Crouching on the very top of the High Tor, in fact. As close as he could get to God. The sun showed it to be well into afternoon. How long had he been out? How did he get there? Castor grazed lazily nearby, so he must have ridden. He could not remember riding. He could not remember anything.

Think, man!

Against the pounding in his head, James tried to remember what had happened this time. It had been morning. Good Lord, hours ago. He had gone to Wheal Devoran. Core was changing. Filthy, exhausted night workers joked noisily with the morning core. As he approached the timber yard he saw Ezra Noone playfully tip the hat of Gerens Palk. Barks of laughter rose from the gathering of men when Palk's hempen candle fell off his hat and into his dinner pail. The man shouted as the cloth covering his pasty ignited. A burst of flame shot out from the pail.

That was all. No more memories came, as he knew they would not. After six years and more, James knew the effects of sudden fire or explosion. And after six years and more, he still could not control it. He had learned early on to avoid the mine on blasting days, but small incidents such as today's could never be predicted.

Another long block of hours lost, black hours during which he could recall nothing. A familiar wave of disorientation swept through him, as though he were two people, one not knowing what the other did. It was always the same, yet it never got easier.

He mounted Castor and headed back down the hill to Wheal Devoran. As he approached the main engine house, Kneebone, his chief engineer, leaned against the doorway and mopped his brow. He spied James and walked over.

"Afternoon, m'lord," he said warily.

"Everything all right here, Kneebone?"

"Aye. We got that plunger pump replaced and

now all the shafts are working. And Tregonning's pitch has been reset."

"Good. Nothing else?"

"Everything as usual, m'lord."

If James had made a fool of himself earlier, Kneebone would never mention it. Or anyone else. James knew they all thought him mad. Since he did not know what they might have seen him do—not only today but a hundred times before—he was inclined to agree with them.

He stopped by the count house, checked on the work in the cobbing shed, spoke briefly with the smithy, and made a quick survey of the store buildings. The surface workers avoided him if they could. The rest seemed more guarded then usual. The balmaidens had stopped singing. He wondered again what sort of scene he'd created that morning.

It was possible he'd been in the village during those lost hours. He knew he should return home and forget about it, but he was always compelled to try and discover what he could. The miners and the farmers, though, and even the staff at Pendurgan, kept their silence. Poldrennan assured him he'd done no more harm, but James could never be sure. He turned Castor toward St. Perran's.

He swung wide to the south and west so he would enter the village through the churchyard. He picked his way along the gravel path skirting the fenced graveyard. A babble of female voices stopped him, and he edged Castor behind a small copse of trees near the lychgate.

He watched through the leaves as a group of women appeared at the door of Old Grannie Pascow's cottage, apparently taking their leave. He would stay hidden until they'd dispersed, for he knew how they felt about him. If he listened closely, though, perhaps he might hear something useful, some clue to today's lost hours.

They seemed, however, merely to be discussing their various aches and pains. They were certainly not talking about him. He kept Castor quiet among the trees while the women lingered and lingered. He wished they would leave so he could be on his way.

"I be most grateful, Miz Osborne, and look forward to yer mixture fer my Gwennie."

James froze. Verity? Dammit, what was she doing here?

He watched as Verity's small figure emerged from behind the more substantial one of Borra Nanpean. She wore a gray dress beneath a blue wool cloak and carried a basket on her arm. It was the same blue cloak she'd worn at the auction. Did she know that some of these women had been at the auction? That several of their husbands had actually bid on her? She was smiling and talking to Hildy Spruggins. Did she know Hildy had been there with Nat, probably banging on a kettle as loud as anyone?

She must know. Even if she did not know specifically who had been there, she must realize many of the locals had been. How could she blithely walk out amongst these people, all of whom knew how she came to be at Pendurgan? How could she so calmly face this community of women who would believe her to be no better than his mistress?

Yet here she was, risking their scorn and rejection,

apparently dispensing her herbal remedies. She had faced them head on, and succeeded, for there was no question they had welcomed her. She looked as comfortable with them as any Cornishwoman.

It humbled him to watch her, to see how she faced her demons and won—something he had never been able to do. Her demons, though, had been external forces out of her control. His demons came from within.

Somehow he knew Verity had too much pride to allow that single incident to rule her life. She wore her pride like an armor. It was so easily donned he suspected she had used it often before. Only an occasional flicker of vulnerability reminded James there was no real core of steel beneath the armor.

The distinctive voice of Old Grannie Pascow reached his ears.

"Now 'ee mind what I said, child, and 'ee call on me if ever 'ee be in trouble up there."

Damn. These termagants were rallying around Verity in protection against him. The interfering old shrews! His anger prompted an involuntary jerk on the reins, and Castor whinnied.

The women fell silent and all heads turned in his direction. Muttering a curse, he led Castor forward as though he'd been casually passing by instead of skulking in the trees.

Several stifled gasps met his appearance. Without a word, the women scattered like rabbits to a gunshot. One of them—Dorcas Muddle, he thought—clasped her child to her breast as she scurried down the lane. He wondered again about those lost hours today; but this reaction was typical and likely had nothing to do with anything that might have occurred today.

Verity stood still as a statue in the doorway with Old Grannie. Kate Pascow disappeared inside. The old woman glared at him, her expression formidable and defiant. Verity looked confused and slightly apprehensive as she watched the other women hurry away.

James pulled up alongside the cottage and dismounted. "Good afternoon, Grannie," he said. "Verity." She looked startled at the use of her name, but if he was going to maintain the poor-relation charade, anything more formal would seem awkward.

"Afternoon," Grannie said. After a brief pause, she added, "M'lord." She had known him since he was in the cradle and seldom used his title, except in the company of others.

He turned to address Verity. "I did not know you planned to come into St. Perran's today."

"She did come to give us remedies fer winter head colds an' such," Grannie said in a contentious tone, "fer which we be most thankful, what with that Trefusis feller bein' away an' all."

"That was most kind of you, Verity," he said. "May I escort you home?"

"Yes, of course," she said, apparently flustered at the notion. "Thank you." She turned to Old Grannie and smiled warmly. "And thank you so much for your hospitality."

" 'Ee do be welcome anytime, child. The door always be open an' I always do be home."

"I shall drop by in a day or so," Verity said, "when

I deliver all the remedies I've promised the other families. Now, don't you forget to use that oil I brought."

"I won't be forgettin'. I do thank 'ee again fer it. And 'ee, James." She pronounced his name *Jammez*, in the old Cornish manner. "Take 'ee good care of Verity Osborne, do 'ee hear me?"

"Still watching out for everyone's welfare, eh, Grannie?"

"Someone got to."

He smiled, and her expression softened. "I will take good care of her, Grannie, have no fear. Come, Verity." He reached out and took her basket. Then, holding Castor's reins, he walked beside her along the path.

After a few silent moments, he looked over to find Verity watching him. She dropped her gaze and flushed. "I'm sorry," she said. "You surprised me, that's all."

"By coming to St. Perran's?" he asked.

"No, not that."

"How, then?"

She looked up and met his eyes, hers large and liquid brown and unafraid. "By smiling. You smiled at Grannie."

James shrugged and looked away. "I've known her all my life."

"It's just that I . . . I'd never seen you smile."

Her words, and her soft buttery voice, disconcerted him. It was easier when she was afraid of him.

"I suppose you think me an ogre. Well, it's true, but not all of the time. And I am afraid now is one of those times. What the devil do you mean coming into

St. Perran's all alone? You ought to have taken Gonetta or Tomas with you."

"Oh, but I did," she replied. "Gonetta spent most of the day with me, but left to finish up her chores while I had tea with Grannie and the other women."

"You should have returned when she did," he said. "I will not have you wandering about alone beyond Pendurgan."

"I had not realized you had rules," she said, a note of challenge in her voice.

"Only the normal ones, the ones any *lady* would understand."

"How dare you!"

That had done it. "You know very well how I dare," he said.

"Of course," she said. "How silly of me. I am your property, am I not? I shall take more care in the future."

"Don't be foolish. I do not own you. I thought I made that clear the first night. But I am responsible for you, so long as you remain under my roof."

They walked on in silence. Verity kept up a brisk pace, her strides long and her shoulders rigid. So much pride!

"Damn it," he said at last. "I'm sorry. I should not have scolded you."

"No, you should not."

"I've had a . . . a difficult day," he said. "My temper is on edge. Forget what I said."

"Then I may return to St. Perran's, alone, when I please?"

"Yes, yes," he said, his voice sharp with impatience. "Do as you wish."

"I am only trying to help your people, my lord."

The more she helped, the more entrenched she would become in all their lives. And the harder it would be ever to let her go.

"Why are they afraid of you?"

Her question shook him. He had deliberately avoided being alone with her, all the time believing it was his infernal attraction to her he wanted to forestall. But it was more than that. It was this directness. He had seen it every time they'd spoken more than a few words, from that first night in the library when she had tried to sneak away. Beneath all the other excuses, it was this about her, more than anything else, that made her dangerous. He had feared she would inevitably come to this question.

"Are you afraid of me?" he asked.

"Sometimes."

"You should be." He strode ahead and walked the rest of the way in silence.

During the next several days, Verity often found her heart thrown into a wild disorder. She did not know what to make of James. That day at Grannie's, when he had ridden out of the churchyard on the black gelding, there had been the apprehension that always affected her in his presence, as well as a fleeting moment of fear when the women had run from him. But there had also been a niggling little spark of pleasure at the sight of him.

He had looked magnificent and handsome sitting atop the sleek black horse. It was the perfect mount for him, she had decided as she watched him swing out of the saddle with a fluid grace, for he was equally dark and sleek.

She had no right entertaining such wayward thoughts, considering her situation and his reputation.

All good sense was tossed away, however, when he smiled at Grannie Pascow. Her traitorous heart had melted a tiny bit. He had a beautiful smile, one that broke across the harsh angles of his face like a sunrise. Clearly, he did not often smile. His face did not bear the creases of laughter. Instead, the lines around his mouth and nose were marks of the scowl he wore so frequently. What a pity, she thought, when the smile so much more suited him.

Could a man who harbored such a smile, a smile that went all the way to his eyes, be so very wicked? There was so much she wanted to know, but no one was willing to tell her.

Not even the man himself. He had never replied to her question. It appeared he wanted to keep her at arm's length through fear. He wanted her to be afraid of him. Why? James Harkness was a man wary and watchful. It was as though he held on to his control with a firm grip, afraid to let go, afraid . . . of what?

She had been back to St. Perran's several times, delivering her herbs and remedies, and providing instructions in their use. And the women had opened up to her about many things. She learned a bit about each family, about their joys and their sorrows. She got to know the children. She learned about each tenant farm's capacity and about each miner's pitch. They all seemed to turn to stone, though, on the subject of Lord Harkness.

Even Grannie Pascow was reticent. The oil had worked wonders on her joints, and she claimed to feel as spry as a young colt. Verity sat for hours at Grannie's hearth, listening to colorful tales of Cornish saints and sinners, of piskeys and tommyknockers. Whenever Lord Harkness was mentioned, though, Grannie steered the conversation in other directions.

Since no information was forthcoming from any quarter, Verity was forced to come to her own conclusions.

He had good, loyal servants at Pendurgan. The cottages and church at St. Perran's were kept in good repair. He provided employment for both men and women at his mines. He provided a school for the children and paid the teacher's salary.

If Lord Harkness was so evil, would he take such care of those in his employ, or show concern for the children's education?

And what about her? He still had not come to her bed, and she decided he had no intention of ever doing so. Since he obviously had not purchased her for his own pleasure, it could only mean he had done it to rescue her from a worse fate.

Verity found it difficult to reconcile all this evidence of decency with the general attitude of the local people and their concern for her safety. What did they fear? What did they know that they weren't telling her?

Verity considered the question as she walked up the back stairs to the room where Davey slept. She had discovered a patch of coltsfoot near the river embankment a few days earlier. Pleased to find this herb that could be very soothing to a sore throat, she had prepared a new infusion for Davey.

She knocked quietly before entering. Tomas sat by his brother's bedside and rose at Verity's entrance. The little boy was tucked up to his chin in wool blankets. A shock of bright red hair fell over his forehead, and the freckles splattered across his nose and cheeks stood out like paint flecks against the pallor of his skin.

"Good afternoon, Davey," Verity said. "I've brought something for you." She handed the steaming cup to Tomas, who placed it on a small table next to the bed.

"Hullo, Miz Osborne," Davey squeaked. His throat was still raw and it obviously pained him to speak. "Somethin' good this time, I do hope? No more nasty-tastin' stuff?"

Verity chuckled. "I don't believe this will taste nasty at all, Davey. I've sweetened it with honey for you. It should help your throat feel better. You'd like that, would you not?"

"Sure would," he croaked. "It still do hurt real bad."

"I know. Here, let me help you sit up and we'll see if this helps. Tomas, I will stay with him for a while if you like."

Verity sat on the edge of the bed when Tomas left, helping Davey take the sweetened infusion, one small sip at a time. She chattered to him between sips. She spoke of the Kempthorne children and Gwennie Nanpean and Benjie Spruggins and other children she'd met. Davey knew them all and had his own stories to tell, but Verity kept feeding him sips so he would not talk too much.

After an hour or so, Gonetta entered the room.

"Davey boy, y'ain't been talkin' Miz Osborne's ears off, has 'ee?"

Verity reached up and wiggled her ears. Davey dissolved in giggles, which turned into a hacking cough. Verity held him up straight with a hand at his small, bony back until the coughing subsided. He sank against the pillows, pale and weary.

"You rest now, Davey," Verity said. A rush of emotion for this child welled up in her throat as she tucked the blankets up around his ears.

"Come back?" His voice had become a hoarse whisper.

"Of course I'll come back. But you must sleep now. Gonetta will sit with you for a while, all right?"

He shook his head and offered a wan smile. His eyelids slowly drooped shut, and he was almost instantly asleep.

Verity rose to leave. She told Gonetta about the new infusion and when to administer it again.

"Thank 'ee, Miz Osborne. 'Ee been such a help."

Verity shrugged and smiled down at the boy, then left the room, closing the door quietly behind her. She took the service stairs down to the main level. When she passed the Little Parlor, she saw Anges Bodinar seated on a small divan, an embroidery hoop in her hands. She looked up at Verity's approach and waved her inside.

Verity groaned silently. Encounters with Anges were never pleasant. She gritted her teeth and entered the parlor.

"You've been with Cook's boy again, have you not?"

"Yes," Verity replied. She stood just inside the

doorway with her hands clasped tightly behind her back.

Agnes snorted, then returned her attention to the embroidery. "You spend far too much time with that young scullery rat."

"He's a very sick little boy."

"I thought he was recovered," Agnes said without looking up, a sarcastic edge to her voice. "According to Cook, you miraculously cured him."

"I only helped a little, in the absence of a doctor," Verity said. "But it is a serious illness, especially for a child. He will be some time in recovering."

"And I presume you mean to stay until he is fully recovered?"

"I gave Mrs. Chenhalls my word."

Agnes stabbed at the stretched fabric with her needle. "Too bad," she said. "You ought to have left by now."

Verity walked into the room and took a seat across from Agnes. She was going to get the truth of out of the old shrew if she had to sit here until the sun went down.

"Why are you so anxious for me to leave?" Verity asked. "Is it because of your daughter?"

"Of course it is!"

It had been a shot in the dark, but it seemed to have hit its mark. Agnes must see Verity as a threat to her daughter's memory. Or perhaps she simply did not like the idea of anyone taking her daughter's place at Pendurgan. "You need not worry on that score," Verity said. "I assure you, despite what you may believe, I am in no way—*in no way*—replacing Lady Harkness in this house. Do you take my meaning?"

"Hmph. As if you could."

"You have nothing to fear from me, Mrs. Bodinar. I may have come here under . . . unusual circumstances, but not for the purpose you have supposed."

"Great heavens! Do you think I care if you keep that monster's bed warm at night?" She yanked her needle through the fabric with such ruthless force that Verity thought she would surely ruin the piece. "I only warn you not to trust him."

"Why?"

"Why? Because of who he is and what he's done, of course."

This was the opening Verity had been waiting for. "But I do not know who he is or what he's done," she said.

The embroidery hoop dropped to her lap and Agnes looked up at Verity, astonishment in her face. She blinked like an owl surprised in daylight. "You do not know?"

"No."

"But everyone knows."

"Everyone around here. I am new to Cornwall."

Agnes gave a weary sigh and resumed her stitching. "Then I suppose it is left to me to tell you," she said.

Verity sat silent, hands folded in her lap, perched on the edge of her chair like a pigeon, waiting for Agnes to go on.

"He was fine before the war," Agnes said at last. Her voice had lost some of its sharpness though her eyes remained hard. "They married young, he and my Rowena. They had known one another most of their lives and Rowena was bound and determined to have him. Frankly, I would have preferred it if she'd married Alan Poldrennan. Such a nice young man, and he'd been pining after her for years. But Rowena's heart was set on James." She hunched a shoulder and gave a little sigh.

"My husband's mine, Wheal Blessing, was in the district, not far from here," she continued. "Old Lord Harkness was still alive and running Wheal Devoran with a firm hand. He and James did not always agree on things, so James ran off and joined the army. It was during one of his leaves that he and Rowena married. Wheal Blessing finally played out and was closed, and we lost everything. Soon afterward, my husband died, leaving me nothing but an empty hole in the ground. James offered me a home here, said he wanted me to keep Rowena company while he returned to the army."

Her brow puckered and she stared off into the distance, as though she'd forgotten Verity was even there. After a moment, she literally shook herself free of whatever memory had taken hold.

"He came home on leave as often as he could," she went on. "Trystan was born in 1809. Rowena was blissfully happy. But then James was wounded and sold out. He was not the same man when he came home in 1812. He was hard and cruel. Irritable and vicious-tongued. He made Rowena miserable."

Harsh loathing filled Agnes's eyes. She held Verity's gaze for one long moment before speaking again.

"And then he killed her," she said.

"What?"

"James Harkness killed my daughter. And even worse than that, he killed his own son as well."

* * *

"Are you certain?" Gilbert Russell paced the length of the Turkey carpet in his friend's study. "It is the same man?"

"There is only one Lord Harkness of Pendurgan," the other man said. "It says here he inherited the title some eight years ago from his father. Besides, the father would have been too old to be your Lord Harkness. It has to be the same man."

Gilbert could not believe what he was hearing. He had finally admitted to his friend, Anthony Northrup, what he had done with Verity and where he had got the money to pay off Baldridge. He had thought to unburden himself, to purge himself of this awful thing he'd done to his poor wife.

Tony was one of the few people who knew Gilbert had a wife at all. That's why it had been so easy. A few weeks away in Cornwall and no one the wiser.

But the deed had gnawed at his gut like a tapeworm. He had to tell someone. Who better than Tony, his closest friend and confidant?

But Tony had just made it worse.

Gilbert stopped pacing and pressed his hands to his temples. "Good God, what have I done?"

"It appears, old chap, that you have turned your wife over to a murderer."

Verity sat at the tiny desk in her bedchamber and flipped through her notebook. A single candle illuminated the notes she was reviewing. Rain pounded against the window and the wind howled. She had not been able to sleep. Fidgety and restless, she had finally crawled out of bed and decided to go over the stillroom work for tomorrow, to make sure she had all her recipes in order. She concentrated on the herbs needed for her mixtures, hoping to dispel all thoughts of Agnes's startling revelation.

Had he really murdered his wife and child? Could she believe Agnes? The old woman seemed slightly mad at times, hateful and bitter at most others. Could the words of such a woman be trusted?

Dried betony for Robbie Dunstan's wheezing.

Once she had made the accusation, Agnes had flung her hoop aside and rushed out of the parlor. She had seemed on the verge of tears. She had lost a daughter and a grandchild, so naturally she would be upset. And perhaps there was some reason to blame James for their deaths. But murder?

Rosemary for Izzy Muddle's colic.

If it was true, if he had killed them, why was he not prosecuted for the crime? Why was he still wandering about free instead of rotting in gaol or swinging from a hangman's rope? It didn't make any sense. Agnes must be exaggerating the tale.

Lovage root for Hildy Spruggins's stomach.

But if it was true, it accounted for the way the locals feared him, especially the women. Verity recalled how women had grabbed their children when he had walked through the crowd at Gunnisloe. And how Dorcas Muddle had clasped her baby and run down the village lane. She had not forgotten—would never forget—the whispered words of the people at Gunnisloe, words that had made her fear for her life. The villagers must certainly believe them to be true. But were they, in fact?

Beech leaves for Sam Kempthorne's strained back.

Or was it birch leaves?

How she missed her modern edition of Culpepper. It had been a gift from Edith and was full of Verity's cribbed notes in the margins. When Gilbert had told her to pack everything for the trip to Cornwall, she had not, of course, taken him literally. She had not thought to bring her books.

So far she had been working from memory, and it had served her well. But if she mistook even one ingredient, the results could be disastrous. Blast! If only she had her books.

She pulled her wool wrapper more tightly around her, though it was only the sounds of rain and wind that made it seem cold. Just the same, she moved to the big wing chair and pulled it right up next to the fire so she could rest her toes on the grate. She stared into the flames and willed herself to remember the precise ingredients for the poultice for Sam Kempthorne. No matter how hard she tried, though, she could not recall if it was beech leaves or birch leaves she needed.

What she wouldn't give for a good English herbal.

The library downstairs was lined with books, though she had never ventured in to examine them. It was *his* domain, and she avoided it. But if one of those books was an herbal, it would be a prodigious help to her. What harm could it do to search the shelves?

But what if Lord Harkness was there? She had heard the servant's whispered references to "his lordship's insomnia." What if she went down to the library now and found him sitting there as he had been that first night? Would she be able simply to wander in and casually look for a book?

After what Agnes had told her, Verity doubted anything would be so simple again. Now that she knew the truth, or at least Agnes's version of the truth, she would not be able to look at him again as her handsome, deceptively decent rescuer. He was once again the fearful dark stranger—a murderer?—and she must be forever wary of him.

But she could not stay closeted in this room. She had made commitments. And she needed an herbal.

Verity uncurled herself from the chair and retied her wrapper close about the chest. She put on her slippers, took the candle from the desk, and crept out into the hallway and down the stairs to the main level. She slowed as she approached the library door. It stood slightly ajar, and a flickering light showed beneath it. He was there.

Verity hesitated. Did she really need the book this very minute? She could wait until he was out of the house tomorrow morning and no threat to her.

But why was she assuming he was a threat to her? Should she really place such faith in the words of a grieving and possibly mad old woman?

No, she would not be cowed by such accusations. Verity took her courage firmly in hand and slowly pushed the door open.

James sat there as before, with his back to the fire, and watching her with eyes as hard and cold as blue steel.

James cursed her silently for disturbing him. He had no desire to be alone with her again.

She wore a thick woolen robe, wrapped and tied closely about her. It was a most unappealing garment, but just knowing she had on nothing more than a night rail beneath it set his heart to pounding like the great high-pressure beam engine down at Wheal Devoran. She held a candle in her left hand. She had placed her right hand on her left shoulder, so that the whole arm modestly covered her already woolen-wrapped breast. A thick braid of hair fell over her right shoulder halfway to her waist. She looked very young and very tense and very pretty.

She was most certainly disturbing him.

James and Verity stared at each other for several long, silent moments. A shock of awareness crackled in the air between them. She was the first to speak.

"I've come for a book," she said. Her eyes never wavered from his. "I wondered if you might have a copy of Culpepper or some other herbal."

He studied her a moment longer before responding. "Yes, of course," he said. He pointed to a row of books on the other side of the room. "Just there, I think. Second row from the top. Have a look for yourself."

She hesitated, then walked over to the shelf he'd indicated. She held her candle high as she scanned the titles. She had to stretch in order to reach the shelf. He watched her long, pale neck flex and arch and open itself to his luxurious scrutiny.

James rose quietly from his chair and came to stand behind her. She gave a tiny start at his nearness, but otherwise did not move. She smelled faintly of lavender and hyacinth.

"It is too high for you," he said. "Allow me."

His arm reached around her from behind, brushing against her neck. She flinched slightly at his touch. He pulled down two volumes and stepped away. She set her candle down on a corner table and took them both from him. She flipped open the first one.

"Culpepper's *The English Physician*," she said. "This is the one I especially wanted. It is an older edition than the one I had at home, 1752. But it will do perfectly." She picked up the second and thumbed to the title page. "Meyrick's *The New Family Herbal*. I am unfamiliar with this one. It will be interesting to compare the two." She looked up at him, her dark eyes catching a glint of candlelight. "May I borrow them?"

"Keep them," he said. "I cannot imagine they've been opened in decades."

She cocked her head and gave him a quizzical look. "I may keep them?"

He nodded.

"But I . . . I couldn't."

"I insist," James said. "They were just gathering dust here on the shelf. At least you will make proper use of them. Take them. They are yours."

She looked down at the books in her hand and chewed on her lower lip. "That is very kind of you," she said. "Thank you."

Verity turned toward the table and reached to take her candle, but then swung back around to face him. He wished she hadn't. He wished she would leave before he made a fool of himself. She gazed up at him and tilted her head slightly, giving a delicate arch to the long neck.

"I could give you something to help you sleep," she said.

What the devil? What did she know about his

sleeplessness? Was the staff talking behind his back?

"There are several herbs that could help," she continued. "I could make something up for you, if you like. As a sort of thank you for the books."

He turned away with a dismissive snort. She must think because she'd overcome her own nightmares that her silly little potions would do the same for him. Well, she was wrong. There was no help for him. His shame was too deep.

He heard her walk toward him. "What causes you not to be able to sleep?" she asked.

Dammit, why must she always ask so many questions? He walked away from her and stood before the fire. He watched the glowing embers for a brief moment, shuddered involuntarily, then spun around to face her. Her wide brown eyes begged for an answer.

"It is nothing I wish to discuss," he said.

"Is it something to do with your wife and child?" she asked.

What? A surge of anger shot through his blood like an electrical charge.

"Is it true that you murdered them? Is that what keeps you awake nights?"

The moment she said the words, Verity realized she'd made a terrible mistake.

His eyes took on a savage look, darkening to a deep indigo so they appeared almost black in the dim glow of the dying fire. She took a step backward. James took a step forward.

Good God, what had she done? Why hadn't she kept her mouth shut? Especially after he was kind enough to give her the herbals.

She wished she had kept her nose out of it from the beginning. It might have been stupid—no, it *was* stupid—but in a perverse sort of way she had rather liked the idea that perhaps she alone had discovered the notorious Lord Heartless was really a very decent sort of fellow after all. In the deepest reaches of her foolish, naïve heart, she had wanted him to be her heroic rescuer. But she had pushed too hard to learn the truth, and now she was going to pay.

He took another step toward her, and stood so close his height overwhelmed her. Not wishing to meet those cold eyes again, she lowered her gaze. It was a mistake. She stared at the sun-bronzed skin of his throat, the tight cords of his neck, the hint of dark chest hair revealed by the open collar of his shirt. He exuded a pure unyielding masculine power that threatened to engulf her.

"You've heard that I am a murderer?"

Verity nodded.

"And do you believe it?"

She was not sure what he wanted her to say. She could only stare up at him, taking quick, shallow breaths through her mouth so that she was almost panting.

"Well, do you?" He roared so loudly that she took an involuntary step backward and dropped the books she'd been holding. She bumped against the table where she had left the candle. Reaching behind her, she grabbed on to its edge with both hands.

"I don't know!" Her voice came out thin and strangled. "I don't know what to believe."

He had moved closer until they were standing toe to toe. "You should believe it," he said. Without warning, he grabbed her roughly by the upper arms and jerked her forward. The violence of his movement threw a thick lock of black hair over one eye, giving him the look of a pirate. She began to tremble. Dear God, she wished he hadn't touched her.

"I can assure you," he said, and she could feel his breath on her face, "I am every bit as base and wicked as you've heard." His voice was cold and cruel, slicing through her like a new blade. "More so." He pulled her closer so that her breasts were pressed against his chest. The black brows drew down over eyes bright with anger . . . and something else.

Oh God, oh God, oh God. He was going to ravish her. Despite how repulsive she knew she must be to him, he was going to ravish her. Verity gripped the table edge so tightly she could feel her fingernails digging into the wood.

"In fact," he said, "you will never know the depths of my corruption." He let go of her right arm and took hold of her braid, wrapping it slowly around his knuckles. "But perhaps a demonstration will make a believer of you."

He jerked her braid so that her head was drawn back, and crushed his mouth against hers.

Verity tried to twist away, but he was too strong. He kept hold of her hair with one hand and wrapped the other around her back like a vise, all the while pressing his mouth against hers—brutal, ruthless. Her lips had been slightly parted, and now he forced her mouth open wide and plunged his tongue deep inside.

Startled by this intimacy, and wondering how he could possibly want to do such a thing to her, she squirmed and tried to pull away. But he yanked her hair again, harder, and ravaged her mouth with his tongue. Verity was stunned and frightened and thought she was the one who might be ill this time. But she could not fight him, and so she stopped trying.

She willed her body to relax. If she submitted, perhaps he would not hurt her. She might be able to get through this, if only he did not hurt her. She went limp in his arms.

And all at once, the kiss changed. James pulled back slightly, as though surprised by her acquiescence. He released her braid and wrapped a hand gently around her neck, caressing and stroking it with his long fingers. The arm around her back loosened and he began to move his hand slowly up and down her spine. He withdrew his tongue from the depths of her mouth and began nibbling her lips, slanting his mouth over hers, first in one direction, then another, tasting, exploring, grazing gently with his tongue.

It was a new beginning, as though the other had never happened. He gently coaxed her lips open again and tentatively touched his tongue to hers. She did not retreat, and he followed with a tender stroking, slow circles that set up a treacherous response low down in her body.

The kiss was no longer a punishment. God help her, it was an exquisite pleasure.

Confusion overwhelmed her as his tongue enticed and invited her own timid exploration. She leaned into him and the kiss became more urgent. Their tongues meshed in a fervent dance, while fear meshed with bliss, shame with pleasure, denial with consent. Verity became lost in a maelstrom of warring sensations, and gave herself up to the pure sensuality of it all.

James pulled away at last, leaving her bereft and breathless. He gazed down into her eyes with a puzzled look, then his mouth twisted into an expression of disgust and he pushed himself away.

"You see what I am," he said, his back to her as he leaned against a chair.

Still shaken, as much from her own reaction as from what he'd done, Verity could only stare at him, speechless. She was surprised to find that her hands still gripped the table behind her, had not in fact moved during the whole incredible episode.

"You see!" He spun around to face her, arms held stiffly at his sides, hands balled into fists. "Do you believe now? Do you?"

She felt the sting of tears building behind her eyes. Why was he doing this? She didn't know what to believe and had no words to answer him. She offered an ambivalent shrug in reply.

"Foolish woman!" he shouted. "What will it take to convince you? Ask anyone, anyone in all of Cornwall. Go ahead. Ask them! Every man, woman, and child will confirm the depth of my villainy. Ask them. Go ahead. Go. *Go!*"

Chapter 6

Go!

His words echoed off the old stone walls, bouncing back to envelop Verity in their cruel mockery. She moved quickly to leave, but stumbled over something at her feet. The herbals. She gathered them up with trembling hands and hurried to the doorway. The moment she crossed into the hall, the door slammed behind her with a tremendous crash. The entire household would have heard. She took off for her bedchamber at a half run, then flung herself on her bed and cried. But the tears were few and soon spent. Verity rolled onto her back and tried to make sense of what had just happened.

She brought her fingers to her lips. They felt tender, perhaps a little swollen, and she could still feel his imprint upon them. Verity had never been kissed like that. Good Lord, she hadn't even known anyone ever kissed like that. She could spend the rest of the night lying there reviewing every tiny aspect of it, but such thoughts caused an odd little stirring deep in her belly such as she'd never felt before. It would be easy to abandon herself to the pure physical memory of his arms and fingers and lips and tongue. But there was too much else to consider. Besides, it would be foolish, and useless, to dwell on desires that could never be fulfilled. Not with this man. Not with any man.

She rolled off the bed and removed her wrapper, then pulled back the counterpane and crawled beneath the blankets. She turned onto her side, tucked in her knees, and curled up like a hedgehog. The rain still pounded outside and the windows rattled against the incessant wind. The noise probably would have kept her awake even if her mind, and body, were not in such a mad whirl that sleep was an impossibility.

What had just occurred in the library had been more complicated than a mere—*mere*!—kiss and the confounding and probably sinful responses it wrought within her. The perplexing behavior of James Harkness—rescuer? murderer?—made him more a conundrum than ever.

He had accosted her brutally in the beginning, but had not ravished her as she had feared he would. If he was so anxious for her to believe the worst of him, why had he not acted in the worst possible manner as proof of his wickedness? There might be other reasons why he had not taken her, reasons having nothing to do with him and everything to do with her, but she had no wish to dwell on those at the moment.

There had been an obvious need for him to demonstrate a level of brutality, and yet he had not been able to maintain it. She very likely had bruises on her arms from his rough handling, and it had been extremely painful when he'd pulled on her braid. But when his embrace had changed—changed into something so sensual and wonderful she would surely go mad if she could not get it out of her mind—Verity had sensed a change in his need as well.

Perhaps she had only imagined it, and of course she had no experience whatsoever in such matters. But when the kiss had gentled, she could swear she had sensed a sort of longing, a melancholy yearning that was in no way connected with the need to overpower, to subjugate, to conquer. It was this longing to which she had responded. She felt as though—was it possible?—he needed her.

She was probably reading too much into it, trying too hard to find that decent, misunderstood man beneath the Lord Heartless mask. It was also possible that her lack of experience allowed him to manipulate her into seeing tenderness where there was only artifice and trickery. Was he in fact a fearsome murderer who found her dangerously easy to seduce?

A shudder coursed down her spine. She curled up into a tighter knot and clung desperately to the pillow.

She was no nearer the truth than ever. Ask anyone, he had said. Well, she had tried just that. She'd nudged and prodded and encouraged confidences, but only Agnes Bodinar had provided any information. Yet, because of her relationship to the late Lady Harkness, her words must still be considered suspect. Verity needed confirmation or explanation. She needed to know if she'd just been thoroughly kissed by a man who murdered his family.

Ask anyone.

All right, she would do that. She would go into St. Perran's tomorrow and tell Grannie Pascow what Agnes had said, and ask her straight out if it was true. Verity pounded the pillow into a more comfortable shape and closed her eyes. She ran a finger across her lips one more time. Tomorrow, she would discover the truth about the man whose touch and taste still lingered.

James leaned against the windowsill in his bedchamber and gazed out over the estate. From his high vantage point he could see the formal gardens and the wooded landscape of the lower grounds, the apple orchards and the grain fields, the southern pastures dotted with sheep and the mill buildings down near Pendurgan Quay. A great gusting wind caused even the trunks of the big chestnut trees lining the drive to sway like gilly flowers. Far to the west the stacks of Wheal Devoran puffed white bands of smoke against a morning sky the color of an old shilling.

His father had always loved this room, the only bedchamber in Pendurgan's only tower. When James was a boy, before he and his father had become estranged through endless petty disagreements, they often sat together on this very sill. He used to tell James how he could survey most of his holdings from this single room and how proud it made him to look out over the legacy of several generations. From an early age, he had instilled in James a love of the land and a responsibility for its maintenance and prosperity.

But James was not interested in the extent of his lands just now, or reminiscences and regrets about his father. He had other regrets this morning.

He watched as Verity walked through the terraced gardens, tilting forward into the wind and stepping cautiously along the muddy path. She disappeared from view momentarily when she passed through the archway leading to the lower grounds, but reappeared near the dovecote.

A knot of remorse twisted around in his gut as he watched her walk toward St. Perran's. He had behaved abominably the night before. He had been so upset—with himself for what he'd done and with her for inciting him to do it—that he had drunk himself into a stupor before falling asleep in the library. Lobb had retrieved him at some ungodly hour and dragged him to bed. Eventually the nightmares had overtaken him, despite the drink. Only this time there had been a slight difference. This time his sergeant's face had transformed into Verity's instead of Rowena's. A new guilt to disturb his sleep.

So now his head throbbed from last night's brandy and his stomach churned over his treatment of Verity. He felt like hell, duly punished for his sins. He sipped on Lobb's spiked coffee as he watched Verity disappear down the lane into the village.

He had certainly proven his point, had he not? He was a brute to the core and no woman was safe under his roof. It had been useless to pretend that such an encounter could have been avoided. It had been inevitable from the start. Verity Osborne had got under his skin from the first morning after her arrival.

He'd tried to convince himself that it was her strength and courage and dignity that most attracted him. Utter rot. She was just a damned fine-looking woman, and James had been without a woman far too long. Almost any woman would have affected him the same way.

But was that really true? When he had kissed her he had not been thinking of how the sight of her in nightclothes and with her hair down had stirred his blood. He had been furious with her questions about his wife and son, and wanted to assert his power over her, to provoke fear and loathing.

It had all changed in the space of a moment. She had stopped fighting him and seemed almost to melt in his arms. God, but she had felt good. Soft and warm and responsive. From the moment he had sensed her own pleasure, he had been lost. He had wanted to devour her—in slow, succulent bites. He was about to set his lips on a path down that long white neck when he'd come to his senses.

If he had not forced her to leave, James could not be sure that he would have been able to restrain himself from taking her. Right then and there, stretched atop the table at her back. The thought of her soft, white body beneath his aroused him even now. But shame and guilt had stopped him. He had no right to treat her as though she were a common whore he'd purchased for the evening.

Yet she had fought him only when he had been rough with her. When he had become more gentle, she had responded. Would she have let him make love to her?

The thought of taking Verity as his mistress set his heart to racing. His wickedness was known far and wide. Why continue to deny his own well-deserved reputation? Why not make the tales true? What was there left to lose?

His own reputation had been as black as it could be for over six years now. Through no fault of her own, Verity's reputation was in shreds. There was no redemption for either of them among the solid Methodist stock of this part of Cornwall.

Despite what the world may think of him, he would never take her by force. If he behaved like a gentleman, would she allow it? Would she allow him to make her into what everyone already believed her to be?

There was only one way to find out.

Grannie Pascow's eyes narrowed as she glared at Verity. Her knobby fingers beat a tattoo on the carved wooden arm of the high-backed chair. "So," she said, " 'ee wants to know the truth, does 'ee?"

Verity nodded. The smoldering peat fire in the hearth filled the room with an odiferous smoke that caused her eyes to burn. She looked around at each of the room's other occupants: sturdy, no-nonsense Kate Pascow, proud Ewa Dunstan, and sweet-natured Borra Nanpean. Verity had hoped to speak with Grannie in private, but the old woman never seemed to be alone. Women gathered around the hearth, children frolicked on the dirt floor, and men stopped by to greet

Grannie on their way from the mine or the pastures.

It was easy to understand her status in the village. Verity felt the old woman's strength of character as much as any of the other villagers who'd known her all their lives. She could trust Grannie Pascow. She could not have explained how she knew that to be true. Perhaps it was because the old woman reminded her so much of her beloved Edith. Whatever the reason, Verity liked her and respected her. If she wanted the truth, plainspoken and raw, that is what she would get from Grannie.

Verity blinked against the peat fumes and nodded again. "Yes," she said. "I should like to know what happened. I should like to know what sort of man Lord Harkness is, since I am living under his roof."

Grannie leaned back and squinted down the length of her nose. "T'aint a pretty tale," she said. The others mumbled agreement.

"If what Mrs. Bodinar told me is true, then it cannot be very pretty." Verity steadied herself for the cold, harsh truth and took a deep breath. The peat fumes burned her throat and she began to cough. She made a mental note to ask Mrs. Tregelly about providing firewood for the cottages. "Tell me, please," she said at last. "Did he murder his family?"

Grannie's fingers stilled and she let them hang loosely over the chair arms. "Aye, most likely he did."

Verity's heart sank like a wounded bird. No amount of expecting it had prepared her for this bald truth. "Most likely?" she said. "But you don't know for sure?"

"Nobody do know nothin' fer certain. Couldn't be

proved, one way or t'other." The old woman shook her head and pursed up her lips. "Looked bad from the first, though. Looked like he done it."

"But why?" Verity asked, trying without success to keep the plaintive note from her voice. "Mrs. Bodinar implied that he had been very much in love with Lady Harkness. Why would he have killed her? And their child?"

"Don't rightly know," Grannie said. "But when he come home from Spain, he weren't the same. Sumthin' happened to him."

"Aye, it's true," Kate Pascow interjected. She bounced a pink-cheeked baby on her knee while she spoke. "After he come back, he were as like to bite yer head off as look at 'ee."

"Come home with a real mean streak, he did," Ewa Dunstan added.

"How did they die?" Verity asked.

"Fire," Grannie replied.

Verity shuddered. "Good Lord. And you believe he set it?"

"Could have," Grannie said. "Likely he did."

"Tell me what happened."

Grannie surveyed the room in silence for a few moments before she spoke again. "Well now, from what I do recall," she began, "young Trystan—that were his son—and Digory Clegg's boy Billy was playing in one o' them old stable buildings near the big house. Empty barn, it were, old and ramshackle. The boys did used to play there a lot. Not just Billy Clegg, but other village boys as well. Kate's Charlie. Ewa's Robbie. Lucas Kempthorne. Weren't no children of his own kind fer young Trystan Harkness to play with, so he were left to mingle with St. Perran's boys, nice as 'ee please.

"That day, a fire started in the barn. Nobody do know how, but with all the straw an' such, 'twere bound to go up like kindlin'. Rowena, Lady Harkness that was, she seen the fire and runned outside screamin' for help. Jammez stood watchin' that fire, not movin'. Lady Harkness, she shaked him an' shouted at him to help, but he wouldn't budge. So she runned into the stable herself an' tried to save them boys. But the fire be too far gone. The buildin' collapsed and trapped all of 'em. They be all three killed—young Trystan, the Clegg boy, and Lady Harkness."

"And Lord Heartless, the evil cur, he never stirred an inch to help," Ewa Dunstan said. "Stood there and did nothin' while that pretty wife o' his and them two little boys died."

"My God," Verity said. "Oh, my God."

Silence fell in the cottage, broken only by the occasional soft plop of crumbling peat. Anguish swelled like a tumor in Verity's belly. This was not at all what she had expected. It was much worse. Though he may not have held a gun to their heads or a knife to their throats, his inaction had killed them just the same. How could he have done such a thing? It didn't make any sense.

"But how do you know all this?" she asked, grasping for any thread to stitch it all together somehow. "If everyone died in the fire, how can you know what Lord Harkness did or did not do?"

"Old Nick Tresco, he seen it all," Kate Pascow said, hoisting the restless infant onto her shoulder. "He were the steward at Pendurgan. Been there as far back as I can 'member. He were out in the fields when he seen the fire and started runnin' back. He seen Lord Heartless standing there like a statue, big as you please, watchin' that fire. He seen her ladyship try to get him to help. By the time he got close enough to lend a hand, it were too late. Old Nick do claim his bloody lordship didn't say a word. Only stared and stared into that fire with a sort of wild look in his eye."

"Old Nick left Pendurgan after that," Grannie said, giving Kate a disapproving glance for her strong language. "He wouldn't work for the man no more after what he seen. It fair made him sick, he said."

Verity could certainly understand that; she felt nauseous herself. "What made him believe Lord Harkness had actually started the fire?" she asked.

Borra Nanpean looked up from her mending and spoke for the first time. "He were the only one near by," she said in her soft, shy voice. "Old Nick said it looked like it been torched, with fire startin' in more than one place, like. It weren't natural."

"He done it, all right," Ewa Dunstan added. "Just like all them others."

"What others?"

Silence fell among the women once again. Ewa stared at her hands in her lap and did not respond. Verity looked to Grannie. "What others?" she repeated.

"There been two or three queer fires in the district since then," Grannie said. "No one else never got hurt. But none of 'em ever made no sense, and Jammez—

Lord Harkness, that is—were nearby when each of 'em happened."

"What are you saying?" Verity asked, her voice rising, on the edge of hysteria. "That he is a madman who likes to start fires?"

Grannie shrugged. "Don't rightly know. I just be tellin' 'ee what happened, like 'ee asked. Told 'ee it weren't a pretty tale."

Indeed it was not. Was she living in the home of an arsonist? Oh, God. She'd been kissed senseless by a man who had passively watched while his family died, when he might have saved them. Or perhaps even by a man who had he set the fire himself, deliberately killing them. Was she doomed to forever recalling the passion of that kiss and, God forgive her, how she had enjoyed it? Or was she doomed to much worse?

She wiped the moisture from her cheeks, blinking away the peat fumes that stung her eyes.

The wind had let up and a thin ray of sunshine broke through a patch of blue in the northwestern sky. The hint of clear weather ought to have lifted Verity's spirits, but she hardly noticed the change. She trudged up the lane back to Pendurgan, feeling as though she dragged a heavy weight behind her.

It wasn't anxiety that burdened her thoughts, despite having every reason, she supposed, to fear for her safety. Instead, she felt unexpectedly disconsolate after all she had heard. She had expected she would likely hear some level of confirmation of Agnes Bodinar's words. But why was it so much more difficult to accept danger from possible madness than danger from pure evil?

For surely that was the only explanation for what Grannie Pascow and the others had told her. Or perhaps all evil was ultimately rooted in madness.

She had wanted the truth and now had it. And in having it, she was more confused than ever.

Verity was pulled out of her melancholy reverie by the clip-clop of an approaching horse, muted by the rain-softened dirt of the lane. A moment of apprehension that it might be Lord Harkness was followed by relief and curiosity when she looked up to find a very handsome, fair-haired gentleman riding toward her. He reined in and doffed his hat.

"Good afternoon," he said, smiling warmly.

Verity nodded politely, returned his greeting, and then proceeded up the lane. She had no idea who the gentleman might be, but considering her unusual situation and the rumors it prompted, she was wary of any stranger. She had not forgotten the coarse behavior of Mr. Bargwanath and had no wish to endure another rude encounter.

"Forgive my impertinence," he said as she stepped around his beautiful bay mare, barely a trace of Cornwall in his cultured voice, "but is it possible that you are Mrs. Osborne from Pendurgan?"

"Yes," she said in a guarded tone, "I am Mrs. Osborne."

The gentleman's smile broadened. He dismounted and stood before her. "I beg your pardon," he said. "I ought to have waited for a proper introduction but there has not been the opportunity. I am so pleased to meet you, Mrs. Osborne. I am Captain Alan Poldrennan, ma'am. At your service." He swept her a formal bow, a gesture strangely out of place in the middle of a dirt path.

"Captain." Verity acknowledged him with another nod, but remained wary.

"I have a neighboring estate, Bosreath," he said, waving a hand vaguely toward the west. "The Poldrennan and Harkness families have been friends and neighbors for many years."

"Oh?"

"Yes. I have been a close friend to James—that is, Lord Harkness—since we were boys."

"Oh." She was surprised to learn that the man called Heartless had any friends at all. "I suppose that is how you know of me, then," she said. "You must also know—"

"I know about the auction, yes." He gave her a reassuring look. "But we shall not speak of that. We will keep to the explanation James has given for you, as a distant cousin."

"Thank you," Verity said. A genuine amiability was reflected in the benevolent gray eyes, and his words put her immediately at ease. "That is very kind."

"May I escort you back to Pendurgan?"

"I would appreciate that. Thank you, Captain."

He walked his horse around to face in the opposite direction, then fell into step beside Verity. He was the first person, aside from Lord Harkness and Agnes Bodinar, of her own class she had met since coming to Cornwall. She was heartened to know that he did not think ill of her because of how she came to be there. And perhaps the captain could help dispel some of her confusion about the deaths and the fires, if she could think of a reasonable way to introduce the subject.

"You have come from St. Perran's?" he asked.

"Yes. I go into the village often."

"I have heard of your knowledge of herbs and physicks," he said. "I believe you saved the life of one of the servant children at Pendurgan?"

Verity chuckled. "The story grows with each telling. I merely prepared a few home remedies to help ease his breathing and reduce his fever. I do not work miracles, Captain, I assure you. It is simply common knowledge handed down to me years ago."

"It is good of you to share that knowledge with the village women," the captain said. "They are very fortunate to have you just now, when Dr. Trefusis is away. Have you been nursing one of them today?"

This was the opening Verity had hoped for. "No," she said, "I was not helping them today. They were helping me."

"Helping you?"

"Yes. You see, I went seeking information."

He looked down at her with a quizzical expression. "And did you find what you were seeking?"

"Unfortunately, yes."

His brows drew together in a puzzled expression.

"I am sorry, Captain," Verity said. "I do not mean to sound so mysterious. It is . . . well, it is awkward for me, as a stranger and one who came to be here under . . . unusual circumstances. I had heard it said that Lord Harkness had murdered his family. Naturally I felt somewhat uneasy and wanted to learn the truth."

"Ah. And now you know."

"I was told what happened, but it still makes very little sense to me." She looked over at him to judge if she ought to proceed. He kept his eyes straight ahead as they walked. Though his mouth had tightened slightly, he did not appear to have closed her off, as Lord Harkness had done when they had walked back together along this same lane.

"Tell me, Captain," she said. "You are his friend. Why did he do it? Is he mad, as all I heard today suggests?"

Captain Poldrennan walked on in silence for several minutes, and Verity thought she might have made a mistake in asking him such a bold question at their first acquaintance. A frown played across his face while he seemed to weigh his answer. After a long, uncomfortable silence, he finally spoke. "It is very complicated," he said. "And I'm not sure anyone who has not been to war can ever truly understand."

"Then something did happen in Spain? I was told that he was very much changed when he returned."

"We were all changed by what we saw and what we did," he said, his face still marked by the frown.

"You were there?"

"Yes. James and I were in different regiments but saw much of the same action."

"And yet you seem . . . I do not wish to say unaffected. Doubtless you were. But you are, perhaps, unscarred?"

Captain Poldrennan laughed. "I wish it were so. Unfortunately I took a ball in the shoulder at Badajoz." He sobered quickly. "But that is not what you meant, is it? You are speaking of scars of the heart or of the mind or of the soul. I doubt any soldier survives without his share. But for some the wounds are deeper than for others and the healing more difficult."

"Is that what happened with Lord Harkness?"

He stopped abruptly. The mare snorted and tossed her head in irritation. He muttered endearments and stroked the long neck until she stood quietly. He continued the gentle stroking as he turned toward Verity, the frown back in place. He opened his mouth to speak, then stopped. Verity suspected he was concerned about betraying a friendship by revealing more than he should.

"We were at Ciudad Rodrigo," he said at last. He gazed out into the distance over Verity's shoulder. "It was an ugly siege, mid-winter and cold, the ground frozen so hard we thought we'd never get the trenches dug. We had no tents, so the troops had to be billeted in the village across the Agueda. The half-frozen river had to be forded each day to get to the trenches, the troops constantly buffeted by huge pieces of ice. We worked ten days before the assault began."

He took a deep breath before continuing. "I will not bore you with details of the assault. Suffice it to say it was gruesome. James's regiment was among those storming the larger of two breaches. My own regiment was busy at the lesser breach, so I did not see firsthand what happened. At the Great Breach, the head of the column was cut down by French fire. When the French gunners had been dispatched, James's regiment stormed ahead to the ramparts. A huge mine exploded beneath them, destroying the majority of his company."

Verity's face puckered up in horror. She had never heard the particulars of battle, and even though Captain Poldrennan was relating only the broadest facts without grisly detail, it was ghastly and upsetting to hear.

"Sometime afterward," he continued, "when he was finally able to speak of it, James told me how he'd been knocked down and pinned by the charred corpses of his own men. He had broken a leg and couldn't free himself. He watched his young sergeant and several others explode into flames and fall just a few feet away from where he lay. James has never been able to rid himself of the guilt over the deaths of those men. Though it was Picton's order, he believes he sent his own men into a trap. The fact that he waved his men ahead and took up the rear himself, saving him from certain death, only intensified his guilt."

Verity covered her mouth with her hand while she fought back the bile rising in her throat. The picture painted by the captain was more hideous than anything she could imagine. "I suppose," she said after a moment, "I cannot know what it was like. I hope never to know what it was like. But I can certainly understand his guilt, justified or not. What I do not understand is what all this has to do with the deaths of his wife and child."

The captain heaved a great sigh. "There is more," he said. He waited until she looked up and met his eyes. "I do not think James would appreciate me telling this. It is a very private thing, a shameful thing for many men. But I believe it is best that you know. It will explain much for you."

"Then please tell me," Verity said. "Help me to understand. I am living under the man's roof. I am, for the moment, dependent upon him. I need to understand."

He regarded her thoughtfully. "Very well. But I only tell you this in the strictest confidence. James would have my head if he knew."

"I will not betray your confidence, Captain."

They fell into step together, setting a slow pace up the gentle slope to Pendurgan. "James was sent to hospital," he said, "to recover from the broken leg. He stayed quite a long time. They kept him because . . . he became irrational and often had to be restrained. He had terrible nightmares and would wake up screaming uncontrollably. I believe he would have been shipped back to Bedlam were it not for a few of us who stood by and vouched for him. After several months he finally seemed to have recovered, physically and mentally, and was allowed to return to the regiment. But he had no stomach for it and sold out. I was just recovering from my own wounds and decided to go home with him. I suspected he would need a friend.

"So he did indeed come home a different man. He had not, has never, completely overcome the guilt and shame of what happened."

"But why?" Verity asked, still not understanding. "He did not plant the mine. It was not his fault. It is all a brutal fact of war, is it not? Why should he feel shame?"

"An officer takes his responsibilities to his men

very seriously," the captain said. "James felt he had failed them. But the shame . . . that was different. The shame came from what happened afterward." He paused before continuing, apparently gathering his thoughts.

"It is not uncommon that a soldier is traumatized by memories of some horror, sometimes to the point where he can no longer effectively perform his duties. It happens more often than you might expect, but it is seldom if ever mentioned. It is seen by many soldiers as a sign of cowardice. Many commanding officers have no patience for a soldier suffering from 'nerves' or 'exhaustion' or whatever they choose to call it, and often just send him to the rear guard. Fellow soldiers harass him and label him 'coward.' It is a difficult situation and demeaning for any soldier. That is what James would have faced when he returned to the regiment. That is the source of his shame."

Verity began to understand. "He left the army to avoid being labeled a coward. Yet he branded himself with that label just the same."

"Exactly," he said. "James was so riddled with shame and guilt that he lashed out at anyone who approached. He began drinking. He kept everyone at a distance, especially Rowena. She used to cry and cry over his coldness. And then things started to happen. I would not know of this until some time later, but he began to have long periods of blackout. He would suddenly find himself somewhere with no recollection of how he came to be there. He would lose hours at a time."

"Good Lord!"

"Each episode was brought on by the sight of fire. Not just an ordinary fire in the grate, but something sudden. An unexpected burst of flame, a small explosion at the mine, anything like that might trigger memories of the explosion at Ciudad Rodrigo. And he would disappear back into that memory for hours."

"Oh, my God. That's what happened with the stable fire."

"Yes. Physically, he was there. Mentally, he was in Spain, immobilized by the memories."

"How horrible!" Verity felt the sting of tears building up behind her eyes. "The poor man. He must have been devastated when he realized what had happened."

"He became worse," the captain said. "His guilt was compounded by feeling responsible for the deaths of his family. Beautiful, delicate Rowena and that sweet little boy."

Verity brushed away the tears that trembled on her lashes. Her heart ached for what James had suffered. "How simply dreadful. The poor, poor man. And yet this tragedy has labeled him a murderer? It makes no sense."

"The explanation I have given you," he replied, "is known only to myself and Samuel Lobb, his valet. No one else knows about Spain, about the blackouts and nightmares."

"Why not?" Verity asked. "Would it not help people to understand what happened, to know he could not help what the sight of fire did to him?"

"He would rather be known as a cold-blooded murderer than a coward."

"But that's ridiculous."

"It is hard for a woman to understand, I know," the captain said. "But it is his choice, and his life."

"I wonder why he rescued me at Gunnisloe?" The thought found voice before she could stop it.

Captain Poldrennan cast her a curious glance. "Rescue?"

"Yes," she said. In for a penny in for a pound. "I thought at first his motives were sinister, that I might be in some sort of danger. But I have not been. He has left me alone, for the most part." She would not tell him about last night's kiss.

"He keeps his distance from most people," the captain said. "He still suffers the occasional blackout and I believe he lives in fear of another incident like the fire. He does not wish to put anyone else in danger."

"Which is why I am wondering why he brought me here," she said. "Have there been other incidents? I was told of other fires."

Captain Poldrennan's expression became wooden and he stared blankly ahead. "I have heard of one or two unexplained fires," he said. "But I know nothing about them."

How odd, that this amiable gentleman who had been so forthcoming now decided to hold his tongue. Well, she would not press the issue. She had learned more from him than she could ever have hoped.

"I thank you, Captain, for telling me all this. I realize it was difficult for you, and I appreciate your confidence. You cannot imagine how confused I have been, wondering whether I should be afraid for my life. It is a great relief to know I am in no danger from Lord Harkness."

Captain Poldrennan smiled. "You are a most understanding woman, Mrs. Osborne."

"Lord Harkness is wounded from the war," she said, "just as surely as if he'd lost a limb or an eye. I am a healer of sorts, Captain, so it is not difficult to recognize a body in pain."

His smile became a very engaging grin. "I am glad to know that you care for him," he said.

His words caused a flush to heat her cheeks. Did she care for him?

"Perhaps that is your answer. Perhaps that is why he brought you here," the captain said. "After all these years, you may be the one who can finally help him to heal."

James rode through the back gate and into the western court, a small graveled yard adjacent to the main house. Jago Chenhalls, on the spot as always, was there to take Castor.

"Afternoon, m'lord."

James dismounted and handed over the reins. "Afternoon, Jago." He looked up at the blue sky, streaked with more pink than gray for once. "A break in the weather, do you think?"

"Naw," Jago said. "The rooks do be flyin' low. 'Twill rain by nightfall."

James smiled at the man whose portents of weather tended to be uncannily accurate. He walked through the low, wide archway into the central courtyard and saw two figures approaching the main entrance. Alan Poldrennan, leading his bay mare, walked alongside Verity. He wondered how they came to be together. James watched as his handsome friend's warm smile was returned by Verity, and felt an unexpected stab of jealousy. She had never smiled at him like that. But then, why would she? What had he ever given her to smile about?

He had been to Wheal Devoran and back during the time she'd been in the village. Had she done as he suggested and asked for confirmation of his villainy? What had she learned? Would the women have told her about the fire? Of course they would have, if she had asked. And what about Alan? They seemed to be chatting amiably as though they'd known each other for years. Had she asked him as well? And what would he have told her? Alan knew more of the truth than anyone. But how much would he reveal to a stranger, even a pretty one?

"Pretty" was not the right word, however, to describe Verity Osborne. "Pretty" had described Rowena and her fragile porcelain beauty. Verity's charm was more earthy, but in a wholesome sort of way. She seemed healthy and alive and radiant, more handsome than delicate or dainty. Perhaps it was merely a difference in coloring that made her appear so, however, for as she turned that long, white neck to gaze up at Alan she could not have looked more feminine. Or more appealing. His loins stirred with anticipation.

Alan looked toward the courtyard and caught James's eye. "James!" he said. "I hope you won't think me intruding, but I encountered Mrs. Osborne on the lane and she has allowed me to escort her back to Pendurgan."

"Good of you, Alan." He sounded more gruff than he'd intended.

"Not at all." Alan gave Verity another warm smile. "It has been my pleasure."

"And mine, Captain," Verity said.

"I trust you enjoyed your visit to St. Perran's?" James asked Verity. Despite every effort, he was unable to quell the sullen, clipped tone in his voice. Damn. He had determined on politeness, hoping to undo some of the damage done the night before in preparation for the evening ahead. He even thought to attempt a smile, but then her eyes met his straight on.

She knew. She had heard everything. Damnation!

"Yes," Verity said. There was no fear in her brown eyes. Something else, though. He could not have said what, but he did not like it. "I have been visiting with Grannie Pascow," she said. "Her rheumatism is much improved."

James gratefully took this conversational gambit. "Another victory for your herbs," he said. "I saw your first victory scampering about the stables with his father this morning."

Verity's face lit up with a glow of pure happiness. "Davey? He's up and about?"

Her reaction prompted James to give a half smile, and a new softness gathered in her eyes. "Indeed." He found himself thoroughly entranced by the way her pleasure in the news of Davey transformed her, made her no longer merely handsome, but beautiful. Truly beautiful. Clearly Alan noticed, as well. He could not take his bloody eyes off her, either, damn him.

"If you will excuse me, then," Verity said. "I should like to go see him." She turned to Alan and smiled. "Thank you again, Captain, for your escort."

Alan executed an elegant bow. "I am so pleased to have met you, Mrs. Osborne," he said. "I hope we shall see one another again soon."

Verity nodded to each of them, catching James's eye momentarily—there was that odd, unsettling look again—before turning away to walk toward the main entrance. James watched her progress across the courtyard, admiring the way the fitted pelisse clung tightly to the curves of her upper body. Ever since he had kissed her last night, her every movement, every look, every word seemed imbued with a sensuality he had not before noticed. It was maddening. He could barely wait for the evening.

"You were right."

Alan's words pulled James back, and he turned to face his friend. "About what?" he asked.

"You said she was a frightfully good-looking woman. You were right. She is that, and more."

James's eyes narrowed as he studied Alan Poldrennan. Was he interested, truly interested, in Verity? He had been a close friend to Rowena. James had at one time considered they might have been more than just friends, but had discarded the notion. It had been his own jealousy poisoning him against his best friend. It was happening again with Verity, although James had no cause to feel jealousy. There was no commitment between them, no vows as there had been with Rowena.

"What do you mean, 'more'?" he asked.

Alan shrugged. "Just that she seems a fine, intelligent, caring woman. Good God, James, what can her husband have been thinking?"

"I've often wondered that myself. Can you stay awhile? Stay for dinner?"

"Thank you, but no," Alan said. "I'm late as it is. I must return to Bosreath."

James walked with him back through the main entrance. "I am glad you have maintained your honor where she is concerned," Alan said. James flinched at the words. "Now that I've met her, it seems appalling what she must have suffered at the auction. Can you imagine a woman like that sold to some brute like Will Sykes? Thank God you rescued her. Those are her words, by the way. She said you rescued her."

Rescued? James stared, thunderstruck, at his friend. "She did?"

"Yes. I think she cares for you, James."

He shrugged nonchalantly, though Alan's words almost took his breath away. "I thought she was afraid of me," he said. "Hated me, even."

"She has heard the stories, and I suppose she might be somewhat apprehensive. But deep down, I think she sees you as a kind of hero. You *did* rescue her."

James snorted. "Hero? Ha! A man who—"

"Maybe this is a chance for you," Alan interrupted, "a second chance, to be someone's hero. Don't let ancient guilts get in the way, my friend."

James watched Poldrennan ride away. The man meant well, but he was dead wrong. James could be no one's hero. Ever.

Chapter 7

Verity sat before the makeshift dressing table—a dark, ancient-looking gateleg table with a toilette mirror propped on top—and brushed out her long dark hair. It had been a day full of surprises, not the least of which was the uncharacteristic affability of Lord Harkness during supper. Whereas he normally sat quiet and solemn, he had led the conversation tonight. Still, his manner was far from effusive. He maintained a stiff reserve that had cracked only twice. He asked Verity about her remedies and potions, about her visits to Old Grannie and about the tales she told. Ignoring the frequent snorts of derision from Agnes Bodinar, James had expanded on Grannie's folklore with tales of his own.

"Old Grannie warned you about being piskey-led on the moor, did she?" James had asked.

"Everyone has warned me," Verity replied.

His mouth twitched and she thought he might actually smile. Anticipation caused a strange tingling low in her belly. He looked so different when he smiled. Did he know? He must have, for he made a heroic attempt not to do so.

"Indeed, we have," Agnes had said. She darted an odd look at Verity that reminded her she ought to check such reactions to James's smile, his almost-smile, or to unbidden recollections of his hands and lips and tongue the night before.

"The Cornish love to intrigue foreigners with tales of piskeys and giants and ghosts and such," James said.

"To scare us away?" Verity asked, slanting a look at Agnes.

"No," he said, "but only to let the newcomer know he is in a special and different land, steeped in history and legend quite apart from the rest of Britain. Piskeys are uniquely Cornish. They are mischief makers for the most part, and take particular delight in confusing travelers wandering alone on the moor. Farmers and miners who have lived here their whole lives and know every inch of the land can still find themselves wandering in circles, always ending up exactly where they started. And sometimes they tell of hearing the high-pitched laughter of their tiny tormentors, though they never see them, of course."

"It must be very frightening," Verity said.

"It can be," he said. "The best advice is not to wander alone on the moors, especially at night. If you do, however, there is a remedy."

"Yes?"

"If you find yourself walking in circles, simply turn your coat inside out to break the spell."

"Hmph!" Agnes looked back and forth between them, her mouth puckered in disapproval as Verity smiled broadly. "Piskey-led, indeed. Whiskey-led, more like."

Verity chuckled at this, and James could no longer contain his smile, setting off that blasted tingling once again.

She had never seen James like this, so nearly garrulous. There was something brittle, however, about his manner, something nervous and unnatural. Perhaps he had been trying to make amends for last night's assault. Verity got the distinct impression he was trying to put her at ease.

He need not have bothered. She was no longer afraid of him.

Verity slowly ran the ivory-handled brush through the length of her hair. The brush was part of a set given her by Edith Littleton upon her marriage to Gilbert. It was the last time she'd seen Edith, who had passed away some months later, and Verity never failed to fall into fond recollections of her beloved mentor whenever she used the ivory brush.

But not tonight. Verity's thoughts were all on James. His friendly behavior during dinner could have been simply another trick to confuse her. He would surely know she had learned something from Old Grannie and the other women. Was he trying to confound her again by appearing normal when all she had heard today labeled him a madman?

It was unlikely, too, that Captain Poldrennan would have told James of the nature of their subsequent conversation. It was what she had learned from the captain that had changed everything. Verity no longer found it easy to harbor notions of conspiracies and trickery, despite James's unusual mood tonight and apparent change of attitude toward her. She now found it almost impossible to believe him to be either mad or murderous.

He had been wounded and the scars ran deep. Verity could not help but feel sympathy for him and for all that had happened. It was no wonder he had been driven to the edge of madness. But she could not make herself believe he had pushed himself over the edge. She did not wish to believe it.

The biggest surprise of the day, however, had been her own reaction to what she'd learned. When she had seen young Davey in the kitchen with his mother and he had flung himself into her arms, it was clear the boy was quite recovered. There was no more reason for Verity to remain at Pendurgan. Yet when Gonetta had asked if Verity was still planning to instruct her the next day in the preparation of a lavender decoction for the toothache, Verity had consented without hesitation.

What had become of her resolve to leave Pendurgan?

Verity put down the brush and gazed at her reflection in the mirror. Her cheeks flushed warm with the answer to that question. She suspected that her decision had more to do with James Harkness than with other demands upon her time.

Just as she had been unable to abandon Davey, she was also drawn to help James, for surely he needed healing as well. Verity was not certain precisely what she could do, short of providing him a potion to help him sleep, but she felt compelled to do something.

Verity pulled her long hair over one shoulder and began to section it for plaiting. The one problem that still troubled her was the nature of the other fires. Captain Poldrennan had been so reticent on the subject, Verity wondered if perhaps there was some truth in the stories that placed James in the vicinity of each fire. Yet with James's fearful reaction to fire, it did not make sense that he could be an arsonist.

Verity's hands stilled. She knew nothing about diseases of the mind. Could a fear of fire be transformed into a fascination with fire? Had any of the unexplained fires coincided with James's strange periods of blackout, when he could not recall where he'd been or what he'd done?

If that were true, there was still the very real possibility that her life was in danger, as Agnes had warned her. Maybe she ought not be so quick to drop her guard.

A soft tapping sounded on the bedchamber door. Before Verity could do more than turn around on her stool, the door opened and James walked in.

He stepped into the bedchamber and quietly closed the door behind him. Verity gave a tiny gasp and rose so quickly she knocked over the cross-legged stool on which she'd been seated. She wore a long-sleeved, high-necked white nightgown. Her dark hair, gilded by the flickering firelight, hung loosely over one shoulder. She clasped her hands, one tightly gripping a hairbrush, across her full bosom. The fire behind her illumined the shape of her body beneath the white gown. James's own body, naked under the heavy brocade dressing gown, grew hard at the sight of her.

She looked beautiful. And terrified. Her dark eyes were wide with apprehension.

James stood awkwardly, watching her, uncertain what to say. Words ought not to have been necessary. He had been softening her up all through supper and was almost certain he had succeeded. Still, she looked genuinely startled by his appearance in her room, in his dressing gown. Surely she could have no question as to why he had come.

Her breathing came quick and shallow, causing her bosom to rise and fall beneath her crossed hands. James took a tentative step toward her. Verity closed her eyes, the merest tremor tugging her lips into a downward twist. It was a look of unquestionable pain.

An instant later, she dropped her hands to her sides, straightened her shoulders, and raised her eyes to meet his. There was no anguish or self-pity in that gaze, only resignation. She lifted her chin a notch. Proud resignation. She knew what he wanted and, clearly, was prepared to give in to him. Not willing, perhaps, but ready.

For he had bought and paid for her, and she could not refuse.

She stood before him, straight and tall. Nipples taut with fear or cold—or something else?—peaked the fabric of her nightgown, but she made no more move to cover herself. The heat of desire shimmered out from James's groin all the way down to the tips of his toes. In that moment, he wanted Verity Osborne more than he had ever wanted any woman.

Without uttering a word, she stood there cloaked in little more than her brazen dignity, willing to let him take even that from her.

Because he had paid for her.

In a horrific travesty of a transaction, she had had everything else taken from her: her legal status, her rights by marriage, her identity, her home, her future, her reputation. She was left with nothing but her dignity, which she possessed in abundance. And for the sake of a few moments of pleasure, James was about to strip her even of that.

He could not do it.

"Forgive me." James's voice was harsh and unsteady through tight lips. "I should not have come." He turned and quickly left the room, closing the door behind him.

Verity sank onto the edge of the bed and let out her pent-up breath in a whoosh. She placed a limp hand over her breast and felt the pounding of her heart beneath.

What had just happened?

Lord Harkness had finally come to her, just as she had been expecting since her very first night at Pendurgan. Shocked and a little frightened, she had nevertheless been ready to accept her fate. God forgive her, she had even experienced a prickle of excitement that it was finally to happen, for it was useless to deny the physical reactions triggered by this man.

All the sensations of last night's kiss had seemed

to ripple through her body once again, though he stood halfway across the room and never touched her. The dark red brocade of his banyan picked up the glimmer of the dying fire and gave him a devilish appearance. He looked dangerous and magnificent.

She had been ready to give herself to him, if that was what he wanted. Or needed. If that was the way to help heal his wounded soul, then she was ready to make the sacrifice.

Foolish girl! It had ended exactly as she might have predicted.

Verity slammed her fist against the counterpane. What was wrong with her? She had no call to feel physical desire for any man, but most especially *this* man. Her traitorous body ought not to feel even a suggestion of excitement or anticipation. Her wedding night had taught her what to expect, and there was nothing exciting to anticipate in what might have happened. Only disgust and dismissal. Just as it had been with Gilbert.

Foolish, foolish girl! For a brief moment, her own reluctant attraction to this dark stranger had made her forget to expect rejection. She had long been resigned to the knowledge that she could never be desirable to a man in that way.

The look of agonized distress on James's face just before he turned to leave spoke volumes. Perhaps he needed her, or thought he did. Yet when it came to the point, he could not want her. No man could. She had learned that from her husband. She was not normal.

Verity wiped tears from her cheeks and returned

to the dressing table. She righted the stool and sat down, then began once again to section her hair. The only good that came from what happened was that James had recognized the futility of a physical relationship before it was too late. She did not think she could have endured the full force of his disgust if he had made the attempt.

But that look of anguish on his face haunted her. Verity suspected his need grew from the pain and shame and guilt of what had happened, both in Spain and at Pendurgan. She understood pain in many forms. Though she might not understand his specific type of pain, she nevertheless was drawn to do what she could to ease it.

Perhaps that was the least she could do for two hundred pounds. Even if it meant putting herself in danger.

After a sleepless night, James crept down to the breakfast room earlier than usual. Tomas brought him the usual tea and toast and jam. He never felt much like eating in the mornings, and this morning the bread was dry and tasteless, the jam oversweet. He pushed his plate away and was about to leave when Verity entered.

"Good morning, my lord." Her voice was cheerful and she actually smiled.

What the devil?

He cleared his throat and began to compose an appropriate apology for last night's intrusion when Tomas entered. He served her toast and jam from the sideboard and asked if she'd like tea or chocolate.

"Tea, please, Tomas," she said in a bright, convivial tone. "And a boiled egg, I think. I'm famished!"

Tomas nodded and left them alone. Verity began spooning the jam on a thick slice of toast and said, "It's a beautiful morning, my lord. Clear and sunny. I trust you slept well?"

He gazed at her in astonishment. Was this some sort of playacting? She could not possibly be this cheerful, this friendly after what he'd almost done last night.

"No," he said, "I did not. Verity, I—"

"You still have trouble sleeping? Then you must allow me to make up something for you. I have some valerian root that will make a very effective infusion. Shall I make it for you tonight?"

Thoroughly confused, James ran his fingers through his hair and glared dumbly at her. "Please, Verity, this is outrageous. There is no need to pretend."

"I beg your pardon, my lord?"

He fidgeted in his chair. He had hoped to have more time to contrive an acceptable apology. "I'm sorry," he said, "for disturbing you last night. It was unconscionable of me. I do not want you to think that just because—"

"It is quite all right, my lord. There is no need for you to apologize. I quite understand."

"You do?" How could she possibly? Or was she simply so relieved that he had not gone through with it, that she was willing to pretend it had never happened?

"Even so," he said, "you must allow me to say that I regret my behavior—not only last night's, but also the way I practically mauled you the night before. It was unforgivable and I assure you it shall not happen again."

Verity waved her hand in front of her face as though whisking away a pesky insect. "It is forgotten," she said. "We shall not speak of it again."

Tomas returned with tea and a boiled egg perched in a delicate cup. Verity expertly cracked the shell and spooned a bit of egg onto her toast. As she took a bite, James rose to leave.

"I bid you good morning, then." He wanted nothing more than to make a hasty exit. Her apparent willingness to forgive him made him oddly uncomfortable. Before he could take another step, though she said, "Oh, please wait. It is such a lovely day, I thought I might ask you a favor."

Ah. Here comes the payment for last night, he thought. She was going to leave Pendurgan. A knot formed in his stomach. He managed to utter, "Yes?"

She smiled at him. It seemed a genuine smile. He sensed no masked fear or anxiety. Yet he knew that she had always feared him to a degree. Should she not fear him all the more after he had barged, half naked, into her bed chamber last night?

"You must tell me if it is a great imposition," she said, looking him squarely in the eye. "But it is a beautiful sunny day, and there have not been many since I arrived. And one cannot count on too many more such days before winter sets in."

James nodded for her to continue. "It is just that I have seen as much of Pendurgan as possible on foot. I wondered if . . . is it possible you have a horse I might ride?"

She continued to astonish him. "You wish to ride?"

She gave him a smile so brilliant, it was as if she'd held up a light to dazzle him. The knot in his belly uncoiled into something else altogether.

"It has been so long since I've ridden," she said. "It would be such a pleasure to do so. And to have you show me about the estate."

It was too much. He had to sit down. "You . . . you wish me to ride with you?"

"If it is not a frightful imposition and you are not too busy."

He was not too busy. Within the hour, feeling decidedly uneasy, he rode out of the main stable yard by her side. Jago had mounted her on Titania, a sleek little bay mare. Verity had a good seat, though it had obviously been a while since she'd ridden, and she laughed a good deal before she found her way with the mare. Though sunny, the air was chill with a bite of wind, and after a short time, Verity's cheeks grew flushed with the cold. She looked beautiful, even in the slightly shabby habit she'd donned.

At her request, James showed her over the whole estate. They rode past the home farms, mostly dormant this time of year, and the threshing barns where the girls' voices rose sweetly on the wind as they sang while preparing seed wheat. They rode through the pastures where only a handful of sheep lingered while their relatives met their fates in the slaughtering barns.

"It is not the best time of year to appreciate the farms," James said as they skirted the busy smokehouse.

"I grew up in the country," Verity said, "and enjoy all the seasons of farm life. This season of death and reparation is no less important than the spring rebirth."

He asked her where she had grown up, and she spoke longingly of Lincolnshire and its lush wolds. He learned she was the only child of a country squire. It seemed odd that he knew so little about her, when she surely had been told all the wretched details of his past. He would like to know more about her marriage and how it came to such an ignominious end, but he dared not ask and break the spell of pleasant amity that had so unexpectedly grown between them today.

She looked about her and laughed at the strangeness Cornwall had presented when she first arrived. "But now," she said, her glance sweeping the vista of farmland and moorland beyond, "now I believe I quite like it."

He reined in. "You do?"

"Oh, yes. You may all attempt to turn me away with your piskeys and your ghosts, but I have grown fond of this place and the people and their musical voices. Goodness, but it was difficult to understand the local people at first."

"Ah, but 'ee has no trouble now, does 'ee?" James said in his best Cornish.

Verity laughed. "Not a bit," she said and galloped on ahead.

When James caught up, she slowed and turned to him. "Could we explore the moors?"

"If you'd like."

"Oh, I would indeed."

And so they left the green farmlands and stone hamlets behind and headed toward the rugged boulder-strewn moorland. They slowed as they passed Wheal Devoran while Verity peppered James with questions about the mine and its workings. She seemed mesmerized by the rhythmic rattle and hiss of the great bob engine, and he was only just able to stop her from dismounting to explore the mysterious workings within the engine house. She did, however, extract a promise to do so on another day.

When they reached the High Tor, Verity grew quiet. They dismounted and sat silently for a while atop one of the granite boulders.

"This is all yours, then?" Verity swept her arm in a slow circle over the land below.

"Not all. Just the parts we rode over. The farms. And the mine."

"And St. Perran's."

"And St. Perran's. But over there—see?—is Bosreath. That is Alan Poldrennan's family estate. And beyond that is Trenleven, the Nance homestead."

"But your estate is much more vast than the rest, is it not?" she asked.

"We have been lucky in Wheal Devoran, and Wheal Justice before it played out. Mine profits support the land."

"And the people."

"Yes."

"You are good to your people, my lord."

"I daresay they might disagree with you."

"I do not believe so. Oh, they may dislike you"—she shot him a glance—"but they cannot complain of your treatment. Your mine is successful and employs men and women of St. Perran's and other villages, I'm told. Your tenant cottages in St. Perran's are kept in good repair. The church is well maintained, and the Methodist meetinghouse as well. Your people have a lot to be thankful for. And you have a great deal of responsibility."

"It is late," James said, not wishing to head down that conversational path. "We should be getting back." He stood and retrieved the horses. Verity stood on a boulder and he lifted her into the saddle. When he had mounted, she drew Titania up beside him.

"The name does not suit you," she said.

"What?"

"Despite what you'd like the world to believe, you are a good man, my lord. You are not at all heartless."

Later that evening, as he sat in his usual spot in the library with his chair turned away from the fire, Verity entered carrying a steaming cup. It was the valerian infusion she had promised. Perhaps recalling that other time they had been alone in the library, she set the cup down on the candlestand near his chair and quickly took her leave.

He sipped the bitter brew and considered its maker. Today seemed to have been her way of letting him know that she did not harbor the fear and loathing he had expected after last night. She thought him a "good man" despite all she'd heard to the contrary, despite even the way he had treated her.

He stopped trying to understand why, but he had the distinct impression she wanted to be a friend to him. There was nothing coy or flirtatious about her manner, so clearly she was not inviting another seduction.

God knew, he still wanted her. But he admired her too much to take advantage of her again. He found the notion of her friendship strangely comforting.

He downed the last of the infusion and screwed up his face in distaste. He shook his head and chuckled. Perhaps her friendly manner had been a ruse to set him off-guard so that she could poison him. He shuddered involuntarily at the foul aftertaste lingering on his tongue.

He picked up the book he had been reading when Verity entered, but after a few pages the words began to blur. He set the book down, trudged upstairs, and, to the stunned amazement of Lobb, fell straight into bed.

James slept through the night for the first time in more years than he could remember.

The following days settled into a new pattern, always ending with Verity mixing up her infusion and taking it to James in the library. The day after their ride, when they had met again at the breakfast table, Verity had asked him if the drink had been effective.

"I slept like the dead," he replied and gave that little twitch of the mouth that generally passed for a smile. In an instant, though, his manner became serious and his words faltered. "I . . . I cannot tell you what that means to me or . . . or how grateful I am. I do not recall the last time I felt so rested."

Verity was pleased with yet another success from her herbal skills, but most especially she was happy to have been of help to James. This tiny accomplishment could be the first step in his real healing. She liked to believe so, and therefore continued to deliver the infusion each evening.

She detected subtle but noticeable changes in James over the next week. His eyes took on a brighter appearance and the dark circles beneath them began to fade. He appeared at the breakfast table more often than before, and ate more than his usual tea and toast. He took supper with her and Agnes most nights, and his manner was more relaxed, despite Agnes's increased hostility.

And he actually smiled now and then. Not frequently, hardly more than once or twice. Verity expected no more, for his was a sober, guarded temperament. She wondered if it had ever been otherwise, long ago, before Spain. Nevertheless, the full smile that so transformed his face became less rare, and when he turned it upon Verity it sometimes made her weak in the knees.

On a dreary morning that threatened more rain, Verity worked in the kitchen garden, gathering roots and stalks that might still be useful during the winter months. She had more or less adopted this small garden and tended it daily, trimming dead wood and cutting back plants for spring growth.

She stood and surveyed the rows of plantings, denuded for the winter, and considered all her little medicinal successes with pride. It was not long, it never was, before her thoughts drifted to another sort of achievement altogether, one that gave her even more pleasure.

After her ride over the estate with James, a new kind of relationship had begun to blossom. She savored the friendship, for it was infinitely more sensible than the relationship she had expected when he had come to her bedchamber. But in the deepest reaches of her heart, when she was perfectly honest with herself, Verity knew she wanted more. She knew that her gratitude for his rescue at the auction—for she had ceased thinking of it as anything else—and her instinctive need to heal him were leading her into far more dangerous sentiments.

A canvas bag was slung over her shoulder, and Verity reached in and began to strew bits of straw at the base of some of the more tender plants as a protective winter mulch. The simple task did nothing to interrupt her thoughts of James.

Never before had she experienced the physical sensations James had stirred to life in her body and, God forgive her, she wanted more. Her life had been turned upside down and would never be the same again. Everything that had once seemed improper did not matter anymore. One thing, however, would never change—James's rejection had made that very clear. She would do well to remember that and stop spinning foolish dreams.

It served no purpose to dream of a life that could never be, she thought as she packed the mulch neatly around the base of a santolina plant. How could anything ever be normal again for a woman who was married, yet not married, who, though bought and paid for, was neither mistress nor servant?

As she made progress with the mulching, Verity felt as if she'd also made significant progress in adjusting to a life without an identity. Her skill with herbs had allowed her at least to be useful, to provide some level of meaning to her existence. And now she was building an odd sort of friendship with James. It was more than she could ever have expected as she had stood in the market square with a leather halter around her neck. She ought to be satisfied. She ought not to want more.

Verity straightened and groaned. Stiff from bending, she pressed her hands against the small of her back and stretched. Arching her neck, she looked up at the dark, threatening sky and followed a thin white wisp of smoke wafting from the direction of Wheal Devoran.

James had made good on his promise and taken her on a tour of the mine a few days after their ride. He had shown her the engine house first, and Verity had been fascinated by the massive pump engine with its hissing cylinder and huge iron beam rocking overhead. He had showed her the boiler house and the smithy's shop, the storage buildings filled with odd-looking paraphernalia, the powder house and the timber yard, and the picking sheds where girls called bal-maidens hammered the pieces of ore in a rhythm while they sang.

It was all very strange and dirty and busy, and Verity thought it quite wonderful, but perhaps only because of her guide. As they strolled through the yards, a few of the workers—Zacky Muddle, Nat Spruggins, Ezra Noone—doffed their candle-laden hats to Verity, for she had met them in St. Perran's. Most of the workers barely acknowledged James, scurrying out of his path and avoiding him altogether.

One man, though, had unsettled her momentarily.

Verity had noticed a small, grime-covered man lurking behind one of the outbuildings and watching James intently. James either had ignored him or had not seen him, but when he had stepped aside briefly to speak to one of his captains, the little man had darted out to stand near Verity. His eyes stood out like small white stones in his blackened face. He held up one finger and wagged it toward Verity.

"Tedn't safe fer 'ee here, mistress," he said in an conspiratorial whisper. "Nor anywheres with that man, with Lord Heartless." His mouth had twisted as he spoke the name. "There be only fire and death for 'ee up at that house. Fire and death."

"Be off wid 'ee, Clegg," another man had said. "Get back to yer pitch, man, and don't make no trouble. Go on, now!"

The little man had kept his finger raised, gave it one final shake in her direction, then turned away and disappeared behind one of the sheds along with the nameless miner who'd chided him.

Verity had been rattled by the little man's words. She was startled to find James again by her side, and wondered how long he'd been there, how much he'd heard.

James clearly knew that his own people mistrusted him, even feared him. Yet when he had come upon the group of women in St. Perran's who had scattered in his wake, or when he strolled through his mine works where the men did the same, he made no effort to change their attitudes. He wore a perpetual scowl and a steely glint in his eye, almost as though challenging them to deny his villainy.

Captain Poldrennan had said James preferred to

be known as a murderer rather than a coward. Apparently it was something another man could understand. Well, she was not a man and did not understand. She believed he had allowed all that was good in him to be overshadowed by guilt and shame.

This was the wound Verity wanted so desperately to heal.

She reached in the canvas bag for more straw and resumed her mulching, determined to finish before the rain began. The bag was empty when she felt the first drops of rain on her face. With one last look at her work, she turned and hurried toward the scullery. She slowed at the sound of shouting coming from the direction of the steward's office.

"Hold your bloody tongue!" The familiar voice of James brought her to a halt. He must be arguing with that horrid man, Mr. Bargwanath. The loud, jeering laughter of the steward caused an involuntary shudder as she recalled how he had laughed at her in just the same way.

"I only meant she must be gettin' used to it since no one hears her screamin' in the night anymore. Learnin' to like a rough ride, is she?"

Verity froze. Good Lord, they were speaking of her. She had indeed screamed herself awake with nightmares during that first week or so, when she had not yet put behind her the horror of the leather halter and the banging kettles. But that was not what Mr. Bargwanath meant.

She heard scuffling and wondered what was happening.

"Don't you dare speak of her that way, do you hear me?" James spoke slowly, punctuating each word with a sort of huff, as though he pushed against something. Or someone. His words were followed by a whoosh of breath and a crashing sound, as though furniture was being overturned. Something violent was going on, and it sounded as if the violence was being handed out by James. On her behalf. Oh, God, no.

After an uncomfortably long silence, she heard, "Pack your bags, Bargwanath. I've had enough of you."

"You can't sack me! You'd never get no one else to work here and you know it."

"I don't need you or anyone else who refuses to show proper respect to Mrs. Osborne."

Verity flinched at the sound of her name, but continued to stand still as a statue. The rain had begun in earnest and was dripping over the brim of her bonnet and seeping under her collar down the back of her neck.

"Proper? What's so proper about a bought and paid for dollymop like her?"

More crashing was followed by a heavy thud.

"Out!" More shuffling. "Out, now! And if I hear of you setting foot on Pendurgan land ever again, I swear I will kill you. Out!"

The words were bellowed with such force that Verity was at last driven to action. She pulled her wet skirts about her and ran into the scullery.

She leaned against the old stone wall to catch her breath. After a moment, she removed her drenched bonnet and shook it out. She then ran a hand over her face and wiped away the moisture, not all of it rain.

She did not know what frightened her more, the

vulgar insinuations of Mr. Bargwanath, or the violent reaction of James. One tiny corner of her heart felt joy that he would defend her. But so violently! She had spent the last week and more building an image of him that was good and charitable. She had forgotten, or had chosen to forget, that there had always been a dark side to his character as well. She had pushed aside all thoughts of his rough handling that night in the library, of the sharp, almost cruel tone he sometimes used with Agnes when she pushed him too far, of the unexplained fires in the area.

But he had defended her. No one had ever before done anything like that for her. So he must have some feelings for her, even if only of friendship. That tiny corner of joy in her heart began to spread.

Though she knew he might always make her somewhat uneasy, that he had violent impulses she could never fully trust, that he might do her harm if he fell into a blackout and did God knew what, that he might well and truly be mad—knowing all these things and more, she had still allowed herself to do the unthinkable.

She had fallen in love with him.

Chapter 8

The explosion rocked the ground beneath him. Flames erupted all around, igniting every shrub and bush, catching the coattails and sleeves of his men. Shrieks of pain and horror rent the air and he watched, helpless, while several men of his company burst into flames. The odor of charred flesh hung thick in the air, so thick he could barely breathe.

His men were dying and he couldn't move. He couldn't move.

Suddenly a structure loomed ahead. A barn. His barn. His barn at Pendurgan. Two of the burning men fled into the barn. No, not men. Boys. Little boys. Two tiny bodies engulfed in flames ran into the barn, which had somehow caught fire as well.

And there was Rowena, staring at him in horror. She wanted him to run after the boys, but he could not move. He could not move. "Coward!" she screamed, and rushed into the burning barn, her skirts catching fire as she disappeared inside.

Someone else was running toward the barn. A dim figure. A woman. It was Verity. Dear God, it was Verity. He must stop her or she would be killed, too. He must stop her, but he could not move. He screamed her name again and again, and she moved toward him, arms outstretched, but never seemed to reach him. "I'm here," she said, moving and yet not moving. "It's all right. Everything is all right."

Someone was shaking him by the shoulders. Someone was pulling him free, turning him away from the blaze, away from the stench. "I'm here." It was Verity's voice. He wanted to get to her, to warn her, but, maddeningly, she was always just out of his reach.

"Verity!"

"I'm here." Someone was still shaking his shoulders. "I'm here, James." Shaking and shaking. "James!" Shaking harder and harder. "James, come back. Come back!"

Dizziness washed over him and he went limp.

Verity knelt beside his sagging form, placed her hand on the back of his head, and gently stroked his thick, black hair. "James," she whispered. It did not matter how many times she might have been told about his spells, she could never have been prepared for what she'd witnessed. It had been terrifying, and she still trembled in its aftermath.

She had made up his nightly infusion as usual. When she entered the library, he was not in his usual chair with his back to the grate. The chair had been knocked over on its side and James knelt before a blazing fire. He was shoeless and coatless. His boots had been discarded near an ebony settee where his green velvet coat and crumpled cravat lay in an untidy heap. His hands gripped either side of his head, his eyes were tightly shut, and his breathing was heavy. He seemed to be muttering something, but she could not understand. Startled, and concerned he might have injured himself and be in some kind of pain, she had called out to him, but he had not responded with anything intelligible.

Uncertain what to do, she had dropped to her knees beside him and leaned close to try and understand what he was saying. He seemed to be in a sort of trance. "I can't move," he muttered. "My men. I can't move."

And all at once she had known what was wrong. It was just as Captain Poldrennan had described. James was back in Spain at the time of the explosion.

Some instinct had told her to pull him out of the trance before he could suffer a full blackout and be lost for hours. She had touched his shoulder and called out to him. "No," he muttered, over and over, and then he had called her name. Part of his brain must have known she was there now, in the present, while the other half was elsewhere.

The two sides seemed to war with each other as he fought his way out of the trance. She had shaken him hard by the shoulders and shouted again and again for him to come back, until he had collapsed.

She did not yet know which side had won. Was he

unconscious, or simply exhausted from the battle? "James?"

His head stirred beneath her hand and she heaved a sigh of relief. Slowly, ever so slowly, he raised his head from his knees. Verity's hand dropped to his shoulder and she let it rest there. He would need a human touch to help him re-orient after the trance.

"Verity?" His voice was little more than a whisper.

"Yes, James. I'm here."

His gaze appeared to take in his surroundings with a sort of hesitancy, as if he wasn't quite sure where he was or how he came to be there. Verity's heart went out to him, imagining how many other times he had come out of a spell like this, afraid of what he might find. Or what he did find.

He turned his head to look up at her, and she almost gasped at the devastation in his eyes.

She could never have imagined him like this—helpless, vulnerable, powerless against the fear that would always be a part of him. There was shame, too, in the eyes that looked back at her, eyes more black than blue, set deep behind high-boned cheeks drained of color.

He turned his head away. A man who preferred the label of murderer to having anyone know of this would suffer to realize she had been a witness.

Poor man! All she felt in that moment was a tenderness and a determination to help him.

"Oh, James. It is all right. It is all right." She slid her hand about his shoulders, wrapped the other arm around him, and gathered him in her arms.

He resisted only for an instant, then settled his

head against her shoulder and clung to her, tightly, desperately. After long, silent moments, he began to whisper her name, over and over, just as he had done while in the trance. Verity nudged his head away from her shoulder, her hand still entwined in his hair. She wanted to see his face, to make certain he had not slipped back into darkness.

The effects of the episode lingered in his eyes, but there was something else as well.

"Verity," he repeated—and covered her mouth with his own.

He ravaged her with his lips and tongue, as he had done once before. This time, though, there was only urgency, hunger, need. She offered herself willingly.

James pressed his body against hers as though he could not get close enough, kissing her again and again and again. He kissed her jaw and her throat and her neck, always returning to her mouth, opening his wide and drawing her tongue deeper inside. His hands roamed up and down her back and her sides and her hips until Verity thought she might swoon with pleasure.

"Verity. My God, Verity." If he had not kept repeating her name she might have thought he believed her to be someone else, someone desirable, someone normal. But he knew who she was when he explored every inch of her neck with fingers and lips and tongue. He knew who she was when he touched her breast tenderly, as though it were something rare and beautiful. He knew who she was when he cradled her face in his hands and kissed the corners of her mouth and her eyes and her lips.

A surge of pure joy caused her heart almost to leap

from her breast. James found her desirable. Was it possible?

She did not resist when he urged her down on the rug and lay full length atop her, nor when he pushed her skirts up to her thighs, nor when he nudged her legs apart with his knees.

Verity knew what he wanted; God forgive her, she wanted it, too. She wanted to give this to him, regardless of the outcome, the repulsion he might yet feel afterward. She was ready.

At first he had merely sought her warmth, her gentle touch, her comfort. Muddled and shaken, he had wanted to climb right inside her and forget. Now, he wanted more. Pure lust overwhelmed him and he could not have stopped what was about to happen if he tried.

James wanted Verity, *needed* her. Badly, right now. God help him, he could not keep his promise to preserve her virtue. He had to have her right this minute or he would surely die.

He reached down and fumbled with his breeches—clumsy, rushed, impatient. In his haste he ripped one button clean off the fall and it went pinging across the floor.

He kissed her once more, quickly, while he positioned himself above her. He looked down into her eyes, wide and uncertain, and wished he could have done better by her. But it was too late. He needed her now. Now!

"I'm sorry," he muttered, and then plunged himself full length inside her. Like a gauche schoolboy, he came after only a few swift thrusts.

Only when his own groan subsided did he realize Verity had also cried out, but not in pleasure. Even now, she whimpered slightly and he realized what he'd done. Good God, she'd been a virgin. A virgin? Was it possible? Son of a bitch!

He held himself still and looked at her. Her eyes were closed and tears slid down her cheeks onto the floor beneath her. Her mouth was contorted in pain—my God, how he must have ripped through her—and she tried valiantly not to whimper.

Bloody hell. He'd been afraid of stripping her of the last shred of her dignity, and in the end had stripped her of much more. A cad to the core.

She held herself rigid and seemed unable to breathe. "Goddammit, woman." Lust dissipated, he rolled off her in disgust.

He sat up and turned his back to her while he fastened his breeches, cursing at the missing button that left the fall flapping open at one corner. Verity lay silent behind him, like a wounded bird, not moving.

And so he had lived up to his dastardly reputation after all, taking a virgin like she was a whore—quickly, fiercely, painfully. Lord, how he must have hurt her, this proud young woman who only sought to offer him comfort. Typically, he thought only of himself, his own needs, and ending up using and abusing those dear to him.

Yes, she had indeed become dear to him. In the sweet, shy way in which she offered her friendship, she had worked her way under his skin, despite all intentions to keep his distance and stay uninvolved. He had just blown those good intentions all to hell. Once again, he had ruined everything he touched.

James heard the sounds of movement behind him. He turned to find her sitting up, her face as blank as an egg, hair disheveled, skirts still bunched up around her thighs. His eyes were drawn to a deep red stain on the pale yellow muslin of her dress. The sight ignited his anger, and he wanted to shout. He wanted to throw something. He wanted to strike out.

"What game do you play, madam," he said, "that you hide your virginity behind this mock tale of a marriage?"

She looked away from him, and in a small, tremulous voice said, "You are m-mistaken. My marriage was real and I was not a . . . a v-virgin."

Anger coursed through his blood and bones and took full possession of him. He grabbed her skirts so roughly she recoiled, as if she thought he might strike her. He held out the bloodstained fabric. "Then how do you explain this?"

Verity twisted out of his grasp and adjusted her skirts. "It is not what you think," she said. "It is merely my . . . my time of month. I have been . . . married. It was not my first time."

James did not know why, but she was lying. She had been a virgin, there was no question of it. Damn her, why was she playing this game with him?

He stood and noticed for the first time that his chair was on its side. He righted it, turned it away from the fire, and sank into it. He watched as Verity rose to her feet and shook out her skirts. The stain on the back stood out like a beacon. She reached up and fingered her hair. The chignon had come loose and bobbed limply at the back of her neck. One untidy lock had escaped and fell over her left shoulder.

There was a rent in the neckline of her dress. She looked for all the world like a woman who had been ravished.

He could not bear the sight of what he'd done. "Please leave," he said.

She walked slowly toward the door without a word. He could tell by the way she moved—awkwardly, cautiously—that she was still in some pain. "Wait," he said, and she stopped. He could not just let her go like that, hurt and confused and damaged beyond repair. He forced himself to say the words that needed to be said. "I am sorry for what happened." His tone was clipped and gruff but it was all he could manage without falling to pieces. "I promise it won't happen again. I swear I shall not touch you again."

Verity squared her shoulders, cocked her head at that prideful angle he'd seen so often, and swept out of the room, dignified as a duchess. He hoped to God no one saw her. Despite the proud carriage, she looked a mess. A bloody mess.

James rested his elbows on his knees and dropped his head into unsteady hands. He thought for a moment that he'd never been more miserable in all his life, but that was not true. He had spent the better part of his life making misery for himself. This was just one more chapter in his infamous history: cowardice, murder, and now ravishment.

Was it ravishment? She had not fought him. She had never once asked him to stop. From what he could remember, she had been just as involved as he was, wanting it as badly as he did.

But she had been a virgin.

Hell and damnation, what was he supposed to do now? What if he'd made her pregnant? The notion sent a shudder down his spine. Should he offer to marry her? But she was not free to marry. Despite those two hundred pounds, she was still legally married.

Or was she? Had she ever really been married at all? If so, then why the devil had she still been a virgin? His head began spinning with speculations of collusion and deception and entrapment, of schemes and plots to entangle him . . . in what? If there had been some master plan, it was a poor one that didn't make much sense. Russell had absconded with the two hundred pounds almost two months ago. Besides, neither of them could have known he would be at Gunnisloe that day, or that he would make that blasted offer. If they had been involved in some entrapment scheme, why wait until now?

Of course, she had to wait for him to make the first move. He had almost done it once before, and she had been ready and willing that time as well, just as she had been tonight.

James lifted his head and swore aloud to the room. "No, no, no!" He pounded his fist on the chair arm so hard he surely bruised it. No, he did not believe it. He was spinning fantasies to remove the blame from himself. He did not know why she lied, but he could not make himself believe Verity was deceitful by nature. She was one of the most straightforward people he'd ever known. Everything about her was genuine, from the fear she'd exhibited at the auction and in the days following, to the comfort she had offered tonight.

He rose to his feet and began to pace the room. Why had she lied? Why maintain the foolish pretense that he had not ripped her virginity from her like a raging bull? Why pretend he had not caused her pain?

His steps came to a halt at the library table where a full teacup sat in its saucer. Verity's tea. She must have been bringing it to him when she found him—what? Cowering before the fire?

He picked up the odiferous brew and all at once understanding slammed into him like a howitzer. Verity tried to ease suffering, whether it be a villager's toothache or his own insomnia. He did not like to consider what she might have seen of him tonight while he fought off his familiar demons. But she had offered herself up as a means of easing his torment. She had given herself freely. She was too concerned with *his* pain to allow him to know of her own. She protected him by pretending to be unharmed.

James spun around and flung the cup and saucer into the grate, where they smashed into a thousand pieces. How he loathed himself for what he'd done. How could he possibly make amends to this sweet woman who was only trying to help him in a moment of weakness? And then he had lashed out at her in anger as though *she* had done something wrong.

Verity had bestowed upon him the gift of her virginity, and he did not misunderstand the generosity of that gesture. It nearly broke his heart, assuming he still had one, to know what she had done for him, and he would forever honor her for that unselfish gift.

And he would treat it as a gift. He would not, would never, ask it of her again. He had done enough to compromise her proud dignity. He would do nothing further to erode it.

What was he to do with her, then, as she lived under his roof every day, ate meals with him, rode with him, and brought him foul-tasting tea each night? They could never marry—

The realization burst upon him like an electric storm. He stopped pacing. Marriage to Verity. By God, he *would* marry her if he could. She had already worked her way into his household, his village, and at least a small corner of his heart. There was nothing he'd rather do than spend his life with her.

He'd never meant to let another woman into his life. His relationship with Rowena had been troublesome and volatile from its youthful beginning. But he had loved her with the consuming passion of first love, and in the end he'd killed her. James never meant to allow love into his heart again.

He wasn't prepared to allow himself to love Verity. In any case, he was not ready to admit that what he felt for her was love. But if she were free and if she would have him, he would marry her in a moment.

He allowed the idea to roll around inside his head for a while, touching upon the possibilities of divorce and annulment. But it was pointless. He had nothing to offer but a soiled life, riddled with cowardice and culpability. Verity would end up despising him, just as Rowena had.

James poured himself a brandy, brought the decanter with him, and sank down into his chair again. He hoped to God his lack of control would not result in a child. The thought terrified him more than almost anything else. How could he be depended on to keep a child safe when he still lost untold hours during blackouts over which he had no control, and during which he had no idea what he might have done?

He pushed aside all thoughts of fatherhood, as he always did, for they only conjured up painful images of Trystan, with his big, trusting blue eyes and a mop of blond hair that curled in all directions. James had barely known his son but had loved him desperately. When he returned from Spain, instead of letting the child into his life, he had kept Trystan at a distance. His blackouts were deeper and more frequent then, and he had feared what might happen. He had been right.

James took a deep swallow and let the brandy burn a path down his throat and warm his stomach. How he wished he could have been worthy of a woman like Verity Osborne. She had such courage, dignity, compassion, not to mention beauty. Did she realize how beautiful she was? He doubted it. Ah, but he could never be worthy. He had condemned himself forever in her eyes as a callous, rutting brute.

He downed the glass and poured another. What a worthless excuse for a man he was. He ought to have ended it years ago. In the days after the fire, he had wanted nothing more than to do so. Why should he be allowed to live when he had killed the two people he loved most in the world? If he had any strength of character, he would do so now before he caused any further harm.

But he had not the strength. He never had. He made excuses instead. He poured a third glass and recounted them. His people needed him. The mine needed him. Winter had arrived and the pumps would be pushed to their limit during the rains. The cottagers would need fuel and food and medicine. He must look after the land, since he no longer had a steward. There was Agnes, too. As much as she hated him, she had nowhere else to go, no one else to depend on. And Verity depended on him now, too.

There were endless excuses why he could not take the easy way out. But James knew the real excuse lay in cowardice. Everything about him was based on cowardice. He had never been strong enough to do what any man of honor would have done years ago.

No honor. No courage. No heart. Only another empty glass to refill in hopes of dulling the pain, drinking himself into oblivion and forgetfulness.

Tears soaked the pillow slip beneath Verity's cheek. She had cried and cried—for the pain he had caused, for the anger he had flung at her, for her own inadequacy, for the ruins of her life.

When the flow of tears had ebbed at last, she rolled onto her back and pressed the heels of her hands hard against her eyes. She ought not be so shattered, having known all along how it would end. She had allowed her need to comfort him to overwhelm the knowledge that she could not. Not in that way.

Verity swung her legs over the side of the bed, rose, and walked slowly toward the dressing table. The ache between her legs had subsided somewhat, but she was still very conscious of it, of what had happened there, and she moved stiffly. One glance at herself in the mirror and she turned away. She looked a fright. She reached for the tapes at the back of her dress. After much fumbling she was finally able to slip out of the bodice and allowed the dress to fall to her feet. When she reached to pick it up she saw the reddish stain between the folds of yellow muslin.

A little moan of despair escaped her lips before she balled up the garment and tossed it into the grate. It began to smolder but did not catch fire. A small bellows leaned against the hearth. Verity picked it up and pumped several times before the dress ignited with an explosive rush. She watched as it blackened and curled and finally fell to pieces. There would be no evidence of what had occurred downstairs.

James had been more furious over her supposed virginity than her other inadequacies. How could he know for sure? Was it possible for a man to be certain about such a thing? She had explained away the blood; how could he possibly have known?

It did not matter. Verity would never admit the truth to him, or to anyone. She had never told a living soul that her marriage had not been consummated. To do so would mean admitting to the humiliation of her wedding night, admitting the fact of her undesirability, admitting a man could never really want her in that way.

It had been difficult enough to admit to herself, but over the years she had come to accept her shortcomings. She did not dwell on it, and she had become resigned to a life without physical love. Or children.

Until she had come to Pendurgan.

When she found herself reluctantly attracted to

James, the old failures returned to haunt her. Every time her body reacted to him—to his touch, his kiss, a look, his mere presence—Verity had been reminded of all she could never be.

The extent of the pain the act had caused surely vindicated the truth of Gilbert's implications. There was something wrong with her, physically, that made sexual relations difficult, if not impossible, and made her sexually undesirable.

Tonight had been an accident of circumstance. James had been needy, and she had been the only one there. Any woman would have done. For that moment, though, Verity had been available and, God forgive her, willing.

She walked to the basin stand and poured water into the bowl. The water was icy cold and she relished its prickly sting as she splashed her face with it.

In the deepest reaches of her heart she had hoped that she might be allowed to experience what other women experienced routinely. For one fleeting moment, she actually believed she could be desirable to a man, to know what it was like to have a man want her.

She rinsed her swollen eyes one final time, then rubbed her face roughly with a towel, hoping to dissipate the last vestiges of foolishness. The sweet moment she had coveted had been fleeting, indeed, for as soon as James had entered her—stretching and tearing so she thought she must be ripped to shreds—he could hardly wait to be done with it. Had she somehow caused him pain as well? He had cursed her, then rolled away in disgust, unable even to look at her.

How could she have pretended it would be different this time? How could she have allowed herself to respond to his kisses, to believe they spoke of desire rather than simple need?

Worse yet, how could she have allowed herself to fall in love with a man who could never want her, who tonight vowed he would never touch her again?

Verity sat, carefully and slowly, on the stool in front of the dressing table and began to unpin her hair. She had lost several hairpins downstairs and the tight coil at her nape had become an untidy mess. She let it fall down her back and began the nightly ritual of brushing its thick length.

She remembered speaking with Edith when she was very young, about her dreams for the future, dreams of a home in the country, a husband, children. Ordinary things dreamed by most young girls. But it had all gone wrong somehow.

There had been nothing ordinary about her marriage to Gilbert, who, after being violently ill on their wedding night when he'd attempted to consummate the marriage, had abandoned her in a tiny, ramshackle house for more than two years, never to come to her bed again, seldom setting eyes on her until he'd come to take her to Cornwall. There had been nothing ordinary about being led to auction like a dray nag. And there was certainly nothing ordinary about falling in love with a man who needed her but didn't want her.

Verity stopped brushing and stared at herself in the mirror. "Stop it!" she said aloud and wagged the brush at her reflection. "Stop it. Stop it."

She hated it when she gave in to self-pity, even for

a moment. She had never allowed the unexpected turns in her life to get her down, and refused to let the world see her as a victim. She had even adjusted to her new life at Pendurgan, however uncertain its nature. She had never been much of a fighter, but neither had she worn her disappointments on her sleeve. She quietly tucked them away and went about her life, head held high, as if they had never happened.

Just as she had told no one of her disastrous wedding night, neither would she speak of what had happened between her and James. Her love for him would remain a precious, close-guarded secret—unspoken, unacknowledged, unrequited.

There were, however, other ways in which she could act upon her love for him.

After what she'd witnessed tonight, when he'd been in the strange trancelike state, she realized James needed a friend more than ever. Not only to help him overcome his guilt and grief and shame, but also to help him rebuild his life, reestablish his ancestral position in the district, restore his good name. Anyone who saw him immobilized during such an episode could not possibly blame him for what happened in the Pendurgan fire. More likely, they would sympathize with the extraordinary pain he must surely have suffered from the deaths of Rowena and the children, when he realized he had not been able to help them.

It was sheer pigheaded male arrogance that drove him to foster his own black reputation. There was nothing to stop *her*, though, from trying to repair more than six years of damage. It should be easy enough to do as she moved about the villages with her herbs and remedies. The local people had begun to accept her and, she believed, respect her. She would begin talking to them about James. Just a word here and there, but over time she hoped those words would take root and wipe out all the old bad feelings that had spread like a thicket through the community.

Verity finished plaiting her hair, then removed her undergarments and donned a nightgown. She felt much less like crying when she returned to bed at last. She had pushed aside what had happened that evening and come to a decision. Though she could not give James what he needed, there were two things she could give him: her friendship and his reputation. They were all she had to give.

James sat on the side of the bed and sipped Lobb's special coffee. His head throbbed and he felt more hung over from drink than he'd ever been in his life. Drink and conscience and self-loathing. All of it had exaggerated the effects of last night's alcoholic binge.

He had hoped to drink himself out of the despair he felt over what he'd done to Verity. It had not worked. The more he drank, the more despondent he'd become. The drunker he got, the more beautiful, the more compassionate, the more passionate Verity had become in his mind. By the time he had passed out in the chair, he had been sick with love for her.

In the reasonably clear light of day, he realized how foolishly maudlin and sentimental he'd been in his cups. He admired her, to be sure, and lusted after her as well. But guilt over what he'd done to her had magnified his feelings all out of proportion. It would be exceedingly foolhardy to fall in love with Verity.

He rose slowly to his feet, the creaking of the bed frame painful to his ears. He grabbed the bedpost to anchor himself.

"You all right there, m'lord?"

James stood perfectly still while the ringing in his ears quieted and the throbbing in his head subsided to a dull roar. "Yes, Lobb," he said at last, "I'm fine. Just help me dress, would you? I'm not feeling too steady on my pins this morning."

He washed his face in bracing cold water, but when he started to shave himself, Lobb took the razor from James's shaking hands and did the job himself. Afterward, James stood useless as a rag doll while Lobb got him dressed, all the while thinking of what he would say to Verity. For once in his life, he wanted to do the right and noble thing. He would offer her marriage, if such could be arranged, or at least a marriage of sorts if it could not be legally done. Perhaps he could contact Gilbert Russell and discuss the possibilities of a parliamentary divorce. In any case, James was bound and determined to pledge himself to Verity, legally or not, especially if he had made her pregnant.

When he finally made his way down to breakfast, he found Verity there, as expected, looking as though she had not slept. The sight of her brought on a renewed wave of desolation, a self-loathing as deep as any he'd ever known. Agnes was there as well. She glowered at him as he took his seat across from her.

"You look terrible," she snapped. "I suppose you've been drinking all night again."

"Good morning, Agnes," he said. "Verity."

Agnes snorted and Verity nodded, attempting a wan little smile. Agnes then set off on a diatribe on the evils of drink, and how it was simply one more sinful nail in his wicked coffin. James tried not to listen and allowed the pounding in his head to drown out her shrill voice.

After half a slice of bread and a few sips of black coffee, he rose to his feet, interrupting Agnes mid-sentence, and excused himself. He turned to Verity before leaving. "There is a matter I must discuss with you," he said. "Would you join me in the library at your convenience?"

He immediately wanted to bite his tongue. The library! What sort of monster would she think him, to force her to return to the scene of last night's debacle? Before she could speak, he amended the request. "No, not the library," he said. "The Old Drawing Room. I'll have Tomas lay down a fire. Will you join me there?"

"Of course, my lord," Verity replied, without the slightest trace of awkwardness or hesitation. But then, he had never yet seen her lose her composure in public. "Shall we say in half an hour, then?" she asked.

"As you wish."

After Tomas had laid the fire, James paced the small room. The Old Drawing Room was seldom used and so he could expect reasonable privacy. Located on the second floor in the tower wing, it was approached by old stone stairs dipped in the center from centuries of wear. It was in the oldest part of the house, built in the fifteenth century, and retained many of its Tudor furnishings.

Two rows of mullioned windows on the north and east walls provided ample light in the afternoon, but on this gray morning, the room was dark and cheerless. And cold. Perhaps it had been a mistake to meet Verity here.

Tomas's entrance startled James out of his thoughts. "Seemed awful cold in here, so I brung more kindlin' to build up the fire."

James kept his back turned while Tomas went about his business. He did not wish to chance another episode by catching sight of newly ignited kindling, but he heard the rush of flame and felt the warmth against his back. When the red-haired youth left, James resumed his pacing and rejected the temptation to pull out his pocket watch to check the time.

When at last he heard Verity's approach, James stopped pacing and stood with his back to the fire, so that when Verity walked in she found him facing her straight on. She paused in the doorway.

"Come in, please," he said. He moved one of the straight-back wooden chairs from along the wall and placed it before the grate. "Sit here by the fire. These older rooms can be quite cold this time of year."

She looked at the chair but did not speak or move away from the door. Damn. He ought to have chosen a more suitable room. Not only was it cold and dark, but the furniture was ancient and not at all comfortable.

Verity took a tentative step into the room and gestured toward the chair. "Will you join me?" she asked. "Or did you intend to remain standing? I should much prefer it if we were both seated."

"Of course," James said. She would not want him

looming over her. He brought another chair and positioned it opposite the first.

Verity walked toward the first chair and turned it so that its back was to the fire. "You take this one," she said. Then she moved the second chair so that it faced toward the fire, several feet away from the other, and sat down.

The small gesture almost paralyzed him. It took a moment before he could bring himself to take the chair, and a longer moment while he composed himself to speak. She did not allow the awkward silence to hang in the air.

"I have never been to this room," she said. "It must be quite old. I've only seen that sort of linenfold paneling once before, in an old Tudor home in Lincolnshire. It sets off the tapestries beautifully, does it not? You have a lovely home, Lord Harkness."

Bless her for opening the conversation with banalities. "Do you really think so?" he said. "Do you not find it dark and forbidding?"

Verity smiled. "I did at first," she said. "I thought the same of you, too."

James flattened his spine against the hard back of the chair. So much for banalities.

"But I have since discovered," she continued, "that Pendurgan is not as dark and forbidding as it looks. Neither is its master."

"Verity." He shook his head in disbelief, then rose from his chair, too agitated to sit. He began pacing once again and wringing his hands in frustration. She was going to make an apology very difficult. "How can you say such a thing, after what happened last night?" He stopped pacing and stood before her. "I cannot tell you how much I regret my behavior." He was looming, so he sat down again. "It was inexcusable. How can I ever—"

"Please, my lord." She held up a hand to stop his words. "You must not trouble yourself over what happened. Besides, it is I who should apologize to you."

"You? Why on earth would I need your apology when I was the one who—"

"You only needed comforting and I was not able to provide it." Chagrin, or perhaps it was sadness, gathered in her eyes. "I wish I could have done so, but you must know that it is impossible. I am very sorry."

Good Lord. Verity was actually apologizing to him, and after he had practically raped her the night before. It was more than he could bear, and he leaped to his feet again, too unsettled to sit still. "Verity, I treated you abominably last night. I . . . I hurt you."

Her gaze dropped to her lap. "It was my fault."

Her fault? What was she talking about? Did she blame herself because she had not warned him of her virginity? Yet she had denied being a virgin, despite all evidence to the contrary. "I do not understand."

"It does not matter." She looked up again. "Perhaps we should just try to be friends?"

He could hardly believe what she was saying. "You wish to be my friend? After what I've done to you? And after all that you know, that you must surely know, about my past?"

"Yes, of course," she replied, as though it was the most ordinary thing in the world.

James sank down onto the chair again. "I do not understand you, Verity Osborne. Why do you not hate me for hurting you, or at least fear me, like all the rest?"

"Recollect, my lord, that I was there last night. I saw what happened to you."

He flinched as though she'd stuck him. Dear God, what had she seen?

"I know that in your mind you were back in Spain," she said, "fighting that battle again."

James gripped the wooden arms of the chair. "And how the devil do you know about that?" he asked, furious that she should know about Spain. What else did she know?

"Please do not be angry, my lord. I wheedled the information out of Captain Poldrennan."

"Damn him!"

"Do not blame the captain," she said. "You must blame me for being too meddlesome. I wanted to know, after the other things I'd heard."

"From Old Grannie and the rest?"

"Yes."

James heaved a sigh. "Then you know what I've done. You know the harm I've inflicted. And now I've done harm to you, as well."

"I only know what I saw, my lord," Verity said. "I saw firsthand how what happened in Spain—and here—still tears you apart after all these years. I would like to help you, if I can."

Damn her interference. Her attempt at compassion had become intrusive and he didn't like it one bit. He was unable to keep the irritation out of his voice. "How can you possibly help me?"

Verity smiled, apparently oblivious of his building anger. "By standing your friend," she said. "By making up valerian infusions to help you sleep without nightmares. By being there when the visions overtake you again. By listening, if you wish to talk about it."

"*Talk* about it?" Was she mad? "Good God, I want only to forget it. That, of course, is impossible. Talking about it is the very last way in which you might help me. Stick to your possets and potions, Verity."

She pressed on, unfazed by his words. "But keeping all that terror inside is eating away at you. I do not know about the visions or blackouts or whatever it is that happens to you."

Lord, please make her stop.

"But I do know about nightmares," she continued. "I know the shock of seeing and feeling the terror all over again, just as sharp as the first time, so that you wake up with a scream in your throat. And it happens again and again until you think you will die of it."

James reined in his temper and watched her face closely. She spoke from the heart. He thought she had overcome the horror of being sold in the market square. He had even resented her for it. Had he overestimated her strength? Was she plagued by nightmares still?

"What happens to you must be a thousand times worse," she continued, "since it occurs while you are awake. I saw what it did to you."

James squirmed in his seat.

"What set it off this time?" she asked, apparently determined that he *would* talk about it.

He had not often spoken about his blackouts. Only to Lobb, who knew of them firsthand from the beginning, and once or twice to Alan Poldrennan. But the resolute look in her eyes told him she would not let up until he had told her everything. Damn her.

"My lord?"

He tossed her a look that he sincerely hoped reflected the intense displeasure he felt at her well-meaning persistence. In the end, though, he was helpless against those gentle brown eyes. He wrenched his gaze from them and stared at a spot on the wall above her shoulder.

"I had just finished reading a letter and tossed it into the grate behind me," he began. "Some minutes later, I got up to get a brandy, assuming the paper would have ignited long before. It had not. Out of the corner of my eye, I noticed it lying at the edge of the grate. I think it burst into flames just then. I don't know. I can't remember anything else."

Verity remained silent for a moment and then said, "It is indeed a thousand times worse than a nightmare." When he looked up at her, she caught his gaze and held it. "I'd like to help you."

"Why?"

"Because I suspect there is a good man beneath all that pain," she said, "beneath the Lord Heartless façade."

By God, he'd had enough. "Madam, you go at me like a miner with his pick, chipping and chipping at solid rock where you think you've spotted signs of a rich vein. But there's no shiny ore to be found here, my dear. I suggest you leave it alone. You will only disappoint us both."

"I merely want to help."

"You cannot help!" he shouted. "God's teeth,

woman, this is not some winter ailment to be healed by your herbs. Don't you understand?"

Verity gazed at him with those liquid brown eyes, doleful as a hound and full of hurt. Blast it all, he had no right to shout at her.

James ran his fingers through his hair and made a effort to curb his anger. She did not deserve this surly treatment, but neither did he deserve her compassion. He had done her irrevocable harm and yet she still wanted to *help* him. It was almost more than he could bear.

He lowered his voice. "No, of course you do not understand," he said. "How could you? How could you possibly understand what it's like to live a life riddled with shame and guilt? To endure the fear and hatred of everyone around you until you become the monster they make you out to be? To wake up each morning and wonder how you can possibly make it through one more day? To want so badly to put an end to it all and yet be without the courage to do the deed? What can you know of any of that?"

Verity sat quietly, hands folded in her lap, the firelight reflected in the depths of her dark eyes as she watched the flames behind him. After a moment, she lifted her gaze to his and spoke, very softly. "You are right," she said. "I can probably never understand the pain you have suffered. I am sorry if I presumed too much. I only hoped to be able to offer you my friendship, if you would have it."

She devastated him with her benevolent words and her gentle eyes. She offered him yet another precious gift, and he had almost been ready to toss it back in her face. Anger dissipated, James leaned forward in his chair, reached out, and took her hand. "My dear Verity, there is nothing I would rather have than your friendship, and I accept it gratefully. But I confess you confound me. Here you are offering kindness to one who behaved no better than an animal last night, taking you against your will."

Her gaze dropped to her lap once again. She kept her eyes on their clasped hands. "It was not against my will," she whispered.

"Perhaps not at first. But it was badly done. I caused you pain and I deeply regret it. It shall not happen again, I promise you."

"You've done me no harm, I assure you, my lord."

He doubted that, but did not press the point. "If we are to be friends, will you at least call me James?"

"James, then."

He squeezed her hand and released it. He did not wish her to think he wanted more. "Verity Osborne, you are a remarkable woman. You humble me, and I would be proud to call you friend. But you must not press me on certain matters. Just as I will not press you on matters I know you do not care to discuss." She winced slightly at his words. He had her there. It was a sort of blackmail—her silence on Spain for his silence on her virginity and the state of her so-called marriage—but it was necessary.

"Agreed?" he prompted.

"Agreed."

"You will stay at Pendurgan, then?" he asked.

She chewed on her lower lip as though considering a negative reply. James realized it was now he who presumed too much.

"Verity, as I told you on that very first night, you

are not bound to stay here if you do not wish it. You are free to go whenever you choose. You always have been."

She released her lip but her brow remained furrowed. He wished to God he knew what she was thinking. Did she wish to leave? She had at one time, of course, but he had thought . . . he had hoped . . .

"Yet I suspect," he said, "you have no place else to go. You told me that your parents are both dead, and that you have no brothers or sisters. The woman you were so fond of, the one who taught you about herbs, she is also dead, is she not?"

"Yes."

"Then let me offer you a home at Pendurgan," he said, trying to keep his voice even, to keep from sounding as pathetically plaintive as he felt. The thought of her leaving had set off a despair howling around in his head like a chill wind.

"I do still feel responsible for you, Verity," he continued, "despite my recent behavior. You are welcome to stay, my dear. You shall remain my long-lost cousin. Will that suit you?"

She smiled, and his despair dissolved into a warm breeze of hope. "Yes, James," she said. "I would very much like to stay. Thank you."

He smiled in return. "And we shall be friends, you and me," he said. But there was one more sticky issue to deal with, and he found himself squirming slightly as he prepared to bring it into the open. "Yes, we shall be friends," he said at last. "But you must allow me to be more than that, Verity, if I have . . . if you are . . . if there is a child."

Her mouth dropped open and she quickly brought

up a hand to cover it. She blushed scarlet and glared at him wide-eyed, stunned and unbreathing, as if a fist had knocked the wind out of her. Clearly, she had not considered the possibility. By God, she really was an innocent.

"You will tell me?" he asked.

She looked away, and suddenly he wanted nothing more than to take her in his arms, to comfort her the way she had done for him. He struggled against the unexpected rush of tenderness. "Verity? You will tell me?"

"Yes," she said in a voice barely above a whisper.

"Promise me."

She lifted her head, cheeks still flushed, and for once did not look him square in the eye. She was as flustered as he'd ever seen her. "I promise," she said. "But do not forget that I have a fair knowledge of herbs. I . . . I know how to prevent such things."

James sagged back in his chair. A profound relief that there would be no child swept over him. Profound and apparently quite obvious relief. A flicker of pain crossed Verity's face before she composed herself.

"You needn't worry about that, James," she said, her protective armor of pride and dignity firmly back in place. "Now, I have much to do in the stillroom. If you will excuse me." She practically ran from the room, without a backward glance.

Bloody hell.

Chapter 9

"You want me to do *what*?"

Verity smiled at what must surely be a look of sheer horror on his face. "I thought it would be nice if you went along with me to deliver Christmas baskets to your tenant farms and the cottages in St. Perran's."

James schooled his features into the stern glare he had perfected during his army days. He would have none of this nonsense from her. "You have no need of me for that," he said in his best Major Lord Harkness voice. "The staff has always taken care of it."

"Always?"

"Yes, since . . . since Rowena's death. She saw to all those sorts of things."

"And so now you send the servants in her stead?"

"Yes." He did not trust the direction of this conversation. "What of it?"

Verity lifted an eyebrow. "Do you not think it is a trifle . . . impersonal?"

"Impersonal?"

"Yes. I would have thought it fitting that one of the family deliver the gifts, and wish all the tenants—*your* tenants—a happy Christmas in person. I had thought perhaps Mrs. Bodinar might wish to accompany me, but she declined as well."

James had difficulty suppressing a smile. "You asked Agnes? To visit the cottages in St. Perran's?"

Verity smiled in return. "Yes."

"Ha! You are a brave woman, Verity Osborne. I suspect Agnes did not appreciate the invitation."

"No, I do not believe she did. That is why I am hoping you will come along instead."

His smile twisted into a frown. "No."

"It is your largesse we will be delivering, after all."

"No."

"It will be much more appreciated coming from you."

"No."

"Oh, James. It is Christmas!"

And so it was that James found himself on a frosty Christmas Eve driving out to each of his tenant farms and all the cottages on his land, distributing baskets prepared by Verity and his staff.

Verity ignored the shocked faces and frightened children as she led James from cottage to cottage, as though it were the most normal, everyday occurrence. "Lord Harkness wanted you to have this," Verity would say, and then press the basket into his hands, forcing him to be the one to bestow it.

It was awkward. It was difficult. James was certain the tenants felt every bit as uncomfortable as he did.

It had not always been so. He had done this with his mother when he was young, and once with Rowena when he'd been home on leave. His wife, however, had always been a trifle condescending when she visited the plain stone cottages and farm-houses. Perhaps aloof better described her manner, for she was not unkind. Verity, on the other hand, knew each family member by name, had a smile and a touch for every child, and a personal word for each adult—more often than not having to do with some ailment or other, as he ought to have expected. She presented her own offerings of clove-studded oranges and prettily tied bags of scented herbs—incongruous luxuries for such simple folk, but effusively appreciated.

It was altogether less hateful a task than James had anticipated. Some of Verity's goodwill among his people spilled over onto James as well. He was thanked by each family. Uneasily, awkwardly, often reluctantly, but he was thanked in every case. It was the first time in more than six years he'd had a civil word out of most of his people, and it was quite strangely satisfying.

Christmas passed quietly as usual. He had been afraid that Verity, in her obvious efforts to redeem him, would make more of the occasion, attempting to revive some of the old traditions. She did not. She stood by quietly when he went through his usual awkward machinations to have someone else light the great mock. Young Davey Chenhalls was more than pleased to do it again, but asked Verity to help, and the two of them had held the charred faggot from last year to light the fire while James maneuvered to keep his back to them. Verity had then raised a glass of punch with the household, and had sent him a look that told him she understood how difficult the whole ordeal was for him.

She went to church on Christmas morning with Agnes and did not object when James declined to join them. She did not so much as mention any other holiday traditions, though James suspected she had once been accustomed to much more gaiety this time of year. He imagined she had been one to fall into the annual traditions with great enthusiasm. Her natural generosity of spirit would shine during the Christmas season.

Yet she did not attempt to impose any long-lost sentimental custom on this wretched household. She did not ask any more of him this year than the awkward delivery of baskets.

James was relieved, and a little disappointed. He had secretly hoped Verity might have resurrected the kissing bough, though it was probably best that she did not.

Their unlikely friendship settled into a comfortable easiness. Verity never knew, or at least he hoped she never knew, of the deep longing he still felt for her, as he made a deliberate effort to keep his desire in check. More foolishness than simple desire was involved, but James knew there was no point in going down that path. He was determined to keep her virtue, what was left of it, inviolate. That he had ever thought to make her his mistress seemed absurd. The very idea of further eroding that stalwart dignity was unconscionable to him.

She held true to her astonishing offer of friendship, keeping their relationship strictly within the bounds of propriety. Even so, he found himself drawn to her in ways that seemed beyond his control, and in more ways than the merely physical.

It often took him completely by surprise to find himself longing simply to be with her, to be in the same room with her, to find her at his side while they walked or rode over the estate, to speak with her, to be silent with her. Was that, after all, why he had made that offer for her in Gunnisloe? Had it been simple loneliness that had prompted that impulsive bid?

They rode together when weather permitted, and James took her all over the vast stretches of the moor, pointing out stone circles and other ancient monuments to her obvious delight. When the weather kept them indoors, he showed her all about the house—through the oldest parts and the unused wings, explaining the stages of building over the centuries, the history of the family.

Throughout all of their wanderings, they talked, mostly of their childhoods, their families, their friends, of books and poetry and politics. She loved to hear tales of Cornwall and he was happy to oblige. It had been years and years since he had indulged in such easy, untroubled conversation, and he relished every moment.

He knew she wanted to talk about Spain; he wanted to talk about her nonmarriage. Neither forbidden subject was broached.

Verity strayed close to the prohibited topic only once. They had ridden to the High Tor one chilly but clear morning, left the horses at the bottom, and hiked to the top. They sat perched on a fallen boulder and enjoyed the view until an icy wind made it too cold to remain outdoors. Verity had laughed and gamboled down the hill like a girl, and James had been thoroughly charmed at the sight.

She had slowed her pace when she reached a particularly craggy spot, and James took her gloved hand to help guide her down the rocky hillside. Though there was nothing improper about taking her hand in this way, he could not deny the almost electrical warmth that seeped through the leather of their gloves. A look passed between them and he knew she felt it, too.

Verity had not let go when he had led them onto smoother ground, but had pulled him down the slope, laughing all the way. When they reached the horses, they'd both been panting, their breath creating white puffs in the air. Her smile was brilliant and she looked positively irresistible. James had been hard pressed not to take her in his arms and kiss her breathless. That bloody promise of his was becoming excruciatingly difficult to keep.

"Don't you simply love this time of year?" she said. "With the air so clear it crackles and so cold it makes your skin prickle?"

"No, actually," James said, "I have always hated winter." Until today, he thought.

She sobered and let go of his hand. "I'm sorry," she said. "Captain Poldrennan told me about—"

She gave a tiny gasp and brought a hand to her

mouth, clearly aware she was skirting forbidden territory. But he was feeling particularly in charity with her, though he would have liked to keep hold of her hand, and decided to allow her this one small lapse. "What did he tell you?" he asked.

Her eyes widened in surprise. "Oh!" She stared at him a moment, obviously rattled, studying him to determine if he really meant her to go on. He gave a slight nod of encouragement, and she took a deep breath and continued. "Well," she said, "he told me about that awful winter in Spain, about the frozen ground, about the trenches, about . . . about everything."

"Yes, it was quite miserable," he said, then gave in to his impulses and kissed her briefly on the mouth. "Now, let's get back to the house before it becomes as miserable here."

She smiled and his heart flip-flopped in his chest. She had not objected to his kiss. For a moment, he considered taking her into his arms and doing the thing properly but decided, reluctantly, against it. He did not wish to spoil what was between them. Perhaps she would consider the kiss no more than a chaste salute between friends. He would leave it at that, for now.

They mounted their horses and raced back to Pendurgan in perfect amity. When they reached the house and had discarded their cloaks and hats, he had followed as she bounded cheerfully into the drawing room in search of warmth.

They had found Agnes instead.

Garbed in her usual black—her constant reminder to him that Rowena and Trystan were gone—Agnes had looked up from her needlework with a glare so cold and vicious it stopped them both in their tracks. She laid aside her embroidery, stood, and swept past them without a word.

James was accustomed to Agnes's fits of pique, but he could sense Verity's dismay. "Come," he said. "Let us try to get warm. I will ring for something hot to drink."

Mrs. Tregelly arrived almost at once. James went about ordering tea and biscuits, and when he turned, he found that Verity had moved two chairs near the fire—one, as always, turned away from the hearth. She was already seated in the other.

"Thank you," James said. "You are most indulgent of my . . . my problem." Now *he* had skirted the forbidden topic. He must be getting soft. He waited to see if Verity would ignore the issue and pretend he hadn't spoken of it.

She did not.

"Has it . . . has it happened again?" she asked. "Since that night?"

"No."

"I'm glad," she said. "Does it . . . does it happen often?"

He ought to put a stop to this conversation, but he was weary of the battle. He decided to allow her a gentle probe. "Not so often as the years go by," he replied. "But I never know when to expect it. At least my dreams are less disturbed, thanks to you. Perhaps the blackouts will continue to decrease over time, as well."

Verity reached across from her chair and rested a hand briefly on his sleeve. "I pray they will go away forever," she said.

Mrs. Tregelly arrived with the tea, and their conversation became more general.

James grew used to having Verity around—to seeing her across the dining table, to hearing her laughter with young Davey in the kitchen garden, to catching a whiff of her familiar lavender fragrance as he entered a room, to awaiting her appearance in the library each evening when she delivered her tranquilizing drink. He began to forget how bleak his life had been before her arrival.

January heralded a wet winter. There had been a brief snow flurry just after Christmas, but no more since. The temperature remained brisk and rain fell nearly every afternoon.

The most pressing matter for Verity, though, had been resolved. She was not with child.

When James had mentioned the possibility it had shocked her to the core. She had not even considered it. The very notion that she might be able to bear a child, like any other ordinary woman, was almost too wonderful to comprehend.

She had lied about her knowledge of herbs in that area. That afternoon, she had pored over the herbals to find what information she could. It had not been heartening. Where on earth was she supposed to find pomegranate seeds?

In the end, it had not been necessary. It was a good thing, for how could she possibly have explained a child? Even so, she had cried for the lost hope when she learned there would not be one.

Verity took advantage of each clear morning either to ride with James or to visit the women of St. Perran's. She began taking Titania into the village after once getting caught on foot in a sudden downpour and having to slog through the mud uphill to Pendurgan. On Titania, she could also venture farther afield.

It was in late January, as she returned from the Penneck homestead, the largest and most distant tenant holding on the Pendurgan estate, when she saw Rufus Bargwanath. It unsettled Verity to see good-natured Mark Penneck leaning on a fence post chatting with that horrid man. She spurred Titania into the opposite direction, every instinct warning her that he was trouble.

She never had told James of what she'd overheard the day Bargwanath was dismissed. That would only remind her that James's action on her behalf had been a defining moment, the precise moment when she realized she was undeniably and completely in love with him. She was careful to keep such foolish emotions to herself.

The path away from the Penneck farm took her southwest, into an area unfamiliar to her. Verity tried to keep the rabbit-eared tower of St. Perran's Church in sight so she would not get lost, but after a few twists in the path, it suddenly disappeared from view and Verity found herself thoroughly disoriented.

She slowed Titania to study her surroundings when she heard an approaching horse. Captain Poldrennan soon rode into sight.

"Mrs. Osborne!" He reined in his mount and removed his hat with a flourish. "What a surprise to find you on this path. Were you by chance coming to visit Bosreath?"

Verity looked around in confusion. "Oh, is Bosreath in this direction? I did not know."

The captain smiled. "Are you lost, Mrs. Osborne?"

"I'm afraid so. I've lost track of St. Perran's Church, my point of reference. Or perhaps I've been piskey-led at last."

Captain Poldrennan threw back his head and laughed. When he faced her again, a lock of fair hair fell over his brow and he reached up to flick it into place. "So," he said, still grinning, "you've been warned of the little folk, have you? Here, follow me. I'll guide you back to St. Perran's."

He turned his horse and led her down a trail Verity had not even noticed. Within minutes, the church tower was once again in sight.

"Were you on your way to the village?" the captain asked.

"Not by design," she replied. "I intended to return to Pendurgan. I do not like the look of those clouds. I've just come from the Penneck farm."

"The Penneck farm? In this direction?" He laughed again. "Good heavens, you certainly were lost."

"It's just that . . . I saw someone I did not wish to meet." Verity kept her eyes on the path ahead and wondered why the former steward had been hanging about Pendurgan. All sorts of implications came to mind and she did not like any of them.

The captain's voice broke into her thoughts. "Do you mind if I ask who you were trying to avoid? I realize it is none of my business and you need not tell me if you'd rather not. But if someone has been bothering you . . ."

"It was Rufus Bargwanath."

Verity slanted a glance in his direction and saw a frown crease his brow. "Bargwanath?"

"Yes," she said. "I thought he had left the area after James let him go. He was a very unpleasant man."

"So I thought as well," he said, still frowning. "Always wondered why James kept him on. Has he replaced him yet?"

"No, not yet," Verity said. "He's doing all the work himself. He was busy enough with the mine, what with all this rain and the extra strain on the pumps. Now he's working doubly hard, poor man."

Captain Poldennan fell into silence and Verity looked over at him to find him gazing at her with a curious look in his gray eyes. She raised her brows in question and he smiled.

"You seem to have settled in quite comfortably at Pendurgan," he said.

Verity felt the heat of a blush color her cheeks, as though his words hid a deeper meaning. "Yes," she said. "I suppose so."

They rode on for several minutes, negotiating the twists and bends in the path, before Verity spoke again. "Why do you suppose Mr. Bargwanath is still about?" she asked.

"Does he worry you?"

She chose her words carefully. "He made some rather . . . unpleasant insinuations about me."

"Ah."

"I would not like to think he is spreading ugly rumors."

"I do not think you need worry," the captain said.

"Bargwanath is a malcontent looking to stir up trouble. But James will be the target of his venom, not you."

That's as may be, she thought, but what is to stop him from attacking James through implications of an improper relationship with me?

"I can think of no one in the district who would be willing to hire the man," the captain continued. "He is known to be an unsavory character. Most folks would be glad to see the last of him. He will be on his way soon enough, looking for work where he is not so well-known."

"I hope you are right, Captain."

He rode ahead where the path narrowed, and waited for her to pull up beside him when they reached the lane to St. Perran's.

"There's the village," he said. "I defy any malicious piskey to make you lose your way with the church looming just ahead. They wouldn't dare."

Verity smiled at his teasing words. If her heart was not already engaged, she might be tempted to develop a fancy for the handsome captain. He was so different from his dour friend.

"Captain," she said, "may I ask you something?"

He grinned. "Let me guess. More questions about James?"

"In a way. You see, I am determined to help repair his reputation."

He whistled through his teeth and frowned at her.

"It is not fair," she said, her voice rising in dismay, "that everyone should think him so cruel for something not his fault. It is not fair!"

One look from Captain Poldrennan and Verity realized how horribly petulant she must sound. Another embarrassed blush warmed her cheeks and she shyly looked away.

"I know how you must feel," the captain said. "And how badly you want things to be different. But so much damage has already been done . . ."

"I know that," Verity said. "And maybe there's really nothing I can do to clear his name. But I have to try."

Their horses grew restless as they stood in the path and Captain Poldrennan reached down to stroke the long neck of his mare. His eyes never left Verity's. "Yes, I suppose you do," he said at last.

"I was hoping you might be able to help in some way." She went on quickly, before he could object. "You are known to be James's friend, and yet your reputation seems to have suffered no ill by association. I thought perhaps among your other acquaintances you could . . ." She never finished the thought for she really had no clear idea what the captain could do.

"Mrs. Osborne," he said, "it is not the gentry you need to reach. They are less willing to paint one of their own so black—or at least more willing to forgive. Or ignore. Whatever the reasons, James would have no difficulty mixing in society if he wished. But he does not wish, or so I believe. He has remained isolated up on that hill for so long that few outside the nearest vicinity know anything of him."

Verity clucked her tongue in exasperation.

"The way to clear his name is through those who live and work on his own land. It is the miners and farmers you must reach. They are simple folk, some of them very superstitious. Theirs will be the most difficult minds to sway."

"I thought as much," Verity said. "It is what I hoped to do."

She told him about the Christmas baskets and smiled at his look of amazement. "I believe they were as surprised as you appear to be. As you might imagine, none of them offered much of a warm welcome. He wore his usual tight-lipped scowl, after all. Some of them looked positively terrified. But they behaved politely, and all expressed their gratitude, however reluctantly. Even so, it was a difficult ordeal for James."

"I do not doubt it," he said. "It cannot be pleasant for him to look upon the faces of men and women who purport to hate him, though, God knows, he must be used to it after all these years."

Captain Poldrennan shook his head. "Poor old James," he said, "has taken on the legendary evil of one of our giants or demons. Or like Tregeagle, who sold his soul to the devil."

He edged his horse slowly forward and Verity did the same with Titania. She was anxious to keep moving; if she read the weather correctly it would be raining very shortly.

"It did not help matters," the captain continued, "that one of their own, the Clegg boy, was also killed in the Pendurgan fire. Tales of James's wickedness have grown with years of exaggeration and outright fabrication, but the general belief in his cruelty has held firm. We Cornish, you know, are loath to let go of long-established dogma, especially where evil is concerned. We need our bogeymen to keep the children in line."

Despite the flippancy of his words, a note of despondency colored his voice. Verity leaned slightly in the saddle, tightening her knee on the horn, and reached out to touch the captain's arm. "I am glad he has you for a friend," she said.

He covered her hand briefly before she withdrew it. "I believe he has a friend in you as well, does he not?"

"Yes, he does."

The captain smiled. "You care for him, don't you?"

"Yes, of course," she replied, though she would never reveal the depth of her caring. To admit to friendship was enough. "And I do not believe he is evil," she continued. "I have seen what the sight of fire can do to him."

"You have?"

"Yes, I have." She would not elaborate. There were certain details that ought to remain private, even among friends. "He is ill, not evil. He deserves compassion and understanding, not hatred."

The captain's smile broadened and a distinct twinkle brightened his gray eyes. "My dear Mrs. Osborne, it was a fortunate day that brought you to Pendurgan. Perhaps old James will have another chance at happiness, after all."

Her cheeks flushed again. They were almost through the village and the clouds had darkened to the shade of gun metal. There was little time to obtain the advice she needed, so she pressed on, blushes or no.

"How do I reach the local people?" she asked. "How do I help him?"

"Start with the one they trust most," he said without hesitation.

"Old Grannie Pascow."

"Convince her and the others will follow soon enough."

Throughout the wet days of February, Verity took every opportunity to ride into St. Perran's. She sat at Grannie's hearth, chatting and drinking tea with the other women of the district who gathered there. Verity made a point to bring her own tea, since she knew it was very dear, and because most often Grannie's tea leaves were used over and over, so that they may as well have been drinking hot water.

Sometimes Verity brought an herbal mix she'd made up herself. Though some blends were more successful than others, Grannie and the other women always appreciated the offering. Once she brought a good, strong Darjeeling from Mrs. Chenhall's pantry. She had asked James's permission to raid the larder, claiming she did not wish to put a strain an Old Grannie's meager resources, and he had not objected.

"His lordship sends along the tea, with his compliments," she announced when she handed Kate Pascow the fine India blend.

Kate's eyes narrowed with suspicion. "Did he, now?" she asked, one skeptical brow arched expressively.

"Don't 'ee go mockin' Miz Verity," Grannie said in a stern voice. "She be not the type to come round tellin' tales. Recollect, she did bring Jammez on Christmas."

"How could I forget?" Kate said. "Like to've caused me an apoplexy, he did."

"He come to our farmhouse, too," Borra Nanpean volunteered in her soft, shy voice. "I thought it 'twere right kind o' him to come wid 'ee, Miz Verity. He never done that afore."

"He be doing a lot o' things he never done afore," Grannie said.

" 'Tis so," Hildy Spruggins said. "I do hear tell that he be helpin' with the lambin' this year. And Nat's brother Joe seen him plowin' up the north field, steering them big ol' oxen all by hisself."

"That is because he has no steward right now," Verity said. "Even so, you surely cannot believe he is above a bit of hard work? He cares for his land. And his mine. And all of you, as well. He always has."

Kate gave Verity a sidelong glance as she poured boiling water into Grannie's old brown teapot. "I do think the lady be sweet on Lord Heartless."

That set all the women to laughing, and Verity knew she must be blushing to the roots of her hair.

Grannie did not laugh. A frown deepened the creases between her brows as she glared at Verity in a most uncomfortable manner. Hers was not going to be an easy mind to change.

Verity let the conversation veer into other directions. She did not want to be any more obvious than necessary in her attempt to sway opinion. On subsequent visits, she simply continued to drop hints of James's hard work and sense of responsibility when the conversation allowed it. The rest of the time she went about maintaining her own credibility with the women. If she won and held on to their trust, perhaps they would more easily accept her views on James.

Strange as it seemed, this very small, very insulated community had in four short months accepted her, a "foreigner," into its bosom. Verity prayed for the soul of Edith Littleton each night, for if that fine lady had not been so willing to share her knowledge of herbs, Verity might not have found it so easy to be accepted here in Cornwall. Her remedies had helped many of the local families through bouts of winter colds, fever, and sore throats. Most popular of all, though, had been her Christmas pomanders and potpourris.

"We been gettin' a Christmas basket from Pendurgan long as I can remember," Tamson Penneck said. "But they always be filled with food—smoked meats and jams and pies and cider and other things to help us through the winter. It all be most welcome, to be sure. But it were a real pleasure to get somethin' that just be pretty to look at or nice to smell—a bit of extravagance, like. It made Christmas right special for me, I can tell 'ee."

So Verity's small effort at thoughtfulness had paid off. She now appeared to be accepted in a sort of lady-of-the-manor role. Despite her local heritage, Agnes Bodinar was not looked upon with any degree of affection. In fact, Verity got the impression she was actively disliked throughout the district.

Verity enjoyed sitting around Grannie's hearth with all the other local women. She had never been one to covet solitude, and it was sometimes very lonely for her at Pendurgan with only the waspish Anges for company while James was busy about the estate and the mines.

Agnes had grown particularly irritable lately; clearly she disapproved of the new amity between Verity and James. She had not seemed to mind nearly so much when she believed Verity to be James's mistress. Any real affection between them, though, would be seen as a threat to Rowena's memory.

Verity often wished she could make Agnes understand that there was no possibility of her usurping the role of Lady Harkness. But Agnes, when approached, refused to speak of the matter. More often than not lately, she refused to speak at all. She could be found silently perched on the edge of a chair, like a black crow in her worn and faded mourning clothes—stiff-backed, silent, grim, disdainful.

From the start, Verity had suspected Agnes was slightly unbalanced. She became more convinced of it as the winter wore on and the older woman's hostility grew more pronounced.

One cold evening in mid-February when she delivered her nightly infusion to James in the library, Verity approached him about another favor for the villagers. She asked if there was firewood or coal to spare for the cold stone cottages in St. Perran's.

"You are taking a great interest in the local families," he said, eyeing her speculatively.

"I do spend a lot of time with them, you know," Verity said. "I have nothing to do up here and there is no company, save for Mrs. Bodinar. I enjoy chatting with the local women. I only notice that they seldom have firewood and burn peat most of the time."

"They need only ask."

"But they won't, as you well know."

"Yes," he said, "I do well know. So they have asked you to intercede on their behalf?"

"Certainly not," she said. "It is my idea, not theirs. The peat fumes sting my eyes, so it is for very selfish reasons that I ask for firewood."

He cast her a knowing look and the half smile that still had the power to make her weak in the knees, no matter how hard she fought it. "I doubt that very much," he said. "But it shall be as you ask. I shall have Tomas load up a cart and distribute the wood."

For a moment, she was lost in the blue depths of his eyes, hardly hearing his words. When she was finally able to respond, her voice sounded too husky. "You are most kind, my lord."

He held her gaze for a long moment and she wondered if he, too, was thinking of that kiss on the moor. Or those kisses in the library before he'd . . . taken her. "I am nothing of the sort," he said at last. "I am simply helpless against any entreaty of yours, as I am sure you have discovered. I have not forgotten about Christmas. You fight hard when you want something, do you not? The villagers shall have their wood."

When she next visited Grannie Pascow's cottage, the sweet scent of woodsmoke filled the room. "I 'spect we do have 'ee to thank fer this, too?" Kate Pascow asked.

"Oh, no," Verity said as she seated herself beside Dorcas Muddle and reached out to stroke the soft cheek of her infant son. "You must thank his lordship. He wanted to put the Pendurgan surplus to good use. It was his idea, I assure you."

"Hmph." Kate's scornful snort was echoed in the faces of the other women.

Grannie kept a scowl firmly planted on her face, as she did whenever James was mentioned. Something about that recalcitrant look, after yet another generous offering from James, caused Verity to snap. She sprang to her feet.

"What is wrong with all of you?" Her voice rose almost to a shout, and she looked straight into the eyes of each of them, one after the other—Grannie, Kate Pascow, Ewa Dunstan, Hildy Spruggins, Lizzy Trethowan, Dorcas Muddle. "Why must you always think the worst of Lord Harkness?"

"For good reason," Ewa Dunstan said, "after what he done."

Verity fixed Ewa with a hard stare. "And what do you know of anything he may or may not have done? Except to give your husband a good job at Wheal Devoran. Or to keep your cottage in good repair. Or to look the other way, Hildy, while your Nat poaches game from his lordship's land. Or to allow your rents to go into arrears when the crops are bad—yes, Lizzy, I know about that, too."

She had spun to face each woman she addressed, pounding the air with her fist. The women looked at her as though she'd gone mad. "I ask you again, what do you know of what he may have done? What?"

After a long moment, Kate Pascow cleared her throat. "We done told 'ee," she said in a hesitant voice. "Old Nick Tresco, him what used to be steward at Pendurgan, he told us."

"Yes, I recall what you said about Nick Tresco," Verity said, facing Kate with hands on her hips. "But he did not see James start the fire, did he? He did not see him toss the two boys and then his own wife into the fire, did he? No, he only saw him standing there, watching. Standing there!" Exhausted by her unexpected outburst, Verity sank back into her chair. The six women eyed her skeptically. She took a few breaths to compose herself, then continued in a softer voice.

"Just standing there," she repeated. "Did it never occur to any of you how strange that was? Even if he had started the fire deliberately, when a witness came on the scene would he not have pretended to help, to deflect suspicion from himself? Grannie, you have known James since he was a boy, have you not?"

Grannie's small, dark eyes narrowed. "Aye," she finally said, "I done knowed him since he were borned. Everybody here," she said with a sweep of her hand, "done knowed him all their lives."

"And was he a vicious, evil little boy?" Verity asked.

Grannie lifted her chin a notch. "No, he weren't."

"What was he like, then?"

Grannie's posture relaxed a bit. She took a swallow of tea before answering. "He were just a normal little boy. Full of life. Him and Alan Poldrennan, they done be thick as thieves, always up to some mischief, but nothin' vicious, like. Just good-natured devilment. He were a nice young feller, too, as he growed up. Heard tell he did butt heads with old Lord Harkness often, though. That be why he left for the army, or so it were told."

"And it wasn't until he returned from Spain," Verity said, "that he changed into . . . something else?"

"Aye, he did come home mean and spiteful as the devil," Grannie said. "It were a sad thing to see what did become of him, how bad he turned out."

The other women nodded and mumbled agreement. Verity reined in her anger.

"He did not turn out so badly," she said, trying with great difficulty to keep her voice even. "You have all forgot about the lively young boy you once knew and created a monster out of him. Did it never occur to any of you that he might have suffered greatly in the war?" She had to be careful here. She wanted their understanding, but she could not reveal all she knew without betraying James in a way he would never forgive.

"Did any of you consider that he might have been wounded in ways you could never understand?" she went on. "And is it not possible he has been made to feel like a criminal for something he did not do?"

Once again, it was Kate who finally spoke into the awkward silence that followed Verity's words. "I do think, Miz Verity, that the man done bewitched you."

"Hush, Kate!" Grannie's stern voice brought a flush to Kate's cheeks. "Let Verity Osborne have her say," the old woman continued. "Now, what is it 'ee be tryin' to tell us?"

Verity managed a wan smile and spoke directly to Grannie. "You say he was a normal little boy and a decent young man. In your heart, do you really believe the boy you knew could have killed the woman he loved and their child, and the Clegg boy as well?"

Verity watched Grannie's face as she considered a response. The old woman set her mouth in a grim line while a knobby finger tapped against her lips. The only sound in the room was the crackling of the wood fire and the occasional gurgle from Dorcas Muddle's baby.

When at last she was ready to speak, Grannie Pascow leaned over to place her cup of tea on an old stool. She sat up straight, placed her plump forearms squarely along the chair arms, and faced Verity with a direct, piercing gaze.

"Old Nick Tresco done be the only witness to that fire," she said. "He told his tale and left Pendurgan, along with half the servants. Jago and Athwenna Chenhalls, them an' their family do know their place and don't never go tellin' tales of goin's on up to the big house. And Mary Tregelly, she do be loyal to the grave. So we only did have Old Nick's word for what did happen there."

Her eyes narrowed slightly as she seemed to weigh her thoughts. When she finally spoke again, she leaned forward, one hand fisted on the edge of the chair arm. "I tell 'ee true," she said, and looked hard at each of the other women, as though daring them to challenge her, "that I never did believe it at first. Not at first." She fixed her gaze on Verity. "But then Jammez, he did act like he done it. He never did seem to be sorry. Just got meaner and meaner. He did act like he done murder, so he were treated like he done murder. He ain't never denied it, all these years."

Verity collapsed back against the chair like a deflated balloon. Relief so overwhelmed her that she felt the sting of tears building up behind her eyes. Success was within her grasp, for Grannie Pascow had once doubted James's guilt.

She took a few ragged breaths, determined not to cry and give any credence to Kate's suspicions about her motives. "Just because James never denied it," she said in a voice more tremulous than she would have liked, "does not mean he did it. You say he got meaner. Have you considered perhaps his fearsome manner was simply a way of masking his pain? I tell you all that I know—I *know*—what happened that day of the fire. I cannot reveal what I know. But I will tell you that he is not to blame. He could not have saved those boys, or Rowena. It was impossible."

"How impossible?" Kate asked, her voice scornful. "He were there. Right there!"

"I cannot tell you more," Verity said. "Only that it was impossible for him to act. He could not save them, and that fact has tortured him for almost seven years."

"But—"

"I do think I understand," Grannie said, interrupting Kate with a raised hand. "I think 'ee be sayin' that somethin' happened to Jammez in the war. Somethin' more than a bullet in the leg."

So they knew of his leg injury, but not how it had actually happened. "Yes, something did happen, but I can say no more. Just remember the boy you knew, and consider how he could possibly have become the monster you created, the monster he allowed you to create."

"He were always a proud one," Grannie said.

"Not likely he'd let on to some . . . some weakness. I take yer point, girl." The old woman gave her a look that made Verity feel as though she could see straight into her heart. A blush heated her cheeks and she dropped her gaze before the old woman could see more than she ought.

"My, my," Grannie said. "Jammez done found him a fine champion in 'ee, Verity Osborne."

Chapter 10

At Alan Poldrennan's request, James had ridden out with Verity to Bosreath. "She must be bored silly at Pendurgan," he said. "I'm sure Mother will be pleased to have the two of you for tea."

The day had been arranged and the weather had cooperated. They saw Alan awaiting them at the entrance of the modern brick house. Growing up in a place as old as Pendurgan, James considered any house only a few hundred years old as modern. Bosreath had been built something less than one hundred years ago, during the reign of George I. Its lines were clean, compact, and symmetrical—about as different as it could be from the sprawling granite mass of Pendurgan.

"My goodness," Verity said as they ambled down the granite drive. "It looks like home."

"Home?"

"My father's house in Lincolnshire had a very similar look—red brick, rows of white paned windows, a pillared porch topped with a simple pediment. How lovely." A note of melancholy colored her voice and a wistful smile tugged at her lips.

"It makes you homesick," James said.

Her smile broadened when she turned toward him. "A little," she said. "But our brick house was set in lush green wolds. Beyond Bosreath's manicured lawn are the same rocky moors we see from Pendurgan. It is not at all like Lincolnshire."

Her words brought a frown to his face and she hurried to add, "I did *not* say Pendurgan, and Cornwall, are not as lovely as Lincolnshire. They are so. But also very different. If you will not tell the captain I said so," she added in a conspiratorial tone, "I will confess to you that Pendurgan suits its setting far better than does Bosreath. Pendurgan seems to have sprung up straight out of the ground beneath it. Bosreath, charming as it is, looks as though it had been carried from some other place and dropped here."

James smiled at the image of some great bird dropping the house on the moor as it flew past. Or perhaps Cormoran or one of the other legendary giants. The notion tickled him so that he was actually smiling when they reached the entrance.

Alan called out, "Good afternoon!" as they reined their mounts to a halt. He reached up and placed his hands on Verity's waist to lift her from the sidesaddle. Was it James's imagination, or did Alan's hands linger a trifle longer than was absolutely necessary?

Perhaps James was overly sensitive because of how very beautiful Verity looked today. He had been aware of it from the moment they left Pendurgan. She wore the same outdated green habit and black beaver hat with its faded short green plume that she always wore when they rode, yet there was a new sort of glow about her, in her eyes and in her voice, that unnerved him.

Had she taken extra pains with her appearance for the visit to Bosreath? Did the green velvet hug her curves more tightly than usual? Did she have to smile so brilliantly for Alan? Did Alan have to be so effusive in his welcome?

His good mood shattered, James dismounted and handed the reins to a waiting groom. By the time he climbed the porch steps, Alan had Verity's hand tucked firmly in the crook of his arm, leading her into the entry hall.

They were met in the modest drawing room by Alan's mother. The tiny birdlike woman fluttered across the room to meet Verity, chirping a string of nonstop greetings and inanities. "How lovely. So good of you to come. Isn't this nice? At last we meet. Won't you sit down? Such a lovely shade of green. So pleased to meet you. How kind of you to call."

Mrs. Poldrennan's fidgety movements matched her nervous chatter, her hands and fingers constantly in motion. James hoped Verity was not put off by her manner, thinking she somehow made the woman uncomfortable. Alan's mother had been nervous and jittery ever since he'd known her. She was like a high-strung terrier nipping at your heels whenever you entered the house. James thought her a trial, but

Alan always laughed and used his gentle persuasions to quiet her, or to politely dismiss her when he and James preferred to dine alone.

Verity handled Alan's mother remarkably well. Her calm patience seemed to soothe the woman somewhat. She even tactfully offered to pour when Mrs. Poldrennan's shaky hands had sloshed tea over the rim of the first cup poured. "For you must have worked all day," Verity said, "to keep this lovely house in such good order. Allow me to relieve you of at least this one small task."

Mrs. Poldrennan was delighted to do so, and embarked on a monologue of how easily exhausted she was these days, how quickly she became winded, how her bones were affected by the cold, and on and on. Verity appeared quickly to have determined that the woman enjoyed complaining. She never once offered one of her herbal remedies as solace, but only nodded and smiled sympathetically.

Still irritated by Alan's marked attentions to Verity, and equally piqued by the way she positively basked in those attentions, James sat silent and sullen throughout the brief meal. Alan steered the conversation away from his mother's complaints to more general topics and Verity drew in Mrs. Poldrennan as often as possible. She tried to draw in James as well, but accepted his rebuffs with an indulgent smile.

After three-quarters of an hour had elapsed, Alan suggested a walk through his small garden. The day was clear and sunny, so they all agreed to the plan. Alan was able to dissuade his mother from joining them, warning she might take a chill and that she really ought to lie down and rest. Mrs. Poldrennan agreed without argument, though she fussed over the rest of them, especially Verity, to make sure they were wrapped up warm enough to venture outside. She dashed upstairs and returned with a stack of woolen scarves, insisting each of them take one. She gave Verity two, and helped her to wrap them about her neck and shoulders.

"You must forgive my mother," Alan said once they had left the house. "She tends to dither and fuss, but she means well."

"I found her quite charming," Verity said.

Alan looked at James and winked. "A born diplomat," he said.

When Alan indicated the path to the garden, to James's utter astonishment Verity moved to his side and took his arm. All of a sudden, the day grew warmer, the sun shone brighter, and James's black mood melted away. He bent his head to look at her, and she gave him a smile that sent a bolt of heat coursing through his veins like a shot of whiskey.

A flicker of surprise lit Alan's eyes for the briefest moment. Then he moved to Verity's other side and offered his arm. "You shall have a double escort," he said, "as we wander through my vast and spectacular garden."

James felt not a twinge of jealousy that Alan held her other hand on his arm. She had approached James first, after all, and he felt ridiculously cocky for it. Her only motive might have been simply to reassure him she had no designs on Alan. It did not matter. He had been so circumspect in his behavior, had so seldom allowed himself to touch her in any untoward manner, that he relished the soft pressure of her gloved fingers on his sleeve. He reached over and covered her hand with his.

The garden was small and not terribly impressive in its sparse winter foliage, though a few early primroses bloomed brightly. They circled its perimeter three times before Alan suggested they be seated on two facing stone benches on either side of the path. Verity released Alan first, so that it was a simple matter for James to draw her down beside him on one of the benches.

James's mood had brightened considerably during their walk. They had all talked and laughed—yes, even *he* had laughed—about every subject that came to mind. It was one of the few completely contented days he'd experienced in many years: comfortable, unguarded, frivolous conversation with the only two people in the world he could call friend.

When the subject of some activity or other in the village came up, it triggered a memory. "Speaking of St. Perran's," James said, "the damnedest thing happened yesterday."

Verity's head bobbed up like a cork. "Oh?"

He eyed her quizzically. "Yes. I had been out in the fields with Mark Penneck and rode back through the village. Old Grannie Pascow stood leaning out her half door and waved me over. Said she wanted to thank me for the firewood, and to tell me how the family had enjoyed the Christmas ham. Later, as I reached the end of the lane, Ewa Dunstan called at me. When I pulled up, she stood there in the lane and thanked me, too, for the firewood, and told me how grateful she and Jacob were to have had the roof leak repaired."

Verity chewed on her lower lip and looked away. Alan raised his brows in question. "What is so strange about that?" he asked.

"Alan! These are the same women who gather their children, close the doors, and draw the curtains every time I pass by. Now suddenly they are anxious to express their gratitude to me. Old Grannie never speaks to me but to chide and berate, or to hiss some epithet at me. Ewa Dunstan hasn't spoken more than three words to me in all her life, and more often than not makes a surreptitious sign of the devil when she sees me. Yesterday she still found it difficult to look me in the eye, but she seemed compelled to speak to me. I cannot imagine what has got into them. Can you?"

They both looked at Verity. When she lifted her head, her eyes were overly bright and her lips, though smiling, trembled slightly. "Is it not wonderful?"

James knew in that moment that what he had suspected was true. Verity had been the instrument of the changes he sensed in the village. Her influence had begun to break down barriers he thought could never be breached. If Alan had not been there, James might have been tempted to enfold her in his arms and never let go. What spark of goodness in his wretched life had earned him the right to such a sweet advocate?

Verity walked into St. Perran's the next day, for there was no threat of rain. As she ambled down the lane toward the village she savored memories of yesterday, of the ride to Bosreath, of the walk through the garden, of James's warm hand covering hers on his arm.

It had been the first physical sign of affection she had received from him since that brief kiss on the moor. All throughout the evening and again today she had cherished the remembrance of the sheer pleasure of his touch. If this was all she ever had from him, it would surely be enough.

Verity walked to Grannie's door. The upper half was open as though it were a warm, summer day. Kate saw her and waved her in.

Grannie's parlor, as she liked to call it, was uncharacteristically empty of visitors. Kate and Grannie had moved a long table near the hearth and were busy making what appeared to be pancakes in a black iron skillet balanced on a tall trivet over the fire. Dozens of the thin cakes were stacked on a pewter plate at one end of the table. Verity stood in the doorway, uncertain if she should intrude.

"Come in, come in," Grannie said, waving her inside with a spoon. "We do be about done. Kate can finish up." She wiped her floury hands on her apron and sank down on a bench that had been pulled up next to the table. She indicated Verity should join her. "*Re'm fay,* I do be worn to death. I be glad you come, Verity Osborne. It do give me an excuse to rest my weary bones."

"Is there something I can do to help?" Verity asked.

"Thank 'ee, no, Miz Verity," Kate Pascow said. "It only do need a bit o' jam to finish up, then we be done."

"They look delicious," Verity said as she watched

Kate drop a spoonful of jam in the center of each pancake, roll it up, and sprinkle it with sugar.

"Aye, and they'll be gone soon enough," Grannie said.

"Oh, I *am* intruding," Verity said, and rose to leave. "You are planning some sort of family celebration. You must forgive me for getting in your way."

"Sit yerself down, Verity Osborne," Grannie said. " 'Tedn't no celebration. Only the nicky-nan boys."

"The what?"

Kate laughed at Verity's confusion. "Don't s'pose they do have nicky-nan boys up-country, eh?"

"Not that I know of."

Grannie added her laughter to Kate's, her plump form shaking with mirth. Verity grinned at both women.

"Poor ign'rant foreigner," Kate said, smiling broadly. "Best 'ee should tell her, Grannie, afore she do make a fool o' herself."

Grannie wiped her eyes with the back of a hand, and leaned slightly forward on the bench, hands on her knees. "It be Shrove Tuesday today," the old woman began.

"Ah. So it is," Verity said. "I'd forgot."

"Every rascally boy in the district do come on Shrove Tuesday, callin' theirselves the nicky-nan boys, threatenin' mischief if 'ee doesn't give 'em pancakes."

"Aha. No wonder you've been working so hard," Verity said. "I suppose that's where all the other women are. At home making pancakes?"

"Aye," Kate said. "Else no tellin' what them boys'll do."

"Goodness, I hope Mrs. Chenhalls has made up a batch, too."

Kate's busy hands froze and she shot Grannie a sharp look. The old woman shook her head and clucked her tongue. "Ain't no nicky-nan boys goin' up to Pendurgan, Verity Osborne."

"Oh, of course," Verity said. "I ought to have known. But do you think—"

"Ea! Ea! Ea!"

Verity almost jumped out of her skin at the sound of the strange, high-pitched cries.

"Ea! Ea! Ea!"

"Here they be," Kate said. She placed the last of the filled cakes on the plate and brushed the sugar off her hands. Grannie rose and leaned out the door, glaring at the large gathering of boys outside. There must have been thirty or more of them, all ages and sizes.

"What do 'ee pesky wags want, eh?" Grannie said.

To Verity's delight, the boys began to chant a rhyme.

Nick, nicky, nan,
Nick, nicky, nan,
Give me some pancake and then I'll be gone.
But if 'ee give me none, I'll throw a great stone
And down, down, down your door shall come!
Nick, nicky, nan.

"Take the pancakes, then, if 'twill keep us safe o' yer mischief," Grannie said. She opened the bottom half of the door and stepped just outside. She held the plate high amid the pushing and shoving and shrieking and giggling, and made sure every boy had his share. In little more than the blink of an eye, the plate was empty.

The rowdy group quickly dispersed, calling out thanks around mouthfuls of pancake. A tiny red-haired figure who'd been hidden in the crowd stepped forward and grinned impishly, red jam stains framing his mouth.

"Miz Osborne!" Davey said. "I be a nicky-nan boy!"

Verity bent and tousled the mop of red hair. "So you are."

"Pa say I be old 'nuff this year. Did we scare 'ee?"

"Almost to death," Verity said. She gave a mock shudder and Davey squealed with delight. "You'd better run and catch up with the others or you'll miss your cakes."

Davey gave her a quick hug, then tore off down the lane toward the next cottage. "Ea! Ea! Ea!"

Verity helped Kate tidy up the room from the cooking and then move the table against the wall where it usually stood. They pulled up three chairs close to the fire and sat with their toes outstretched on the hearth. Kate had saved three pancakes, and they enjoyed them along with a cup of tea.

"That little redheaded tacker sure do take to 'ee," Grannie said.

"Yes," Verity said. "Davey and I are great friends. I am glad he was able to come down from Pendurgan to take part in all the fun."

"They always do," Grannie said.

"Did James?"

Grannie gave Verity a sidelong glance. "Jammez

again. It always do be Jammez with 'ee, Verity Osborne."

"I'm sorry," Verity said, bending her head in hopes of hiding the blush that heated her cheeks. "But you said you knew him as a boy. I just wondered . . ."

"Aye, he were a nicky-nan boy, just like the rest," Grannie said. "Didn't matter none that he come from the big house. He run wild through St. Perran's along wid all t'others."

"What was it like at Pendurgan before all the troubles began?" Verity asked. Gonetta had told her about old Christmas traditions of mummers and the caroling at Pendurgan, community traditions that had lapsed since the tragic fire. It was another way in which James had encouraged his dark reputation—putting a stop to old customs. She had learned in her short time here that the Cornish people set great store by customs. Might it not be a good step toward changing attitudes if some of those customs were revived?

"I assume," she continued, "that people actually came up to the house at times, during special occasions. They must not have always avoided it the way they do now."

Grannie crossed her arms over her ample chest and pursed her lips. It was a long moment before she spoke.

"No, 'twere not always like 'tis now," she said. "All my life, old Pendurgan be the great house in the district where the great people gathered. How we did love it when we did be invited to come up. We'd get all cleaned up and put on our Sunday best and feel so proud to be goin' up the big house."

"I remember that, too," Kate said. " 'Twere always a grand time."

"When did you come?" Verity asked. "At Christmas?"

"Aye, at Christmas," Grannie said. "And also fer the annual tenants' breakfast, and o' course fer the—"

"The midsummer's eve festival!" Kate said. "Oh, my, what fun that was."

"They held a festival at Pendurgan?" Verity asked.

"A grand one," Kate said. "Every year at midsummer's eve. 'Twere lovely. I do miss that, I tell 'ee."

"Tell me about the festival," Verity said. An idea had come to her—a wild and wonderful idea—that took root and began to grow, nurtured by the stories that followed.

"You must be out of your mind."

"I hope I am not," Verity said in response to Agnes Bodinar's outburst. "Indeed, I believe I am not. I have heard that the Pendurgan festival was the highlight of the year in the district, and even beyond. It seems a shame such a fond old tradition should have lapsed."

Agnes gave a disdainful snort. "It lapsed because no one in the district—in all of Cornwall—will have anything to do with Pendurgan now." She glared at Verity as though challenging her to deny it. "Forget about the wretched festival. No one will come."

Ever since Verity had blithely announced her intention to resurrect the midsummer's eve festival, James had been stunned into silence. He knew what she was about, of course. For reasons still incomprehensible to him, Verity had set out to change the hearts and minds of the local people, to repair his blackened reputation. This idea of the festival moved him more than he could ever have imagined.

A revival of the midsummer festival was a significant enterprise, one that could have major results, one way or the other. If Verity's plans failed it would hurt her more than it would James, who was accustomed to the fear and loathing of his own people. But if her plans succeeded . . . The very notion tied his stomach in knots.

It had been so long, so long since anyone other than Alan Poldrennan had visited Pendurgan. James had preferred to keep himself apart from local society. Did he still?

"Can you really be so sure no one would come?" Verity asked. She looked at James, inviting his response. "Did you hold a festival that no one attended?"

"It was not necessary," Agnes replied, her tone waspish and scornful. "There has never been any question that the entire district would avoid Pendurgan at all costs."

"But are you certain?" Verity asked.

Agnes pressed her fists hard against the edge of the table and leaned forward toward Verity. "Of course I am certain." She spoke through clenched teeth, her jaw rigid. "You silly little fool. Have you not lived here long enough to realize how thoroughly ostracized we are up here? Do you not know that the very names Pendurgan and Harkness are loathsome throughout the district?" She tilted her head back, slanted a glance toward James, then curled her lip into a sneer. "Or has he got you so besotted you cannot see the truth?"

Verity held Agnes with her forthright, unflinching gaze. She had backbone, to be sure. That quiet courage was one of the things he most admired about Verity. Admired and envied. For she had the courage to fight for the vindication of his name, when he had long ago given up hope that such a thing was even possible.

"I understand what you are saying," Verity said, her voice calm and controlled, "though, of course, you have lived with the . . . the aftermath much longer than I have. I can never know what it must have been like for you all those years ago, when the tragedy occurred. But perhaps as an outsider, I can see what those of you closer to the situation cannot. It occurs to me, for example, that elimination of some of the old traditions like the Christmas mummers and the midsummer festival may have simply aggravated any bad feelings in the district. It may have done more harm than good."

James stared at Verity, captivated by her tenacity. He wondered if there might not be some truth in what she said, though in his gut he knew Agnes had the right of it. It did not matter. Verity's belief in him, however misplaced, was something he would always treasure, even if he ultimately discouraged her from acting on those convictions. He was not at all sure he wanted her to go through with this idea of the festival.

Agnes crossed her arms over her thin chest and

peered down the length of her nose at Verity. "You came here under circumstances that would oblige any sensible woman to hide in shame," she said, her voice brittle and sharp as broken glass. "And yet you . . . you interfere and meddle in business that does not concern you, insinuating yourself into village life, dredging up old wounds, making a nuisance of yourself. Somehow you think you can make a difference by reviving the festival. Well, you're wrong. You have no idea what you are talking about. I tell you no one, *no one*, would have come."

"You may be right," Verity said. "Six years ago, so soon after it happened, people may have stayed away. But is it not time to leave the past behind? It is not simply a matter of restoring festivals and the like." She turned to look at James. "It is the distance you maintain, the way you've withdrawn from everything that has allowed all manner of foolish tales to spring up. I have spoken to some of the villagers, and they have told me they would be pleased to see the festival revived. They *would* come, I feel sure of it."

"Hmph," Agnes snorted. "So they claim, but I do not believe it for one minute. They would plan some sort of mischief, to be sure. Or more likely, they may simply pretend to go along with you, all the while laughing behind your back, laughing at how you have come under *his* spell."

"Agnes!" James had finally had enough of her spiteful tongue. "You go too far, madam."

"Do I?" Agnes glared at him.

"Yes, you do. You have no cause to say such things

to Verity. She is our guest and . . . my friend." His eyes met Verity's, and she smiled so sweetly he had to look away.

"Your *friend*?" Agnes gave a derisive sniff. "Call her what you will. Everyone knows what *she* is, but clearly she has been seduced into believing *you* are something other than you are. And now that you have her under your control, you have set her to clear your name for you. Well, it cannot be done." She rose so quickly her chair almost toppled over behind her. "Go ahead, missy, do your best for your . . . your lover and see what good it does. But do not expect me to be any part of your foolhardy schemes." In a swirl of black skirts, she left the dining room.

James watched her exit with exasperation. He was used to Agnes's behavior and had made every effort over the last several years to ignore it. After all, she had more cause than anyone else to thoroughly despise him. There were times, however, when her incessant venom became intolerable.

He gave a weary sigh before his eyes met Verity's. "You must forgive Agnes," he said. "She—"

"Oh, I understand, my lord." She smiled in response to his lifted brow. "James. I understand her anger. She is only throwing out words in anguish, poor thing. She lost her only daughter and now thinks that I . . ." Verity's cheeks flushed and her gaze dropped to her dinner plate. She said no more, though they both knew what words had been left unspoken.

"It is more than just that," James said. "Agnes has suffered more than anyone these past years. Not only has she had to deal with the deaths of her daughter and grandson, but she is forced to depend upon the man who killed them."

"James." Verity raised her head and shot him a concerned look. "You must stop saying that. You did *not* kill them. You know you did not, yet you seem to want everyone to believe you did. I do not understand you. Such remarks only encourage the villainous legend of Lord Heartless to prosper and grow."

He regarded her gravely. "Agnes is right, you know. It is too late. My name is too black to be restored." He reached over and touched her hand briefly. "But I do appreciate the effort."

Verity looked down at the hand where his fingers had brushed hers. "It is worth the effort," she whispered. "I owe you . . . that much."

It became more and more difficult to ignore the affection for her—or was it more?—that had begun to blossom in his heart when her words caused the damned organ to dance a jig in his chest. "You owe me nothing," he said. She had already given him more than he deserved, while all he could do was take. He had nothing to give in return. "You owe me nothing."

"Nonsense," she said, dismissing his words with a wave of her hand. "Besides, the festival will give me something to do. I prefer to be busy at something, and there is only so much I can do with my herbals. It will give me pleasure to plan the festival, truly. Please, do not ask me to abandon the idea. I would so enjoy doing it, and I *know* people will come. They will." Her eyes were ablaze with enthusiasm and her voice had become decidedly impassioned. She was almost irresistible.

"Yes, I suspect you will be able to convince any number of people to come," James said, thinking she could probably charm the piskeys from their faerie grove if she set her mind to it.

"Then you will allow it?"

He gave her a sidelong glance. "If you must know, the whole idea scares the bloody hell out of me."

She pulled a face. "Then you are indeed afraid they will not come?"

"On the contrary. I am very much afraid they will."

"Oh." She knitted her brows as she puzzled over his words. She looked so adorably confused he had to bite back a smile.

"It has been a very long time, you see, since people gathered at Pendurgan," he said. "I am not quite sure I'm prepared."

Her face lit up like a thousand candles. "You will see, my lord. You will see. If you open your home and your heart to these good people, they will not scorn you. A resumption of some sort of normalcy in the district can only be a good thing. If you will but begin to set things to right once more, they will smile upon you with gratitude and be happy."

He could no longer restrain himself. James reached for her hand and brought her fingers to his lips. There was much he would like to have said. "Thank you," was all he could manage.

She slowly—reluctantly?—retrieved her hand. Her cheeks blushed rosily and she looked away briefly. When her eyes met his again, they were fired once more with excitement. "This will be so much fun, I declare. You must tell me, James, the sorts of entertainments people would most enjoy. I can guess about the general sort of thing, but there are perhaps Cornish games and customs that I know nothing about. There must also be music, of course. And dancing. Are there any traditional Cornish dances we should plan for? And how do we go about arranging for booths and sellers of various goods? Oh, and the food! We must plan ahead for lots of food. You must tell me if—"

"Verity!"

She stopped chattering and gazed at him quizzically, head cocked to one side. He smiled broadly and noted how her eyes softened to a liquid brown as she watched him. He had not failed to note her frequent use of "we" as she spoke of her plans. It gave him a strangely heady feeling.

"You have almost three months and more to prepare," he said. "There is no need to rush into it this very minute. Mrs. Tregelly can answer many of your questions on the games and dances and such. She has helped plan many a midsummer festival at Pendurgan. And Mrs. Chenhalls can advise on the food and drink."

"Wonderful!" She leaned forward in her chair and gazed at him with infectious eagerness. "Then we shall—"

"But I must warn you to be careful of Agnes."

His words brought a hint of apprehension to her eyes.

"She already has some notions about our friendship," James said. "You know what she thinks." Verity nodded. "Agnes will make this very difficult for you. She hates me, and with good reason. Because of what she thinks is between us, she no doubt has as little love for you as she does for me. She will not like to see you try to mend my fences for me. She will use her own venom to tear them down again. Be careful of her. It was Rowena, you know, who always arranged the festival, even during my absences. Agnes will take no pleasure in watching you take Rowena's place."

A look of profound sadness gathered in Verity's eyes. "Poor woman. How it must pain her. But what about you, James? Your pain must have been greater even than Agnes's. Will it be awkward for you to see me planning the festival, just as Lady Harkness had done?"

Her question took him aback. Perhaps he ought to have felt some twinge of regret that someone else now took on tasks Rowena had once done, but he did not. He had loved Rowena, and there would ever be a dull ache in his heart for the loss of her. In truth, though, he had spent so many years consumed with despair over his role in her death that he had often forgot simply to miss her.

But Verity was not Rowena. She was as different from Rowena as she could possibly be—in looks, in temperament, in character. A comparison of the two had seldom even crossed his mind.

"No, it will not be awkward for me," he said at last, though in truth his unrequited desire for her, and his promise not to act on it, made her mere presence exceedingly awkward for him at times. Like now, when frustration was so painful it was a physical ache. "I have never thought of you as Rowena's usurper, Verity. You do not even bring her to mind. She was so . . . Well, you are nothing like Rowena."

An unreadable emotion flickered briefly in Verity's eyes, but she smiled quickly and the expression disappeared. "Then if you have no objections, my lord, I would ask your permission to proceed with plans for the midsummer's eve festival."

"You have it," he said. "Along with my gratitude for your efforts. But I must ask one more thing of you."

"Yes?"

"If Agnes is right and no one comes, you must not blame yourself."

A smile wreathed her face and lit her eyes, almost taking his breath away. "No one come? Don't be silly, my lord. *Everyone* will come!"

For her sake, James hoped she was right.

Verity threw herself into the planning of the midsummer festival with abandon. She was determined to succeed. After quizzing everyone at Pendurgan and all the ladies of St. Perran's, she had a pretty clear notion of what the festivals had been like in the past. She had discarded the fantasy of making this one the grandest of all. It was enough that it be familiar. Everyone seemed to have fond memories of the Pendurgan festivals. If nothing else, those memories alone would bring them back. Verity was sure of it.

One constant thread in all the recollections of the festival, though, had made her uneasy. It was the custom in Cornwall to light huge bonfires at midsummer's eve. There could be no festival, she was told, without a bonfire, and for that reason Verity had been ready to cancel all festival plans.

But James convinced her to proceed. "If I know it

is there, I will be fine," he assured her. "It is sudden, unexpected blazes that seem to affect me. I shall simply be cautious when the fire is lit. After that, there should be no problem." No matter how many times she offered to call it off, James had insisted she go on with her plans.

One afternoon, Verity invited Mrs. Poldrennan to tea, and when the captain came to collect her afterward, she had the opportunity to pull him aside and ask about the wisdom of the festival.

"I am so concerned for James," she said, "and how he might react to the bonfire. It is the only aspect of the festival that truly makes me nervous."

"I would not worry about it," the captain said. "James is no doubt right. If he is prepared for it, he will have no trouble. You and I can both stay close at his side, just to be sure. Besides, I think the whole idea is splendid. It is long overdue."

"I'm sure you are right," she said, "though I cannot help being concerned. Not only are there . . . sad associations with fire, but James—"

"Is it not fitting," Agnes said, her approach unnoticed by Verity, "that the master of a festival of fire is himself so well linked with fire?"

The spiteful remark brought an awkward hush to the room, silencing even the tittering Mrs. Poldrennan. The captain was the first to respond. "Come now, Mrs. Bodinar," he said, "I doubt the people will associate the bonfires with what happened here almost seven years ago. Besides, it is too much a part of tradition. I do not believe the festival would be a success without the fires."

"I suspect you have the right of it," Verity said, ignoring Agnes's disdainful snort.

"As for me," the captain said, "I think the fires make the whole thing so much more festive. Once, when I was in Penzance at midsummer, flaming tar barrels atop tall poles were placed throughout the streets of the town. It was the most spectacular sight. I say, why don't you do that for your festival, Mrs. Osborne? Flaming tar barrels throughout the estate. What do you say?"

"I don't know, Captain," she replied. "I am still trying to accept the notion of a bonfire."

"I think it is a lovely idea, Alan," his mother said, plucking at his sleeve. "It is something I should certainly like to see."

"I agree," Agnes said, smiling at the captain. "The more fires the better. Perhaps the old place will burn to the ground."

Verity frowned at her. She had hoped Agnes would be more polite in company, but apparently not. She seemed to be getting more vicious, determined to see that the festival was a failure.

"I hope it will not come to that," Verity said. "I am willing, though reluctant, to agree to a bonfire, but I will have to think about the tar barrels, Captain."

"I am at your service," he said, "if you decide in favor of them."

"Did you know," Agnes said, "that the fires were meant to strengthen the sun at the beginning of its long journey down toward the winter solstice?" She gave a mirthless chuckle. "Fire to feed the terrible pagan god. Again I say, how appropriate."

Verity wished they would get off the subject of fire. "I recollect some business about lights and candles at midsummer in Lincolnshire," she said. "But it was not the focal point of any celebrations. Mostly I remember picking St. John's wort to make into wreaths. But even it is a sun symbol, is it not, with its bright yellow flower. Did I tell you, Mrs. Poldrennan, that I plan to make wreaths this year?"

"To ward off evil spirits?"

Verity smiled at the serious tone in Mrs. Poldrannan's voice. "No, ma'am. Just to look pretty. I am hoping to enlist Mrs. Bodinar's help in weaving them this year."

Agnes frowned, but did not reject the idea. Verity bit back a smile. Edith Littleton had once said, "If someone doesn't like something you're doing, ask them to help."

The Poldrennans stayed for a short time longer, but declined the invitation to stroll the gardens. Mrs. Poldrennan was feeling tired and wished to return home, and the captain acquiesced.

When they were gone, Agnes turned on Verity. "What do you mean, trying to involve *me* in your horrid little festival?" she said. "I told you once, I want nothing to do with it."

"I hoped you had changed your mind," Verity said. "I could use your help. I have always admired the flowers you embroider so beautifully. I thought perhaps weaving a few real ones might be something you would enjoy."

"Hmph. We shall see."

Verity cast her a brilliant smile. It was the first real sign that there might be a chance to win over the old woman.

The rest of the Pendurgan household had thrown themselves into the planning with obvious pleasure. Verity was the center of all activity, coordinating every aspect of the event. She took notes and made endless lists of things to do and ideas to consider and questions to be answered. She sat for hours with Pendurgan's cook and made lists of foods to prepare. Mrs. Tregelly helped make lists of vendors and food stalls and planned a trip into Bodmin to approach various shopkeepers about setting up stalls at the festival. Gonetta volunteered to make bunches of herbs tied with colored ribbons for girls to throw in the bonfire.

Young Davey was determined to help as well. His father, who had agreed to help organize sports and contests for the men and boys, enlisted Davey's help in finding local boys to compete in the foot races.

Even James, though busy with estate business in the absence of a steward, did what he could to help. He worked with Jago Chenhalls to build rudimentary structures for food stalls and wrestling matches. He even volunteered to go into Bodmin, or farther if needed, to engage a troupe of players.

Verity's lists began to grow. She had lists of food, lists of games and contests, lists of materials to make or buy, lists of entertainments, lists of potential helpers to prepare food and fairings, lists of tasks requiring workmen, lists of schedules, lists of questions, and on and on. She carried them about in her pockets and was liable to pull one out at any moment when a new idea or question came to her.

"I ain't never seen the like, Verity Osborne," Grannie Pascow said when Verity next visited her.

She watched Verity unload her stuffed pockets and laughed so that her plump bosom jiggled like aspic. " 'Ee do got a list fer everything. I declare I never did see so many lists."

"It is a big project, Grannie, and I need to be organized if I am to pull it off. Now, let's go over the entertainments once again, to make sure we haven't forgotten anything."

Verity spread out a list on Grannie's trestle table. She had ruthlessly taxed Grannie's memory on past festivals, and listed all the various entertainments that had ever taken place. She had no notion of introducing all of them into her plans. She merely needed to understand what sort had been offered over the years in order to help her select the most appropriate for this year's revival.

It was difficult to keep Grannie's concentration on the task at hand. She tended to become sidetracked with wistful recollections of festivals past. As on several previous occasions, Grannie's reminiscences sparked others by Kate. When Hildy Spruggins joined them, she had memories to share as well. Verity surreptitiously took notes when some story inspired an idea. She was more than ever convinced that the festival would mark a new beginning for Pendurgan and for James. There was already a spark of excitement in the air of St. Perran's. Verity had no doubt the women carried that spark home to their own families. By mid-June, the district would be agog with anticipation.

And perhaps the tragedy of 1812 could finally be put behind them. James would be able to hold his head up again, to walk proudly among his own people, to turn his life around.

When the question of her own role in his future tugged at her reason, she pushed it aside. The festival was all that mattered for now. She had a mission, and it consumed her. When it was over . . . well, she would think about that later.

Chapter 11

Spring came early to Cornwall and by April was in full bloom. The sharp tang of chamomile and the limelike fragrance of bracken tinged the air when Verity strolled the lower grounds. Even the village of St. Perran's had been transformed. The squat little cottages with their ugly slate roofs took on a special charm as the flat slates became covered in a yellow lichen burnished gold by the afternoon sun.

Once the roads had recovered from the incessant March rains and become more passable, James took Verity and Mrs. Tregelly into Bodmin. He had agreed to meet with the manager of a troupe of local players, and Mrs. Tregelly wanted to confirm plans with a few tradesmen. Verity wanted to come along for no other reason than she hadn't been farther than Bosreath since she arrived at Pendurgan.

Feeling as giddy as a child at Christmas, she had dressed in her best kerseymere pelisse and Angoulême bonnet, with little care for how unfashionably outdated she must appear. Perhaps Bodmin was a small backwater town, several years behind London in style, and would find her quite the thing. It did not matter. She was happy to be going somewhere new, and secretly glad Mrs. Tregelly had come along. It was to be a long day, and to spend it alone with James would have been exquisite torture.

It was a glorious sunny day and the town was bustling. It was not a grand town, to be sure, though it boasted the Assize Court and a lovely old church missing its steeple. But the main street was crowded with shops and businesses and inns as it climbed its long way up to the top of a hill.

James left them to go about his business. "After I meet with the stage manager, I have an appointment with my solicitor," he said, giving Verity an unreadable look. They agreed to meet at the White Hart for tea in two hours.

Verity and Mrs. Tregelly spent a great deal of time with two notions sellers who each agreed to bring a stall to the festival for selling ribbons and lace and other trinkets for the ladies. They also made arrangements with a toy maker to set up a stall of carved wooden toys for the children. Verity discovered the Pendurgan housekeeper to be a persuasive and formidable negotiator. She had exacting requirements and brooked neither unnecessary extravagances nor economies. When Verity pulled her into an herbalist's shop to pick up a few herbs she had not been able to locate at Pendurgan, Mrs. Tregelley was able to cajole the dour proprietor into setting up shop at the festival.

The two women were on their way to a pie maker's shop when they realized the time, and set off for the White Hart instead. James was awaiting them, and led them to a small parlor he had engaged, where fresh tea and cakes were laid out.

"The players are set to come," he said as Verity poured their tea.

"Oh, famous!" she exclaimed. "The people will be sure to come now." She caught an uncertain look in his eye as she handed him a cup. Though he never said so, she knew he was still wary of the whole festival idea. Yet he went along with her wishes without complaint, not only securing the acting troupe, but engaging the local kiddly keeper, Old Artful, into providing ale, setting the St. Perran's blacksmith to making extra quoits for the games, and rounding up workers from the tenant farms to build stalls and wrestling rings and a makeshift stage. Most difficult of all, he had not ignored the bonfire. He set Tomas to the task of rounding up enough wood to build the huge pile.

Verity wanted to throw her arms around him and thank him for all he'd done, despite his misgivings.

"Verity?"

She jerked herself to attention. Good Lord, she'd been staring at him. What must he think of her? "I beg your pardon," she said. "I was woolgathering."

"I asked how your day progressed. Were you able to engage a few sellers?"

Verity pulled herself together and told him what they'd accomplished. She kept up a lively chatter, regaling him with more detail than he probably cared to know. But at least it kept her mind from wandering to foolish fantasies.

"There are still several others to visit," she said, pulling out her list of Bodmin vendors and tradesmen. "First, there is the pie maker and then—"

"Mrs. Tregelly," James interrupted, "I trust you can manage with the baker and the others on your own?"

"Yes, of course, my lord."

"I thought as much. Here, you take Mrs. Osborne's list. I should like to borrow her for a while, if she has no objections."

Verity experienced the merest tingle of anticipation. After a confirming nod from Mrs. Tregelly, Verity said, "I have no objections."

"Good," he said. He made arrangements to meet the housekeeper in one hour, then rose and offered his arm to Verity.

He led her along the main street, obviously with some destination in mind, though he said not a word. Something in his manner made her decidedly nervous. What was he up to?

"Did your meeting with your solicitor go well?" she asked, too jittery to allow the silence to continue.

He glanced down at her and gave her one of his enigmatic half smiles. "Yes, I believe so. I found out what I needed to know. Ah, look there, Verity. What do you think of that hat?"

He had stopped before a shop window that displayed hats and shawls and reticules. He indicated a charming leghorn bonnet trimmed with flowers, with an up-to-the-moment broad brim and low crown. It was the most gorgeous thing she'd ever seen. She gave him a questioning look. "It is quite lovely."

"And would look even lovelier on you." He flashed one of his rare smiles in response to the startled look she must surely be wearing. He reached up a hand and briefly touched her cheek. "My dear Verity, you are still wearing the same dresses, the same cloak, and same two bonnets that you brought with you to Pendurgan. And I suspect none of them was new even then. Let me buy you something new to wear."

She colored up. "Oh, James, I couldn't let you do that. I already owe you—"

"If you are going to mention that two hundred guineas, I will let you walk home to Pendurgan!" The laughter in his eyes belied his harsh words. "You owe me nothing, and you certainly deserve a new dress for the festival. And a new bonnet as well, I think. Shall we see what Mrs. Renfree has to offer?"

It had indeed been so long since she'd had anything new to wear—since her marriage to Gilbert, in fact—that Verity was tempted once again to throw her arms around his neck. Though she attempted a smile, her lower lip began to tremble.

"Now, don't get all weepy, I beg you. You'll have the whole town thinking I beat you."

She gave a quavery chuckle and blinked away her tears until she felt more composed. "You really don't have to do this, James."

"Yes, I do. You've been working so hard and I know why you're doing it. You deserve much more than a few dresses."

"You are too good to me."

He pressed his hand against the small of her back to lead her into the shop. "Not as good as I'd like to be," he mumbled under his breath.

"What are you going to do?"

Gilbert Russell stopped pacing and gazed down at his friend. Anthony Northrup sat sprawled on the sofa as calm as you please while Gilbert's life threatened to crumble into pieces.

"I need this position, Tony," he said. "You know I do. But Beddingfield is as stiff-rumped as they come. If he were to find out . . ."

"He won't find out."

"How can you be so sure?"

Northrup swung his legs down and leaned his elbows on his knees. "In the first place," he said, "don't assume the old poop is such a puritan. The man went to school. He would have experimented just like everyone else."

"Even so—"

"Besides, you have the perfect cover. All you need to do is present yourself as the traditional family man in public. So long as you have a wife to trot out to the occasional affair, no one cares what you do on the side."

Gilbert felt the blood drain from his face. "A wife?"

"You do still have a wife, don't you? Assuming that Heartless fellow hasn't murdered her."

Anxiety simmered like acid in Gilbert's stomach. Ever since he'd learned the reputation of the man who'd given him two hundred guineas for Verity, his conscience had gnawed at him like a dog with a bone. He knew he ought to have done something, but instead he simply tried to ignore it, to forget it. "Dear God, Tony, are you saying I should—"

"You want to stay in Beddingfield's good graces, do you not?"

"Of course I do." He ran agitated fingers through his hair. "I'm all done up. I need that position on his staff."

"Then keep his suspicions at bay. Get your wife back."

"Ain't he wunerful, Miz Osborne? Ain't he?"

Davey Chenhalls stared at the new moorland foal with total infatuation. It had been love at first sight a week ago when the pony was born. Every day Davey had dragged Verity out to the old stables where the ponies were kept to admire the new foal.

"He certainly is wonderful," Verity said, tousling the boy's bright hair. "Have you thought of a name for him yet?"

"I been thinkin' and thinkin'," the boy said. "It gots to be special, 'cuz he be my very first pony. I gets to ride him, Da says, soon's he do be old 'nuff and big 'nuff."

"He'll be a fine pony for you to ride."

"He sure will!" Davey said. "If he'd a been a girl, I did be gonna name him Verity, 'cuz that be yer name."

"Oh, Davey!"

"But that don't be soundin' right fer a boy pony. So I do figure to name him Osborne, 'cuz that be yer name, too, and it do sound more like a boy's name."

Verity knelt down on her haunches and hugged

the little boy, blinking back tears. "Davey, my dear, I am so honored that you wish to name your pony after me."

"Well," he said, squirming out of her grip to gaze again at the tiny foal, "it did have to be a special name, like I said, and you do be the most specialest person I do know."

She kissed the top of his head and thought how she'd grown to love this impish little heartbreaker. "Come along, Davey," she said. "The festival is only two days away and I have lots of work to do. Do you want to go to the village with me? I must see if the smithy finished those quoits."

"You bet I would! Could I go see Benjie Spruggins, too?"

"Yes, of course. You may visit with Benjie while I have a visit with Grannie Pascow. Come along, then."

With a final glance at the foal, Davey skipped down the path that snaked through the western pastures before it joined up with the lane to St. Perran's. Verity watched his high-spirited gamboling and a sudden wave of longing swept over her. Idiot! She had years ago abandoned dreams of having children of her own. What had brought on such foolishness? Was it simply Davey's endearing attachment to her? Or something more?

When they reached the edge of the village, just before the Dunstan cottage, Verity's thoughts were interrupted by a sharp whistle. She spun around to find Digory Clegg beckoning her, and heaved a weary sigh.

"Mr. Clegg, I know what you are going to say and

I do not wish to hear it." Ever since she had thrown herself into the festival plans, the dark little man had been plaguing Verity, going out of his way to spew his words of doom. She had recognized him at once as the man who'd approached her at Wheal Devoran, warning her even then. She felt sorry for the man, but his constant prognosticating was becoming tiresome.

"I just do be warnin' 'ee, mistress," the little man said, eyes narrowed, finger wagging. "An' this little 'un, too. And ever'one else up to that house. There do be only fire and death in that place, mistress, fire and death."

"Good afternoon to you, Mr. Clegg."

"Fire and death," he repeated as Verity walked quickly away, dragging Davey by the hand. "If 'ee has that festival up there with that demon lord, there'll be fire and death, mark my words. Fire and death!"

Verity was almost running to get away from his horrible words. Davey looked up at her in confusion as he scurried along beside her.

"Who is that man, Miz Osborne?"

"Don't pay him any mind, Davey. He's just a sick, crazy old man. You stay away from him."

"I will. He looks scary."

"You run along to Benjie's cottage. I'm going to stop in on Grannie. Come by in an hour or so and we'll go get the quoits together. All right?"

Verity stood in the lane and watched until she saw him safely inside the Spruggins's cottage. She hoped to God Digory Clegg stayed away from him. She did not at all appreciate that he had included Davey in his predictions of doom. It so upset her, in fact, that she wanted to sit with Grannie Pascow a while and allow the old woman's easy company and wise counsel to calm her.

"Here come Verity Osborne," Grannie said when Verity arrived, "with her festival lists. Don't know how her pockets be big enough to hold all them lists."

Verity chuckled at the old woman's teasing as she entered the parlor. Kate Pascow and Borra Nanpean were there as well.

"What do be ailin' 'ee, Verity Osborne?" Grannie asked when a mug of weak tea had been passed to Verity.

"Hm?"

"Sumthin' on yer mind, child?"

"Oh, it is just Digory Clegg. Davey and I saw him as we came into the village."

"Still spoutin' gloom and doom?" Kate asked. "Preachin' fire and death?"

"Yes, but this time he included Davey in his ranting and it made me especially uneasy."

"Oh, dear," Borra said.

"What am I going to do about him, Grannie?" Verity asked. "I've worked so hard to make this festival a success. What if he scares people away?"

"Don't 'ee be worrin' 'bout that," Grannie said. "Ever'one do know about Digory Clegg. They'll likely feel sorry fer him, but they won't listen to what he do say. Most folk think his mind do be gone, anyway."

"Do you think he might be dangerous?" Verity asked. "Liable to cause some sort of mischief?"

"Poor man," Borra said. "It must be hard to lose a child."

"Aye, and that child were all he did have," Kate

said. "After his Gracie died, he doted on that boy. That fire at Pendurgan might as well o' kilt him, too, fer all the misery it did cause. The man ain't never been the same."

"Kinda like what did happen to Jammez, ain't it, Kate?" Grannie said.

Kate snorted but did not reply.

Verity stayed and chatted until Davey returned and dragged her to the smithy. The quoits were ready, and they soon set off back up the path to Pendurgan. Before they had reached the main drive, they saw Captain Poldrennan coming from that direction. Verity sent Davey on ahead and waited for the captain's approach.

"Good afternoon," Verity said, offering a cheerful smile. "I did not expect you today or I would have come back earlier. Would you like to come in again and share a pot of tea?"

He looked somewhat surprised, and not especially happy to see her. His smile did not quite reach his eyes. "What an unexpected pleasure to see you, Mrs. Osborne," he said. "And I thank you for the offer, but I have just had tea with Agnes."

"With Agnes?"

"Yes. I visit her from time to time. She and I are old friends, you know."

"No, I did not know," Verity said, and wondered how she could have been unaware of his visits. "I am pleased to hear it, though," she said. "Poor Agnes always seems so lonely and does not seem to want to be friendly with me, much as I try. And she's become more and more irritable as the festival nears. I worry about her."

"It is hard for her to see someone taking Rowena's place."

"But I am not—"

The captain cocked a brow. "Aren't you?"

"When I offered to plan the festival," she said, "it was not with any thought of supplanting the memory of Lady Harkness. It was merely to help James restore his good name in the district."

"Ah, yes. The festival. I am so looking forward to it. How are plans coming along? It is but a few days away, is it not?"

"Indeed it is. And the planning has gone extremely well. Have you not heard of my famous lists?"

He gave a genuine laugh that softened the look in his eyes. "I have, actually. Wellington could have used you on the quartermaster general's staff."

"I sometimes feel like a general directing my troops."

"Then may you have the luck of Wellington at your midsummer siege."

"Thank you, Captain."

"I predict it will be the most brilliant event this district has seen in many years."

"I certainly hope so."

"Oh, it will be." He flashed her a broad smile. "Believe me, it will be."

Verity told him how she had found enough local musicians so that none had to be hired from outside the district. He told her how he had arranged for the tar barrels to be delivered the morning of the festival and how they would be set up all about the estate. He seemed to have lost the oddly strained manner he had shown at first, and was now the amiable gentleman she'd come to admire. They continued chatting for what must have been a half hour before Verity recollected they were standing in the middle of the path. She again invited him back to Pendurgan but he declined, and they parted in high spirits.

Verity's mind was thoroughly distracted on the walk back to Pendurgan. There were so many details, so much to be done in the next two days. She did not even notice the carriage on the far side of the central courtyard.

She pushed open the big oaken doors and entered the Great Hall. She turned toward the corridor leading to the main staircase, but was halted by Mrs. Tregelly's voice.

"Pardon me, ma'am," she said. "But there's a gentleman here to see you."

Verity stuffed a list back into her pocket and looked up at the housekeeper. "Pardon?"

"A gentleman, ma'am. He asked for you. I put him in the New Drawing Room."

"A gentleman?" Verity stared at Mrs. Tregelly, her brows lifted in question. Surely there was some mistake. She had met no gentleman other than Captain Poldrennan and he had just left Pendurgan. Who could it be, then?

"Do you know who it is?" she asked.

"No ma'am. But he was adamant he would speak only to you."

Verity sighed. Whoever he was, she would simply have to deal with him. She hoped he would not take much of her time. But perhaps he had come to discuss something about the festival. Perhaps he had heard of the plans, which were spreading like wildfire throughout the district, and represented some troupe of players or musicians or merchants, someone who wanted to participate in the event.

"I must certainly see him, then," Verity said. "Would you take my bonnet please, Mrs. Tregelly, and my pelisse. Heavens, I am dusty from the walk. Do I look a fright?"

"Not a bit, ma'am. There is one loose curl, just there. That's it. Now you look fine as five pence. Shall I send in tea and biscuits?"

"I don't know," Verity said. "Let me see what his business is first. I will ring if I need you."

"As you like, ma'am."

Verity checked her reflection in the high polish of a Civil War breastplate hung on the wall. She plumped her hair as best she could, shook out her skirts, and rubbed the toes of her half boots against the back of her stockings. It was the best she could do. She proceeded down the opposite corridor to the east wing.

The door to the drawing room was open. She could see the flickering light of a fire inside. She entered and found a man standing with his back to her, facing the fire.

"Sir? I understand you wish to see me?"

The man turned, and Verity gasped as she looked into the eyes of her husband, Gilbert Russell.

Jago Chenhalls was oddly quiet when James returned from the fields, but James was so exhausted he did not have the energy to wonder about the man's strange behavior. James and Mark Penneck had been mowing hay and it had been a long, tiring day. It was on days like this that he most missed having a steward.

James had depended heavily upon Mark Penneck over the months after Bargwanath's departure. It had been uncomfortable asking for help since Mark's attitude toward James had been no different than that of the other locals. But the Penneck holding was the largest on the Pendurgan estate and Mark was the most experienced farmer, so James had approached him.

The partnership had been awkward at first. Over the months of working side by side, however, the two of them had gained a new respect for each other and the work had gone well. It occurred to James that Verity's reasoning in regard to his black reputation might have some validity. Keeping his distance might indeed have merely increased the hostility toward him. What Verity did not seem to understand, however, was that keeping his distance had never been a choice. It was necessary.

James ducked beneath the low archway into the central courtyard and then stopped to stretch his back. His muscles ached like the very devil and he was likely to be stiff as a corpse in the morning. He pushed open the heavy oak doors to the Great Hall, and groaned at the effort. Lord, he was getting old. He would like nothing better than to soak in a hot bath. Perhaps Verity had some herbal remedy to soothe the strained muscles in his back and shoulders and hips.

Before facing the climb up the long staircase to his tower room, James wanted to check the day's post.

He was expecting a letter from Woolfe regarding an enlarged steam cylinder, as well as a new issue of *The Edinburgh Review*. If they had arrived, he could take them both upstairs and leisurely read them while soaking in a hot bath.

He walked into the library and over to the desk where Mrs. Tregelly always left the daily post for him to review. A fat leather purse sat on the center of the desk. *What the devil?* James lifted the purse. It was heavy with coins. He drew aside the leather thong holding it closed and saw a mass of gold coins inside. There must have been well over a hundred of them, maybe two hundred.

A cold shudder of fear crawled down his spine.

A folded and sealed note lay next to the pouch. He picked it up gingerly, as though it might scald his fingers, terrified of what it would say. His throat dried up so that he could hardly swallow and his breathing became ragged. He stared at the parchment for several long moments before garnering the courage to break open the seal.

A second folded paper fell out and dropped to the desk. James ignored it as his eyes scanned the brief words written in a spidery scrawl.

I am taking my wife home. You will find a purse reimbursing you for the £200 outlaid in November along with an additional portion for your trouble. I enclose the original bill of sale. Let us consider this transaction null and void. I regret any inconvenience.

Yrs,
Gilbert Russell

It was as though a large fist had punched him in the gut and knocked the wind out of him. He could not breathe. He could not move. He could only stare at the words on the page, reading them again and again, as though another reading would somehow change their meaning.

I am taking my wife home. James studied each word, the way the letters were formed, the way the ink broadened here and thinned to wispy lines there.

He stared and stared until a huge knot of despair began to twist in his belly and worked its way up through his chest and into his throat and out his mouth.

"No." It was little more than a hoarse whisper, almost a whimper. "No. No. No."

She was gone. Verity was gone.

His fingers closed slowly around the crisp parchment, which crackled as he crushed it into fanlike folds. James looked about him and felt lost, disoriented, the way he sometimes felt after a blackout.

She was gone. He could not seem to get his mind around the idea. She was gone. Russell had taken her home.

But *this* was her home. She belonged here as surely as James did. How could she be gone?

How could he go on without her?

James closed his eyes tightly, fighting against the pain building up behind them. Misery and despair threatened to overwhelm him. Those few penned lines had ripped a vast hole through his soul, leaving him dry and empty and dead inside.

He had no right to love her, should never have allowed himself to fall in love with her. But he had, and now she was gone. He wanted to die.

"No!" He crushed the parchment into a tiny crinkled ball and tossed it across the floor. He picked up the money pouch and flung it as hard as he could against the opposite wall. It struck a Chinese vase and sent it flying to the floor with a thunderous crash amidst a rain of gold sovereigns.

"My lord?"

The noise had brought Mrs. Tregelly. Oh, God, he was not prepared to face anyone just now.

"My lord?"

He took a deep breath and concentrated on the anger flickering in his breast. Anger was something he understood. He knew how to deal with it. He knew how to use it. He knew how to take refuge in it. He tested it, enticed it, savored it until it had spread throughout him as pure, unadulterated, all encompassing rage.

He spun around to face his gentle housekeeper. The raw fury in his eyes sent her retreating back a step.

"What the devil happened here while I was gone?" The roar of his voice reverberated against the thick stone walls and shook the very air with its rumble.

Mrs. Tregelly flinched slightly, but kept her sweet, sorrowful eyes on him. "She's gone, my lord."

The words tore through him like a blade. "I know she's gone, goddammit," he shouted. "What happened?"

"She left with that young man, Mr. Russell. She said he was . . . her husband. She was quite upset, my lord."

"Good God. Did he use force? Did he—"

"No, my lord. She went quietly with him, took all

her things, too. It was a dreadful thing to watch. Gonetta and Cook sobbing to break your heart, and little Davey clinging to her neck and begging her to stay. Poor Tomas had to pull the boy off her. By then, Miz Verity was crying as hard as Davey."

Her voice trembled and she paused to wipe a hand across her eyes. "She hugged every one of us," Mrs. Tregelly continued, "just like we was family. She wanted to wait until you returned, but Mr. Russell wouldn't have it. Said they had to leave then and there. She left a note for you, though. On your desk. Did you see it?"

"No." James whirled around and bent over the desk. He picked up the paper that had fallen out of Russell's note, but it was only a copy of the bill of sale, the same receipt James had kept safely locked away all these months. "I don't see it," he said and riffled through the papers on his desk. "Where *is* it? Where is it?"

"Here, my lord." Mrs. Tregelly pointed to a sealed note propped up against the inkwell on his father's silver writing set.

James grabbed at the note, upending the pounce pot and spilling the fine powder across the desk. "Lord Harkness" was written on the folded sheet in an elegant, flowing script. Not even "James," only the formal title. He choked back disappointment, ripped open the seal, and read hungrily.

James,

I am sorry to have left without a chance to say good-bye. My husband has returned for me and, because the law is on his side, I am forced to leave Pendurgan. Please accept my gratitude for your kindness and your friendship and the chance to know the good people of Pendurgan and St. Perran's. I shall miss you all. I regret that I will be unable to be here for the midsummer's eve festival. It is sure to be a great success. The people are so looking forward to it.

To have known you will remain one of the greatest pleasures of my life.

Yrs in friendship,
Verity Osborne Russell

James turned his back to Mrs. Tregelly and read it again, savoring each word, seeking hope beneath the pain. He found it glimmering in the last line. *One of the greatest pleasures of my life.* Oh indeed, he thought, and you were that to me.

James stood for several long moments, mining each word for precious meaning. She was sorry to leave. She was grateful for his kindness—ha!—and his friendship. She had wanted to say good-bye. She would miss him. No, she would miss them all, but he was certainly included in that sentiment. She would miss him. She was sorry. She was grateful. She cared.

Surely that was the meaning to be read between the lines. She cared. Perhaps she even loved him. No, that was stretching it too far. But she did care for him. He had known that for some time.

But what good did it do to realize she cared, now that she was gone? To give validity to the ache in his heart?

In such a short time, Verity had made an impact on

his life, on the lives of everyone at Pendurgan and St. Perran's. She had wrought so many changes in this grim house. It would never be the same.

The biggest change of all was James himself. She had begun to bring him back to life, back to living. It might be only the tiniest seed buried deep within his wretched black soul, but it struggled to break through and send its shoots toward the sun. That it struggled at all was because of Verity, because she believed in him, because she offered hope when he never dared to dream.

She had made him want to live again, to take control of the demons that plagued him, to reclaim his life. Verity had planted that seed, and by God, he was not ready to let it wither and die. He knew, though, just as surely as he breathed, that there would be no other chance for him. She had been his last chance. And she was gone.

I am forced to leave Pendurgan. She had not gone by choice. That bastard Russell had waved the law in her face and forced her to go. He had not cared much for the law last fall, when he had led his proud young wife to auction at Gunnisloe. The wife whose marriage had never been consummated.

By God, he was not going to let Russell cause her any further pain and humiliation. He might have legal marriage lines, but he did not have the right. James, of course, had no rights at all, except that he loved her. Russell could never have loved her. James was not about to let that blackguard jerk Verity around like a marionette. James would fight for her, for her right to make her own choice.

He would go after her. Perhaps he would make a

widow of her, if that's what it took. But by God, he would fight to get her back.

"Mrs. Tregelly?"

She had quietly left the room, leaving him to his solitary misery.

"Mrs. Tregelly!"

His bellow brought the poor woman scurrying as fast as her plump legs would carry her. "Yes, my lord?" she asked breathlessly.

"How long ago did they leave, Verity and Russell?"

"Oh, well. Let me see, now." She pursed her lips and tapped her chin with a finger while she considered the matter. "It must be several hours ago. Just afore eleven, I'd guess."

"Eleven?" James checked the mantel clock. It had just gone three. They'd been gone at least four hours, a hell of a head start. "What sort of carriage did he have?"

Mrs. Tregelly looked puzzled. "What sort of carriage?"

"Yes, yes," James said, unable to keep the impatience from his voice. "How many horses? Two or four?"

"Oh, I believe it was four, my lord. Yes, I'm sure of it. Four horses."

They would make good time, then. But on horseback, he might be able to catch up with them. He would ask Jago Chenhalls for more detail on the carriage so he could follow its trail. There was no time to waste. He tucked Verity's note in his waistcoat pocket and rushed toward the door.

"My lord?"

He paused reluctantly. "Yes, what is it?"

"Are you going after her, my lord? Are you going to bring Miz Verity back to Pendurgan?"

"I am certainly going to try," he said.

Mrs. Tregelly heaved a sigh. "Thank the good Lord."

James cast her a broad smile then hurried to the main staircase. He bounded up the stairs, heedless of the stiff muscles that had so troubled him earlier, and was headed for the tower stairs when he came face to face with Agnes Bodinar. She stood in the main corridor, silhouetted against the dim light of a wall sconce. She moved to block his path to the tower.

"You're going after her, aren't you?"

"Yes, Agnes. Let me pass."

"You do not need her, Harkness. Let her go."

James tried to move around her, but she sidestepped him and continued to block his path. "Agnes, please."

"Don't be such a fool. She's not worth it."

He stopped and looked into his mother-in-law's steely gray eyes. "Ah, but she is, Agnes." He thought of the two hundred and more gold sovereigns scattered on the library floor. "She's worth every penny."

Verity shifted on the carriage seat and tried once again to find a more comfortable position. It was useless. Her muscles were cramped and stiff from endless hours spent bumping along rutted and muddy roads. Gilbert had insisted they travel into the evening hours. He seemed anxious to reach London.

If she had to leave Cornwall, Verity would have preferred to go back to Berkshire, to the ramshackle house nestled in the downs where she had spent the first two and a half years of her marriage. Gilbert had told her, though, that he had sold the house in order to pay back Lord Harkness, and now had only a small leased townhouse in London.

He needed her there. He had come in line for a government post and could not afford an investigation into his wife's disappearance.

Verity had been wretched with despair as their carriage had wound its way through the rough, granite-strewn landscape of Bodmin Moor.

"What a bleak and dreary land this is," Gilbert had said. "I am more sorry than I can say that I have forced you to live in such a godforsaken place. You must be happy to see the last of it."

His words had caused a flood of tears that he misunderstood as relief. She was far from happy to see the last of it. She had never been more miserable. Except perhaps when Davey Chenhall's skinny arms had to be forcibly removed from around her neck, or when a sobbing Gonetta had returned Verity's hug with such force she'd thought her stays would crack, or when she had watched the gray mass of Pendurgan disappear from view for the last time.

Verity would forever recollect with profound regret the thick, cold, stone walls of the old house, fraught with the desolation of its master and the tragedy of its recent past. She had grown to love the old place and had so looked forward to seeing its gardens in full summer. She would never get to see what became of the tiny green seedlings she'd planted in the kitchen garden that had just begun to sprout. Nor would she ever know if the midsummer festival took place as planned. She would forever regret leaving all that behind at Pendurgan.

She would regret leaving its master most of all.

"I should not have done what I did to you, Verity," Gilbert said as she silently wept. "I do not suppose I can ever explain it to you, explain why I did it. That doesn't matter now. But when I heard who it was I had . . . I had left you with, well, I tell you I was devastated. Lord Heartless of Pendurgan!"

Verity had let him prattle on about how contrite he was for turning her over to a renowned monster, a wife murderer. He never once used the word "sold." But he *had* sold her—something Verity would neither forget nor forgive.

Gilbert had convinced himself he was rescuing her from a horrible fate, some unnamed terror at the hands of Lord Heartless. For Verity, though, the real monster in all this was Gilbert. So quiet, so reserved, so unassuming, and yet a monster who had sold his wife without a qualm, until he'd learned the reputation of the buyer. He might convince himself of the noble act of rescue. Verity would never forgive him for taking her away from the only man she'd ever loved.

It did not matter that James had been dark and angry and brooding and potentially dangerous. She had grown to love the man beneath the mask and to understand the root of his anger and self-loathing. Even recognizing the cause of his pain, though, Verity could not really be sure that she could ever have helped him, that she could have helped heal his wounds.

But, oh, how she would like to have tried. The ache in her heart was for that more than almost anything else—that she would never know if her love for him could have made a difference.

She wiped her eyes and straightened her spine. She would *not* be done in by this new twist of fate. She had survived all the rest, though this was the most painful change she had yet endured. To leave behind all that was unfinished at Pendurgan, to leave behind James . . .

She would survive. She always did. What she must remember was that James had not felt anything beyond friendship for her, and one night of something more. It was her own arrogance that caused her to hope and dream of things that could never be.

You are nothing like Rowena. His words had reminded her that she could never fill that special place in his heart.

She had hoped there had been some affection between them, that their friendship mattered to him. But in the end she could never be that important to him, for she was nothing like Rowena, the one true love of his life.

Throughout the long, uncomfortable carriage ride, Verity brooded over all that had happened, coming to grips with her broken heart, her shattered dreams. She rebuffed Gilbert's attempts at conversation. She had nothing to say to him and preferred to be alone with her thoughts. He had finally recognized that fact, and fell silent.

Verity closed her eyes but could not sleep. Her mind was in too much turmoil and her body too stiff. How she wished they would stop for the night. It had been dark for hours.

When the carriage began to slow and pull into yet

another posting inn for a change of team, Verity was finally compelled to speak.

"May we not stop here for the night?" she asked. "It is late and I am tired and uncomfortable. May we not rest for a while?"

Gilbert looked out the carriage window. "Yes, it looks to be decent enough. Let me see if there are rooms available."

Verity would have been agreeable to sleeping on a bench in the taproom if necessary, but she kept quiet. Gilbert bounded out of the carriage and closed the door behind him. Verity was too tired to watch and leaned her head against the squabs and closed her eyes. She heard the voices of ostlers and the rattle of harnesses, and felt the jostling of the carriage as the horses were unhitched.

Gilbert returned after a few moments and reached out a hand to help her down the folding steps of the carriage. "They have one small bedchamber and a private parlor. We can have a quick meal before retiring, if you like. I will stretch out on a chair in the parlor. Or the taproom."

He need not have added that last bit of information. Verity had no fear that her husband would finally seek her bed after all these years.

She found that, as tired as she was, she was nevertheless hungry, and so they ordered a cold collation to be served in the private parlor. Gilbert seemed to find her continued silence oppressive, and once again he attempted conversation.

"I hope we can start over, Verity," he said, and passed her a slice of cold ham. "I hope that we can view this as a new beginning for us. I know our marriage has not been . . . has not been much of a marriage. And I have not been much of a husband. I will try to do better by you this time, my dear. You will see. We will live in London together and start over."

Verity spread butter on a piece of grainy bread, and reached deep within herself to locate the courage she had nurtured over the months at Pendurgan.

"I do not wish to start over with you, Gilbert," she said. "I have no wish to live with a man who has seen fit to sell me at auction for two hundred pounds."

Verity marveled that she was able to say the words. There had been a time when she would have bitten her tongue out rather than cross her husband. She had certainly kept her silence when he led her to the market square at Gunnisloe and placed a leather halter around her neck.

Something had happened to her, though. Something essential deep inside her had changed. She would go where life took her, as she always did; but she would no longer be silent about how she felt, about what she wanted. Somehow, during the months at Pendurgan, she had developed a bit of backbone. Not a terribly strong one, to be sure, or she would not have gone with Gilbert at all, legal rights be damned. But she would no longer be the silent little mouse she'd been before.

Gilbert stared at her wide-eyed. He had difficulty swallowing his food and seemed almost to choke on it. He took a long swallow of ale and it appeared to calm him. He continued to stare at her, a hint of apprehension in his hazel eyes.

"Verity? Do you mean you would rather have stayed with that . . . that murderer?"

"Yes," she replied without hesitation, "that is what I mean."

"Why, for God's sake? The man's a monster."

"I was happy there. I was useful. And he is not a monster."

"Oh." Gilbert looked thoroughly abashed. "I see. Well, I am glad, at least, that it was not as bad as I had believed. You cannot know the unspeakable horrors I imagined were being inflicted upon you."

"And yet it took you eight months to come for me," Verity said. "Eight months of unspeakable horrors. You must have been astonished to find me alive."

Gilbert paled at her words. His hands began to fidget nervously. "I . . . I did not have the funds to . . . to . . ."

"To buy me back?"

He fumbled with his neckcloth and squirmed in his seat. "I had to repay the money Harkness had given me. I could not simply steal you away without worrying that he would come tearing after us."

"And you had already spent the two hundred pounds."

He pushed away his plate, though he had hardly touched his food. "Yes. There had been debts, you see. I used the money to help repay them."

"Ah, I see. You sold your wife to redeem your vowels. Others might have sold a horse or a painting. How clever of you to think of selling a wife you never wanted."

"Verity." He looked miserable, as though he might actually break into sobs. "It was hateful and wrong. I know it. I must live with what I've done. I don't expect your forgiveness. But I will make it up to you, I promise, once I have this position in the Home Office. You will see, Verity. I promise you will never want for anything ever again."

Really? And how was he going to make her stop wanting that dark stranger she'd left behind?

She fell silent again. She had made her point; there was no need to pound it into the ground. Gilbert was her legal husband and she was bound to do as he wished. Perhaps she would forge a new and interesting life in London. If she could be occupied and useful, perhaps it would be enough.

But would it ever be enough to quell the ache in her heart for all she'd left behind—for Cornwall, for Pendurgan, for the red-haired Chenhalls family and sweet-faced Mrs. Tregelly, for Grannie Pascow and the women of St. Perran's, for James?

No. Nothing would ever be enough to dull the ache in her heart for James.

Chapter 12

He'd found them.

It had taken twice as long as he'd hoped, but James had finally tracked down Russell's carriage at the Bull's Head in the village of Alston Cross. Russell had hired a post chaise, a typical Yellow Bounder that looked like every other private coach on the road, and so it had been easy to lose track of them.

The biggest loss of time had begun at Liskeard when he had followed a false trail north toward Tavistock. It had been some time before he realized he'd been chasing the wrong coach, and then more hours of backtracking to discover Russell had gone south toward Plymouth. The long summer twilight had begun to fade into dark before he spotted the lone yellow coach in the yard at the Bull's Head.

He almost hadn't dared to hope it would actually

be Russell's hired chaise, but when the innkeeper confirmed that a Mr. and Mrs. Russell were indeed guests, James had been ready to collapse with relief. And exhaustion. He was tired to the bone. Somehow he had to garner the strength to face Russell, to fight for Verity's freedom.

James had to bribe the innkeeper to reveal the location of Russell's rooms. He led James through a rabbit warren of corridors and narrow stairways until finally indicating a door up two steps at the end of a hallway.

"That be the parlor," the man said. "The bedchamber be the door just over there. They was just served a late supper, so they most likely be in the parlor. Though a young couple like that, can't be so sure." He gave James a lurid glance before taking his leave.

A bubble of excitement began to expand in James's gut. Verity was behind one of those doors, and he was ready to fight for her.

It had been a long time since he'd been seized by the spirit of the fight, a long time since anything in his life had been worth fighting for. But the spirit was on him now, pumping through his veins like quicksilver. The possibility of smashing Gilbert Russell's face into a bloody pulp inflamed him with a kind of battle fever.

He marched up the steps to the parlor and turned the door handle, prepared to kick it in if it was locked. It was not. The door swung into a small room with whitewashed walls and dark wainscoting. A fire blazed in the grate. Verity was seated at a table before the fire. Russell stood warming his hands over the flames, his back to the door.

Verity looked up and gasped, her teacup clattering to its saucer. Russell swung around. "What the devil?" He saw James and sputtered, "Oh, m-my God." He moved behind Verity and placed his hands on the back of her chair.

James's eyes had not left Verity's. He read a series of emotions there—surprise, apprehension, relief, joy—that kept his gaze locked firmly to hers. His own anger and joy combined to make him want to pick her up in his arms and carry her out of there. But the fierce pride in the angle of her jaw and the set of her shoulders reminded him of all she'd been through. Much as he wished it, he would not allow himself to take control of her life for her. This time, she must be allowed a voice in her own fate. Here, at last, was something he could give *her*.

"Wh-what are you doing here?" Russell asked, trying his damnedest to look cocky but failing miserably. "I thought our business was completed. D-did you not find the purse I left?"

James reached inside his greatcoat and withdrew the leather pouch. He'd collected all the coins scattered over the library floor before leaving. He wanted to fling the bloody thing in Russell's face, but the coward stood protected behind Verity. Instead, James threw it down on the table with such force the serving dishes bounced and rattled and a meat fork danced to the edge and fell clanking to the floor.

"I do not want your bloody money," James said. He kept his temper under control as he took Russell's measure. The young man looked like a frightened rabbit trying to stand up to a fox. There would be no sport in fighting such a man. He had all the earmarks of a sniveling coward.

"Th-then why have you come?" Russell asked. He gripped the back of Verity's chair so tightly his knuckles flared white. "You cannot mean to j-just take her away with you, to take her by force?"

"I have no intention of forcing anyone to do anything," James said. He put as much steel into his voice as he'd ever done in Spain. The man was so easily cowed by a sharp word and a fierce look, he wouldn't have lasted five minutes in James's regiment. "It would appear to be you, sir," James said, "who is doing the forcing."

"Wh-what?"

James turned his attention to Verity, who had not moved a muscle since he'd come into the room. He tried not to lose himself in those soft brown eyes, resolved to maintain control. "I gather from your note, madam, that it was not your choice to leave Pendurgan?"

She slanted a quick glance over her shoulder, then looked back at James with a smile in her eyes. "No, my lord," she said, "it was not my choice."

Exhilaration flowed through James like a shot of whiskey. He wrenched his gaze from Verity and skewered Russell with a piercing glare. "I have come, sir, to ensure this lady has a choice in what happens to her."

"B-but she is my wife. I have the ri—"

"You gave up your rights when you sold her like a blood horse at Tattersall's!" James's bellow must surely have been heard throughout the inn. He could have sworn the small paned window rattled in its casement.

"I regret that wretched bit of business," Russell said. "But you must know the transaction was not legal."

"And neither was it moral."

Russell deflated like a pierced bladder. His whole body took on a woeful slouch. He moved to lean heavily against the broad mantel over the fireplace, as though he did not have the strength to hold himself upright. When the young man raised his head, James thought he'd never seen eyes more full of misery, except on occasion staring back at him from a mirror.

"No, it was not moral," Russell said in a tremulous voice. "It was vile and hateful and I have never regretted anything so much in my life. I have made my apologies to Verity, though I do not expect forgiveness. I was simply hoping that we . . ." He paused and slammed a fist against the wooden mantel. "Blast it all, I could never get anything right. My whole life has been a series of failures. I'm not fit to live on this earth." His voice had trailed off into a quavering whisper. He turned his back to them, propped a forearm on the mantel, and lowered his head to rest on it. The slightest tremor shook his shoulders.

James was thoroughly taken aback. He'd come expecting to find Verity in the grip of a brutish, cocksure husband ready to reassert his rights. He would have welcomed a contest of wills against such an enemy. Russell's anguish knocked all the fight out of James.

He studied Verity as she watched Russell, her expression a mixture of compassion and confusion.

"Verity?"

She looked up at him, and all the joy he'd seen earlier had gone out of her eyes. James suddenly found himself uncertain what he should do. But it was her choice, he reminded himself. She must decide what to do, and he must accept it. He was no longer so sure, though, what her choice would be.

"Verity, you must tell us what you want." He spoke directly to her and kept his voice as even and unemotional as possible. "I did not come to spirit you away against your will, I assure you. But I had to make sure that Mr. Russell was not doing so, either. You have been buffeted about in all directions, dancing to everyone else's tunes. It is time you were allowed to make your own decisions, regardless of who has legal rights to do what. We have all trampled over the law these past eight months and more. None of us has the right to call upon it now to justify our actions. Russell?" He raised his voice, instilling it with the command that had once sent troops scattering to do his bidding. "Would you agree with me on this?"

Russell did not lift his head from the mantel, but muttered his agreement.

"And so, Verity," James continued, softening his tone once again, "disregarding the legalities, tell us what it is you would prefer to do. Do you wish to return with Russell to London, or return to Pendurgan?"

Russell raised his head. "But—"

"Let her speak!" James roared.

Verity's gaze darted back and forth between her husband and James. She considered her words for several long moments before speaking, moments during which James's stomach tied itself into knots. "I am sorry, Gilbert," she said at last, "but if I am truly given the choice, I would prefer to return to Pendurgan. I have found some small measure of happiness there, you see."

Russell turned around to look at his wife. His face wore a mask of utter despair, and it was a wonder Verity's natural compassion could withstand such a plea.

"You must understand, Gilbert," Verity continued, "that Lord Harkness has been a true friend to me. And, given the choice, I would rather live with him in friendship—for as you are well-aware, no man could ever desire me for anything more—than with you in marriage."

It was a monumental effort for James to hold in check the flood of emotions brought on by her words. His heart thumped in his chest like the great steam cylinder at Wheal Devoran. He would not have to live without her after all.

But this was no time to succumb to sentimentality. He had to put his plan in action before Russell tried to assert his legal rights again and talk her out of leaving. He was going to make Russell a proposition, one that would free Verity from this sham marriage once and for all.

The sight of James bursting into the parlor had caused Verity's heart almost to stop beating. He had looked so large and menacing framed in the narrow doorway, like a bull ready to charge. Though tall and well-muscled, James was not a particularly large man. Yet, enveloped in the capes of his greatcoat, with his black hair falling piratelike over one eye and a day's growth of beard darkening his face, he was a powerful sight to behold. She had never been so happy to see anyone in all her life.

He had been so full of anger, she could almost feel the tension tightening his muscles like a whipcord. For a moment, she had been afraid he meant to do violence, to attack Gilbert; but his restraint had been formidable.

Everything would be all right now, though. She was going back to Pendurgan. She was going home.

"Verity will return to Pendurgan with me in the morning," James was saying. "And I want you gone from this place tonight. But first, I must speak privately with you. Wait here, if you please. Verity, come with me."

Keeping a firm hold of her arm, James led her silently down the parlor steps and through the labyrinth of hallways and stairs down to the taproom on the ground floor. It was noisy with the chatter of patrons and the clanking of mugs. James asked the barman if there was a private parlor nearby. He was directed to one and led Verity there. When she stepped into the empty room he did not follow, and she turned to face him.

He filled this doorway just as he had the other: large, indomitable, dear. They gazed at each other in silence for several beats of her heart.

"Verity."

She was never sure which one of them moved

first. Within another heartbeat, they had walked into each other's arms.

Verity burrowed her head against James's shoulder and rubbed her cheek against the wool of his greatcoat, crushing her new bonnet and not caring. They simply held each other for several long moments.

"Verity," he said at last, still holding her tight against his chest. "I thought I'd lost you."

She shook her head and he seemed finally to recognize the awkwardness of embracing a women in a full-brimmed bonnet. He stepped back and allowed his hands to linger over her shoulders and trail slowly down her arms until he reached her hands. He took hold of them both and gazed at her with an expression of something like desire, though she did not fool herself into thinking it was any such thing.

"Thank you for rescuing me once again, my lord," she said. "You are very kind. I never expected—"

He stopped her words with his finger on her lips. "Kindness had nothing to do with it, my dear. It was pure selfishness. Your leaving has thrown my entire household into an uproar. Especially with the festival tomorrow. You have never seen such a hangdog, weepy group. I don't . . . we would not have known how to get on without you."

Ah. The household needed her. Not James.

"I wanted to speak with you privately, away from Russell. I want to be sure you do not feel coerced, by either of us. I must ask you one last time." He began to stroke the edge of her jaw with the same finger that had pressed against her lips. "Are you certain, absolutely certain, this is what you want? To return to Pendurgan?"

"Yes, of course," she said. It surprised her she could sound so normal when his touch caused her heart to flutter in her chest like a bird's wing. "As I said earlier, I have been happy there, content. Besides, I have no wish to go anywhere at all with Gilbert Russell."

"No, I do not imagine you do."

"Thank you, James. For everything."

"Verity." He cradled her face in his hand, his thumb brushing the corner of her mouth. Then he dipped his head beneath her bonnet and kissed her.

It was not a passionate kiss, but soft and sweet and so full of tenderness it made her ache with longing.

He lifted his head and his lips twitched into a half smile. "I'm sorry," he said. "I promised never to do that again. Forgive me."

He released her and stepped back, leaving her bereft and wanting more. "If you are quite sure, then, I must ask you to give me a few moments alone with Russell."

"James, you are not going to . . . to hurt him, are you?"

He smiled. "I wanted to. Hell, I wanted to kill him. But there is something pathetic about the man that takes the fight right out of me. No, I won't hurt him. I just need to speak with him about something. If you will give me a few minutes alone with him, perhaps you can find the landlord and arrange to have any of your baggage still in Russell's coach transferred to mine. And ask if he has another room available that I could have for the night. Thank you, my dear." He kissed her hand and dashed back in the direction of the stairs.

Her head still reeling from the effects of his kiss, Verity sought out the landlord and set about arranging for the transfer of her trunk and hiring a second bedchamber for the night.

She then returned to the private parlor and ordered a pot of tea. Though she had been warmed by James's insistence that she make her own decisions, Verity was quite sure he and Gilbert were upstairs making some decisions that involved her. She had no idea what James could possibly have to say to Gilbert that did not involve her. She had given her word, however, and would therefore allow them a few moments alone. But only a few moments.

James knew he ought not to have kissed Verity, but he could not have stopped himself if he tried. And he did not regret it. If Russell cooperated, James would ultimately do more than merely kiss her.

Refusing to dwell on that, James opened the door to the private parlor where he'd left Russell and walked in. The young man had taken Verity's seat at the table and sat with his head bowed in an attitude of total dejection. James could almost feel sorry for him, but he was resolved to do this.

Russell looked up at James's entrance but said nothing. James removed his greatcoat and tossed it on a settle near the window, and then did the same with his gloves. He sat down at the table opposite Russell, pulled over an empty plate, and speared a slice of ham from a serving platter.

"You will forgive me, Russell, but I find I am famished."

Russell shrugged his indifference. James took a bite of ham and then continued. "Tell me, what made you come for her? A pang of conscience after all these months?"

Russell eyed James warily. "My conscience has plagued me for some time now, especially since I learned I had sold her to a wife murderer."

"Ah." James sliced off a large portion of bread from the fat loaf on the table. "So if I had been the slovenly blacksmith, Will Sykes, you would not have returned for her?"

"I would have returned."

"Why? Why now?" James placed a thick slice of ham on the bread and took a large bite.

Russell's response was a long time coming. "I have come in line for a minor government post, if you must know. I need this position. I need the money it pays." He expelled a breath through puffed cheeks. "Questions were asked about my wife."

"I see. And you were not prepared to announce that you'd sold her for two hundred pounds."

Russell bowed his head and said nothing. His cheeks colored slightly.

"You hoped to take her to London and parade her about as your wife, in the most ordinary fashion."

Russell still did not speak.

"The strange thing is," James continued as he sliced off another piece of ham, "that Verity never really was a wife to you in the ordinary fashion, was she?"

Russell's head jerked up and his eyes widened

with what looked like fear. "What are you talking about?"

"I think you know very well what I am talking about. Your marriage was never consummated."

Russell's face turned crimson. "And how would you know that?"

James raised his brows in a look of mock incredulity.

"You bastard!"

James shrugged and reached for an apple. He began to cut it into sections with the ham knife. "You sold her, Russell. What did you think would happen?"

Russell rose so abruptly his chair went crashing to the floor. James had struck a chord of some kind. He just might get that fight he'd been spoiling for earlier, though it was not at all what he wanted now. "I knew she had not been safe with you," Russell said. "I swear I could kill you."

James dismissed his threat with a careless wave of the knife. "Sit down, Russell," he said, pointing to the overturned chair with the blade. "If you will but listen, I think you will see how you can use this situation to your advantage."

"What? What do you mean, 'my advantage'?"

"Sit down and I shall tell you."

He glared at James for another moment, then righted his chair and sat back down. "Well?"

James took one last bite of apple, then laid down the knife and pushed the plate away. "It is obvious that you never wanted this marriage to Verity. You never consummated it, then sold her like a prime bit of horseflesh. Clearly, you have no interest in her and in fact wish to be rid of her. I suggest that you do so, legally this time. I think you should file a divorce action against her."

"What! You must be joking."

"I'm perfectly serious. You have grounds for a Crim Con action. You can accuse her of adultery. With me."

Russell looked thoroughly dumbfounded, eyes wide and mouth gaping.

"It would be a simple, uncontested suit," James said. "Lengthy and expensive, but much less complex than a contested action."

Russell frowned and appeared to consider the matter. "I don't know . . ."

"Of course, if you prefer, I could assist Verity in filing an action against you. I have no doubt we could find witnesses to your own infidelities."

"No!" The word exploded from Russell. All color drained from his face.

"I am certain we could find witnesses who would attest to one or another of your own liaisons. I doubt you have spent these last few years in complete celibacy."

"No! No, please, you cannot."

"Are you so afraid of making public your own affairs, then? I guarantee you, Russell. I have the money to track them down and—"

"No!"

"—see to it that each and every one of them is published."

"No. No. Please, no." To James's utter astonishment, the man covered his face with his hands and began to cry. "You c-can't do this to m-me. Oh, God, pl-please. No."

James was thunderstruck. What the devil was this all about? "Give over, Russell. What is the problem? Every man in London has his paramours. Some are more discreet about it than others, but—"

"You do n-not understand."

"No, indeed, I do not."

"I tell you I would rather die than have any of my . . . my liaisons made public."

James snorted. "A rather dramatic threat, don't you think?"

"No." He sniffed and made a visible effort to regain his composure. "Not so dramatic, actually. I would likely lose my life in any case, if any of it became public."

"What are you—" James sucked in his breath. Dear God. Suddenly it all made sense. "Your lovers are . . . men?"

Russell leapt from his chair, turned his back to James, and braced himself against the fireplace mantel with both hands. "Don't you see?" he said. "I could be hanged if the truth came out. And others as well."

"Good God." James studied the young man's back and began to understand his misery. British society and British law were severe in the public treatment of homosexuality, though heaven knew it was widespread enough in private. No boy could go to school nor a young man go to war without some exposure to men who preferred men. It was not spoken of, of course, and men who followed that path did so in the greatest secrecy. The penalty for conviction on a charge of sodomy was death.

"So that is why you never consummated your marriage," James said. "Does Verity know?"

"No. At least, I do not believe she does." He kept his back turned as though unable to face James. There was still a tremor in his voice, though he appeared to have checked the tears. "I tried, you see. I just . . . I could not do it."

"What happened?"

He gave a soft groan. "It does not matter."

"Yes," James said, "it does. For Verity's sake. I care for her, Russell. A great deal. Tell me about the marriage."

"It was arranged by our fathers," Russell said, his voice flat and lifeless. "We met only briefly once or twice before the wedding. I knew I would never be . . . like other men, but I thought I could go through with it. Others like me do. She was a sweet enough girl, but I had never been with a woman. When I tried, on our wedding night, I was . . . disgusted. I tried to touch her, but it made me . . . I retched and retched until I thought I would die. I left her the next day, figuring she was better off without me."

James tried to imagine the scene—this poor young man trying desperately to be something he was not, and Verity, not understanding, seeing only rejection and disgust.

Suddenly, he remembered once telling Verity that she could never know what it was like to live with pain and shame and guilt. *I can probably never understand the pain you have suffered.*

Ah, Verity.

Other things she'd said suddenly began to make more sense as well. Earlier tonight she had made a comment about how no man could ever desire her. Not understanding Russell's revulsion, she must believe there was something wrong with her, something that made her sexually undesirable. His own actions during the botched attempt at lovemaking would have only further encouraged that absurd notion, the way he had cursed her and raged at her virginity. *It is my fault,* she had said.

Ah, Verity. Sweet, proud, beautiful, eminently desirable Verity. If only she knew how very wrong she was.

But there was more to this sorry tale. "What made you finally resort to selling her at auction?"

"Oh, God, I don't know," Russell said. He pushed himself away from the mantel and began to pace the room. "I left her in my father's old house in Berkshire. Little more than a run down cottage. I'd planned to take care of her financially, even if I could never live with her as a husband. But I never did. I left her in that tumbledown house while I lived high in town. London is full of temptation, you know, and I got myself in a bad way. I'm ashamed to say I'd gone through her dowry and any other blunt I could get my hands on. I'd sold everything else I owned. Then one day I saw a small notice in the *Morning Post*. It told of a wife sale in Cornwall. I must have gone a little mad. I decided I had one more thing yet to sell."

"God's teeth, I would love to wring your bloody neck for that, Russell. I don't gave a damn whom you prefer to sleep with, but treating your innocent wife like that is simply beyond the pale. And you think *I* am a villain?"

Russell stopped pacing and looked down at James, brows raised in question. "I don't suppose it's true that you murdered your wife, is it? Else Verity would never have agreed to return with you."

"I am not completely without blame in the matter of my wife's death," James said. "But I am not a cold-blooded murderer, no." It was the first time he had ever admitted it, even to himself.

"Then you are right," Russell said. "I am the villain here."

"Then I will ask again if you are willing to do the right thing by her and bring this sad marriage to an end, legally."

"My God. You are in love with her, aren't you?"

"I am very much afraid I am." James smiled. It was only today, when he'd found her gone, that he had finally admitted it to himself. He loved her.

"Now look, Russell. You have grounds against her. You need not reveal the details of your own personal life. I will admit that she committed adultery with me. Verity will offer no contest. It should be a fairly simple matter."

"Simple and expensive and horribly scandalous. No. No, I'm afraid I cannot do it."

"Why the devil not?"

"My prospective employer, Lord Beddingfield, is a high stickler. He would never abide the slightest impropriety."

James arched a brow and Russell blushed scarlet. "I'm sorry, the scandal would be too much. Beddingfield would turn me out."

"Bugger Beddingfield!" James immediately regretted his words.

Russell glared at him with such hostility the room fairly crackled with it. "No. I won't do it."

"God's teeth!" James leapt from his chair as though shot from a cannon. "You *will* do it, Russell, or I swear we will file an action against *you*."

"How dare you threaten me," Russell said through his teeth, rising to face him.

"How dare I? How dare I? I'll tell you how. Because you have ruined the life of a perfectly innocent woman, a woman I happen to care about. If it takes airing your private peccadilloes to set her free, that and the fact that you illegally engaged in a wife sale, then by God, that is what I will do."

"You wouldn't!"

"Oh, yes, I would. Just try me."

"How could you be so cruel?"

"How could you condemn Verity to a life in limbo?"

"No wonder they call you Lord Heartless."

James took firm hold of his temper. "Enough. This is getting us nowhere. There is one other possibility we have not considered."

"What?" Gilbert asked.

"Annulment."

"Annulment?" Verity's voice caused both men to look up sharply. She had waited fifteen minutes before returning, and heard the shouting as she approached. "Are you talking about annulling our marriage?" A bubble of hope swelled in her breast. "Is it possible?"

"I do not know," James said, rising and offering her a seat. "I spoke with my solicitor about it, and it seems a difficult thing at best."

He had spoken to his solicitor about it? How long had he been thinking of it? "How difficult?" she asked.

"Unfortunately, there are few grounds for annulment, and I'm not sure if any of them apply here. That is why I never mentioned it, Verity. I thought it was near impossible."

Her heart swelled at the implications of his words. "What sort of grounds?"

"Frankly, I had hoped it could be a simple case of failure to consummate."

Verity blushed at his words. So he really did know the truth after that one time.

"But only the inability to consummate can be used as grounds for annulment. Are you prepared to claim impotence, Russell?"

"No!" Gilbert exclaimed. "Dear God, no!"

"I thought not," James said. "Can we also assume there is no close blood relation between you, or affinity by marriage?"

"No," Gilbert said, and Verity shook her head at James's questioning look.

"Then according to my solicitor," James said, "the only other grounds are based on litigation. I don't suppose either of you had a precontract of marriage with someone else?"

"No."

"No."

"Was either of you under age?" James asked.

"Without written consent of parent or guardian?"

"I was four and twenty," Gilbert said.

"I was only twenty," Verity said, "but my father certainly consented. It was his arrangement, after all."

"That does it," Gilbert said. "We have no grounds. I'm sorry, Verity."

"Hold on," James said. "There is one more remote possibility. My solicitor explained about a tricky loophole in the Marriage Act. Apparently, if it can be proved that any information in regard to name or age was incorrect on the license or in the banns—even the slightest and most inadvertent misspelling or error—it can be used as grounds for nullity."

"I have a copy of the license here," Gilbert said and reached into his coat pocket. He gave a sheepish grin when he saw the astonished looks on their faces. "I thought you might object to my taking Verity away," he said to James. "I wanted evidence that I had the legal right to do so."

"Let us see it, then," James said, and Gilbert unfolded the document and laid it on the table.

Verity bent down to read it. She remembered signing the church register after the wedding, but had never seen the license. Those details had been taken care of by her father.

What she read caused her breath to catch in her throat. "Dear God, do you see?" She stabbed her finger at the parchment. "It says I was twenty-one, but I was five months short of that age."

Oh, Papa. For once her father's absentmindedness had been a boon instead of a maddening eccentricity. The poor man could never remember birthdays or anniversaries or church holidays. He even had to be reminded of Christmas each year, as though it were unexpected.

He must have assumed Verity was twenty-one because she would be so at some point in 1816. He simply could not remember the precise date.

Tobias Osborne had survived his daughter's marriage by only two months. He never knew how badly it had turned out, and she had always been grateful for that. It would have broken his heart. How perfect that it should be her dear scatterbrained Papa who just might set her free.

Chapter 13

Verity paced the length of the small bedchamber, unable to bank the excitement that stirred her blood. Another strange and unexpected twist in the road faced her, but this time she did not fear it. She did not have to steel herself against some unknown fate. This time, fortune was on her side. She was going to be free at last of the marriage bonds with Gilbert, free to make a new life, to make her own choices, to find her own happiness. It would take some months, apparently, but in the end she would be free.

Her heart sang with new possibilities.

A soft rapping on the bedchamber door caused her to turn in time to see James enter.

"He's gone," James said and closed the door behind him. "He can find another inn in this village or the next. I suppose it was harsh, but I wanted him gone." He stepped close to Verity and took both her hands in his. "So much has happened. How do you feel about it, my dear?"

"Elated. Ecstatic. Free!" A gurgle of laughter bubbled up from her throat. She gave a wordless shriek of pure delight, then threw her head back and laughed.

"I'm free! I'm really free!" She flung her arms wide and wanted to soar like a bird. "I'm free!"

Suddenly she was swept up into James's arms, and he swung her around and around, laughing with her. They laughed and twirled until she was breathless. When he finally set her feet back on the ground, she felt dizzy and giddy and perfectly wonderful. She could not seem to stop smiling. She was glad for his hands at her waist for she might have collapsed to the floor without their support.

"Oh, James," she said between breaths, "you do not know what this means to me. You do not know how . . . Oh, it is the most wondrous thing. You cannot possibly understand, but oh, James, I don't believe I've ever been so happy in all my life."

"Verity. My sweet Verity." He brought his mouth to hers and kissed her.

Gently at first, his lips moving over hers, tasting, testing, teasing. She felt dizzy again, this time from the taste of him, the musky smell of him, the softness of his lips that always surprised her. Boldly, shamelessly, she moved her lips beneath his.

He groaned against her mouth and deepened the kiss, clasping her more tightly against him, one hand sliding down from her waist to her bottom, pressing her hard against him. He pushed her lips open with his own and filled her mouth with his tongue, stroking and stroking in a way that set off a strange fluttering down deep between her legs.

Verity did not know what it all meant and did not care and did not want to think about it just now. She gave herself up to the sheer sensuous pleasure of his lips and tongue and arms and body. She was lost to him.

His mouth left hers and began trailing kisses down the length of her neck and underneath her jaw. Verity threw her head back to give him better access and he took advantage.

She wanted this man, desperately wanted him. And she wanted him to want her. When he coaxed her to suck on his tongue as it stroked her mouth, she complied willingly. She would do just about anything to make him desire her. If only just this once.

She lost all sense of time, but they seemed to kiss and kiss forever. When James finally lifted his head and looked down at her, they were both breathless and panting.

"There are no more rooms available," she said between breaths. "Did you know? You will have to . . . to stay here."

"I know," he said and stroked her cheek with the back of a finger. "That is why I sent Russell away. It did not seem right to make love to his still-legal wife under the same roof."

"Are you going to make love to me?"

"If you will let me, I would like nothing better."

"Oh." Verity closed her eyes and thought she must be in a dream. He really wanted to make love to her?

Even knowing how it would be? "Are you sure?"

He pulled back slightly, gazed down at her with heavy-lidded eyes, and smiled. "I've never been more sure of anything in my life. I want you. I've wanted you for a very long time."

"Oh, James. You know how it will end."

"I hope I do, but I don't think you do. I promise to do a better job of it this time. Will you make love with me, Verity?"

"Yes." He could not possibly want it more than she did. "Oh, yes. Yes!"

James smiled at her eagerness, then kissed her again. He wanted nothing more than to let her know how desirable she was. He wanted to undo all the damage Russell's behavior, and his own, had done to undermine her self-confidence. Though his body wanted to take her now with swift, hot lust, he was determined to make love to her slowly, to arouse her with lips and tongue and touch and words, to convince her beyond doubt of his desire.

James buried his face against her irresistible neck and began to nibble and kiss while he twisted a hand into her hair, flinging pins in every direction until it fell loose. He lifted the full weight of it in his hands and ran his fingers through its thick, soft length.

He then began on her dress, kissing every exposed inch of skin as he untied the tapes in the back. She gave a slight groan when his lips trailed lower, to the shoulder he exposed when he pushed aside the neck of her dress. She smelled faintly of lavender and her skin tasted warm and clean. He wanted to devour her. To forget all the complications and past histories of both their lives and bury himself inside her.

He deftly undid the tiny buttons at the front of her bodice and plunged his hand inside, covering her full breast with his palm. She sucked in a sharp breath and pushed against his hand. God, he was ready to explode, but he would take it slow. Very slow.

He kissed her mouth while he stroked her breast, and she melted against him. When he lifted his head, he gently pushed the open dress over her shoulders and let it drop to the floor. He drank in the sight of her in nothing more than a chemise and corset, full breasts spilling out above the stays, while he swiftly divested himself of coat, waistcoat, and cravat. He turned her back to him while he unlaced her corset and let it drop to the floor, leaving only the chemise. Turning her back to face him, he kissed her mouth while he stroked her soft, unconfined breast, and she melted against him again. When he lifted his head, he gently pushed the chemise down her shoulders and let it drop to the floor.

"Oh!" Verity stiffened and made a movement to cover her nakedness, but James took her hands away and held them at her side.

Her thick dark hair spilled over one shoulder, in sharp contrast to the creamy white smoothness of her skin. She was perfectly formed, softly rounded and full bosomed, so unlike Rowena's delicate slenderness. He held on to her hands and drank in the sight of her, his gaze lingering on the ripe breasts, the small waist, the flaring curve of hip, and the thatch of dark curls lower down. Verity kept her eyes downcast as though ashamed.

"You are so beautiful," he said.

She looked up at his words. "You don't have to say that, James. I know I am not—oh!"

He had stopped her words by bringing his mouth down to her breast. He suckled and circled the hardened nipple with his tongue while he stroked her buttocks with his hands. Verity squirmed and made little whimpering sounds, her own pleasure firing his desire. She brought a tentative hand to his head and stroked his hair while he laved her breast.

After James had given equal attention to the other breast, he straightened and tugged the shirttails from his pantaloons. Then he lifted the shirt over his head and tossed it aside. He scooped Verity up in his arms and carried her to the bed.

Verity's body hummed with new sensations as she watched James remove his pantaloons and stockings. She had never seen a fully naked man—not even Gilbert—except in pictures of Greek statues. James was certainly as magnificent, tall and lean and well-muscled. There was not an inch of softness about him. Instead of the smoothness of marble, though, his chest was furred with dark hair. She longed to run her fingers through it.

James stood beside the bed in all his naked glory, and Verity's gaze followed the path of dark hair that arrowed down his flat belly. She gasped at the sight of his fully erect penis. Good God, no wonder there had been pain. He was too big.

Any such misgivings flew right out of her mind when James lay down beside her, gathered her into his arms, and kissed her. The sensation of his solid chest pressed against her soft breasts, his furred flesh against her smooth skin, was an indescribable pleasure. He deftly untied her garters and inched her stockings down her legs, his lips following the silk, kissing each new inch of bare skin, even taking her toes into his mouth, creating sensations that made her want to scream with pleasure.

Fully naked now, she felt her skin tingle and flush as his hands moved over her body, working magic with each caress. Desire tightened deep inside her, becoming an almost unbearable ache. He trailed kisses down her neck and shoulders, teasing her breasts once more, and dipping further to the tender flesh beneath her breasts, to her abdomen and stomach. The dull, throbbing ache inside her became more intense, almost painful.

"So beautiful," he murmured over and over until she almost believed him.

Verity allowed her hands to move over him, tentatively at first, but then more boldly when he whispered his pleasure in her ear. She ran her hands over his chest and shoulders and back, and lower, to the swell of his buttocks. James groaned at her touch and rolled on top of her.

He nudged her knees apart and she felt his erection against her thigh. He took her mouth in a passionate kiss that left her quivering with need. His hand moved down the slight swell of her belly and pushed through the curly hair between her legs.

"Oh, my God," she groaned and writhed beneath him. His fingers kept moving until his thumb discovered a point of pleasure she had not known was there. She shuddered and choked back a scream when he began to rub the hot, wet flesh. He whispered words of desire in her ear, but she barely heard. She clung to him, thrashing restlessly, all her concentration on the extraordinary way he was making her feel.

"Please," she said, not knowing what she begged for. "Please."

James spread her legs further apart with his knees and pushed his rigid sex against her. She tensed, steeling herself against the pain that was to come. He raised himself on his elbows and looked deep into her eyes, then entwined his fingers with hers on either side of her head. Keeping his gaze locked to hers, with one slow, smooth thrust, he pushed himself inside her.

James stilled himself and watched her face. For a moment she had looked like she was preparing for a tooth extraction. He held tightly on to her hands, knowing she was afraid. Now her eyes widened with wonder. He smiled down at her and squeezed her fingers. "No pain?"

"No," she whispered, drawing out the word as though she couldn't believe it. "No."

He kissed her. "Good. Now let me love you properly."

He began to move slowly, to give her time to adjust to the process, to realize there could be pleasure where there had once been only pain. He released her hands and put his beneath her bottom. He set up a rhythm and used his hands to teach her how to follow, rotating her hips in opposition to his thrusts.

She learned quickly and seemed to give herself over to her body's natural response. She moaned and writhed and bucked beneath him. He could feel the tension building in her and understood it better than she did. When her breathing became quick little pants and he sensed her climax was near, he reached down between them and stroked the sensitive bud of flesh he'd teased earlier. She jerked spasmodically and called out his name. James held her tightly as she shuddered beneath him, and only then did he finally relinquish his own control, driving hard and fast and deep until his own climax ripped through his body, leaving him spent and sated and more satisfied than he'd ever been in his life.

They lay together for a long moment, panting and slick with perspiration, James's full weight collapsed atop Verity. She didn't notice. She savored the lingering aftereffects of what had just occurred between them, the incredible things he'd done to her, that amazing explosion of sensation when she thought she might shatter to pieces. He'd made her feel beautiful and desirable, something she had never thought possible. Oh, how she loved him for it. A sting of tears built up behind her eyes.

She lifted her languorous arms and draped them around his shoulders. "Oh, James," she said, unable to keep a tremor from her voice, "I didn't know. I didn't know it could be this wonderful."

He lifted his head and used a thumb to wipe away a tear from the corner of her eye. He kissed her tenderly, and Verity could no longer hold back the tears. James rolled off her, pulled her onto her side, and wrapped his arms tightly about her. "I know," he said as he held her. "I know."

"No, you d-don't," she said, blubbering through her tears.

"Hush, my love." He continued to hold her tightly until she gained control of herself.

"You don't understand," she said at last. "I thought there was something . . . something wrong with me. That I could never have a physical relationship with a man. I thought I was not . . . normal. But now . . . I think I must have been wrong. All this time, I must have been wrong."

James kissed her. "It was never you, Verity. There is nothing at all wrong with you." His hand dipped down to briefly stroke her breast. "Nothing at all."

Verity was so overcome by this revelation she was almost unable to breathe. Of all the astonishing events of the last day—Gilbert's arrival, James's rescue, the possibility of an annulment, this exquisite lovemaking—nothing affected her as profoundly as this new knowledge that she was not, after all, defective in some way, undesirable to men.

The notion had so colored her perception of who she was, it had become a permanent element of her being. To discover she had been wrong was literally breathtaking. How might her life had gone differently if only she had known the truth?

There were still questions, however, that needed answers. It had not been only Gilbert who rejected her.

She looked at James. "And so the pain last time—"

"Was my fault entirely. Had I known you were a virgin, my dear, I would have been more gentle. My anger afterward was directed at me, not at you. I was angry and ashamed at the rough way I'd handled you. If only I'd known, if only I'd done a better job of it, it might not have been so painful for you. It only hurts the first time. The rest of the time—"

"It is quite wonderful." She hugged him close and burrowed her head against his shoulder. In the space of a moment, she was a new woman. The man she adored found her beautiful and desirable. The pride she would now wear would be real and true, no longer a mask for shame.

"Thank you so much, James. You cannot know what this means to me. I—" She almost told him she loved him but bit off the words before she could say them. She did not know how he felt. Just because he desired her did not mean he loved her. It would only make things awkward between them if she declared her love and he did not.

He kissed the top of her head. "It was my pleasure, madam." He extricated himself from her embrace and sat up. "Now, my dear, we have much to discuss. Come under the blankets where we can stay warm."

They rearranged themselves in the bed, propped up against the pillows with the covers pulled up to their chests. James held her hand beneath the blankets.

"I am more pleased than you will ever know," he said, "that you want to return to Pendurgan, that you have found some happiness there, despite the way it all began. But after the annulment, I would not wish to involve you in yet another scandal by asking you to live there with me as my mistress. For I intend to spend many more nights like this making love to you. I thought it would be best if . . . if we married."

Verity's heart lurched in her chest. She did not

know if it could bear another jolt. But this one . . . ah, this one she would endure. "Married?"

"Yes, if it's all the same to you. It seems the best thing to do, don't you agree?"

The best thing to do. Oh, indeed. "I suppose so," she said, keeping her elation in check.

"So you will marry me, Verity?"

"Yes, James. I will marry you."

He reached over and kissed her gently. "Thank you, my dear. I hope you will not regret it. I am not much of a bargain, you know."

Not much of a bargain? For the first time in her life she saw the prospect of a normal marriage, and perhaps even children, with the man she loved. It seemed a tremendous bargain to her.

"I'm not so young anymore, for one thing," he said. "Did you know I am all of eight and thirty? Much too old for a beautiful young thing such as yourself."

She smiled and lifted a hand to touch the silver at his temples. "You are not too old," she said. "It is just that you have wasted too many years believing yourself a murderer."

"If I am not a murderer, then at the very least I am surely mad, for I cannot control these spells that happen to me. I really have no right to ask you to saddle yourself with man whose brain is damaged."

"Your brain was never damaged," she said, "but only your spirit. Your spirit was broken by your inability to help the men under your command, or to help your own loved ones when they needed you. But unlike a damaged brain, a broken spirit can be repaired, James. Only look what you have done for me tonight. By showing me that I am not deformed in some way, by teaching me that I can be desirable, you have washed away all the years of private shame and guilt. You have helped to heal my spirit, James. Let me help to heal yours."

He made an odd strangled sound in his throat and pulled her into his arms, crushing her against his chest. He held her a long time without speaking.

"Thank you, Verity," he said at last. "Thank you for believing in me. I'll do my best to see that you do not regret marrying me."

He kissed her, and the kiss quickly became passionate. They made love again, at first slowly and then frantically. Verity fell asleep in his arms, curled up beside him like a kitten, and as content.

James's carriage pulled into the long graveled drive just as the sun was setting. He let down the carriage window and gaped at his almost unrecognizable estate: Pendurgan had been transformed into a fairground. He could hardly believe his eyes.

Tents and makeshift structures were sprawled in every direction, and people—dear God, so many people!—milled about everywhere he looked. Bright flaming torches seemed to dot the landscape as well. No, not torches. Something bigger. Tar barrels? It was a sight to behold.

"My dear Verity," he said. "You have outdone yourself. I am quite literally overwhelmed. This is marvelous!"

"It is, isn't it?" Her smile was brighter than the bonfire and he could feel her almost bouncing off the seat in excitement and pride.

She had done it for him. He gathered her in his arms and held her tight. His emotions ran so strong that words seemed a poor instrument, so he simply held her and hoped she understood.

As the carriage approached the great stand of chestnut trees, a shout went up from a group gathered around the tables placed on the lawn outside the main entrance. Within moments, so many people surrounded the carriage that the driver was forced to pull it to a stop.

"Welcome home!"

"A fine festival, my lord!"

"Lord Harkness is here!"

Nick Tregonning opened the carriage door and pulled down the steps. Tossing his hat and greatcoat on the opposite bench, James alighted, turned to hand Verity out, and then faced the crowd of men and women wanting to shake his hand. He was grabbed from every direction. Zack Muddle and Gerens Palk and Ezra Noone and Ned Trethowan and Dickie Nanpean and Tom Bedruthan and so many others he could hardly keep track as he was spun in one direction, then the other to receive an astonishingly warm welcome.

His hand was pumped, his back was slapped, and he was tugged along toward the center of the festivities, escorted through the crowd like a king among his people. It was literally breathtaking. These good people, who had hated him, scorned him, even feared him for almost seven years, now treated him like a returning hero. A tankard of ale was thrust in his hand by none other than Old Artful. The grizzled old kiddly minder raised his hand for silence.

"Here be a toast to his lordship," the old man said, "fer givin' us this here fine festival again, and better'n ever. To Lord Harkness."

"To Lord Harkness!" the crowd shouted in unison.

James raised his tankard with the rest and drank, savoring the good, strong local ale. He then raised his own hand for silence.

"I want to thank you all for coming," he said. "I am sorry to be so late, but now that we're here I am pleased to see so many of you. Here's hoping we continue the tradition every year."

"Here, here."

"And one more important toast," he said, and steered Verity to the front of the crowd. "To Mrs. Osborne, for working so hard to make the festival a success."

"To Miz Osborne," the crowd sang out.

Verity blushed with pleasure and James beamed at her. He would like to have announced their marriage plans to this happy crowd, but it was probably best to keep that news private for now, until the annulment was accomplished.

"Please continue to enjoy the festival," James said, "while I take a look around for myself. Thank you all again for coming."

"I'm going to dash upstairs and change," Verity whispered, "and then make sure everything is running smoothly. I will see you later."

She gave him a look so sizzling with promise he almost lost his balance.

Verity enjoyed a tearful reunion with the household, though there was no time to linger over sentiment. Her corps of volunteers had been wonderful, with Mrs. Tregelly overseeing it all in Verity's absence. Word of the festival had spread well beyond the district, and peddlers and trinket merchants and craftsmen had poured onto the estate to set up temporary shop. Even an old gypsy woman had showed up offering to tell fortunes.

Jago Chenhalls and George Pascow, Kate's husband, had organized foot races, sheep-shearing competitions, wrestling matches, and various contests of strength for the men. Borra Nanpean and Annie Kempthorne had organized the children's games. Ezra Noone, who played the fiddle, had rounded up groups of other musicians and lively music had filled the air when Verity arrived.

Mrs. Chenhalls commanded a troop of local women, including Mag Puddifoot from Gunnisloe and a French pastry maker from Bodmin, who had been engaged to help with food preparations. The cavernous old kitchen bustled with activity. Young girls came and went bearing trays of savory pies, saffron cakes, figgy obbin, and other local favorites to be loaded onto several long trestle tables set up near the front of the house.

The troupe of players had brought with them jugglers and acrobats and puppeteers as well. The make-do stage had been scheduled to present performances of all kinds throughout the day and evening.

Verity wandered about the stalls that meandered over the grounds, and was hailed here and there by people who seemed to take her presence at Pendurgan for granted.

"Miz Verity!" Jacob Dunstan called out to her as she passed Old Artful's slapdash temporary kiddly. "Miz Verity, where be his lordship? When he did send word to close the mine for the day, I did think fer certain he'd be here, but I ain't seen him."

"He arrived a short time ago," Verity said. "He is having a look about. I'm sure you will see him soon."

"Glad to hear it," Jacob said. "Did want to raise my glass to him, I did, fer bringin' back the festival."

"He's certain to make his way to the kiddly before long, Jacob. I am sure he will be pleased to know you are enjoying yourself."

"Slap me if I ain't," he said. " 'Tis the finest time we did have round these parts fer many a year."

Verity smiled at Jacob and was about to stroll on when she caught sight of a familiar figure perched on a barrel and leaning against the long board stretched between two sawhorses that served as Old Artful's counter. Rufus Bargwanath. What on earth was he doing here? She thought he had left the district months ago.

He leered at her and gave a lecherous wink. Verity whirled around and almost stumbled over Jacob Dunstan's outstretched legs.

"Careful there, Miz Verity," he said, and offered a hand.

"Jacob," she whispered, "what is *he* doing here?" She tilted her head in the direction of the former steward.

"Bargwanath? Don't rightly know. Likely he do be out o' work again. Or maybe he just did come back to stir up trouble, like he always done. Don't 'ee be worrin' 'bout him, Miz Verity. Me and t'others'll keep an eye on the rotter."

"Thank you, Jacob." She glanced over her shoulder to see Bargwanath grinning at her with those big yellow teeth. She quickly strolled away back toward the stage, where the players were entertaining a boisterous crowd with a broad farce. She was hailed again after a few moments by Gonetta, full of excitement.

"It do be getting on time for the bonfire," she said, barely able to contain her enthusiasm. "Where be them little bundles of herbs we did tie up so pretty?"

"Oh, dear," Verity said. "I left the basket full of them in the kitchen. Come with me and we'll pass them out to the girls."

She had trouble keeping up with Gonetta who practically ran back to the house. They retrieved the basket and swung it between them as they trudged up the rise where the wood and kindling had been stacked in a huge mound. A crowd had already begun to gather as word spread that the fire was soon to be lit.

Verity and Gonetta distributed the herbs to all the young girls—bunches of clover, cinquefoil, vervain, and restharrow, all tied up with colored ribbons. It was a local tradition that each girl would toss her herbs into the fire and make a wish for her favorite young man to fall in love with her.

"I do be takin' one fer meself," Gonetta whispered. "I got me eye on Josh Trethowan."

Verity smiled and surreptitiously took one and tucked it in her pocket. She had a wish of her own to make.

She was glad James did not join the crowd around the woodpile. It would have been a shame if the fire had triggered one of his spells and spoiled his successful reentry into local society. Fortunately, no one seemed to think it strange that James was not present. George Pascow, Nat Spruggins, and Cheelie Craddick carried torches to the mound of wood and used them to light it all around the bottom, then threw the torches on top of the pyre to great shouting and applause. The blaze took off quickly, and within minutes the flames were soaring to the sky.

Girls, giggling and squealing, threw in their herbs, and soon all the young people began to "thread the needle" around the bonfire. When she thought no one was looking, Verity tossed her own bunch of herbs into the fire. She looked up to find Grannie Pascow smiling at her from across the flames. The old woman winked, and Verity grinned sheepishly.

" 'Tis a shame James wasn't here to start the fire."

Verity spun around to find Agnes Bodinar standing just behind her. It was the first time she'd seen her, though she showed no surprise to find Verity had returned. Verity assumed she would have remained inside the house and ignored the festival entirely.

"To start such a great, huge fire would have suited him," Agnes said. "Don't you agree?"

Verity protested Agnes's words with a click of the tongue. "You are not being fair," she said. "After all these years under his roof, you must surely know how fire affects James."

"I only know he shows an uncommon fascination

for the flames," Agnes said. "Whenever there is a fire, he always seems to be there. A pity he should miss this one."

Verity had had more than enough of Agnes's vicious tongue.

"I think you are hateful," she said, almost spitting out the words. "I know you lost your daughter, but it was not James's fault. He cannot help the way he is."

"He cannot help being a murderer? An arsonist?"

"No! You know that is not what I meant. He is neither of those things and you must stop saying he is. He has torn himself to pieces with guilt over the deaths here at Pendurgan. He loved Rowena. And Trystan."

"He never loved her. He simply wanted her because Alan Poldrennan wanted her, and he was always in competition with Alan. I tried and tried to convince her to marry Alan, but Rowena was bound and determined to be Lady Harkness."

"I think you are wrong, Agnes," Verity said. "James loved Rowena. I know he did." In fact, Verity doubted he could ever grow to love her as much. She was nothing at all like Rowena.

"You think you know him so well," Agnes said, her lip curled into a sneer, "but you don't know anything. It doesn't matter anymore, though." She gave Verity a strangely intent look. "Things are going to change soon enough, are they not?"

She walked away, leaving Verity confused. But she had no time to ponder the matter, for Davey came bounding up against her knees so fast he almost knocked her down in his enthusiasm.

"Miz Osborne? Can we go see the pony now?"

"My goodness, Davey. With so many fun things to do here, you want to go see your pony?"

"I ain't been out to see him all day," the boy said. "I did be havin' too much fun. But I done ever'thin' there is to do. I wanna go see Osborne now, afore he do go to sleep."

Verity looked about to see if she was needed anywhere, but it looked as though the festival was running itself. It was winding down now that the sun was setting, but the adults might drink and sing and dance until all hours. She could spare a few minutes for Davey.

He took her by the hand and tugged her along through the stalls and the livestock and the games. Flaming tar barrels had been placed all along the way, lighting their path. They really did look lovely, reaching all the way to the farthest edges of the estate.

When they left the main area of the stalls and headed toward the western stables, neither of them noticed the person following close behind.

Chapter 14

"Quite a sight, i'nt it?" Mark Penneck asked as his gaze swept over the festival grounds. "Looks like a real fair. Just like Morvah or one of them places."

"It is nothing less than amazing," James said, and meant it. Not just the fair itself, but what it had accomplished was truly astonishing. The people loved it, and seemed ready to welcome him back into their good graces on account of it. It was all due to Verity, and James wanted nothing more than to track her down and show his appreciation by kissing her senseless.

"Now, where the devil is Verity? Have you seen her, Mark?"

"Last time I did see her was up to the bonfire, talking with Miz Bodinar."

With Agnes? Had she actually got Agnes to take part? James had assumed the old woman would stubbornly stay inside and refuse to have anything to do with the festival. He thanked Mark and headed toward the bonfire.

He was stopped all along the way up the slope, for a handshake or a simple greeting. Verity had told him, when she first began planning the festival, that people were unlikely to be discourteous to their host if they were having a good time. He wondered if all this goodwill would last beyond the morning.

When he reached the top of the slope, he circled the huge bonfire, searching faces for the only one that mattered. She was not there.

He walked over to Sam Kempthorne. "Have you seen Mrs. Osborne, Sam?"

"Aye, that I have, my lord," the farmer replied. "I did see her walkin' back down to the stalls with young Davey Chenhalls."

As James trod back down the slope, he was aware of the heat of the fire against his back. It only then occurred to him that he had not even flinched at the sight of it.

He wandered through the stalls looking for Verity but not finding her. He reached an area that looked to have been used for sheep shearing earlier, and caught sight of Tomas Chenhalls. He flagged the boy over.

"Have you seen Mrs. Osborne, Tomas?"

"Not in the last hour or so."

"Damn. I've been chasing her all over this festival but she seems to have disappeared. She was with your brother, I'm told."

"If she did be with Davey, most likely they be at the old stables."

"The old stables?"

"Aye. Where the ponies are kept. Davey got hisself a new moorland foal and can't seem to stay away from the little trotter."

"I suppose it is worth checking," James said, "though why one small pony would hold more fascination for a boy than all this, I'm sure I don't know."

"Are you ready to go back now, Davey?" Verity asked. "Do you not think we should be getting back to the festival soon?"

"Soon," the boy said, but made no move to leave.

Verity wanted to get back to make sure everything was still running smoothly, that there was enough food and ale and cider, that people were still enjoying themselves. She wandered about the barn, waiting impatiently.

It was a long, low barn with two separate wings flanking the central open entry. The wing to the south was closed off with a massive door. The north wing was open and apparently used only for the few ponies on the estate. Besides Osborne, there were just his dam and two others, odd little creatures with small heads, tiny ears, thick necks, and short legs. Verity strolled about the barn to look in on the other ponies when she heard a strange thudding sound, followed by a strong whoosh of air and an unmistakable smell. She spun around and saw smoke and then flames erupting along the far wall near the foal's stall.

Dear life, the barn was on fire.

"Davey!" she cried. "Fire! Get out of here!"

The ponies were screaming and she managed to guide the two nearest her quickly out the main door, slapping them on the rump to ensure they bolted at full speed. She dashed to the other end to get the foal and his dam. Flames licked at the loft above and hay burst into flame with an explosive rush.

Dear God. "Davey, help me, please. We must get Osborne out and his mother. Hurry!"

Coughing and choking on smoke, eyes watering, she urged the dam and her foal, wall-eyed with fright, out of the stall and through encroaching flames toward the main entry.

"Come on, Davey, come on!" But when she turned she found the little boy frozen with fear at the other end of the barn. He had not moved, and fire had erupted all around him. He screamed.

In the next breath, before Verity could take so much as a step toward him, the big door to the central entry slammed shut. There was no other way out.

They were trapped.

James watched in horror as the barn went up in flames.

As he had approached the building, he could see Verity and Davey inside through the open door and windows. Excited to have finally found her, he increased his pace, but came to a stunned halt when the tar barrel outside it suddenly toppled over and ignited the barn wall.

Old nightmares skirted the edge of James's consciousness, temporarily immobilizing him. Explosion. Fire. Burning barns. Charred flesh. Rowena. Verity.

He tried to fight them off but the images tormented him. He had to save her. He had to save Verity. *Please, God, don't let this happen again. Verity*!

With a tremendous effort, he willed himself to move toward the barn. Wanting to run, he could manage only one slow step at a time. His head pounding, his vision blurring, each step brought him closer to immobility, to darkness, to death. *Verity. Verity*. Her name became a litany, a prayer, as he dragged one foot forward, then the other. He pushed everything else out of his brain. There was only Verity. No fire. No darkness. No pain. Just Verity.

He caught a glimpse of her again, running toward the back of the barn—away from the door! No! He wanted to scream. No, please God. There was no exit that way. She was going back into the fire. No!

Another figure, silhouetted black against the flames, darted around the front of the barn and into the central entry. Thank heaven. Someone to help. Did they know she was inside?

He had to get to Verity. He could not lose her now. *Please, God, don't let me fail again*. One more step. Another. Another. He could do it. For Verity. He could do it. One more step. One more.

When he reached the central entry at last and saw Alan Poldrennan standing inside, James sank to his knees, panting, shaking, dying.

"Alan! Verity is inside," James gasped. He took in a deep gulp of air but inhaled only smoke and started coughing. The throbbing in his head was beyond bearable. "And Davey Chenhalls. Quick. Help me. Help me to get them out." He struggled to his feet again, fighting the darkness that clouded the perimeter of his vision. He would not give in to it. He would not lose Verity.

Alan turned to look at James, a strange, almost wild expression in his eyes. "I'm sorry, Harkness," he said in a maddeningly calm voice. "I'm afraid I cannot do that." Then he lifted the heavy wooden bolt and locked the door.

James stared at him, incredulous, confused. "What? What do you mean? Quickly, lift the bolt, Alan! Verity and Davey are inside."

"I know." He took the torch he'd been holding—why hadn't James noticed it?—and set fire to the bolt and all around the perimeter of the door.

"Alan! My God!"

From some secret resource, James found the strength to lunge at his friend, but Poldrennan swung out and struck him, knocking him to his feet again. James now had his back to the wall, and Poldrennan held the torch inches from James's face.

Oh, my God.

"I'm afraid poor Mrs. Osborne has to die, James." An eerie light shone from the depths of Poldrennan's eyes, like those of a mad dog.

"No."

"Yes. She was making you forget. Agnes thought you might even marry her. I couldn't let you do that, James. You have not yet finished paying for Rowena's death. My darling Rowena."

Poldrennan swung the torch back and forth in front of James's face, taunting him. But fire no longer held the power over him it once had. The man's words had shattered the blackness completely. Somehow James had to save Verity from this madman.

"Rowena's death was an accident," James said. "You know that."

"Yes, I do." Poldrennan's voice had become high-pitched and singsong. "She was never meant to die. The fire had been meant for you, James. You never deserved her. I was the one who loved her. But, yellow-bellied coward that you are, you let her die for you. It is only right that everyone should blame you for her death. Just as they will blame you for Verity's death. But you will die here with her and become just another Cornish tragedy to feed the folklore. I shall not fail this time."

He waved the torch back and forth. Back and forth. James grew dizzy at its hypnotic pull, but the heat of the close flame kept him alert, kept him from succumbing to its spell. That, and the urgent, desperate need to get away from Poldrennan. The door was now completely engulfed and flames had spread to the rafters. There was no hope of rescue through the door.

Verity!

"Look at the fire, James. Look at the fire. You know what it says to you." The flame swung back and forth. "Look at the fire. You know what it will do. Look into the fire."

Good God, what was he to do? Poldrennan had him trapped, and soon the whole place would be ablaze and come falling down upon them.

Verity!

"Look into the fire, James. Let the fire take you. Hear the men screaming. Smell their flesh burning. Look into the fire."

No. He must appeal to what was left of the man's

rational mind. He must not give in. "We cannot let Verity die, Alan. We must try to save her. *Help me*!"

"No. She must die. She is dead already."

Oh, God, no. Was his beautiful, sweet Verity dead? The one person he loved in all the world? The one person who had brought meaning back into his life? Was she dead?

It would be so easy to give in to the darkness again, to let it pull him in. If Verity was dead, he would sink comfortably into the dark and not have to feel the pain.

But the blackness would not come. He had fought it and won. It was gone forever. He would not be spared the agony of Verity's death. Grief swept over him, intensifying with each pass of the flame. Back and forth. Back and forth.

No! She could not be dead. He hadn't even told her he loved her. Dear God, he hadn't told her. She would never know. Why hadn't he told her?

But she was *not* dead. She could not be.

"She is still in there, Alan. We can still save her. Let me pass so that we can try to get to her."

"No. You cannot save her. It is too late."

"What about the boy? You have no quarrel with the boy."

"An incidental sacrifice. It could not be helped. Just like before, with Trystan and the Clegg boy. It doesn't matter. Look into the fire. Let it take you."

"Baassttarrrddd!"

Digory Clegg flew into the barn and, taking Poldrennan by surprise, knocked him to the side and straight into the flames. The torch flipped out of his hand and landed at Clegg's feet. Oblivious to the flames licking near his trousers, Clegg cried out, "You killed my boy! You killed my boy!" He picked up the torch and began to pummel the fiery, flailing, screaming form of Alan Poldrennan.

Within a heartbeat, both men were totally engulfed, and became a single ball of flame, a single piercing, wretched cry into the night.

Sickened by the all-too-familiar smell, James wasted no time on remorse, but ran outside where he found Clegg had not been the only witness. A small number of horrified spectators had gathered, and a group of men were shouting at the north end of the barn. He ran toward them.

Jago Chenhalls, Cheelie Craddock, and Jacob Dunstan wielded heavy axes, breaking down the outer wall of the barn, while others passed buckets of water brought up from the river to throw on the flames. Just as James approached, a sizable breach in the wall was obtained, spewing out great billows of gray smoke and heat so intense he had to cover his eyes.

"Are they still in there?" James shouted above the roar of the fire. "Verity and Davey?"

"They are, God help 'em," Cheelie shouted back.

Jago kept swinging his axe, a ferocious glint in his streaming eyes. It was his little boy inside.

"I'm going in," James said, taking off his cravat to protect his face.

"No, my lord, let me." Jacob Dunstan eyed him warily.

James ignored him and headed toward the breach. Verity was in there somewhere. Dead or alive, he would bring her out himself. He dipped his cravat in a bucket of water, wrapped it around his face, dumped the rest of the water over his coat, and plowed headfirst through the opening.

Tongues of fire licked at him from the edges of the breach, and a thick wall of smoke almost knocked him backward. His eyes watered and burned so badly he could hardly see where he was going. Barely able to breathe, he pulled the wet cloth away from his mouth and shouted for Verity, over and over.

The raging inferno beyond swallowed up the sound of his voice, so he replaced the cloth around his mouth. She would never be able to hear him, and he couldn't see where he was going so he simply held his hands out straight and inched his way through the smoke.

He bumped into the railing of one of the low stalls and the wood was so hot it scorched his hand. "Damn." At the same moment, his other hand connected with something soft, something moving, something alive. "Verity?"

A rasping cough was the only response.

It was the most beautiful sound he'd ever heard. She was alive.

He grabbed on to fabric and tugged her toward him. He could just barely make out her form in the smoke. She had the boy bundled tightly beneath her chin. James removed the already dry cloth from his face and wrapped it about hers. She had probably already inhaled too much smoke for it to do much good, but she needed it more than he did.

He was startled by another moving body at his side. One of the ponies. *Damn.* He felt for the animal's rump, and gave it a slap. Scared to death, it did not move.

James swiftly shrugged off his coat and put it over the pony's head. Then he moved toward the opening, pulling Verity along with one arm, the pony with the other while flames nipped at their heels and fireballs of burning hay dripped down from the loft above. The men had widened the breach in the short moments James had been inside, and the four of them—man, woman, child, and pony—burst through and into the cool night air like an explosion. James was only vaguely aware of another small figure following close behind. The young foal.

Verity handed Davey into unknown arms, then collapsed on the damp grass and sucked in great gulps of cool air. This set off a fit of coughing and sputtering until her throat was raw and she was wracked with dry heaves.

She lay crumpled in a ball, her head bent over her knees. It was some time before she could finally take a breath without choking, but even then she didn't seem able to move. As if from a distance, she heard Agnes's shrill voice and she seemed to be crying. "I'm so sorry," she repeated over and over, and Verity felt a sort of vague curiosity about whom she might be speaking to and what she was sorry about. But she could not keep her mind on anything immediate. People were shouting and running around, but she could only lie there, thinking of the flames. And the heat. And the smoke. And Davey's screams. And how it had felt as though her skin were melting. And how a falling beam had sent a shower of cinders into her hair. And the blocked exit. And the burning in her eyes. And how she grew dizzy from lack of air. And how she had thought she was going to die.

She began to shudder uncontrollably.

Before she understood what was happening, she was enfolded in strong arms that held her tightly while a dear, familiar voice crooned her name.

James.

She tried to respond, but managed only a hoarse, unintelligible whisper. He crushed her to him so tightly it almost hurt. It didn't matter. She had thought she was going to die without seeing him again. He could bruise every inch of her as long as he never let go.

For a long time, she thought he never would. But finally, he held her away from him so he could look at her. Tears left white tracks through the black soot on his face. "I thought I'd really lost you this time," he said, his voice husky with smoke and emotion. "Dear God, Verity, I thought I'd lost you."

She swallowed and attempted to speak again. "Never." It was weak, but it worked this time. She swallowed once more. "You could never lose me," she whispered.

"I'm glad," he said, and ran soft fingers along her jaw and throat. "You see, I never told you I loved you, and my heart was breaking because I thought you might die without knowing."

Her own heart soared. "You love me?" The words squeaked out like a mouse.

"More than life," he said, and kissed her tenderly, oblivious of the crowd of people milling about and surely watching.

They both tasted of smoke and soot, and laughed when the kiss ended and each of them spat out bits of ash. James removed a handkerchief from his waistcoat pocket. He wiped her face and then his own. The square of linen was black when he finished. He tossed it aside and took her in his arms again. For a long time he just held her.

"I love you, too, James."

"Verity."

"I have for the longest time but was afraid to tell you."

"And I was afraid to tell you." He laughed. "What a pair of idiots we've been." He kissed her again.

She gazed into his eyes, devouring the sight of him, the wonder of him—and then she realised what had happened.

"James! You saved us. We were trapped in there and you saved us!"

A pained look flickered in his eyes.

"You charged into a burning building to save us. A *burning* building."

"So I did." He looked down at his filthy clothes, reeking of smoke. "And not too much the worse for wear. But what of you?" He ran a finger over her left eyebrow. "You've been singed."

"Have I?" She reached up and felt the charred ends of her brow, then dismissed it with a wave. "James, do you know what this means? You faced fire. You were not immobilized, you did not black out. You faced it. James!"

He looked inexplicably sad when Verity thought he should be ecstatic. Something was wrong.

"I believe I have shed my demons at last," he said

in a somber voice. "But I have lost something in the bargain."

"Tell me."

And he did, in as few words as possible.

"He was my closest friend, except for you," he said. "And yet he killed my wife and my son, and Billy Clegg. All for hatred of me, because I had the woman he wanted." He gave a great, shuddery sigh. "So much that I'd believed in was a lie. I thought he was my friend. I thought I was a murderer."

He shook his head as though to clear it, then studied her up and down, taking in her scorched and tattered skirts, examining her hands and arms. He touched her bare shoulder through a rent where the sleeve had been ripped away from the bodice. "Are you sure you are all right? You are unharmed?"

"My throat is raw and I have a singed brow; nothing more. And I am heartsore at what you have learned of your friend. But I cannot be unhappy. We have both survived this night. I have discovered love where there had been only hope. You have conquered your fears and seen your good name restored. Despite all that has happened, there is much for which we must be grateful."

"It is a bittersweet triumph, though," James said, "to have my good name back at the cost of Alan's betrayal and death. And yet you believed in me all along, when everyone else, including me, believed I was the culprit. For that, I will always honor you. Verity, my love, I do not know how I could have come through all this without you. Let me ask you once again, in front of all these friends who are doing a poor job of pretending not to watch us, and just for the pleasure of hearing your answer: Will you marry me?"

"I would be honored to marry you, James. Honored and proud and full of joy. It is the least I can do for two hundred pounds!"

A cheer went up from the crowd as James took Verity in his arms once again.

Epilogue

She was ready when he came for her.

Verity had asked James to escort her downstairs to breakfast. She wanted to be with him, to see his surprise, when he saw what awaited them in the Great Hall.

She had dressed in a new gown of figured sarsnet silk with a soft flounce of French lace appliqued to the hem with a narrow band of embroidery. The sleeves were long and full, confined at the wrist with a band of the same embroidery. The falling collar, trimmed in French lace, left bare a V of throat and revealed the gold chain and tiny gold cross that had belonged to her mother.

In honor of her new, though temporary, unmarried state, Verity wore no cap.

James stood back and gave her an admiring

glance. "You look beautiful, my love. Is that a new dress?"

"Yes." She spun around for him to admire the entire package. "It cost the earth. I hope you do not mind, but I wanted to look especially nice today."

He cupped her face in his hands and kissed her. "Why should I mind? You did not have a chance to be much of a bride that first time. I want you to feel like a bride today. You look beautiful."

So did he. He wore a blue tailcoat with notched collar and wide lapels, a striped silk waistcoat, and gray ankle-length trousers. He looked every inch the gentleman of fashion.

"Oh, James, I am so excited."

"So am I, my love. We have waited many long months for this day. I confess I began to despair of ever seeing your wretched marriage annulled, but it is done and you are free. Have you changed your mind and prefer to savor your new freedom?" He grinned, for he knew she wanted no such thing.

"Freedom does not suit me," she said. "I find I prefer the married state after all."

"Good. Then let us go down to breakfast. The Reverend Chigwiddon should have arrived by now."

And not only the vicar, Verity thought as she bit back a smile.

James offered his arm and led her down the stairs and through to the Great Hall, where he came to an abrupt halt. "What the devil?"

The old hall was teeming with people—his tenant farmers, his cottagers, their wives—all dressed up in their Sunday best. The hall was laid out with three long tables in a U shape, set for breakfast. At the bottom of the U, in the center, sat the old seventeenth-century Great Chair, imposing as a throne, where the master of Pendurgan always sat.

James was stunned. Verity had revived another old Pendurgan custom. He turned to her and smiled. "I'd forgot," he said. "It's the annual tenants' breakfast, is it not?"

"It is indeed. Always on St. Perran's Day."

"And always filled with bleary-eyed tenants hung over from the St. Perran's Eve revels." He squeezed her arm. "But a fine tradition, too long lapsed. Thank you, my love."

As he made his way toward the Great Chair, he stopped to speak to each farmer, each miner, and each of their wives. These were all the people who lived on and worked on Pendurgan land. It had long been the custom to entertain the tenants at a lavish breakfast banquet once a year, in thanks for their efforts to keep the land profitable. There had not been an annual breakfast since his father died, but James would make sure that this tradition, too, would live on.

James found the Reverend Chigwiddon and pulled him aside. The men laughed over the confusion James's note had caused, since the vicar had long before received his invitation to the breakfast. James gave him the license and told him they wished to be married there, that morning, at Pendurgan, surrounded by his tenants. The vicar was pleased to oblige, as long as the bride and groom agreed to walk to St. Perran's Church after breakfast to sign the register as was the law.

"Believe me, Mr. Chigwiddon, I know more about

marriage law now than I ever cared to know," James said. "I will not risk a single error, I assure you. The register will be properly signed. I'll even drag along two witnesses to sign as well, for I know that is also the law."

James signaled to Verity, who was speaking to Borra Nanpean, and she came to his side. He then held up an empty goblet and struck it with a knife blade several times. The chimelike sound brought silence to the big room.

"Dear friends," he began, and almost had to stop right there, his voice nearly cracking. He had lived so long in isolation, he never thought to call anyone his friend. Except Alan Poldrennan, who had been no true friend at all. But since that fateful midsummer's eve, he knew these people gathered here to be his friends indeed. Another old notion turned upside down.

"Before we commence with the banquet," he continued, "there is something else I would like you all to do. As some of you know—actually, I suspect all of you know—Miss Verity Osborne"—he slurred the "miss" a bit so it might be heard as "miz"; there was no need to explain about the annulment—"has agreed to be my wife."

Shouts and cheers resounded throughout the hall, those gathered clearly hanging on to the celebratory mood of the previous evening.

James raised his hand again for silence. "Mr. Chigwiddon has agreed to perform the ceremony right now, this morning, here in this fine old hall. I would be honored to have you all as witnesses, and then to join us in a wedding breakfast."

More cheers rang through the hall, but the crowd became silent during the brief ceremony, which the reverend spoke from memory, not having his prayer book with him. After the vows were spoken and James had slipped a beautiful sapphire ring on Verity's finger, he shocked them all by taking Verity in his arms and kissing her soundly. The old hall rang out with thunderous applause.

When everyone was seated and ready for the banquet, James stood by the Great Chair with Verity beside him.

"There has been much tragedy and sadness in this old house these last several years," he said. "That is one tradition I do not intend to uphold. I have loved two women in my lifetime. The first I lost to fire." He looked down at Agnes, who sat at his other side, and briefly touched her shoulder. "I almost lost the second, Verity, in the same way." He reached over and ran his finger along the spot where Verity's singed eyebrow had never quite grown back. "But the days of tragedy are over. The Harkness family has been too much touched by fire, but we are now rescued by love—the love of a woman who is not even Cornish."

The crowd laughed, and James continued. "Let this be a new beginning for Pendurgan, and hope this fine old house will soon be overrun with children born of the love we celebrate today. Now, let us dine in friendship, *onen hag oll*, one and all."

When he sat, he brought Verity's hand to his lips. "Thank you for healing my spirit, my lady, and for bringing me back to this life and this land and these people. And"—he whipped out a folded parchment from his waistcoat with a flourish—"I intend to have this auction bill of sale framed and hung prominently in this Great Hall, for it is surely the sweetest bargain any Cornishman ever made."

They smiled into each other's eyes, Lord and Lady Harkness, then turned to their guests and began to celebrate the first day of their new life together.